THE WEDDING THIEF

Helen Adam

Published by

Llyfrau Cambria Books, Wales, United Kingdom.

Cambria Books is a division of

Cambria Publishing.

Discover our other books at: www.cambriabooks.co.uk

This book is dedicated to:

The Wild Welsh Women Who Write, with thanks and love.

Flora

Isn't it funny how all brides want a unique wedding but end up with almost the same event? As a wedding planner, I'm not exactly discouraging this trend, and I have become an expert at organising and packaging the "perfect day". I create a bespoke fantasy for each bride (almost identical to the last). A fantasy that will live and take wing one glorious morning, like a long-cocooned butterfly, be caught on camera and pinned down firmly in a heavy cream leather album. A fantasy that over time will ripen to sweetness or sour to gall.

A Cotswold barn conversion is the scene for this morning's bridal action. So far, so original. Picking my way across the freshly laid gravel on this bright May morning, I scan the outside approvingly. It is perfect for the chic country life idyll that is my speciality. Crumbling walls of honey-coloured stone are gloriously dressed in climbing white roses and inside are the obligatory exposed beams, set off by expensively neutral plasterwork and a huge fireplace filled with flower-strewn logs. I stride briskly in, imagining it through the eyes of the guests who will soon be following me and admiring my choice of bay trees in tubs at the entrance.

Inside, the décor is 'shabby chic, kind of boho', just as the bride requested. Each table is a tasteful mass of subdued whites, artfully natural wildflower displays and twinkling tea lights.

I wave brightly at the makeup girls on their way to the upstairs suite to prettify today's bride. I take a moment to enjoy the room, my handiwork. It is perfect now, before the guests arrive. They will come soon, to smear the glasses and squash the flowers. They will scatter the tea lights as they reach for the wine, disrupting the layout as they discard tight shoes and over-heavy bags. They will drop red onion marmalade on the white seat covers and smear chocolate mousse into the tablecloths, despoiling the beauty and symmetry of my perfect creation.

'It's a shame we have to have guests,' says a voice beside me, echoing my thought. A quiet voice, from a gentle looking man. Tall and skinny, with flopping dark hair pushed back from clearly needed glasses.

'I'm, er, Luke, the, er…' he gestures at the oversized camera and lens slung round his neck.

There is something endearing about him despite his awkwardness, so I give him a warm and hopefully encouraging smile.

'Flora,' I say. 'Lovely to meet you. Yes, get plenty of shots now before the little monsters come in and start showing off.'

'God, kids are the worst,' he winces and, smiling in sympathy, I move off to continue my checks. I head to the top table and then to where the cake is already laid out, an elaborate castellated edifice of carved white sugar, a feast for the eyes rather than the mouth. Today's groom, Dan, had pulled me away from his bride-to-be last night after the wedding rehearsal and asked me to do him a little favour. He has a personal extra gift for her, he had said. I must remember to put it beside the cake later and now I am curious about what it is he has chosen. I can't resist pulling the little box out of my pocket to look.

The box is light and stylish. I'm telling myself I want to be sure she will love whatever it is, but really, I am captivated by this romantic gesture. Almost as though it was a gift for me, my fingers curl round the so tempting lid and gently prise it open. It is jewellery, of course. The piece that nestles inside is more stylish and edgy than I gave today's safe-looking groom credit for. An exquisitely made silver chain sets off a bejewelled skull pendant, whose eyes glow red and suggests Damian Hirst's gem encrusted art. I turn it over gently in my hands. This is not costume jewellery, this is the real deal. Those sparkling stones are actual diamonds. And are those rubies in the eye sockets? It glitters irresistibly in my palm. Oh, she is so lucky. Fancy having a man who adores you so much.

Well, my part in the surprise is easy. I've just got to keep the box safe and then put it on this table before the cake is cut. I can look forward to watching her delighted surprise.

Chloé

Oh, my lord, here I am with the hottest jewels in my hands. I'm getting chills looking at them. Delicate enough for a wedding, expensive and edgy as fuck. What a fortunate little bitch is today's wedding princess, whatever her damn name is. But, I think, glancing around the room at the scene unfolding around me, but fuck it all, why should one girl (her) have all of this? This beautiful room, this perfect day, hundreds of people rushing around working to make her happy, all on top of an adoring and generous man and loads of friends and family. Even the bloody sun is obliging her today and smiling roundly and warmly on the spoilt brat. And then, hello world, just over here, feeling tired and thirsty and quite unloved. Here is another perfectly nice girl (me) who is working her arse off trying to get everything just so and nobody is making a fuss of *me*.

Yeah, damn right, I haven't noticed anyone asking if I would like a drink or making sure I have a fresh hot croissant, though I can clearly smell those that the bridal party is enjoying; a bunch of indulged layabouts the lot of them. Not one adoring young man is telling me how fantastic I am or showering me in gifts and no crowds of stylish and excitable friends are cooing and fussing over me.

The balance of things is too skewed. Nature abhors injustice. I straighten up and square my shoulders as I come to a decision. It is up to me, right here and right now, to correct this injustice. I don't think miss prissy-pants shiny new bride is going to miss one extra thing tonight, is she? Not when she is standing beside her handsome new husband after a whole day of being worshipped, cutting into the cake's gleaming edifice, dazzled by the flash of cameras all focussed on her, her, her.

No way is it right she gets this too. I gently tip the jewels from one hand to the other and decide I should try them on. There is a mirror in the hotel lobby.

I tuck the little skull, already warming with my touch, into the palm of my hand and saunter through. Fuck it all though, the place is now full of early arriving guests, faffing around with coats and presents. I don't want to talk to them. On an impulse I head out through the front door and across the gravelled drive to my car, my feet slipping on the loose stones in my hurry. Opening the door, I slide in. My pulse is racing in excitement at the treasure in my hand. I fix the clasp around my neck and look at myself in the driver's mirror.

And oh, my sweet fucking Lord, it looks good! The skull rests on the top of my collarbones at the perfect length and the ruby eyes glint a look of pure money, sex and privilege back at me. My own eyes are shining now to match, and my cheeks are flushed. You know how it feels when you go into a shoe shop in your scuffed and street soiled shoes and try on some gorgeous new ones and suddenly become a more pulled together and better version of yourself? This is what happens to me now when I try on this necklace. That is what this

4

outfit, which I had thought was perfectly fine this morning, really needs. This new edge and sass is how I should look all the time.

Well, they do say diamonds are a girl's best friend, don't they? And I could certainly do with a new friend or two, I tell myself, unclipping the clasp and sliding the necklace carefully into the depths of my glove compartment.

2

Flora

I shake my head to clear it as I leave the dining room, checking my phone for the next item on my 'to do before 3pm deadline' list. I feel dazed and shaky, not even sure where I am. Maybe I should grab a coffee and biscuits while I'm checking the canapés downstairs. Though, checking the time as well, I'm running later than I thought and will be lucky to stop at all. A whole hour has disappeared, and a shiver of unease runs through me as I realise I have lost time again.

I tell myself I'm edgy today because the last few weddings have all gone wrong, and that is surely co-incidence. There was the townhouse wedding last month at which a bridesmaid swore blind that £200 in cash had been taken out of her little clutch bag, the otherwise charming country wedding on a family farm at which a wealthy young stockbroker had the bonnet to his car savagely keyed, the series of complaints I received after a dull hotel event when the bridal couple were missing a few presents from the pile.

These things do happen occasionally, I know, but after a run of such weddings, I am feeling jinxed. Maybe I've been working too hard and need to take a holiday.

I drag myself back to the present, gulp down a tepid coffee and Danish in the kitchens and over the next few hours am kept busy earning the large fee that I command. I calm today's bride, Evie; produce my own emergency make-up supplies and encourage her out of her dressing room despite the blotchy red rash that has come up all over her chest mid-morning. I banter patiently with the tipsy best man and bride's brother and compliment them on their choice of

6

kilts. I prevent two small children from destroying the fragile wedding cake castle. I mix up jugs of Pimms when supplies run low out on the terrace in the heat. Mopping the sudden tears of the bride's mother, I make sure she gets a salmon sandwich inside her to soak up the three large glasses of white she has swiftly knocked back. I position the harpist out of the sun and fetch her water and an envelope of crisp twenty-pound notes.

I am on hand when the evening dance band turns up, banging their boxes of gear into my carefully positioned troughs of gardenias and scattering the roosting doves in the nearby barns. I watch as they set up with elaborate care, monitoring the screeches of feedback. Once they are coaxed in off the darkening terrace after a pre-gig smoke and once the beat of their first song stirs the quietening evening, I know my work is nearly done. So far, despite my earlier forebodings, everything has gone perfectly.

Now I need to check the evening coffee service is on schedule, help an over tired elderly couple to their rooms, check the buffet is still looking fresh, that the toilets have soap, hand cream and clean towels and that no one is getting too drunk and mouthy in the bar. I am slowing down now, my feet hurt, my cheeks are numb from smiling, my mouth is dry.

One more set-piece to go and then I can safely slip away. It is The Cutting of the Cake, completed by many photographs of the couple adorably feeding each other sweet and sticky mouthfuls. All the guests must be given a slice, most of which will later be cleared up by the late-night cleaners, who hopefully take it home to their families.

Everyone gathers in anticipation, and I glance at the table on which the cake is waiting. Yes, Dan's little box that I put out earlier is still there. That's good. Suddenly I had had a stab of anxiety, that maybe I had forgotten it, or put it in the wrong place or something. What *is* worrying me about that box? Half my mind is working on this niggle and the other is checking the choreography of the last piece of wedding theatre as I scan the room, absent-mindedly chewing on my thumbnail as I do.

Yes, the two principals are there, gleaming sliver knife in hand. The photographers are posed, as well as an expectant semi-circle of family and friends all with their phones ready.

The cake is cut to oohs and camera flashes, which catch the widest smiles yet on the faces of my bridal pair. I finally relax and allow myself a second to enjoy my success. Today *has* all gone well. They are both so happy and everything is picture perfect. I stayed in control and nothing went wrong.

Dan takes Evie's hand to pull her back to the table. Everyone is talking and exclaiming over the cake, so I watch his lips moving, as he hands her the small white box. Evie looks surprised and delighted and before even opening it she blushes and reaches up to give him a big spontaneous kiss. Oh, they are so sweet. My anxieties melt away and my eyes are damp as I watch them.

Chloé

Fucking hell, I thought today would never end. And all that fuss at the last minute! Never mind, it is all pretty much a wrap now and I can fuck off out of it. The party is in full swing with most guests half pissed, so I can head home for a drink myself. Let's hope there is some decent wine in my flat. I certainly need it.

Alone in the cloakroom, I shrug on my jacket and then pop to the ladies before I leave. I am in a cubicle when I hear two women enter, talking excitedly. I'm pretty sure one of them is Dan's sister, Marie, who has been bossily acting as an unofficial 'best woman' all day.

'I can't understand it either, but it gives me a really creepy feeling, you know?' Marie is saying.

'Oh, my God!' her friend responds, 'are you thinking what I'm thinking?'

I have frozen since they entered the room, but I can hear them both at the sink, opening bags and clattering make-up on the worktop.

'You don't think that someone could have taken it, do you? Nobody here would do that, surely?'

'Well, Dan *said* to Evie that he must have left it on his desk at home in all the rush and he does need to check that out, but yeah, otherwise, I suppose someone must have done,' Marie continues in tones of horrified triumph.

The other woman gasps.

'I suppose there *are* lots of people going through the rooms all the time, in a place like this…'

'Yeah,' Marie interrupts, 'if it was taken it might have been a member of staff, or another hotel guest, it could be anyone. The management is going to have to look into it because Dan said he was sure he gave it to that wedding planner. You know, the blonde girl with the heels who has been rushing around organising things all day?'

I freeze in my cubicle. Now I've been in here so long I don't feel I can come out or it will look like I've been listening in on their conversation. And can they see my feet? If so, they will know it is me in here. I lift my legs as high as I can and try not to breathe. Maybe they will think this cubicle is always locked. Why does this sort of shit always happen to me? I suppress an urge to giggle. I always do that when things cock-up.

9

Just when I thought the situation couldn't get any more awkward, my bloody phone trills out loudly from my jacket pocket. In a panic to stop it, I nearly fall off the toilet and I jab at it frenziedly. I mean to turn it off but in my haste press answer by mistake and some posh woman says.

'Am I speaking to the Wedding Planner please?'

Oh, this is fucking brilliant. What am I going to do?

Luckily, at that moment, another girl comes in, exclaiming loudly about how drunk she is, and strikes up a conversation with the others. Soon all three head off back to the dance floor, shrieking with laughter.

As the clatter of sharp shoes on tiles dies away, I try to focus on the caller on the end of the line, who – amazingly – is still there.

'Can you hear me now? it's extremely busy here,' I say, sounding, to my surprise, quite the controlled professional.

'I apologise,' says the woman, not seeming at all sorry. 'I hadn't thought you might be working. I'm interested in setting up a meeting with you to discuss my upcoming wedding.'

I ask her to email me the details and assure her I would be delighted to help and then furtively exit the cubicle, checking that the room is empty. Alone in front of the mirror, I stare at my reflection. My hair is a little mussed, but I look pretty hot, eyes sparkling, and face flushed with the excitement of my new 'borrowed' jewels that just *might* be missing and *might* be in my car right now.

Smiling broadly, I grab my bag and mouth a cheery 'Goodbye and I'll email you tomorrow' to the hotel manager as I swing out through the door as fast as I can.

Back in my car, my heart is pounding. I open the glove compartment for a peek at the skull, which sparkles back at me in welcome. Seeing it there gives me a buzz that wipes away any fear of getting found out. It's not like I'm going to go back to that hotel for a few months, is it? I don't think I have another booking there this summer, so it *will* all blow over. Once the lovebirds set off on their honeymoon, they will forget all about a little bit of jewellery, once they are sunning and shagging in the Seychelles or wherever. All will be well. The scales of justice have weighed the balance in my favour and the right girl has been rewarded.

Flora

Back in my car at last, I stare blankly into the darkness in an exhausted stupor, before stirring myself to start up the engine. The edgy, lost feeling is back. It *did* go well today though, didn't it? Apart from the fuss right at the last minute about some jewellery that was supposed to have been in a box but wasn't after all.

What could have happened there? Did he forget? Did some guest steal it? Thinking about this makes me fuzzy-headed and sick. Why did another bad and weird thing have to happen at *this* wedding as well and after everything had been so perfect? I try to shake my building anxiety and remind myself how happy the couple had looked. Perhaps tomorrow the jewellery will turn up safely after all.

After talking all day, I am too emptied of words to formulate a coherent thought. The deserted road curves blankly ahead and darkness weighs down my eyes.

'Pay attention and keep your mind on your chores,' says a stern voice inside my head, quite clearly. *'You are always daydreaming, child, now use what little sense the good Lord gave you and get back to helping your mother in the kitchen.'*

A shiver of fear shakes through me. It is when I am

11

nearly asleep that I hear that voice. I wind down the window to let in a rush of inky early morning air. The present comes back, a welcome return. Soon the roads I am driving through become feature-filled, with streetlights dimly showing graceful Georgian buildings as I enter the outskirts of Cheltenham.

3

Flora

It is a late sunny Sunday morning, my favourite kind of morning. It is such an effort to remember where and who, I am each morning though. Does everyone get that? To remind myself, I focus on the tall, shuttered windows of my first floor flat and am soothed by the expanse of expensively understated paintwork. My eyes drift around the room, taking in polished wood floors, scattered rugs, a few pieces of antique furniture, a bunch of orange peonies. The peonies cause me to frown, because, lovely as they are, I cannot remember buying them. I'm not quite awake yet. To reassure myself, I reach for the diary by my bed and for today's date. Four years ago, when I bought this flat, I started to make detailed notes of each day's appointments. That was after an exasperated call from the solicitor to say I had missed yet another appointment to come and sign the deeds. My shaky memory is something I try not to think too much about. Everyone forgets things, don't they? Luckily for me the kind if nosy woman who lives in the flat below, Elena she's called, she took a bit of a fancy to me and in the end helped a lot, talking me through filling in the paperwork and even helping to carry stuff up the stairs when the flat was finally mine.

She can be a bit much though, always ready to get to know me better. That is not something I need in my life.

To banish thoughts of curious neighbours, flat buying hassles and swirling background anxieties, I focus on breakfast. After yesterday when I hardly had time to eat, I am starving. Stretching out, I admire my perfect pedicure before flinging on a silk kimono and padding into the kitchen to put on some coffee.

'Ok Flora,' I say out loud to myself, as I often do when alone, 'coffee, fruit and muesli first, then a long soak in the bath.' My handbag is slung across the kitchen counter, and I pull out my phone to check for messages.

My hand lands first on bottles. Why are they in my bag? There are definitely bottles in my bag. Three in fact. I pull them out. A single-malt whisky miniature, a full-sized cream liquor and then a bottle of perfume, which has already been opened. I stare blankly at these and then reach back in to find two blueberry cupcakes wrapped in an embossed napkin, a silver chain and a couple of crumpled twenty-pound notes, sticky with cupcake icing.

Chloé

It's dark as fuck in here. Bloody weather. One minute it's sunny and then there is rain lashing down and shit going on outside. And it's way too quiet in this flat. Sticking on some tunes, I wander to the kitchen for more cake. Why do people bother to eat all that healthy crap, all that birdseed tasteless shit, when there is cake in the world?

I slide the second muffin onto my plate, adding chocolate ice cream from the freezer. Some of it spills onto the kitchen table, so I scoop it up with my fingers, whilst scrolling through Netflix on my phone. I need another drink, so slop the rest of the cream liquor into my glass and go in search of a proper amount of wine.

I know there was some here. I remember bottles in the fridge. I don't know where stuff goes some days. I swear there is a poltergeist moving my stuff around.

So, I've got a tipsy ghost wandering round the place out of sight? I decide it must be that and find myself giggling at the image of a drunken spirit lurching around, pouring wine

14

into itself. Without a proper body, it would go straight through, wouldn't it, onto the floor? Like that last lot of wine did. Fuck it though, it will dry. At last, I am warm and safe. This evening I'll get takeout and watch trash non-stop. It is Sunday after all.

Miriam

Sunday after all. A bell tolls inside my head. It is Sunday, the holy day. Why am I not at prayer? Why am I not in the Meeting Hall now with my sisters in the Lord, my head bowed, my hair (naturally light brown, now blonde and highlighted), plaited and firmly covered by a cotton scarf? Not attending on a Sunday is surely a mortal sin. Am I going to go to Hell as the Elders warned me? Have I committed too many unforgivable trespasses? Or am I already in Hell? Am I trapped in an empty flat with only my guilt to haunt me? The room spins. The sweetness of cake and alcohol in my mouth is sickening. I fall to my knees in prayer, hearing again the harsh voice in my head. *'Seek always the plain way, never strive for worldly success. Daughter, you are not of this world, you must set yourself apart, for you are a chosen servant of the Lord.'*

4

Flora

The doorbell's sudden blare has me scrambling to my feet in alarm. I am chilled and stiff. The room is dark and messy. There are cake crumbs all over the table, a pool of liquid darkening underneath, half-empty wine bottles and a designer perfume I don't recognise, are open on the counter. Why does someone have to come round now? Can I ignore them? God, I hate unexpected callers. I'm not keen on expected callers. People always ask so many questions.

I'm pretty sure I know who this is and I'm right.

'Hi, hi Flora, can I come in for a second?' says my downstairs neighbour Elena, hovering smilingly at the door. 'I heard you come in late last night and I thought you hadn't been out today, so I wanted to check you are alright.'

That is so Elena. She knows every time I enter or leave my flat. A warm-hearted and talkative Argentinian, she lives with her ailing parents. Despite being inquisitive, she is too kind to dislike, though I do wish she hadn't come up now and caught me at such a bad moment.

'So, you look pale today, cherub. How are you feeling?' She advances into the room, switching on the lights, her dark eyes quickly flicking over my undressed state, my unbrushed hair, the chaos of food and bottles.

'Was it a good wedding last night? You do have such an exciting life,' she burbles on, starting to gather up dirty dishes and running warm water into the sink. 'Much more so than me. I've been to Mass today, of course with my mother. Papa was not feeling too well again. You know how he has been

16

lately with his chest. Nothing exciting to report from church, I can assure you. Only the priest asking for more help with the flower rota and for running the Sunday school' she chuckles. 'I thought he was quite good looking when we met him first, but there's no point looking to a Catholic priest for any fun, is there? Dear God!' She crosses herself after this use of the Lord's name. 'Fancy vowing to celibacy all your life. It's not like I get much attention these days,' she gestures down at her round figure encased in a floury smock, 'but I couldn't imagine saying "never again". I'm not like you dear' she turns back to me, with bright and teasing eyes. 'You must meet lots of nice men at all these smart events you do. Surely that's half the point of weddings, a chance to meet people when everyone is dressed up in their best?'

'They never look at me,' I protest. 'I'm just the hired help, part of the backstage machinery. No one is interested in me.'

'And I know for a fact that is not true, you funny girl,' Elena retorts, smiling at me. 'It is fine, don't worry. I'm glad to hear people having a good time. But I do know that you had some pretty noisy male company last Saturday night. Nice-looking boy he was, though he made a poor job of leaving quietly. I had to help him open the front door at about five in the morning before he woke my parents. He'd clearly had a few drinks up here and maybe a few before. So don't give me that "no-one's looking at me" line,' she laughs.

I try to join in through a familiar mix of fear and puzzlement. What boy? Elena calls all men under fifty boys, so he could be any age. At five am? I cannot remember last Saturday at all. Maybe I should go to the doctor about my memory. The days all run together sometimes, don't they? I'm not going to let Elena see my concern, but this conversation is making me uncomfortable. I take the cloth that she is using to wipe the tabletop from her and become a little cooler, hoping she will leave without any more questions.

'It is really nice to see you,' I say, 'but I do have quite a lot of paperwork to catch up on.' I gesture lamely in the direction of the squashed cupcake cases, 'and I have a busy week coming up.'

This is a lie, and she must know it. I have clearly not been working today. I don't have much to do tomorrow. I don't care how it sounds though. I just want her out of my flat. I can't deal with people.

Elena looks disappointed. 'You are always so busy, darling. You need to make time to see friends and family. I've never seen you have any family over, or girlfriends? I'm sure you must have loads. *And* you need to look after yourself better. Well, anytime you want a cuppa and a chat, you know where I am.'

She is suddenly distracted by a small box that is open on the counter. Before I can say anything, she has peeped inside.

'Ooh, what a fancy necklace! That skull looks quite sinister, doesn't it? Staring up at me like that. You are so stylish and unusual, darling. Wherever did you find that? You always have such nice things. So, tell me, where did you buy that, or did some nice young man give it to you?'

And this is why I don't like visitors. Because where did I get it from? At this moment I have no idea at all.

5

Chloé

My belly is fucking huge from the food I've eaten today but I still want more. Nothing left in here though, just some hard and greasy pizza crusts spilling out of the takeaway box. I rub my stomach as I flop back onto the sofa, skidding the castors back into the wall, my hand moving lower. I'm feeling horny and dissatisfied. I'm clearly not going to get any action *this* weekend, so let my mind wander back to the lad who was here last. What the fuck was his name? Ben? Zane? Something like that. Not that it matters, it is not his face I am remembering now.

For a uni student, he was well built. I like them like that. Firm strong shoulders muscled back and a proper hard cock. And he had some weed in his pocket and we had both leant out of the window, smoking and drinking and pissing ourselves laughing. Shame he is not here this evening. He would have done nicely.

How did he come to be here? The still-functioning part of my mind tries to remember. Oh yeah, it had been a good wedding, and I'd been loading up my car at the end with a few little extras that no one seemed to need. And then this Ben, Zane, whatever, had been parked next car along and he had started the chat straight off. It was him being keen, not me. He was a right flirt. And he had a full bottle of champagne that he had picked up from the wedding breakfast table, so he had good taste. We'd ended up here on this sofa, drinking his fizz. Damn, I could do with him or another like him right now. He had a great arse. I lose myself in imagining his eagerly pumping buttocks in my hands and his hardness pushing me down into the cushions.

19

My last thought before dozing off is that it is time I got more fancy underwear for my next hook up, something saucy. Must go into town this week and pick some out.

Flora

My dreams are filled with dark shawled figures, with flickering lights and with long shapes on windowless walls. I wake with a start, tangled up in my sheets and with a pounding heart. To calm myself, I do my usual checks till the dreams recede into the cool grey light of early morning. I am Flora. I am 36. I am a successful wedding planner. I live alone in this smart flat, for which I have a too large mortgage.

I think back over the weekend. I did do a good job on Saturday for Evie and Dan's wedding, didn't I? Despite that missing jewellery at the end, which was unlucky. It *had* gone well, hadn't it? Why am I anxious? I log onto my phone messages to bring me back to earth and there is a lovely email from the happy couple thanking me. I have also been sent copies of shots that the photographer took. That shy but sweet new guy. Luke Sanderson, I see his name is. Well, he might not be great at small talk, but he can take a good picture. Scrolling through the images, I see these are exactly right; lots of informal groups and the unguarded but charming solo shots that are so current. I drop a line to the photography agency he works for asking to use him again.

I also have emails about my next wedding booking this coming weekend, as well as a long message from a woman who said she rang on Saturday. She is called Laura and she is marrying Tom. Glad of a new job, I reply at once and set up a meeting with her.

This week's wedding is in one of those large old-fashioned hotels in the centre of Gloucester. The bridal couple, though they booked me for a 'Flora Miller Special' have clearly now had some other influences. They have added a few incongruous touches, requesting a croupier and blackjack tables for the evening, a pig-roast for the evening guests, a pick and mix sweet cart for the kids and a pop-up photo booth. None of these fits with the tasteful and classic styling I had planned for them. Pulling it all together as a coherent look is going to need careful re-arranging and diplomacy, so I decide to go to the hotel first to plan where everything could now go. If I do that this morning, then I can go clothes shopping in Cheltenham on the way back.

Thinking about this upcoming trip I chew my nails reflectively, drawing blood as I go in too hard. Something about this wedding venue is making me uneasy but I can't work out what it is. I frown at my ragged manicure and tell myself to get a grip.

Driving into Gloucester, the sultry weather breaks, with heavy chilly rain spilling from dun-coloured skies. Pedestrians struggle with umbrellas blown inside out whilst cars splash dirty water against their bare legs. Now I'm here I understand why I was anxious. I have been here before. Many times. I remember this rain-soaked street very well. I remember staring at the damp concrete on the way to and from the Meeting Hall, hand in hand with my elder sister Martha. It is so familiar, though as if from another life. I even spot familiar patterns and patches of grey and dull pink studded stones in the pavements that we would hurry down. I can remember walking past this very hotel, the hotel I am about to go into today, all that time ago with Martha. Our heads would have been bowed, trying not to attract any attention from the strangers all around us, but we were always unable to resist peeking in through the large glass doors.

Lost in the past, I watch the doors swing open, as they must have done that day, what would it have been? maybe twenty-five years ago. I slip back easily into the past. My nose pricks at an elusive evocative smell, a sudden gust of warm and scented air emerging from inside the hotel. My footsteps had slowed down that day too, my breath catching, enthralled by a glimpse of an unimagined world of colour, light and warmth.

'Child, Child, stop staring at those ungodly people. They are not like us, they are not our people. You must not let yourself be distracted by worldly sights and places. Make haste now, we need to get back to prepare for the service. And then you still have scriptures to learn and you must help me make food for the brothers and sisters tomorrow.'

Rooted to the pavement, a ten-year-old child, I had squeezed Martha's hand; she had seen what I saw too. Through the open window, we had gazed at an enormous tree. A real tree, growing inside and as lush and green as the trees in pictures of the Garden of Eden from my old and still loved Children's Bible. Lights had hung from the roof, shining a golden glamour onto the well-dressed people below. A smiling woman behind a high desk had laughed down at a pair of excited children playing by the door who had run in towards her. The smells were irresistible. I remember standing and sniffing like a hungry dog, eyes wide with excitement.

Following the excitement comes another feeling, less welcome and more intense. A hot drench of shame. Shame, that made me stiff-legged and clumsy with self-consciousness, that brought redness to my face and turned my tongue into a lump. Shame that made all our trips into town or anywhere away from the safety of our own people a miserable ordeal.

Those two children, happy and ordinary and dressed as they are in jeans, trainers and colourful jackets, make me see how much we stand out. *My* legs are not comfortable in jeans but are hidden under a full-length dress. *My* feet are not

22

running free in bouncing springy trainers (and oh how much I want those trainers) but are imprisoned and weighed down in sturdy sensible brown lace-up shoes. *My* long hair is not flying messy and free, with a flowery clip in it, but hangs in heavy plaits down my back. My head is covered with a triangular scarf tied firmly by my mother this morning and now pinching a band of tightness over my forehead. How I wish I was not me but was her, that unknown girl, who looks my age but is from a different world. Imagine being able to run and shout and to be inside that hotel.

But the hotel is full of ungodly people. My father has told me so. And so that girl and her brother must be ungodly too. They are sinners and they are going to go to hell. I should feel sorry for them and should pray for them, not be envious of their worldly pleasures. If I were a better child, I would not feel this way. If I could only keep the teachings in my head, I would not be full of envy. I would be grateful to be different, *'We are not of their world, we do not live as they do.'* I should be proud to be showing that there is a better way to live and to be bearing witness to our faith. I am not though, I want to be that other girl with her loose messy curls and her bouncing feet, about to go for hot chocolate in that amazing hotel. I want to be her so badly and I am so ashamed of who I am that I feel I will break into pieces.

A man hurries into the hotel, leather bag under his arm and bangs against me, rooted as I am to the spot. He glances at me in half-apology. I shake myself.

Come on, Flora, I tell myself. This is not a place to be daydreaming and you're getting wet. I step firmly through the revolving doors and walk briskly up to the smiling receptionist.

'Good morning. I am Flora Miller. The wedding planner for Saturday's 3 o'clock?'

The shadows at the edge of my mind recede as I struggle to focus on the receptionist's face. I am swept up into activity, am introduced to the hotel manager, given a coffee and taken to look at the ballroom. Quite back to my professional self, I go through my notes for the event, discuss timings and put in a quick call to the photographic agency to confirm the photographer they are sending is my new favourite, new boy Luke, with the badly cut hair and the surprisingly good eye.

6

Chloé

I'm *so* bored after that dull as arse morning and I bloody well need something to cheer me up. I'm going shopping and I'm going right now. I've got to get out of this pissy weather anyhow, so it will have to be this department store here, what the fuck is it called, oh yes, Partingtons. It is all a bit 'grandmother's sitting room' style, but once I've dodged those weird, orange-faced make-up pusher types in the front, there will be some better stuff behind. Moving into the first clothes hall I flick through some dull formal work dresses, my heart speeding up as I realise that now is a chance to practice my shop-lifting skills.

God, I love this! Getting one over on the pompous fuckers who run these places. Getting some shiny new things that I can't afford. Whose fault is that anyway? It's certainly not mine. I work my arse off every day. All these rich entitled bitches in here are just wandering around picking out stuff that they don't need. Why the hell shouldn't I get some as well? I'm clever enough to get it for free.

We all do it right, sometimes? Don't tell me you don't. But not everyone is a fucking genius like me. I can get pretty much anything I fancy these days, so long as it is small. The problem today is finding something here in this crappy temple of all things dull and middle-aged that I want. Damn it, there must be *something*.

Now *tha*t is nice. I finally spot something I totally have to have. Top shelf there, along with all the Missoni and Victoria

25

Beckham and designer shit. That cute leather bag, cut in a circle and in cool reflective black. That bag is *so* me. I need that in my wardrobe, no question. I lift it down, turning it over in my hands. No way should it be stuck in here waiting for some posh entitled cow to snatch it up. Poor bag, it must feel terrible put next to that olive green tote, navy satchel type thing with fake leather trim and about a million and one black and beige bags on the shelves below.

I stroke the glossy skin of the little beauty. 'I'll rescue you' I murmur to it under my breath. It is only right, isn't it? The poor thing, stuck up here on the shelf like that. It is like re-homing an abandoned puppy and people think that is a great thing to do. And it would go perfectly with that new expensive- as-fuck biker style soft leather jacket I picked up last week on another successful 'shopping' trip. My fingers turn over the price and care ticket, just to see what they want.

And what the bloody hell? Someone is taking the absolute piss here, aren't they? How can they try and charge that much for this tiny thing? It's a total cheek them asking that price, there's nothing to this bag, you could barely even fit your phone in it. I'm in this store all the time; they get plenty of money out of me and I'm going to be buying stuff in the food hall afterwards. This bag belongs to me, as a perk for being such a good shopper. It is all factored in anyway, the pissing rich dicks upstairs expect to make losses like this, so what the hell.

I wipe my palms down the side of my pencil skirt, deciding on the best way to liberate it.

Yeah, I know, I'll try on a dress, to create a distraction. One of those butt ugly ones I saw earlier will do fine. I scoop one up and add another couple for good measure. Holding them up against me in turn and hanging the bag off my shoulder, I examine myself in the mirror before heading to the changing rooms, trying not to wince. And of course, the bag that I am rescuing drops between the folds of gross clothes and when I come back out of the changing room, smiling in polite refusal at the assistant as I hand back the dresses, it is tucked safely out of sight.

Later, out in the street again, the sun has come back out and I can feel the bulge of that new bag against my hip inside my loose summer jacket. I'm buzzing with a job well done. I'm so good. Despite all the cameras and expensive security, no one spotted little innocent me. Light fingered rescuer in action, I am. I'm thirsty now after the excitement, I'd bloody kill for a large glass of something chilled. Spotting a streetside bar I turn sharply in and check out today's special deals.

Flora

Oh my, what is the time? I've just woken from a completely unplanned nap. I know I didn't sleep well last night but this is ridiculous, falling asleep in the street. My head is full of drowsy fog and for a moment I have no idea where I am, or how I got here. I blink and take some deep breaths, re-orienting myself.

Think, Flora, think. What have you been doing today? Oh yes, I had a hotel meeting this morning and then must have decided to stop off for a drink. And here I am now sitting outside under a striped umbrella with empty wine glasses on the table in front of me. There is a gap in my memory of today though and anxiety twitches at my throat. I can't shake off the sense of a dream that is somehow too real. Drinking in the day will do that, I tell myself. What had I been thinking ordering wine on a working day and more than one glass by the looks of it? I must have got carried away into a holiday mood by the warmth of the sunshine, which has now steamed away all this morning's rain.

27

The bar just along from mine fills with a crowd of young professionals spilling from a nearby office. They have been undergoing some sort of team-building exercise and it seems to have worked by uniting them in noisy condemnation of the group leaders. After their first round, swiftly knocked back, they grow increasingly uninhibited and friendly with each other. Absentmindedly I start listening in and turn to look at them. One of the group, a tall dark-haired woman, glances over and spots me eavesdropping. Half-frowning at me, she pointedly turns away to focus more intently on the man by her side.

And that small movement, that turning away, that subtle rejection, unlocks another unwanted flood of sensation. In an instant, I am back as an awkward girl again, this time hovering outside the school gates. Memories, stirred this morning by my location, come to the fore as I look away, embarrassed.

'Shunning,' the meeting called it and it was a severe punishment. If you, as a good sister in the Lord, did something that the elders, the grand men of the meeting, deemed to be wrong, they could cast you out. You were cut off from everything you knew and thrown out into the darkness of the world. You were rejected by your whole family. Your mother and father would cross the street if they saw you coming. Friends and relations would be forbidden from speaking to you.

It had been my greatest fear. I had watched it happen to other members of the Meeting, had seen the self-righteous turning from them in disdain and seen the poor sinners, one by one, disgraced and cut adrift, left to drown in their loneliness, unable to understand the alien world in which they found themselves.

Martha and I had a regular foretaste of how shunning would feel, of what it was to be rejected. Of course, as girls, we didn't go to school that much, as there was no need for us to have more than a basic education. My brothers travelled each day over fifty miles by taxi to attend a religious private school, leaving the house at 6.30 am and arriving home in time for prayers and supper, but for a few years, Martha and I were simply sent to the local comprehensive to acquire what education we could. During that time, each weekday started and ended with a sharp reminder of our social status as pariahs, with every walk to and from school.

Each morning after prayers and chores we would set off briskly, eyes down, keeping closely in step together. Our covered heads and long loose clothes marked us out as easy targets for teasing. I desperately wanted not to be noticed.

I used to break the walk to the end of the road into manageable sections in my mind to deal with the fear.

Get to the point on the pavement where there is a red car parked, that is quarter of the way gone. Nothing bad has happened so far. Look ahead now, right at the end of the street, just past that bus stop, that will be halfway. My body would be stiff like a jointed wooden doll that someone else was moving. As we crossed the road, another mental landmark relief would rush over me briefly.

Three-quarters of the way there and nothing terrible has happened yet. Then the terror would really kick in over the last two hundred yards. The worst was still ahead, which was the walk past the shop right by the school. Kids would always be hanging around, swinging on the railings, shouting to each other and sucking sweets from bags they had just bought. Though I kept my eyes straight ahead, fixed on the school gates, I could hear the percussive rattle of crisp packets opening, the fizzing sound as cans of drinks were opened, the acrid tang of illicit cigarettes. My bladder would tighten in fear as the curious children's gaze hooked on us both.

'Off to church, are you? Hurry up or you'll miss prayers,' a boy would shout and the other kids would collapse in giggles and walk behind us, mimicking our stilted movements, swinging in their hands imaginary versions of our plain brown leather briefcases.

On bad days, we were shoved into the road and puddles and arrived at school with soaking feet and legs. Some days, hands would pull at our plaits and mocking faces push into ours and one day Martha found dog poo smeared on the back of her coat. She, with the fervour of young religion, welcomed it all. She meekly submitted to the shouts and mockery, as all you could expect from the ungodly ones and as a test sent by the Lord to strengthen her fortitude. She told me to do the same. And each night I prayed for grace, as my mother taught me to do, telling me, 'It is a good opportunity to bear witness to these unsaved children, to show that we are not of the world and that there is a Godlier way.'

The pavement wine bar is filling up now and music begins to play inside.

'Mind if I take these?' says a young waiter, eyeing me curiously as he scoops up my empties. I am the only person sitting alone and I am headachy, cold and stiff. I fumblingly pay my bill and set off home. There are more shopping bags than I remember.

Not such a good idea drinking wine in the afternoon, Flora. I chide myself and plan a healthy dinner of sushi and vegetables, followed by an evening with my spreadsheets to prepare for Saturday's event.

7

It's now Tuesday morning after the Gloucester wedding. Nothing bad happened there, thank goodness, despite my forebodings. The couple seemed happy, and their cash is now helping to fill the hole in my bank account. I can relax a little, hoping the run of jinxed events is over.

This morning I'm driving out of town to meet those new clients, Laura and her soon to be husband Tom, who want an 'at home' wedding. They live just outside Cirencester, at Laura's parents' place, 'Chalk Hill Farm.' Laura's appearance matches her patrician telephone voice. She is a tall brunette, dressed in Barbour and jodhpurs from trotting out the family's horses, fitting this meeting in before heading to her job in a law firm in Cheltenham. Tom seems at home in the lush surroundings of pale stone outbuildings, expensive horses and rolling fields, but it is less clear what he does. Tossing his dirty blond hair off his face like one of the stable ponies, he pads barefoot to the Aga and pours me a coffee.

'We're going to have it here,' Laura gestures out to the lawns in front of the house, 'and Mummy's friend Lucinda is organising the catering. I'll give you her details, so we only need you to sort the entertainment, flowers, placement, invites, favours, novelties, some fun ideas for the children and of course the cake. We thought with all the clean eaters coming we might need two, a raw food one and a conventional one, mightn't we darling?'

She looks across at Tom, who is fiddling with his phone and then continues, 'I have loads of ideas. I've got several mood boards and all the themes are planned to tie in with the outfits of the principals. Mummy has replanted all the herbaceous borders specially to match. It was all supposed to be next year, but,' she smiles coyly and smooths her flat stomach, 'we've found out we are expecting. It really wasn't planned, but luckily Tom can be very hands-on and so can Mummy, so that does mean that we are bringing all our plans forward by a year and now we want the wedding in July, which is only eight weeks!' she finishes on a rush of words and breathes deeply.

There is a short pause in which I try to decide if it is going to be possible to arrange the complicated wedding of her imaginings in less than two months and in that pause, I glance across at Tom. A fleeting expression of panic is crossing his face. A half-smile twists his lips as he realises his emotions are on show. This is followed by a closer look at me. I feel his eyes catching on my newly cut and highlighted blonde curls, held off my face with designer sunnies I picked up a few days ago. His gaze slides slowly down my green wrap dress, lingering at my hips and finally drops to check out coral-painted toes peeking out of my open-toed heels.

Oh, hang on a minute, is this guy giving me the eye? The cheek of the man. He's just got his super successful fiancée pregnant; he's going to be running the family farm by the looks of him and now he's giving me hot looks? Well ok, young Tom, two can play at that game. I can be up for a bit of fun as well. I flash him my best sultry look. All these cocky straight men are so easy, I think triumphantly, watching a faint flush rise in his cheeks.

'So, Miss Miller, I hope I can call you Flora?' Laura breaks into my daydream, reminding me who I am and, more importantly, why I am here. 'If you take us on, we are going to be seeing a lot of you for the next few weeks.'

'Of course,' I smile. I'm only a few years older than her. After a shaky start, my career developed fast, as I discovered creative talents and business drive my early life would never have suggested. And it wasn't like I had any friends or family life to distract me.

Laura's voice is buzzing on, and I tune back in.

'So, I bought this piece of fabric when we were on holiday in Provence' she says, again trying but failing to catch Tom's eye and get him to take an interest. 'I'm imagining that you could pick up all the colours in this bit here, this sludgy green and look, this dusky pink and this almost silver and incorporate them into the place settings so it creates a sense of style? I'd like you to intimate an aura of faded grandeur, but with a contemporary twist. I'm thinking Louis Quinze through a decadent smokescreen of film noir, with a quasi-melancholic post-hedonistic mood. Do you see what I'm seeing?'

I'm not at all sure that I do, but I make plenty of notes and dutifully photograph the fabric. I am conscious throughout of Tom, drinking his coffee, tapping on his phone and looking at my legs.

We agree a price for my work. With all her quasi-melancholic fantasies in mind, I aim high, and Laura agrees at once. She has clearly realised she is up against it if she hopes to pull off her vision in time and is relieved to find someone who will take her on. Then she must dash off for her meeting and departs, her Range Rover spattering gravel as she reverses down the drive at speed.

As the sound of the car disappears, Tom swings off the kitchen table on which he has been perched throughout my conversation with Laura.

'So, Miss Miller,' he says. 'Funny kind of job you have. Making all our dreams come true, is that it?' He sounds sarcastic. 'How did you get into this line of work?'

I decide on an edited version of the truth. It's easier that way.

'I was brought up cooking for weddings' I say. 'My mother used to do all the catering for the, for lots of local weddings and I got interested in the flowers and the photography and how the whole thing was put together.' Actually, I had set up on my own doing weddings as far removed as possible from those I had helped at as a child, ones which would horrify my mother, if she ever knew. But she never will.

I realise I've tailed off a bit and Tom is waiting for more.

'I just like making people happy, creating that perfect day and I'm good at organising' I add, sounding extremely lame even to myself. Tom clearly thinks so too.

'Ooh, proper Little Miss Sunshine aren't you,' he says. 'Well, I'm sure it *will* all be perfect, and you will make us very happy. I mean, it's pretty nice here, isn't it?' He gestures out as Laura had done towards the lawns, borders and orchards of the garden, which roll off expensively into the Cotswold countryside.

'And of course, Laura has such amazing taste, everyone says so. She's always helping friends out with ideas for their weddings and as for her own, I think she's been planning it all her life. If she wasn't about to be made partner at her firm, she'd be after your job herself,' he adds, managing to make me feel both anxious and inadequate in one sentence.

'Anyway, I'm sure you girls are going to have a fabulous time together until the wedding, planning the colour of the napkins and where to put Aunt Vanessa. Don't forget about the...' here he gestures an imaginary little bump over his belly. 'She'll be getting hormonal pretty soon as well.' His voice trails off. 'I'm gonna be in charge when it lands apparently. Laura is at such a "crucial stage in her career"', he makes speech marks in the air as he says this, 'that she says it's only fair that I take on most of the childcare to start with. I don't know how that's going to go. I have literally no idea what a baby even is really,' he laughs, seeking my complicity in his ineptitude.

Tom could talk for both of us and seems eager to chat, but I remind myself that my clients' personal lives are not my concern. After a brief walk round the gardens to see where the marquee will go, I wave him a perky goodbye and set off back to town.

8

I'm going to be very busy with Laura's wedding for the next few weeks and it has come at the right time. Despite my brave professional front, my diary had been too empty this summer and the mortgage on my lovely flat is more than I can afford.

Over the next week, I am in daily and sometimes hourly contact with Laura. One of the ideas she presents to me (via emails, instant messages, voice messages and texts) is that she would like a photographer to document the process of preparing for the wedding, as well as the day itself.

'It's going to be such an intense time and I'm so incredibly busy with work with this big project coming off and I want to capture memories of this golden time for the rest of my life,' she writes. I think of the touching and informal shots that Luke created at last week's soulless casino wedding and decide if anyone can make this work, it will be him. I dash him off a message, relieved he is polite and respectful to work with, not like that snarky young smoothie Tom, who I will have to watch.

The wedding at Chalk Hill Farm will take most of my time for the next few weeks, though I have a few smaller jobs to finish off, including an alternative outdoor pagan wedding in a meadow and a gay couple's civil ceremony. Today I wake up with my head full of to-do lists as well as my usual morning checks (I am Flora, I am 36, I own my own flat and, oh my God, I have a stressful wedding to plan).

I make coffee and write a to-do list, deciding to focus first on Laura's extremely specific colour scheme. This morning I'll head back to the department store in Gloucester, the same one I was in last week looking for work dresses, with the photos of Laura's chic French fabric as a guide to choosing table dressings and props.

As I pass Elena's door on my way out, she pops her head out. She must have been listening for my steps on the stairs, but my irritation at being checked up on fades as I see how upset she looks.

'Papa is really not good today,' she says. 'I'm trying to get him to see the doctor, but he's worried he will have to pay and we don't have much money. I'm trying to explain about the health service here, but you know, he is getting a little confused,' she smiles at me. Through the open door, I can see the elderly couple, Mr and Mrs Varela. They are sitting close together, surrounded by tiny tables covered in framed photographs, potted plants and coffee cups. It is such a homely and comfortable domestic scene (no one is praying, no one is cleaning, no one is angry), that I am tempted to follow Elena inside and join them on the saggy brown sofa. I wave at them both and promise Elena I will call in soon and try to explain once more about care being free at the point of contact, though I know Mr Varela's head is still in a country ruled by the Junta, in which every man needs to look out for themselves.

This image of Elena's family life stays with me as I drive to Gloucester, triggering trails of sadness that drift through my brain and distract me from the day's work. I park and enter Partingtons department store trying to focus and decide to start in glassware, where there just might be some champagne flutes and jugs in Laura's specific shade of romantic muted green.

Chloé

So here I am in my newest freebie-gathering place, Partingtons. It is a bit of a crap fest generally but does have hidden treasures. In its favour they are lax about security, I haven't spotted any cameras at all, if they are going to be so fucking lame, I might as well take advantage, mightn't I? At least I am brave enough to shoplift, I bet most of this lot here would love to but just don't have the balls. That's not a problem for me. I've a few items already tucked away today, minus their tags, at the bottom of my oversized handbag. Now I want to pick up one of those new watches that I spotted on my way in, and the job will be a wrap.

For some reason though today, I don't pull things off that well. There are always people all over the fucking place pretending to be shoppers who are really store detectives. I usually spot them, no problem, and there is not much I don't know about sleight of hand when it comes to small items. I could have given that rubbish magician who was fumbling around at last Saturday's wedding a few tips for sure.

But today, what happened? I'd moved from the dull-as-fuck homeware section into jewellery and new arrivals and was eyeing up those watches. Not that I need a watch. My phone is always in my hand, but one of these would look chunky and good on my wrist. So, my signature move is to pick up a couple, try them on loosely, let the security tag catch on the strap of my bag and then obviously fumble to free it. This allows time and cover to remove the tag with the tiny penknife that I always keep with me and then one of the watches (still tagged) goes back on the rack, but the other one can now be tucked away at the bottom of my bag.

That was my plan, except today, for some reason my sleeve got caught on another hook on the rack, pulling it over. Then something else fell, banged the stand next to mine and before I knew it, I was holding onto a whole teetering pile of display stands, with watches and bangles and fuck knows what all slipping off in all directions, clanging onto the glass-topped counter and the watch I'd wanted disappeared down behind the assistant's table completely. Stupid thing, I didn't like it that much anyway.

Flora

So, one minute I am in glassware looking for the right colours for super particular Laura and then I must have spaced out again. Now I feel like I've just come round, and I am in the jewellery section. I have had a clumsy moment as well. A whole display stand is knocked over. Why am I even looking at watches and bangles? I really don't like this zoning out that keeps happening. I *should* see a doctor, but what would I say? It is going to be hard to explain and the thought of going to see a (probably male, probably patronising) doctor makes my stomach clench with fear. I struggle to put right the upended stands while swallowing down a wave of panic.

Nearby shoppers have turned in my direction as I've startled them. One big guy is staring and moving quickly towards me. Perhaps he is an in-store detective.

Why am I so clumsy? My cheeks are boiling, and my hands feel like I'm wearing gloves as I struggle to put everything back. A shop assistant comes to my side briskly and takes over, giving me a cold nod as she does so. It doesn't seem like anything is broken, so I decide to slip away without drawing any more attention to myself, giving a limp smile in the general direction of that possible store guard. He is staring at me hard, and I am obscurely guilty.

'Come on, Flora,' I say to myself. 'I am here shopping for Laura.' Tidy and super controlled Laura, who has everything planned. Laura whose life is about to spin *out* of control, once her flat stomach starts to curve, her perfectly neat ankles to swell and her keen lawyer's brain to soften with maternal hormones.

I feel a momentary sympathy for her, especially with that wandering eyed fiancé and resolve to give her the best possible wedding within her impossible time frame. Finally focused on my mission I gather a collection of glasses, flower vases and glass bowls for floating candles in the subtle muted shades she specified. I'll mix these with vintage plates and antique silverware to dress the tables. Next stop is the flower stall in the covered market to source some nearly black flowers, which mixed with sun-whitened branches and under the flickering candlelight will add a Gothic vibe and supply some of the film noir, quasi- whatever- it -was that Laura told me she wanted.

9

Monday morning has me back at my desk. In a patch of sun streaming through the tall Georgian window and with a fresh pot of coffee beside me, I work through a series of messages from an increasingly fraught Laura.

'Please can you check in with the band? I do need to know what they are planning on wearing. They mustn't turn up in something clashing like bright blue, or slogan t-shirts.'

'Tom and I had a cake testing session yesterday, but we are concerned about the gluten-free offerings. Also, one of Tom's cousin's children has a nut allergy, so we need a complete list of everything that will be in the kitchen.'

'I don't think the gerberas that the florist suggested for the bouquet in the hall are going to work there. Gerberas are a little common, especially the bright orange ones. Could you have a word to see if we could get something more classic?'

'Mummy is getting quite fretful trying to sort out the placement. It is *such* a nightmare. Any chance you and that nice photographer could pop over in the next day or so and take some lovely images of her making up wedding favours or choosing her hat to get her back in a good mood and onside again?'

I respond to this last request, mainly to put off having to call the band to discuss their shirt choices for a wedding that is still a month away. Luckily, Luke is free, and I arrange to pick him up on the way over to Chalk Hill Farm. I am happy to have a reason to drive out into the Cotswolds this lush July morning and it is a chance to get the top down on my second-hand convertible and feel the country air blowing through my hair.

I've been in touch with Luke a lot since taking Tom and Laura's booking, but we haven't met up much. I know he has been back out to the farm and has been documenting the construction of a new summer gazebo. He has also chronicled further work in the garden, the clearing and refurbishing of the raised pond and its fountain and the transformation of a shabby outbuilding into an 'orangery.' We chat about this in the car, and I tell him about the damp debacle that was my recent outdoor pagan wedding, with guests in party dresses, wellies and waterproofs supping Pimms and canapes inside a stinking cowshed. Luke laughs out loud at my stories.

'I wish I'd been there to get pictures, at least they would have been different to usual,' he says, sprawling untidily in the seat next to me, his large and rather dirty boots filling the front of my two-seater Mazda MX-5, but his warm smile and gentle manner lifting my spirits despite my twitchiness about mess.

'Yes, it was funny when the guests started falling over in the mud, especially the poor girls in heels. The couple were cool about it all, they were *very* chilled people, but I think this lot today will want everything to be perfect.'

I'm starting to worry about the new list of tasks from Laura this morning. Luke shoots me a consoling look but says nothing more. He is *very* quiet and a bit gauche, with his frame that seems too large for my small motor, but I've enjoyed his company this morning and feel calmer than usual as we crunch up the freshly raked gravel drive.

Laura greets us hastily. She is just off to check the progress of her bespoke dress before heading to London for a 'terribly important' meeting.

'I've asked the dressmaker for a waterfall of seed pearls down my back, flowing into the train, but I'm worried now it may be over-emphasising my bottom,' she frets, before hastily introducing us to her mother Annabel and rushing off.

Annabel is an old-fashioned gentlewoman, with a cut-glass accent and is flanked by two shaggy golden retrievers. She is eccentrically dressed in multiple colourful layers of clothing, a unique mix of moth-eaten cashmere, Peruvian cotton and high-end sportswear.

'My dears, do come in,' she welcomes us. 'There is still some China tea in the pot. Would you care for refreshment? My daughter is anxious that we should have some photographs taken as you know, which is not my thing at all. First, perhaps I could ask your opinion, as members of the younger generation, about a small matter?'

'Of course, Mrs, er,' begins Luke.

'Oh, call me Annabel, dear. In truth, I am a touch reticent about this, but Laura and that handsome young man she is marrying, I'm sure he has made an impression on you?' she turns to me, smiling slightly, 'they have suggested that I should read a short extract from the Bible at the wedding ceremony. They have persuaded the local vicar to let them marry in the village church. It is fourteenth century and very fine, so perfect for photographs,' she smiles at Luke.

'Are either of you religious at all?' she continues, gesturing vaguely with open hands. 'Not that it matters these days, does it? I haven't been to church for years, honestly decades, my dears, so I asked an old uncle who is very devout for suggestions. I wonder what you think of his choice? Here it is, look, St Paul's letter to the Ephesians Chapter 5, verses 21-33.'

'Child, child, listen to the words of the Apostle. "Wives, be subject to your husbands as you are to the Lord. For the husband is the head of the wife just as Christ is the head of the church, the body of which he is the Saviour. Just as the church is subject to Christ, so also wives ought to be, in everything, to their husbands.'

I know these words so well. I know without even looking at the open Bible what Annabel is showing us. I know every word that is on that page. There is a roaring in my ears, and I feel I am falling.

'Hey, Flora, you OK?' Luke's voice breaks into my awareness. I focus on him through the sudden mist in front of my eyes; he is smiling at me uncertainly. Annabel is also watching me closely. I shake my head to clear it, straighten my shoulders and smile at them both.

'That *is* a powerful passage' I say, trying to hide the effects of sudden and unwanted memories and pretending to be deep in thought. 'Hmm, maybe though, it would be nice to use something that speaks of love and gentleness, as well as obedience. How about here?' I rifle through to Colossians Chapter 3, verse 12, my fingers feverish on the familiar pages. 'Here, look' and I read, carefully keeping my voice quiet and steady.

'As God's chosen ones, holy and beloved, clothe yourselves with compassion, kindness, humility, meekness and patience. Bear with one another and, if anyone has a complaint against another, forgive each other; just as the Lord has forgiven you, so you must also forgive. Above all, clothe yourselves with love, which binds everything together in perfect harmony. And let the peace of Christ rule in your hearts, to which indeed you were called in the one body.'

'Oh, that's much better,' smiles Annabel. 'You are clever, dear, to know so much about St Paul. My Biblical knowledge is only what I can remember of Sunday school, and I don't need to tell you how many centuries ago that was. Those words will suit Laura better as well.'

Luke is still looking at me with concern, as though I am about to do something unexpected. I give him a small shove to lighten the mood.

'Are *you* impressed by my biblical knowledge?' I ask. 'It's only in marriage related texts. I'm clueless otherwise! Anyway' I add to Annabel, 'Luke is here with all his camera equipment,' (currently cluttering up my pristine car) 'to get some pictures of you preparing for the wedding. What would you like to be doing?' Laura suggested...' Here I scroll down the list of recent emails on my phone, 'oh yes, "I think it would be charming if you could get some pictures, just nice informal ones, of my mother tending the flower borders ahead of our garden party, or on the phone to the caterers, or sorting out towels and linen for the guests who will be staying over..."'

My voice tails off, as Laura has continued, "she can be stubborn and eccentric, maybe get Tom to help you if it's not working out and please try to suggest she wear something relatively non- offensive."

I smile at Annabel, wondering if today's outfit in a mix of raspberry red, purple and neon yellow qualifies as relatively non-offensive and then decide that Laura doesn't need to get her way in everything.

In the end, we set her up in the cool and musty smelling pantry, with dribbling dogs in attendance, pretending to be sorting through after-dinner cheeses. Luke snaps away busily, chatting more to her than I'd heard him do before. I find myself at a loose end in the kitchen and idly check out the cards and photos on the large corkboard. My eye is caught by a collection of tiny silver filigree ornaments on the mantelpiece; galloping horses, women with water urns, nesting birds, whimsical and delicate. I feel an almost overwhelming urge to pick up one and slip it into my pocket. The room seems to have become larger. Dizziness washes over me. Voices are clamouring in my head.

'Look how much stuff she's got; this house is stuffed with goodies. It's not like she'd miss a tiny thing, is it?'

'You are a sinner and will be cast out for your wrongdoings. The evil one has you in his grip.'

I hesitate, hand half outstretched towards the mantelpiece, as though paralysed. Another louder voice disturbs my inner dialogue.

'Hellooo, little Miss Miller, are you about to steal the family silver? Anything take your fancy?'

I spin round to find Tom laughing at me and, taking advantage of having caught me unawares, he lurches close to me. Brushing his hand over my shoulder, his lips touch my cheek in a clumsy and slightly over-familiar greeting.

'Oh hi, Tom. Great to see you,' I say, recovering my professional pose. (What had just been going on? I had spaced out there for a minute). 'Just admiring your mother-in-law's lovely things. And she is doing very well in there.' I gesture towards the larder 'let's hope all the family is as good as her in front of a camera.'

'Nearly mother-in-law.' Tom corrects me rather unnecessarily. 'I'm so tired of all this wedding crap,' he continues, quite rudely given that I am his wedding planner. He then smiles disarmingly at me.

'You must see it all the time,' he says, 'perfectly sensible women turning into bridezillas and demanding their every whim be granted. We are getting on with it quickly, because of the bump, but she's been plotting and planning wedding nonsense since before we met. I'd sooner just pop down the registry and then out for a pint or two.'

My warning look down the kitchen alerts him and he pulls himself up and puts on a cheery smile as Annabel and Luke finish the cheese-choosing shoot and emerge from the larder. 'Well done all,' he says, clearly trying to be pleasant. 'This looks like coffee all round.'

10

Flora

Saturday already and today's wedding is for two tech professionals, Victor and Max. After arriving late, though I was sure I left in good time, nothing is working out right. I was tongue-tied rather than reassuring with the bridal pair and the hotel staff seem off-hand with me too. What if something goes wrong again today? I don't think I could bear it. Was I late because I lost time again this morning? And why am I wearing such unsuitable shoes?

I plaster on a fake bright smile to take a last-minute delivery of bunches of cottage garden blooms. Hurrying into the pantry, I use them to fill the waiting vases and jugs. My hands are shaking, and my arrangements look amateurish and lumpen rather than charmingly informal. I poke and frown at them and then decide they will have to do, as I need to keep a close watch on the timings of the catering and to greet arriving guests.

Why is nothing working out right? Have I lost my touch? I feel like going to hide in the garden and having a good cry.

'Come on Flora, just get a grip,' I tell myself. I *am* going to have to go and see a doctor. There is something about doctors, especially the male ones I always get that scares me. I can't bear the thought of trying to explain to one how I am feeling, but today it seems as if my brain is unravelling.

I'm standing in front of the wretched flower arrangements, a forgotten hydrangea bloom in my hand when I feel a gentle touch on my shoulder. Spinning round in panic, I catch my breath in relief when I see it is only Luke.

'Hey, Flora,' he says gently. 'Are you ok? You're really pale.'

He takes the hydrangea from me and frowning in mock concentration, shoves it at a comically bad angle into the failed flower arrangement. It makes me smile despite myself and I move to straighten it, squaring my shoulders as I do so and taking a deep breath.

Luke pours himself a glass of water from the kitchen sink, pours me one too and then, looking out at the well-dressed crowds milling outside, sighs.

'Well, I'd better get out there and catch some shots of all the million and one bridesmaids before they get too pissed and sweaty. It's not going to take long for them to get tanked up today. Take it easy now,' he adds, giving me a warm smile and hurrying back to work.

I take a deep drink of water and wave my thanks at Luke, calling after him to make sure to take a picture of the top table before the meal and find I am feeling better. To my pleasure, the flowers magically become cooperative and arrange themselves into pleasing shapes. Triumphantly carrying the heavy jugs of blooms to the conservatory, I give the drinks waiter a cheeky smile, my good mood quite restored.

After their ceremony, Victor and Max are also relieved and exuberantly joyful and introduce me to some of their coupled-up friends who might be getting married soon. My mood continues to lift as the day turns out beautifully after all. By early evening I am basking in the glow of a job well done and good prospects of future work. Nothing has gone wrong, not a single thing. In a burst of optimism, I decide I don't need to bother going to any miserable doctor. What was I worrying about? there is nothing wrong with me. I am a success, popular and in control. Just look at today.

The party continues to warm with the evening sun,

reaches the sweet spot where it tips over into merriment and slides easily along. It is oiled by the grooms' obvious happiness, by copious bottles of Bolly, the scent of warm young flesh and freshly spent money and, I think, watching the energy levels continue to rise and inhibitions to lower, by some added illegal party fuel. I'm pleased the photography agency sent Luke along again, he is so good. He has been slipping in and out of the guests all afternoon, gently nudging them into poses, but so gently that no one feels self-conscious.

Towards the end of the evening, we both find ourselves on a stone balustraded terrace above the main party who have spilled out into the garden and alone apart for a few smokers at one end. I call Luke over to admire the scene below and together we lean over the low stone wall, looking down into the candlelit garden at the tops of the shadowy trees and the guests laughing, drinking and skinny-dipping in the raised pond below.

After a spell of comfortable silence, Luke speaks.

'I was, um, I was thinking about my grandfather today,' he says, as though he is choosing his words carefully. He smiles at my surprise at where his thoughts have taken him. 'He died four years ago today, which is why he was in my mind so much. We were quite close, in an odd way.'

I smile, pleased that he is talking about something other than work, as he continues. 'He had been a captive in the Second World War in the Far East. God, that sounds like something out of a history book, but it is true. He nearly starved to death out there. He rarely spoke about it, but he only survived by living on his wits and had to do things he wouldn't usually have done to stay alive.'

Luke stops speaking, takes a deep breath and looks at me closely as though to assess my reaction to his story so far. I'm enjoying listening to this more talkative Luke and am caught up in hearing about his grandfather. I smile at him encouragingly, 'Go on,' I say, and he continues more slowly.

'He spent the rest of his life haunted by what happened. I think that is why he ended up drinking so much. It was as though there was still an enemy just behind him and danger beyond every closed door. He would jump in alarm at the slightest noise.'

I do that, I realise. I am always jumping out of my skin. Why is Luke telling me this? Is this more than chat about his family? I make an uneasy movement as though to stop the conversation, but he is in full flow and looks away from me as he pictures his grandfather.

'It made him defensive too and he often would attack first, you know, rather than wait to be attacked. It didn't make him easy to be around, he could be a right pain in the arse. I came to understand why he was like that though, especially after he started opening up in the last years of his life.'

I shiver in a sudden chill as the sun sinks below the horizon. The mood has changed between us as well and become more sombre. Goosebumps are prickling on my arms as much from anxiety as from the cooling evening.

Luke is still looking away from me and down into the garden as he adds, more slowly, 'sometimes we would be sitting together with a beer and he would be there in the room with me, but it was like he had left his body behind and his spirit was somewhere else altogether. He was off fighting a long-lost battle or facing down a dead torturer. At times, he got so lost in the past that it was as though he had no idea where he was. Or who I was either.'

I am definitely worried about where this is going. I find out, as Luke takes another deep breath, almost a sigh. Looking across at me, his glasses glinting slightly in reflections from the lanterns overhead, he says, very gently, 'it is just that sometimes, Flora, there is something about you and how you zone out as you did earlier in the kitchen with the flowers, do you remember? that reminds me of him.'

There is a pause. So, *he* thinks there is something wrong with me as well. Coldness runs over me. The back of my neck prickles with tension and alarm and my mood plummets. Luke's face is half in shadow now in the dimming light and his expression is unreadable behind the blankness of his glasses, but I can tell he is waiting for a response.

I start to say something about how I am just forgetful and always have been but as I begin, I remember the long moment a few days ago when we stood with the open Bible at Annabel's house and the way both he and Annabel had been looking at me when I came round. How long had I not been there for? Fear is moving closer now.

I think back then to this morning and how lost and scared I had been. Had I been frozen in front of those stupid flowers for ages before Luke touched me on the shoulder? I want to ask him but am too frightened about what his answer might be.

Unable to answer at all, I try instead to brush off his serious mood by lightening things up. Forcing a smile, I playfully punch him on the arm.

'Well, thanks a lot, Luke! I'm so glad I remind you of your old Granddad. It must be my dodgy moustache that I thought I'd got rid of. Oh, and maybe the beige polyester trousers I like to wear so much!'

Luke glances involuntarily down at my legs and smiling, concurs.

'I never saw my grand pop in a pink pencil skirt, that's for sure, or gold sandals. You do have a varied wardrobe, you know, Flora, you almost look like a different person some days. Though you always look nice,' he adds hastily and then blushes slightly as though he has been too personal.

I was already feeling uncomfortable, and these last remarks don't help. I remind myself that it is best not to get close to Luke, or indeed to anyone, not if they are going to start trying to talk like this. How do other people do it? How do they cope with the whole making friends and chatting to workmates stuff? It is dangerous to let anyone see anything other than my super bright and in control "Flora doing a wedding" act. There are so many questions once you start talking. How does anyone risk sharing their secrets?

Chloé

I need to go and check out that pile of handbags and shit I saw earlier. There is something there that I've got to grab before some other posh bitch swans off with it. I need a treat now, right this fucking minute. I've been working damn hard all day whilst being pissed on from a height by over-entitled guests. I'm not sure what I've been talking about with young Luke here, but it doesn't feel like I was exactly having a ball. Muttering a quick excuse and waving airily at him, I hurry away.

I'm panting in my haste and slipping in my heels on the stone floor tiles as I re-enter the hotel. I remember now what it was I wanted, in that pile of bags and belongings in the conservatory. I hope whoever came with the grey fur stole that was thrown there has not yet left. It is not my usual style, a bit safe maybe, but I can tell it would totally work with my outfit today. I've been aware of being under-dressed all evening, among the stylish crowd in here. That always puts you at a disadvantage, doesn't it? No wonder I'm feeling crap.

As I reach the pile, I think I'm too late but then I spot a

glimpse of grey fur, half-buried in a mass of handbags. There are fake and real Gucci bags, Vivienne Westward, Kate Spade and Chloé, as well as a lot of high street rip off shit stacked up together.

Oh, hang on, back up a minute. A Chloé handbag! Look at that. That is *my* bag. A beautiful bag with my actual name on it. I snort out loud in pleasure and surprise. I don't know why I picked the name I have, but Chloé I am. And tonight, the perfect gift to myself (which I fucking well deserve after all my grafting) would be a perfect new bag.

This handbag is the real deal. It is certainly not a fake. Perfectly sized, in soft grey, but with a tough edge of glamour to it that screams money, class and success. My heart starts thumping like a drum machine. This is an exciting find, better than usual. This is hitting the jackpot. Forgetting the grey fur stole altogether (an everyday trifle and far too soft and girly, what had I been thinking?) I focus my attention on this handbag. The bag that will make me happy. The bag that will take away my nagging anxiety and make me fit in with this fashion-forward crowd. Anyone who carries a bag like this is a success, right?

I quickly scan the room. It is gone eleven and all the guests are outside in the garden, apart from a few oldies in one corner who are shouting at each other over the sound of the DJ. The lights in this main reception room are dim and whoever owns the bag is probably drinking or dancing in the moonlit and really should take more care of their stuff.

I don't want the things inside it. Those are far too grubby and personal. I open it with a satisfyingly expensive click and tip the contents out without looking at them. Then, in an instant and almost by accident, the bag is buried inside my capacious tote, safely tucked underneath a bunch of invoices from the bar and caterers.

It is important to look busy, so I fussily tidy up the messy pile of belongings, rearranging and hanging jackets on the back of a nearby chair and smoothing them down as I do. Resisting the temptation to look around and behind me, I am hyper-aware of the conversations and noises in the room. There are always these groups of old biddies at weddings, as much of a fixture as the daft man-in-a-kilt who fancies his own fucking knees and the cute kid upstaging all the dancers.

This lot seem to be discussing supermarket shopping of all boring things and I tune into their chat about their favourite post-shopping cafes whilst I finish tidying the pile.

I'm on top of the world. What a great wedding this has been. And what sweet people these are, nattering away harmlessly together. I can see Luke is back at work again. He works fucking hard, to be fair. He is now taking arty shots of couples cuddling and smoking under the fairy-light strung trees. I find myself checking out the breadth of his shoulders now revealed in his plain black t-shirt and impulsively decide to ask him for a drink when he's finished.

Bouncing up to him, I give his muscled shoulder a playful slap.

'Come on babes,' I laugh. Leaning in, I whisper in his ear, 'You've already got more than enough shots of this lot and they won't want all their old aunties to see photos of what they are going to be doing later, will they? Stop being so good. Why don't we escape now, and I'll buy you a lovely cold beer?'

Luke's attention jerks off his shot and on to me.

'Flora, what has got into you? You were the one asking for lots of party shots. I'm just trying to do a good job for you here.'

'Um, though, well,' he gives me a cheeky grin as a couple

wander past giggling frantically and with their hands under each other's shirts, 'maybe I have got enough, now. You're right, the next bit won't make it into the albums, will it? I could certainly use a beer. Okaay, I'll just wrap up in here. See you outside in ten?'

There is another reason I want to get out quickly, apart from wanting a drink. The treasure in my tote bag needs to be safely stashed away. It has got to be good for Luke's ego though if he thinks I can't wait to have a drink with him and that will be good for his work as well, I reason, hazily, as I bustle around air-kissing and fitting in a final flirt and cuddle with the happy couple. I am going to be sending them a very large final invoice next week, after all.

Luke and I head to a nearby pub. I pull off my gold shoes under the table with a sigh of relief and sink half a large gin and tonic. As the alcohol hits my empty stomach, I feel the buzz and smile broadly across the table.

'Okay, let's swap stories. You give me your worst wedding disaster story and then I'll give you mine and the best one wins a drink.'

I'm bubbling away and exuberantly good-humoured, knowing that I have *the* best present to myself hidden in my car. I am damn good. I have talent. Before I hid the handbag, I hadn't been able to resist getting it out to admire it. It is bloody gorgeous and looks expensive as fuck. Probably worth a grand at least, though I'm not planning to *sell* it of course. It is all mine to enjoy.

Luke is looking shell-shocked by being abruptly kidnapped from his job, but my mood is infectious. He gets in a couple more drinks and starts to tell me about a recent wedding at which the couple had decided the bride should arrive by horse-drawn carriage. Unfortunately, she had never been that close to a horse before and didn't realise she was violently allergic. By the time she arrived at the church she was swollen faced, purple and blue; and gasping for breath. He ended up snapping photos of her being helped into an ambulance for a trip to A and E rather than processing into her marriage.

'Whatever happened to the horses?' I'm giggling to Luke, trying to picture the scene and he is leaning in close to me so he can be heard over the din of the crowded bar. My attention shifts when several text alerts come through on my phone. I pick it up, expecting thanks and adoring feedback from the wedding group. My blood chills as I read and my mood changes at once. There *are* several new messages, but none of them are happy or congratulatory.

Flora

It seems there has been a theft at the wedding. One of the female guests has discovered her new designer handbag is missing. The hotel manager has messaged, asking for a list of the names and addresses of all the guests that I know. The guest is apparently hysterical and says her bag is worth over a thousand pounds. She is determined that the thief will be caught, and the hotel manager has promised to help. His immediate concern I know will not be to spoil the end of the evening for our two grooms who are picking up the tab and for the rest of the party. He is not going to be keen to call the police tonight either, as he knows as well as I do that there are party drugs on his premises. I give him a quick call, encourage him to try to calm down the angry woman with free drinks and the offer of a room and promise her assuredly that we will all investigate the theft.

Turning back to Luke, he is watching me carefully, with an assessing look on his face. Just like he was doing earlier.

Abruptly, I feel tired and flat. I no longer want to talk to him or to anyone. It has been such a long day. I want to get home to the safety of my calm flat.

Being with people is so confusing and tiring. I don't know now why I ended up going out for a drink at all tonight. It's not like me to be so social. Usually, I am chatty whilst on duty and 'on show' but it switches off as soon as the job is done. I'm going to go home now and shut the door on everyone and turn off my phone and not look at any messages or speak to anyone for the weekend. That might make me feel safe again.

11

On Monday I awake sweating, the echo of screams in my ears and my throat raw and dry.

Where am I? *Who* am I? Still shaking with the nightmare that is knotted around my thoughts, I lie and wait for my heart to slow. Finally, I remember my morning mantra. I am Flora. I am 36. I am a successful wedding planner. I have an important wedding this week.

Oh God, yes. I jerk awake fully and check the date on my phone. It is only five days till Laura and Tom's wedding. That is too soon. I am nowhere near ready; how did that happen? The days have slipped away from me. I am instantly twitching with anxiety and there is something else niggling as well. On top of the long list of urgent tasks and the sticky remnants of sickening dreams, there is a new feeling. A dirty shifting is deep inside my stomach, a churning of guilt and paranoia. It is as though there is something bad with me right here in my flat. Is it something that I've done that I can't remember? I'm trying to shake off these forebodings by focusing on what I must do that day when I hear a familiar tap at the door.

'Hi darling, hi Flora, it's only me,' calls Elena.

What time is it? Is it late? Yes, it is gone eleven. And it is Monday, I just checked that. So why is Elena not in work?

'Just a second,' I call, staggering to the door, trying to demuss my hair, wipe my eyes and pull my nightie down. There is no time to do anything else.

Luckily, Elena is too preoccupied to pay attention to my appearance.

'It's papa,' she bursts out. 'He's not well. He's not

breathing properly at all and he's shaky and can't stand up. I should be in work this morning,' she looks anxiously at her watch, 'but I can't leave him and mama. She is terribly worried too… but they both are trying to pretend nothing is wrong. Could you possibly come down and help me try to persuade him that he needs to see a doctor? He thinks I'm fussing, or that's what he says anyway, though I think he is frightened. But he always likes seeing you darling and he might listen to you when he won't to me.'

Her kind words make me feel even worse. Not only am I totally untogether, but I have been avoiding Elena and her parents for days now, cherishing my privacy closely like a security blanket to protect me from the dangers of friendly neighbourly enquiry.

Elena looks at me more closely.

'Darling, are you ok? You look very peaky and it's, um, quite late. It is not like you not to be out and about when you've got a big wedding coming up.' She tactfully tries not to look at the mess around us, piles of dirty clothing, half-drunk coffee cups, an empty wine bottle. What have I been doing this weekend? Did I make all this mess on my own?

'Oh, it's just been super busy,' I reply, gesturing generally at the room, trying to create the impression of a woman in the midst of productive activity but wishing that for once I could have even a short chat without these time gaps tripping me up. The fear and paranoia from this morning is creeping back. To distract myself, I try to be neighbourly. I take a deep breath.

'I'll just have a shower and then come down and see your father. Try not to worry.'

Elena squeezes my hand with her warm one. I find myself wanting to hold onto her and not let go, though at the same time a part of me is pulling back. Why is she doing this?

Why am I letting her touch me? Why am I getting involved with her life and that of her parents at all? Didn't I decide when I moved here to remain on nodding terms only with the neighbours? Didn't I create the perfect self-contained space free from the demands of other people? Despite these misgivings, I am secretly glad to be invited down into her warm and cosy flat again.

Spurred into action, I whirl around the flat in a flurry of tidying and sorting. There is a handbag I don't recognise on the kitchen counter.

It is a very nice bag.

A beautiful grey Chloé bag. I should focus on why it is here and whose it is, but at this moment I'm caught up in Elena's anxiety and my own stress about Laura and Tom's wedding. I know there will be a barrage of messages from Laura waiting for me. I'll think about it all later, I tell myself, forcing the anxiety away as I hide the unwanted bag on a high shelf and hurry out, relieved to get away from it.

Mr Varela is very poorly today, grey-faced and wheezing. I'm sure it is a worsening of his lung disease, after years of chain-smoking Camel cigarettes. Gently I explain again to him that he will not be asked for money if he goes to the hospital as he has dual citizenship, but that they will all be very nice. I hope this latter bit is true and that someone will have the time to talk to him. He reluctantly consents to me calling for medical help, which shows he must be feeling very unwell. Elena fusses tenderly over both her parents as we wait for the ambulance, wrapping them in scarves against any possible chill and making up a fresh flask of matté tea and sandwiches to take to the hospital.

Have you had any breakfast?' she turns to me suddenly. 'I'm sure you haven't. You don't take proper care of yourself, dear. Here, try this,' she hands me a mug of tea and a slice of bread covered with a soft brown sweetly scented spread.

'It's like mother's milk for us Argentinians and papa will always eat this, however bad he is feeling.'

I take a cautious nibble, unsure what it is I am trying. The spread is like treacle and caramel and is so creamy and comforting that I want to be able to eat it forever.

Elena laughs at my expression. 'Dulce du leche', she explains. 'It's what we make with the leftover milk from all those herds of cows. It is really good, isn't it?'

I nod wordlessly, lost in taste sensation, and she gestures to the open jar.

'Have some more,' she offers. 'Look, I've got another jar,' and she points to the shelf above the sink. 'I have to keep that one though because it is papa's absolute favourite. I order it for him specially, because there is only one kind that he thinks is good enough. When I was growing up, he always made me a snack of this when I got home from school, and we would eat it together out on the terrace with the dogs.'

Smiling at her memories, she bustles out with the sandwiches and flask. I hear her gently chivvying her parents in the other room. I am still holding the half-eaten bread. As I take another bite the sweet and comforting taste of the dulce du leche fills my mouth with pleasure and a craving for more. I try and fail to imagine a childhood in which my father would have made me a snack and chatted to me after school. All I can remember is the coldness and quiet of the family kitchen and the anxiety whenever I heard my father's footsteps coming down the stairs from the study where he spent most of his time. I was bound to be corrected for some small fault or set chores to do. Those were the only times he spoke to me, apart from when he was reading scripture or praying with the whole family.

61

Chloé

I am completely starving, and I *need* some more of that bread and spread, whatever the fuck it is called. It is like solid ice cream and I'm going to faint unless I eat some more right this minute. Elena has a whole unopened jar sitting there. Well, it looks like there is plenty in this pot and she can get some more soon, can't she? I need this stuff in my life. I can't walk away and leave it here. I can squeeze the new jar into my pocket, just about, and then I'll be able to have a load of it later. It is probably better not on bread but with a spoon straight up. I'm helping these people out anyway, aren't I? Why can't I have something bloody nice for once? Why does everyone else have all the good stuff?

Flora

I come round out of a daydream, still holding an uneaten crust. What had I been thinking? Something to do with coming home from school as a child? Elena is calling gently to me from the doorway, so I swallow the bread and join her and her father. He and I have always got on well and I enjoy letting him ramble on about his early life as a musician in Argentina. Today there is no chat though and every breath is a struggle. We are all relieved when the ambulance crew bustle in with their medical kit and cheerful banter.

He needs to be admitted to hospital and as the family set off Elena gives me a quick hug. 'Thank you for coming this morning. You are really kind. Now you take good care of yourself today and I'll see you soon, I hope.' Mr Varela in his wheelchair lifts his arms to me for a weak and cologne-scented hug.

'Bless you, wedding girl,' he mouths faintly at me. I'm not sure what to make of all this. This is me, Flora, who never gets involved. How come I'm being embraced and thanked by neighbours? And how come when he was hugging me, I wanted to cling on to him and burst into tears? I can't get a handle on today, but I need to focus on work, that usually sorts me out, and there is certainly enough of it.

Turning on my laptop, I begin to read the latest emails from Laura.

'I am worried about the flower girls' outfits,' I read. 'I don't feel they are the right shade of pink; they don't have the fin de siècle look that I'm after…

Tom's mother has still not said who she is bringing with her as plus one. Tom says it could be an old racing driver called Roger, it could be her gardener, or her friend Rosie, but it won't be his father…'

'Also, I'm worried about the timings for the evening. And do we know yet what colour shirts the band will be wearing?'

I turn from the screen with a sigh. Laura is not getting any easier. I fire off a few emails and then set off into town to buy some last items.

As I reach the main shopping street, I remember there was a reason why I wasn't going to go into the large department store, Partingtons, the place I bought that nice green glassware recently. There *was* a reason but now I can't remember what it was, so like so many other things this morning, I force it to the back of my mind.

At least in here, I should be able to get flower girl ribbons to match, as well as wedding favours for some last-minute guests. Mentally I curse Laura's over-complicated colour scheme. I wish all clients were as easy to please as Victor and Max had been. I'm unsettled by this upcoming wedding. Something is going to go wrong; I just know it.

Chloé

That uptight bitch Laura is getting on my tits. Her and her damn 'Louis Quinze, fin de siècle nonsense. Who does she think she is, Marie Antoinette? Who is going to give an actual fuck about the colour of her flower girls' ribbons? No one is going to be looking at them anyway. They will be clocking her new baby bump, or they will be admiring the groom. Now *he* is quite tasty. Lounging around as cool as anything, using all that 'why little Miss Miller' stuff. It's a waste of a hot man him getting tied down with snotty cow Laura. He could have had more fun chasing *me* around.

Why do all the good men get snapped up? Why do none of them decide that it is me they would like to marry? Why is Laura so special? Yes, she's got rich parents and a good job. She should be counting her blessings and not take the only good looking single straight man left in Gloucestershire. She is a greedy cow. Why does she have to have him as well?

I am stressed out and my shopping is erratically matching my whirling thoughts. I grab up some spools of ribbon without checking the colour matches the swatch. I add more arty shit for the cake table. And these are nice. This pair of tarnished silver candlesticks would be great as a centrepiece.

Actually, I think the candlesticks are too cool for Laura, but they would look great in my flat. They could be my treat today. But not at the inflated price they are asking.

Let's get these guys home with me then. It is going to be easy. All I've to do is tuck them under the ribbons and napkins already in my basket, fuss everything around and now it all looks totally natural. There is no-one standing too close to me pretending to be a shopper, so I'm good to go.

Fuck it all! Out of the corner of my eye, I catch the flash of a camera.

Now that wasn't supposed to happen. All I can do now is style it out. I turn to the camera, look fully at it, smile broadly and then flick it the finger. That will give anyone watching a surprise. Poor fuckers having to sit there all day watching boring people wandering about a boring shop. They'll be glad I smiled at them, to break up their day. I giggle out loud and a young couple in front of me turn round and look at me in surprise. Time to get out now. And luckily right in front of me, I can see an open door and not one that customers use. It is a fire exit opening into a service bay, full of bins and crap. I can see into an unloading area. Surely beyond that will be the street.

Well, I'm not going to walk past an open door, am I? If the shop is being so stupid as to leave a door to the outside swinging open the only sensible thing to do is to walk through it surely? I wrap the contents of my basket inside the summer jacket that's over my arm. The candlesticks cause a bit of a problem because they are long, so they stick out of the makeshift parcel. Succeeding in the end, I casually drop the empty basket to one side and stroll out. I pick through the rubbish-strewn service area, avoiding dirty puddles. As I'd hoped it pops me out into a backstreet just off the main shopping drag.

'Fuck I'm good. Talk about the light-fingered fantastic.' I'm laughing out loud now, as there is no one here to give me odd looks. I do love a freebie and I can charge snotty-pants Laura for the things I'm using for her wedding that I didn't pay for so I'm coining it here. The candlesticks are mine, though. She doesn't get to have those.

Flora

I am outside a back entrance to Partingtons and I am totally confused about how I got here. I've that feeling again,

65

the one I keep getting. Like I've woken from a heavy sleep. Except I'm dressed and outside and apparently have been shopping, so I can't just have woken up, can I? What am I doing in this street? I don't recognise it at all. I must have been shopping in Partingtons and then got lost inside and come out a different way. I try to shake my head clear. The waves of panic from this morning are back and lapping closer now.

'That *was* a blank moment, Flora.' I mentally chide myself. 'Get a grip.' I must find out what is causing these absences. It is not good that they seem to be happening more often. I'm spaced out and groggy and can't think straight. I'll go and see the nurse at the surgery soon, even if I can't face a doctor. I check inside my bag for a snack to see if that helps and to remind me where I am in the day's errands. Good, I've clearly just bought the ribbons for the flower girls. Before I can consult my to-do list, my phone rings. It is Luke.

'Hi Flora,' he murmurs, sounding subdued. 'How are you feeling today?'

"I'm fine, thanks Luke,' I reply, surprised by his solicitous tone and still trying to orient myself. 'How about you? Are you all ready for Saturday?'

'Yes, I think so,' Luke answers slowly. 'I've got all the preparation shots I need, so it is just the wedding rehearsal tomorrow and then we will be having a hell of a long day on Saturday. By the way,' he continues, sounding odd again, 'I had a call from the police earlier. About the handbag that got stolen on Saturday. It turns out it was very valuable, so though the contents were left behind, the woman who lost it reported the theft and called in the police after the hotel manager didn't get anywhere. They asked me a lot of questions about the evening. I expect they'll ask you too, they are being pretty thorough.'

'Oh, I can't wait,' I say sarcastically, though a chill has run through me on hearing the police will be in touch. Police are like doctors, worse if anything. I'm starting to sweat in panic and my thoughts are jangled, spinning away from the conversation with Luke, who I forget is still there. In my head, I am in an empty room and the burn of guilt is hot in my throat.

'Miriam, are you a common thief? You have broken the Lord's commandments. Have you such a depraved heart that you would put a glittering piece of nonsense ahead of your immortal soul? You will stay there and pray until you repent.'

'Hi, Flora, you still there?' I hear Luke's voice faintly. 'Are you okay? Did we get cut off there? Look, take it easy, try not to worry. Focus on Laura's wedding, you've put a lot into it, it should be a good one. I'll see you tomorrow at the rehearsal? I hope that poser Tom shows up and can remember his lines.' I can hear him smiling down the phone.

Luke *is* being nice. And he is sharper and more interesting than I'd first thought. But what do I know about him? Apart from that story about his grandfather that he shared the other day. Does he live alone? Is he in a relationship? What about his parents? I've never thought to ask. I've been so wrapped up in my own worries. But that is what people do, isn't it, if they are becoming friends? It does seem that despite my intentions; we are becoming friends. Somehow quiet, Luke seems a safe enough person to allow into my life a little and I look forward to the times we meet.

'Thanks, Luke, I'll see you in the morning. You have a good day now,' I reply shakily, making a mental note to ask him more about himself tomorrow.

I need to get safely home, to think. There *is* something wrong. I can't pretend there isn't. The time gaps are happening more, and I don't know what I have or haven't done. This isn't just work stress or tiredness or low blood sugar. The fear is back again, like an ugly gargoyle that hovers in the shadows. It whispers that I am going mad, that I do not know what I am doing and that they were right about me all along.

12

Back in my flat, it is the mess that hits me first. In my head, my home is a sanctuary of calm and serenity, but it seems like the place itself has other ideas.

Or maybe I do? Do I live differently in the missing time and make all this mess? I've been assuming I blank out as in suspended animation, but what if I am carrying on acting, talking and creating consequences? This thought brings me up sharp and I catch my breath in alarm.

Why else is my flat a mess when I'm such a tidy person? I've half pretended to myself that it is Elena popping in and nosing around, or even that a burglar has ransacked the place, but deep down, I know I've been avoiding the situation. Why do I feel that Luke knows something about me that I don't know myself? And, I think, looking round the chaos in confusion, whose lovely grey handbag is that and why is it here?

For a moment, the panic suffocates me. I struggle for certainties, repeating my familiar mantra. I am Flora; I am 36. I am a successful wedding planner.

But a wedding planner with someone else's designer bag in her flat? And no idea how it got there?

Scanning the room, I decide the first thing to do is to tidy. Once the place looks as pretty and neat as it should, I'll feel more like myself again. I pull out the cleaning stuff from under the sink, open bin bags and run hot soapy water, full of energy to tackle the mess.

For the next few hours, I work calmly and steadily. Dishes and cups are washed and put away. I change my bedding, noting that I have been drinking red wine in bed and eating something red as well. Doughnuts? Jam sandwiches? Something sticky. Finally, all my clothes are hung up, sorted and folded. I take out the rubbish and recycling, put away the hoover and spin around watering parched plants and plumping up cushions. Finally, I light a scented candle and collapse exhausted on my cream sofa to admire my handiwork.

The grey handbag is still on the counter. It is daring me to think. It is daring me to understand why it is there and to remember how it arrived.

It should *not* be there, that is the problem. This is surely the same bag that has been reported as stolen. A cold dread washes over me again and I taste bile in my throat. As I've been tidying, I've noticed that there are other things that should not be here. When I opened a bedroom drawer that I've not used for ages I found it stuffed with items I do not recognise, scarves and shrugs, clutch bags and bangles. And in the kitchen, there is a cupboard that I thought had empty bottles in which is again completely full. When I open it out cascades a pile of wrapped gifts. Other people's gifts; wrapped and with their names on as well as bags of chocolate and fudge, bespoke-flavoured artisan tea and gold-coated coffee beans in gauze bags. At the back is a jam jar stuffed full of crumpled twenty- and fifty-pound notes. None of these things should be here. I sit back on my heels and stare blankly into the cupboard and the fear moves closer and squats on my shoulder, chuckling and pointing at the piled-up gifts.

Something is very wrong, and that thing is me. Me, Miriam Miller. No. Flora Miller. The girl who is always at fault. The girl who lacks grace and is full of greed and covetousness. I'm still full of those things it seems. Even though I'm no longer Miriam, of course.

70

I blink. It's been such a long time since I even said that name to myself. Where did that come from? Why do I think I am called Miriam?

'Come on Flora,' I tell myself. 'Stop sitting in the dark and imagining all kinds of nonsense. The main thing is, get Tom and Laura's wedding over with, make a success of it and then decide what to do about that wretched bag next week.'

Chloé

Flora is being thick as usual. She can be fucking dumb. Why is it always me who has the good ideas? There is no reason to be so worried about that stupid bag. All I need to do if the police ask about it (and they probably never will) is to say that the bloody thing got left behind at the wedding and I'm looking after it for the owner. That sounds like the action of a careful and considerate wedding planner. Honestly, what is all the fuss about?

Now back to business and I need to pick out a hot outfit for tomorrow's wedding. I want to look good because that Tom is tasty. Maybe we can have a bit of a flirt before he devotes himself to Laura. For life. Fuck it, why would anyone do that? She is such an uptight cow; she's not ever going to kick back and relax, is she? She'll be trying to keep everything under control all day tomorrow and I'm already about to scream. Honestly, I deserve some fun with Tom.

This dress is perfect. Low scooped neckline to show off my tits, check, short enough to show off my legs, double check, and strikingly patterned with bright pink and orange flowers. It is very body con, too body con for work, but who cares? I look good in it and sexy too. And I need fuck me heels. Damn it though, that 'lost' bag sitting there on my countertop would be perfect to finish the look. I wish I could take it out tomorrow. Hopefully, everyone will shut up about it soon and I can.

13

Flora

I wake up feeling confident on the morning of Laura and Tom's wedding. Everything has been planned so carefully for today that surely nothing can go wrong. The early sunshine and clear morning skies cheer me still further. Even the weather is on my side today. I decide to make a good start by getting to Chalk Hill Farm before anyone else and by eight am I am turning into the long drive to the house, stopping to tie a beribboned 'Laura and Tom's wedding' sign at the entrance. Once there, I find a visibly twitching Laura, who looks like she has had no sleep at all. My first job is to calm her down, so I make her a cup of camomile tea and suggest she joins me in some slow breathing exercises.

'I don't think the weather is going to plan at all' she worries, leaving her tea to go cold while she looks out disapprovingly at the gardens, where the sun has yet to burn off the morning mist. 'And I don't think the gardener did a good job with the lawn mowing. Look, those stripes are not straight. I'd better have a word with mother.'

I manage to reassure her that the perfect summer day she had requested will appear within the hour and that the garden looks incredible (which it does) before handing her over to today's make-up girls Jess and Daisy.

They patiently flatter and cajole her into better humour, whilst managing to disguise the dark circles under her eyes and her morning sickness pallor. The seamstress has put an extra panel in the front of her dress. She fusses constantly about how pregnant she looks, but we reassure her that if she holds her trailing bouquet carefully, no one will be able to see that she is expecting in the wedding photos. I tell her Luke will be careful not to photograph her from the wrong angle, whilst wondering why it seems to matter to her so much.

Thinking of Luke reminds me I was so worried last night that I had decided to talk to him about the designer handbag sitting ominously in my flat and about my recent episodes of 'lost' time. This morning, in all the bustle of activity, it is hard to imagine how I would begin that conversation or whether I even should. I'm being overanxious. Everyone forgets things, don't they? People are always telling me how much I get done. Look at this event today. I wish that wretched handbag wasn't in my flat though and whenever I think of it, my mind clouds over in confusion.

Stop worrying right now, I tell myself firmly. What was I thinking about before? Oh yes, Laura and her determination for people not to realise she has got Tom's baby growing inside her. It's an old-fashioned concern, but she does seem at heart to be an old-fashioned girl, despite her high-flying career. She is about to have the ultimate old-school "happy ever after" fantasy completed today, with a picture book perfect white wedding, a handsome husband, lovely home and soon a baby as well. She could be a bit more cheerful about it all. Maybe even be grateful for my hard work.

Despite her demanding behaviour, when I see her and Tom having their first pictures taken as a married couple, under the arch of pink roses in the garden, with Laura at last smiling radiantly and waving at her guests, I get a sense of satisfaction at a job well done.

It is Tom who is looking strained and tense now. Earlier I had caught him knocking back a couple of brandies in the kitchen with his morning coffee and had edged away quickly when he leerily invited me to join him. He is not the safest bet as ideal husband material to fulfil her romantic dreams, but he will probably play along. Who knows, maybe he will adore being a father.

Annabel has done a great job with the catering and is supervising table laying and final preparations with genteel aplomb. She gives me an onion scented hug, smiling warmly from underneath a monstrous and moth-eaten black and yellow hat. Laura won't like that hat, I think, smiling back conspiratorially. The guests move slowly out onto the lawns, gasping in satisfactory admiration at the views, sipping champagne and enjoying my selections of gluten-free, paleo and dairy free canapés.

I even have time for a chat with Luke. Not about the handbag and scary stuff, but after deciding the other day to find out more about *his* life, I seize the chance of a quiet moment. Once the crowds are all outside with drinks in their hands, I grab a couple of coffees from the kitchen and seek him out.

Luke takes a big gulp gratefully.

'Hey thanks, Flora, that's kind. It has been a long morning already. I really need this.'

This gives me an opening.

'Yes. I was wondering, Luke,' I say, 'I think you said before you live out of town, near Prestbury, isn't it? That is quite a drive in. Are you on your own out there?'

Luke laughs wryly. 'Yeah, just me. It is a bit of a dump to be honest. The problem I've got is my cat. He was not even my cat, though I suppose he is now. He used to be my grandfather's. Remember, I told you about my grand pop?' He checks that I have remembered, 'well my grandma died last year too, and they had this big cat and no one else in the family wanted him. I couldn't let him go to a rescue, so he ended up with me. He's a great useless ball of black fluff, but you know....' he tails off. I enjoy the picture he paints and

75

smile. Pleased to see his softer side.

This is the only moment of respite in the day and from then on, I am running non-stop. Cursing my high heels, I oversee the extended pre-lunch drinks and rush in and out of the kitchen, trying not to make the sweating cooks any crosser. Lavish piles of presents need to be stacked (wedding lists at the White Company and Fortnum and Masons) and people encouraged to write messages in the wedding day guest book. Children are racing happily around on the lawns. They will no doubt become whiny before the day ends but so far are sweet.

The seven-piece trad jazz band with whom I have exchanged so many emails arrive and slowly begin to set up their gear in the orangery, trailing leads and strumming chords as they check sound levels. Luckily, Luke is now doing the formal wedding group shots on the front lawn, so I am spared Laura's frowns of disapproval. I go to offer the musicians a drink and am pleased that they have all defaulted to basic black shirts and jeans so there is no danger of a hissy fit from Laura.

As usual, I keep a low profile throughout the day but make sure that everything goes exactly how Laura wants, her many requests and reminders ringing in my ears as I work. Once the drinks and formal photos are over the guests wander into the marquee for the wedding breakfast of smoked salmon salad, Hunter chicken, Crème Brulee and raspberry sorbet, followed by cheese, biscuits and port. I am relieved when the lengthy best man and father of the brides' speeches are over, and the evening party can begin.

The sun has dipped now behind the laden fruit trees in the orchard, so I walk round the garden lighting the evening lanterns. The caterers arrive to set the hog roast turning for the buffet and the band plays the first set. It is all still going well. So far, I tell myself, despite my nerves, everything has gone perfectly. Maybe I've just been having a run of bad luck and that is over now. A few more smooth events like this and I can put aside all those worries about my memory and about handbags going missing and then turning up in the wrong places. I smile at a passing guest and as my tension slips away. I decide to go and check on how Luke is doing and see if he needs a sandwich.

14

As I walk back from the gardens, I am thinking that there *is* a shadow over the day despite its outward success. It is uncomfortably clear that the marriage we are busy celebrating is not the happy union of two people in love. Not the way the principals are behaving. I noticed how straight after the staged smiles for the camera they seemed to be having some kind of row, snarling at each other out of the sides of their mouths and from then on they have not been seen together. It is not just me who has noticed. Whenever I've been close to groups of guests gathered at the bar or standing on the terrace, I have seen strained smiles and heard muttered worried comments as they glance at one or other of the bridal pair. During the day, Laura has gone beyond tension and stress into a rigid paralysis and her face is now set in a rictus of simulated pleasure and enthusiasm. Her voice has risen too, and she is braying manically at her friends and relations.

Tom, by contrast, looks bored and disengaged, as though he would sooner be somewhere else entirely. He does scrub up well and certainly looks the part today in a dove grey morning suit with floppy blond hair gleaming. With his expensive watch, boots and cufflinks, he has all the outer trappings of a well-bred country gentleman, but his expression and demeanour are at odds with his appearance. He looks as if he is in a dentist's waiting room about to have root canal treatment.

Chloé

He smells bloody good though, as I discover when I almost run smack into him on my way to the pantry where

I'm checking the vintage port has been decanted. He is leaning out of the back door, smoking a fag in the fading light. It looks as though he is hiding out here to get away from the crowds of new relations and congratulating guests.

My pulse thumps on seeing him. He looks bloody sexy and a bit sad. I never can resist a hot guy in distress. Surely this is the chance I've been looking for to make a move. All thoughts of sorting boring evening drinks leave my brain and for the first time in what, just fucking ages, I start to feel properly horny.

Umm, I breathe in deeply, enjoying a waft of his expensive woody fragrance and of warm and pampered masculinity. How come someone who is a bit of an arse gets to smell so good? I wobble, half on purpose, and lurch closer to him, pretending to have lost my footing in the dim corridor. And how does he get to have such sexily darkening eyes? Eyes which are now laughing down at me as Tom puts his hand on my bare arm to stop me from losing my balance, just as I'd planned he would. His hand is warm, dry and firm and as I dimple fake-demurely up at him, his gaze is fully focused on me.

Nature is a bitch, I decide, making this player so damn cute, but why should I care about his personality? I am after a bit of fun, not a relationship. I do care that he has turned from the door to face me fully, thrown away his cigarette and now catches both my hands and pulls me towards him.

I turn slowly, feigning reluctance, as he steadies me with one strong arm, with his other hand stroking from my elbow to my fingertips, pausing to briefly massage the inside of my wrist with a fleshy thumb. Ooh, that is a *very* hot move. He is a cheeky bugger, with his bride so close, just outside in the conservatory. When I left there just now, she was keeping a sharp eye on the bar staff. She looked pale again and awkward in her over-tight dress, with hair escaping wispily onto a damp forehead. Tom's mother had turned up with a scruffy young man and they were swinging around the dance floor whilst swigging a bottle of wine, with Annabel watching tight-lipped from a side table as she sipped a coffee.

I've just about had it with this family. And especially with Laura. If she expects me to behave, she should have been nicer to me earlier, shouldn't she? Like would it have killed her to offer me a coffee when I arrived early this morning? But no, she was so focussed on herself there was not even a flicker of a welcoming smile. So, if her newly hitched partner wants to play naughty, he has found a willing playmate.

'Hey, little Miss Miller,' Tom says breathily. I lean in closer to hear him. He is slurring his words and his movements are a little too wide. He is plastered and is going to be easy pickings for a woman on a mission. With my head full of sexy fantasies, he is perfect. Time to swoop in for the kill.

Putting on my best 'professional' voice I ask him if he has had a good day and is happy with his wedding. All the time I am batting my lashes up at him and making sure he gets a good eyeful of cleavage.

'Yeah, well, the thing is, Little Miss Sexy Pants Miller,' answers Tom, swaying even closer to me. 'I've not had such a good day. In fact, it's been a fucking travesty. I mean this whole thing,' he gestures out to the garden full of sparkling lights and to the crowds of guests. 'What's it all for? We've just spent over thirty grand on utter crap. No offense to your work,' he waves in roughly the direction of the marquee, brushing my shoulder with his firm and warm hand. 'I've only known that girl, my wife, Laaura,' he makes her name sound like an insult, 'about five bloody minutes and three-quarters of that time we have spent discussing fucking table napkins and

80

placement and all that nonsense. I fancied the pants off her when we met, mind. I asked her to marry me as it was the only way to get her into bed. I couldn't get her out of my head, even though I've shagged half the other women here tonight. Then she promptly went totally mental and has spent the entire time deciding what kind of cake and what colour flowers to have. And now what, now the fucking what?' A note of desperation is in his voice. 'What are we going to talk about now? I've got no damn money, never have, it's all hers and her families. We haven't had sex the last three months as she's sick and sensitive the whole time. We're going to have to live with her bloody mother to start off with and then the thing; the baby. God I'm not ready to be a dad, it will be here, and I'll be the one having to look after it. How did this happen?' he finishes pathetically. 'I'm so not ready. I wish we'd just shagged and then called it a day.'

Well, that is saying it like it is. I glance around to check he has not been overheard, but everyone else is in the main room. Peals of laughter and clapping drift faintly through the double doors. I consider my next move.

Tom has put me off a bit now. He is more bitter and unhappy than I expected and less up for mindless fun. In the back of my mind, an alarm bell is ringing. But when I look up again at him, he is staring down at me with flattering intent. His eyes are holding mine and his head is dipping towards me. It seems like he has warmed up just as I was cooling off. I get another waft of that sexy scent from his body which bypasses my brain and arouses me again. He covers my cool hand with his hot one and angles even closer, so we are facing each other and only a breath apart.

Now I do want him, right here and now. Why can't it be *my* turn to get the guy? Why shouldn't he kiss me? Bloody Laura is out there being adored by all her smart friends and has her mother and father and sisters all running around after her. The spoilt cow has the most fantastic pile of gifts as well. I reach up and give Tom an open lipped kiss. Not a kiss of congratulation, commiseration or friendship but a sexy kiss with a promise of more.

First move. A girl has got to take what a girl wants; no one is going to give it you.

Tom turns his head towards me so the kiss lands full on his parted mouth. His lips linger and catch at mine while I hear a tiny moan from the back of his throat. Now his hands are sliding over my bum and his body presses so close that I can feel the hardness of his cock.

So, the boy is ready to play; that *is* a good sign. For a minute I'd worried he might be too drunk. But this is a man who has not had a shag for three months. A man full of self-pity, feeling trapped and ready for something fast and daring and dirty. And I am here beside him, ready to join the ride.

Now we are so close I realise how young he is. He must be ten years younger than me, but that doesn't seem to have put him off. Fiery warmth floods my cheeks as my pulse rate rises. He is looking down my dress now, so I do a little shimmy, breathe in deeply and push my tits against his chest, glad that I wore my best cleavage-boosting bra. On cue, he reaches out and strokes the top of my breast. I stroke him back on his forearm, enjoying the toned muscles moving and twitching beneath my touch, on his flat belly and then let my hand slide lower onto his rock-hard cock.

I am abuzz with triumph. I've got the man! I have stolen him right from under the nose of his new wife. Forget handbags and gifts and money; this is a prize worth having. Dizzily I contemplate a string of gorgeous men, stretching into the future, all whose weddings I will organise, all of whom will be ripe for picking on their big day itself. I forget about all the dull grooms, the much older ones, the gay ones, and I lose myself in a fantasy in which I am a combination of supreme organiser and irresistible seductress.

Back to the present and this clinch. Tom really fancies me, there is no doubt. Both of us are swept up in the tides of lust that have risen in our bodies, and we have lost any sense of where we are.

I think if we had been able to stop after the first kiss, then everything would have been alright, and events would not have taken the turn they did. It was just an ill-advised bit of flirting up till then. It could have been seen as me congratulating Tom too enthusiastically and his pissed brain taking it too far. If we had stopped then there was still the chance we could have straightened our clothes, grinned at each other with embarrassment and got on with our lives. But we don't stop there.

Young Tom has got his blood up now and giggling like a fool, he pulls me away down the corridor and into the larder, the earlier scene of Annabel's staged cheese-choosing shot. A quick flicker of memory of Luke standing there smiling in his shy way half brings me back to myself, but Tom is all over me, his warm firm hands on my arms and back. I nuzzle into his neck to get a better sniff of his scent. God, money talks the bollocks when it comes to smell, doesn't it?

My hands are reaching further, and I explore the muscles of his shoulders and back, hard and pumped under his fine linen shirt. At the same time, he is reaching soft-tipped fingers up under my short-skirted dress and stroking my inner thighs and my body is softening and melting. Ooh, he *is* good. I can see why Laura is keen. But this guy needs a real dirty woman to take him on, not some workaholic "every hair in place" kind of a girl. And at last, in me, he has found one.

Flora

The larder door behind me flies open suddenly and a high-pitched scream makes every nerve in my body jangle. At the same time, my arm is painfully pulled from behind and I am thrown halfway across the room. What is happening? I am dazed and disorientated and the pain in my arm takes my breath away. I am not sure where I am. Have I just hit my head? It feels like I am waking up from a heavy sleep or coming round after a faint.

Struggling to orient myself, I find myself staring at ten bottles of vintage port. Ah yes, I remember choosing this brand, as middle of the range, not anything special or too pricey, but good enough to please the lawyers and uncles. So that is why I am in here. I remember now; I had come to check the port. But why is my arm in agony? Why does my face feel like it is just been rubbed by sandpaper and why is my dress rucked up and sticking to the tops of my thighs?

I have less than seconds to try to work all this out because another scream rings out. Ghastly confusion is both inside my head and in the room itself. The person who screamed and hurt my arm was Laura yanking me forcefully off her husband. Now it is not just Laura but also her bridesmaids who are crowding into the larder, jostling and exclaiming and shouting. In the sudden crush of bodies, I fight to steady myself against the countertop, clutching randomly at a bottle. I am trying to pull myself back to my life, the life I should be in, the job that I had come in here to do. Before whatever terrible thing happened that has everyone shrieking; and shrieking; I realise with growing panic, *at* me. Laura is beside herself, her face a ghastly white with livid spots of pure anger in her cheeks. Seeing me looking at her, she rushes at me with her hand raised to slap. I cower away from her, knocking over a bottle of port as I do. It shatters in a sickening crash and a wide pool of dark red sticky liquid mixed with shards of glass forms around our feet.

I'm trying to piece together what has happened. It is not looking good. Laura is yelling at me 'you slut, you utter tramp, you little snake, you bitch!' Tom is frantically straightening his clothing, doing up his half-undone shirt, wiping something, oh dear God no, it is my bright red lipstick, from off his face. He is succeeding only in smearing it further across his cheeks, so he looks like he has been made up by a child. Under the lipstick, his face is flushed, and his guilt is drawn across it. He is the most caught-in-the-act looking man you could imagine, with his cufflinks undone, his corsage crushed and his trousers still bulging. He is stuttering and trying to speak but he cannot meet his new bride's eye.

Annabel is next on the scene, her ringing voice demanding 'whatever is going on in here? Everyone can hear screaming.' Her daughter points to me and gasps 'that bitch, the little cow, she had her hands all over my Tom and was trying to snog his face off.'

As what she is saying sinks in, the shame hits. Shame and horror at what I must have been doing sickens me. My head drops, tears fill my eyes, and my cheeks are on fire. Any excitement has fizzed away like a champagne bubble, leaving a gritty coldness in my throat and the familiar feeling of guilt. The voice in my head is back, louder than ever.

'Miriam, Miriam, how have you sinned again? Such a grievous sin. Truly you have fallen from grace. You have broken another one of Jehovah's commandments, the commandments given to all God-fearing people by the prophet Moses. How much teaching have you had, you Godless child? And yet you forget it all and hurry to join the adulterers and fornicators in their headlong rush to hell.'

Annabel's icy look freezes me with the shock of a bucket of cold water. I am now fully awake and aware of the disaster of my situation. My half memory of being lost in a sexy

85

altered reality only moments before has faded, as quickly as sensations of pleasure have left my body.

Other guests are crowding into the larder. More female friends of Laura. They exclaim and hug her, aghast and excited by the sudden drama. They throw evil glances at me, standing stunned as I am in a pool of crimson wine. They goggle at my ripped tights and rumpled frock and then across the room at Tom, with his make-up smeared face and mis-buttoned shirt. He has not moved or spoken but is standing mute, a helpless spectator to the crashing ruin of his wedding.

Laura's father, Gerard, appears next, disturbed by the noise. Earlier that evening he had warmly thanked me as he shook both my hands in his, saying, 'terrific job you did, young lady. So glad it all went off well, it has been a tough few weeks. I thought Laura would make herself ill with all the rushing around but thank God they are safely married now.'

He had pressed a fat envelope into my hand, containing a handwritten cheque to pay for my services and also a bonus of five crisp twenty-pound notes with a card of gratitude.

The shame rises higher and threatens to drown me. The secret fear that has dogged me that I am evil and immoral turns out to be true after all. This fear that I am sinful and a slut is one that I have edged away from in my waking hours and that has stalked my restless nights. It is now in front of me, real and inescapable. How could this have happened? I've worked so hard to try to create a new life for myself, to live my sinning self behind. A life entirely devoted to work, a life that is a façade of brilliant perfection and immaculate style. A life that is now crumpled around my feet; is shredded and wrecked and soiled beyond repair.

All this I understand, on one level, before a minute has passed. My mind has spun into a desolate future and back into my carefully forgotten past. I am floating above the room watching events unfold but separated by an impermeable barrier from the drama and unable to initiate movement or speech.

In this state, it seems as though the room has become quiet, and the agitated voices of Laura and her supporters have ceased but now I can hear them all again. Of course, they were there all the time, speaking, crying and screeching over each other and repeating in gasps and whispers a tale of my wrongdoing that I can hardly bear to hear. It was just that in those first endless seconds my mind seemed to split away from my body and the minutes and hours that follow are as though through glass. I am cut off from the reality of it all.

Laura also has been in shock but her anger bursts through. Her reaction to a surge of raging energy is predictable and automatic. She rounds on me and before I can flinch away, she gives me a stinging slap on the cheek with her left hand, new rings catching my skin as she does. It really hurts.

'You,' she pauses on the words, gasping for breath, 'you, you conniving little bitch! You are my employee, you wretched little cow. I've paid you good money and he's paid you good money.' She points at her father. 'To give us a proper and well-organised wedding. Is this what you do at all your weddings?' Spit sprays from her mouth as she yells. 'Good God, I will bring you down.' She has not looked once at Tom, who is immobile and rigid. 'I will make damn sure you never work again. I will cover your website with terrible reviews and tell everyone what an utter snake you are...'

Reality overtakes her as her sudden drop in status from envied and adored bride to spurned and cheated-on object of pity and curiosity begins to sink in. She gives an ugly snort, reddens, sobs and shakes. A bridesmaid, Clare, who has been giving me evils, rushes to comfort her. Laura continues to gasp and snort and shake as her mother and other bridesmaids all cluster around her.

If Tom has anything to him at all, he will surely make a move now, to comfort or explain to Laura or to defend me, but he remains frozen. He is shocked too, but maybe he has been wishing for something like this to happen. His lack of action leaves me exposed to everyone else's wrath.

Annabel turns to me again and in her well-bred ringing tones demands. 'And just what are you, young woman? You act like a common slut.' Her lip-sticked mouth is a moue of disgust.

More and more people are appearing, filling the kitchen, peering over each other into the larder to find out what is going on. Pushing and questioning.

'What has happened? Is Laura alright? What's going on? Oh my God!' The band, distantly heard, forlornly play on to an emptying dance floor.

I see Luke now, peering anxiously over the top of the crowd. Oh please, can Luke not have to see this as well. That is just too much. To avoid the sight of him and his puzzled and hurt expression, I close my eyes. The room lurches away from me, the noise dies down and I am in a bubble of blessed silence.

Miriam

If I keep my eyes tight shut, this awful scene will disappear, and I can wake up again and find everything is alright. I am dizzy and I reach my hand out for support towards where I think the countertop is. To my surprise, my hand encounters warm fur and I hear a little mew of greeting. A cat. It must be one of Annabel's cats, I've seen several hanging around the place. This one is probably checking the food supplies to see if any treats have been left uncovered. My hand finds her warm cheek as she nuzzles against my fingers. She is as keen for affection as for food. Still with eyes tight shut, I scratch behind her ears, and she purrs and butts my hand for more.

Oh, I would love to have a cat. It would be so nice. I would come home every night and she would jump down from where she had been sleeping and run to greet me, chirruping a friendly welcome. I would scoop her up and cradle her in my arms and carry her to feed her. Maybe after prayers she would jump onto my bed and snuggle down with me? My hand rests in her warm soft fur and the weight of her purring body is a barrier between me and the world. Wondering what colour she is, I think I would like to have a grey cat, with soft long fur. I would have company then and a safe and loving friend.

Flora

The cat has long since moved away and my fingers are clutching cold marble countertop when something else taps on my hand. The last two human touches on my flesh are still burning with sensation. I can feel Tom's warm eager fingers on my thigh and the slight graze of his nails on my soft skin as he retreated at top speed and my cheek is stinging with the heat of Laura's rage. This touch, an impatient peremptory tapping, causes me to open my eyes at last and I find myself confronted by a different bridesmaid. How many angry women are there here? Pink faced with emotion, she hisses into my face,

'And she's pregnant as well, have you thought of that? What if something happens to the baby now?'

'Do you know how much she did for this wedding?' another woman demands, almost crying herself. 'She's talked of nothing else for weeks and worried herself sick trying to make everything perfect.'

Laura rallies at this comment and turning to the crowd, but with her eyes firmly fixed on me, she calls out. 'So how many lawyer friends do I have? Jason, Clarissa and...' she hesitates for a minute, her usually quick and calculating brain fuzzy with shock. 'Oh yes, Malcolm, dear Mr Hargreaves. Well, I don't think I need to worry about legal representation, but you...' here she rounds on me, 'you are going to find you have no business after this. No business left at all, but some big financial problems. You had better lawyer up damn fast.'

These last words are literally spat at me, but luckily the froth of her venom is partly absorbed by a figure coming between us.

A hand takes my arm firmly. Another touch and this one not as unwelcome. It is Luke. Luke who has fought through the pack of hostile women. He seems angry too and is pretty much manhandling me, pulling me through the groups of gaping onlookers, who reluctantly make way and out towards the back door of the house.

Luke, holding onto me firmly, walks me through the kitchen and out into a small lean-to area full of boots and watering cans. I catch the musky scent of ripening tomatoes from plants filling the windowsills and feel a lurch of nostalgic sadness. At other events like this Luke and I might have by now been chatting comfortably at the end of the wedding, hidden from view in just such a hangout as this. But we are not going to be chatting today. I have never seen Luke like this before.

'What the fuck, Flora? I mean, really, what the fuck? That guy is a total creep. You can't tell me you like him. And what a damn stupid time to pick too. What the hell?' I've never heard Luke swear before and his voice is hard and loud.

He runs out of steam after that, gesturing mutely and furiously around at the carnage of a beautiful summer 'Flora Miller Special' wedding that is going on around us. From the makeshift stage come faint sounds of the band, beginning to pack down their kit. We can hear continuing shouting and crying from the kitchen, a confusion of angry and distraught voices.

Luke's words hang in the air. I think about what he's just asked. Do I like Tom? No of course I don't. The guy is a complete waste of space. Using his good looks and easy sleazy charm to get into women's knickers.

But he almost got into *my* knickers. The touch of his hand against my skin high up on my inner thigh is a brand of shame. The thought of him there is sickening. And Luke, sweet gentle Luke, who I've always felt safe with, is looking at me with an expression that blends disgust, disappointment and incredulity.

For once, I am honest.

'Luke,' I say slowly. 'I really don't know what just happened then. I don't understand *how* it happened either. I don't like Tom.'

It seems very inadequate. I have absolutely no excuse for my behaviour. To make things worse, the events of the last half-hour are already disappearing from my mind, so I can barely remember what it is we are talking about. I am overwhelmingly tired and disorientated, my body still shaking with half-remembered emotion.

Luke looks down at me thoughtfully, his expression changing and softening as he scrutinises me.

'Yes, okay, Flora,' he says in a gentler tone. 'I can see that. Can you remember what's been happening in the last hour or so?'

Before I have time to answer him, Clare, the righteously indignant bridesmaid, has burst into the porch area, scattering a stubbornly dozing cat and some plant pots with the energy of her entrance.

'She's here,' she shouts behind her and turning to me spits out. 'Annabel and Gerald naturally want back the money they have just given you. You cannot expect to be paid for this wedding. The bride is in pieces. She is hysterical. They have just called a doctor. And Tom, that creep, has pushed off somewhere. Bastard has just done a runner.'

This last bit is news. Tom didn't hang around long. Maybe he had not had any serious intention of committing to Laura, though why go through with the wedding in that case?

Clare is holding out her hand and remembering what she just said, I slowly reach into my handbag for the envelope that Gerald had given me only a few hours before, remembering his kind words at the time. With a shaking hand, I pass it to the bridesmaid. Luckily, I've already paid all the suppliers. This was *my* money though. The money I've been earning over the last weeks of hard work. Without it going into my bank account, I have no idea how I'm going to survive financially for the rest of the summer. I seem to have more bills and debts to pay than I can explain and have been putting off payments until this money came through. A lurch of fear jerks through me at the thought of my lovely flat with its expensive mortgage payments. I have made myself a bubble, a sun-filled bubble of style, serenity and flower-filled wedding parties and now the bubble has burst, leaving me soaked in shame and cruelly exposed.

Exhaustion sweeps over me again. It is too much effort to think and there is nothing I can bear to think about. I remain standing still and silent, unable to initiate any movement. My lack of reaction enrages Clare further. She rounds now on Luke.

'What are *you* doing still here?' she demands, sensing that in some way he is supporting me. 'There is no way they are going to want any of your photographs now, is there? I think you can safely assume we no longer need your services anymore, thanks to your friend the marriage wrecker here.' She points her finger furiously at me. I think of the hours Luke has spent recently patiently snapping away as Laura posed for innumerable setup wedding preparation shots. He has pictured her choosing her flowers, posting out invitations, staring misty-eyed into the garden whilst flashing the huge diamond on her finger and trying on myriad different veils.

More images flash through my mind of the last weeks. Laura, tight-lipped with tension and nausea and Tom, detached from the wedding activity but always loafing about nearby, watching me and watching her. I have been flattered by the way his eyes ran up and down my body and by his easy charm, but it is Luke, I realise belatedly, who has been the friend to me and it is his company I have enjoyed.

And now I have destroyed my career and there will be no more comfortable chats with Luke, no more reason to see him at all. My reputation is what gets me work and if I can believe Laura and her supporters, it is about to be trashed. I have just handed back all the money I thought I'd made and have no idea how I will make any more. I have wrecked one of Luke's jobs as well. I have trampled on and treated our developing friendship as though it was nothing. And I have destroyed a marriage and I am still standing in the house of the furious, betrayed and devastated bride.

I accept Clare's fury silently. I deserve it all.

Finally regaining the power of movement and without a further word to either of them, I quietly open the door to the garden and, followed by Clare's baleful eyes, I leave. In a daze

I walk round the house to the tradesmen's entrance by the kitchen garden to where I left my car this morning. I am still outside my body, looking down as it mechanically goes through the motions of starting the car. My mind is empty of thought and my movements are slow. I am cold; so cold; chilled to the bone by the cool night air and by horror at what I have just unleashed.

15

'Miriam, Miriam, truly was it said by the apostle, "God will judge the sexually immoral and the adulterous." Your sins are great, and you have been cast out of the community of the God-fearing. Yet still you persist in your wickedness.'

The voice is loud and melodic with the sonorous cadences of a life-long preacher. It rings in my ears as I kneel by my bedside. How did I get here? How have I ended up in my flat again and for how long have I been praying? My knees are numb on the polished wooden floorboards and my thighs ache with the effort of remaining in my penitent position. I focus on the linen bedcover in front of my eyes, tracing the pattern of pink roses against cream, but although I am looking at it what I am seeing is a kaleidoscope reel of vivid and unwanted images racing through my mind. I struggle to blot them out with yet more fervent prayers, welcoming the pain in my legs as a deserved punishment.

'Lord God, I am your unworthy servant. I have sinned against you and against your holy scripture. I humbly beg your mercy.' The pictures in my mind's eye sharpen and jump into focus, silencing my feeble prayer.

I am leaving Chalk Hill farm with the tyres of my car spinning in the gravel in my hurry to get away; and from the open back door, a trio of women, Laura, Annabel and Clare are silently watching me depart. Laura has pulled off her veil and her wedding ring, which she flung at Tom with a sobbed-out curse. She is still wearing her white dress with the seed pearls down the back. This dress on which she spent thousands of pounds and wore for only a few hours has red wine stains around the hem and ugly black streaks of mascara down the skirt. Her eyes burn darkly in her white set face and follow me down the drive and out onto the open road. More than her threats and screaming, this frozen and devastated look makes me realise the extent to which I have wronged her. It leaves me in no doubt that, as promised, she will pursue me for revenge.

'Lord God, I have sinned. I am not worthy to lift my voice to you.'

Luke, looking exhausted and overwhelmed by the events of the day, packing up his van with equipment and turning to raise his hand to me in a mute gesture of farewell. I have no idea what he will be thinking about me now, but it can't be good. Will I see him again? Could that have been a final goodbye?

Stop thinking about him, you ungodly wretch. For once, forget your carnal desires and your need for worldly success and try to humble your heart to pray.

'Lord God, I am your unworthy servant. I have sinned grievously. I am not fit to lift my eyes to you. Lord Jehovah, if it pleases you, show me how to repent and what I must do to seek forgiveness.'

Parking my car and catching a glimpse of a happy group of people, drinking, chatting and laughing late at night. The evening breeze was blowing open their muslin curtains so for a moment I could see them all clearly. I desperately wished I could step through into their innocent and happy world.

Standing at my front door and unable to remember how to use the key. My thoughts had slowed to nothing, my movements sluggish and confused. Despite the warmth of the summer night, my hands were shaking with cold. I stood fumbling for several minutes and staring blankly at the keyhole and my useless hands, trying to remember what to do with them, until Elena, hearing me scuffling and scratching like a wounded animal, opened the door from the inside. Her exclamations of surprise, welcome and concern dried on her lips as she looked at me. Without a word, I pushed past her and staggered up the stairs to my flat.

'God will judge the sexually immoral and adulterous.'

I know all the words there are to know about sin. The great variety of sin and the details of my particular sins are burnt into my conscience. Stern verses from the Bible and especially the vengeful Old Testament prophets were instilled in me with my mother's milk. They are indelibly embedded. How could I have thought that escape was possible? The body and the soul remember who I am, it seems, even if my flawed recollection does not.

Hours pass in agonised and fruitless attempts to pray. My body is racked with cramps, but I force myself to remain kneeling. My mouth is dry, and I am desperate for water but cannot bring myself to move. I weep until my head is throbbing. No amount of tears will be enough to wash away my sins. I can only beseech the Almighty for help. Again and again, I ask the Lord, the Mighty and Vengeful Lord whom I serve, what it is that He needs me, His handmaid Miriam, to do to atone. No answer comes. Perhaps atonement is not even possible. Perhaps there is no way I can escape the endless fire and fury of His wrath and the descent into a hell I surely deserve.

There is a terrible pain in my legs. God that hurts. What the fuck have I done to myself? I look down expecting to see a twisted and deformed limb at best, but my legs seem normal. I am kneeling and not on a rug or carpet but my hard wooden floorboards. As I start to move blood begins to flood back to my cramped limbs and it is so painful that I roll back and forth on the floor, groaning loudly. Fuck it all. My head bangs hard on the floorboards in my frenzy of pain. Dazed, I lie on my back, staring at the ceiling and trying to work out what is happening.

The thumping sound that my head made as it cracked on the floor hangs in the silent room. Will that thump have disturbed Elena and her parents in the flat below? Thinking of Elena, I remember pushing past her and ignoring her when I came back last night. Was it last night though or the day before? Or was it longer ago?

If it is Sunday, perhaps they are all in church I think vaguely. What time is it? I can see dim light through the linen blinds, but I can't tell if it is morning or evening. I should turn my head to look at the clock behind me but can't bring myself to make any decisive action. If I lie here and do nothing maybe reality will not return. I am not going to like it when it does.

Elena, oh no, now I think of Elena, I have a bad feeling in my stomach. What have I done to Elena? I search my memory, through images that tease and twist away from me as I try to bring them to mind.

Oh yes, her father was ill. Her father went into hospital. I can remember being at hers that morning. I never asked how her father is since he went into hospital. Oh God, what if her father, dear Mr Valera, was so ill he died in there? Or maybe he is still in hospital, and I should be visiting him? Probably Elena needs help now as she has her mother to care for at home who will be lost without her beloved Salvador.

There is something worse than her father's illness niggling me when I think of Elena. Sickly guilt rises in my throat with a tang of sweetness.

What is it I have done? I focus on the sweet taste and try to locate it. That is the flavour of dulce du leche that was her poor father's favourite. I stole it from her kitchen, didn't I? *Didn't I?* And then I came back up here with the jar hidden inside my jumper sleeve hoping she didn't spot the awkward lump. I remember standing by the sink in my kitchen and spooning it into my mouth as fast as possible in a compulsive stupor, not using bread or crackers or a plate. And then I hid the scraped-out jar so that she would not see it next time she called. This is what I do, by hiding the evidence of theft I can tell myself it didn't happen at all.

Now I remember that whole morning clearly, yet it feels as though it happened in a dream. Why did I steal something that had such value to Salvador and so little to me?

For once, I force myself to accept this must have actually happened and to think through the consequences. Elena will have noticed the jar was missing after I left. So, she will have realised it was me who took it, though she is far too nice to challenge me.

Fuck it all, what a terrible person I am. Elena is pretty much my only friend apart from Luke. What a crappy thing to do, to steal from her and her sick father. It is not like they have any spare money. I roll my head around on the hard floor in distress. I deserve everything that is coming to me. I am so self-obsessed that this is the first time I have thought of Elena. She is always nice to me, but I am often rude and off-hand with her. It seems I can keep myself together at work but not at home.

Except I haven't kept it together at work, have I? In despair, I hit my already bruised head again as more sickening memories return. Now I have opened the door the terrible events of Laura's wedding come flooding back. I relive the moment Tom and I were discovered wrapped around each other. I remember Laura's furious and vengeful face and her threat to destroy my reputation.

I have been so proud of my 5-star reviews and the gushing comments of happy clients that feature on my website, but how fragile it all is. One aggrieved bride will be enough to bring it all down. I will not get any more work this summer. Maybe I will never get any more work. Anyone who looks me up will find out what I have done.

I flop back, exhausted, banging my aching head again. The pain is a welcome distraction from my mental turmoil. I tried to create a new life for myself. But now it is all ruined and ruined by me. I shut my eyes and drift off once more. I am Flora, I am 36. I am, no, I was, a successful wedding planner. A tear squeezes out from my aching eyes, pushes under my closed eyelid and slides down my cheek and onto the floor.

16

Fuck, I am cold. Bloody cold. Where am I? I was dreaming I was in a giant freezer, lying rigid on a metal shelf. Now I'm awake, I seem to still be in there. In the pitch dark, I stretch my hands out blindly to check around. It is wood I am lying on, not metal, and judging by the space above me, I am in a room.

What has happened to me? I cautiously feel down my body, which is encased in tight cloth and then stare into the darkness, trying to understand. Slowly my eyes get used to the dark and I recognise my front room. I am lying on the floor near the sofa. Why am I wearing a sleeveless party frock in the middle of the night? Isn't this the dress I chose to excite that hunky Tom? What the fuck happened? Oh, I can't think now. I am so damn cold.

An unguarded movement sends pain shooting through me and I lie back gasping in surprise and shock, shutting my eyes again in exhaustion and despite the cold, I slip back to unconsciousness.

When I wake again, I am no longer cold but thirsty. My mouth is so dry it is sealed shut and my throat is raw and aching. My eyes hurt when I open them, so I shut them quickly again. I need liquid first. That is the priority. Squinting around cautiously, I see an open vodka bottle within reach. Moaning with pain, I shuffle my body towards it.

I focus hard on the bottle and roll towards it. Banging my hipbone as I stretch, I finally have the drink in my hand and take a huge burning gulp. I lie back, gasping for breath until the liquor courses into my empty stomach. It is warming and soothes the throbbing ache in my head.

That feels good. I need more. Slowly, I lift my head and take another deep draft. When was the last time I had a drink? A proper drink that is, an alcoholic one. A fugitive memory tweaks at my taste buds, the smell of roses, the tang of champagne. The picture sharpens into a sunlit garden filled with people. I am there and I have champagne in my hand and am wearing, surely, this same dress.

The bubbles of memory are bursting open. I remember the last time I was drinking. We were toasting Laura and Tom's health at their wedding. I must have been thirsty because for once I drank the whole glass and very quickly. How long ago was that?

It was proper champagne at Laura and Tom's wedding; no expense was spared for those two. Then after that, what happened? There is a blankness that I struggle to fill. Maybe it doesn't matter? I'm not sure I want to think about it. The late afternoon sun, filtered by the closed blinds, is streaming over me and I bask in the warmth. It must be a glorious day outside. I need more vodka.

As I reach for the bottle another memory bubble pops me back to the pantry at Chalk Hill Farm. The smell now is not roses, but cologne. With the scent comes the man. I can almost feel him pressed against me, his hands on my body, his lips on mine.

I lie back, shocked by the scene unfolding in my mind's eye. What had I been thinking? Snogging the groom at his wedding? And I was a trusted person with a job to do. Although I am alone heat rises to my face and burns my chest. I roll in anguish on the unyielding floor, shaking and banging my head to blot out the pitiless images.

It wasn't my bloody fault though, was it? It was that lech Tom. He's been bothering me ever since I took the booking for his damn wedding. Even on the first day, he was creepy. He is such a slimeball. *He* was the one getting married. I was just trying to keep him sweet. He was the one with his eyes constantly down the front of my dress checking out my tits, even when we were talking about poems for his wedding service.

Why couldn't he have left me alone? And what the fuck am I going to do now? I can't get up because then I'll see my phone and all those vengeful cows are no doubt online out for my blood. The only thing is to get off my face on vodka and go back to sleep. I'm sure I can think of a way to fix things tomorrow.

'Miriam, Miriam, remember the words of St Paul. For you may be sure of this, that everyone who is sexually immoral or impure, or who is covetous, has no inheritance in the kingdom of Christ and God. Surely you will be cast out into hell, even as you were cast out from your family for your wickedness. Will there be no end to your wrongdoing?'

The harsh voice is back in my head again as I come round in the early morning light. This time I am too tired to silence it in prayer.

I lie back, defeated. I *am* a sinner and I have turned away from the righteous path too many times. My family were right to throw me out, the Meeting was right to cut me out, like a cancerous growth from its midst. Left to myself, I have turned to sin again. I have sinned against the holy laws of marriage and have wronged an innocent woman. Older memories are coming back now. Memories I usually suppress before they can take shape, but today I am too overwhelmed to filter them out.

My father's voice is louder. I recognise him now. It is he who has been in my head all this time. His voice rises and falls in sonorous phrases. Today, he is quoting the words of Isaiah against me.

'Oh child that I have reared and brought up, but who has rebelled against me. You have forsaken the LORD; you have despised the Holy One of Israel. You will be utterly estranged. Why will you still be struck down? Why will you continue to rebel?'

Before I can stop them, memories that I hoped I had forgotten flood back into my head. I can no longer evade them. All my methods of escape have failed. The memories are real. All the things that haunt my nightmares and that I spend my waking hours trying to chase away. They did happen. My head fills with snapshots from the past, seared in as indelible images.

My family are all here. I see them as they were on the day I was sent from the house, thrown from my childhood home in disgrace. They are standing grouped together to watch me go. I study the mental image carefully, focusing on each person in turn. My father stands in the centre of the picture as befits the head of the family. He is the Meeting Elder, the Preacher and the family Lawgiver. His favourite leather-bound Bible is in his hand. His long beard and patriarchal air are at odds with his nondescript clothes but his worn grey corduroys, brown slip-on shoes and beige polyester pullover do not detract from his solemn appearance. Jacob Miller, my feared and respected father, was not a man with any personal vanity but was possessed by a certainty of his direct connection to God which both sustained and drove him tirelessly.

Beside him and so self-effacingly as to appear in the place of his shadow, is my mother Fidelma. She is dressed in neutral shades with long greying hair tucked away under a brown headscarf. Her tired and patient face is shaded from full view.

Her downcast eyes reflect her wish to shrink from scrutiny and her mouth is firmly shut on any thoughts that do not reflect and echo the words of her husband, Jacob.

My brothers are there as well, standing to the right-hand side of my parents, stiff and uncomfortable in their Meeting suits, their empty hands hanging awkwardly. They are glued together as always. I will not linger on them though. Thinking about them makes my heart thump painfully. I quickly scan their remembered image, looking for clues. Surely something must show on their faces, for after all they too are hiding a secret. A guilty secret and a terrible sin. But there is nothing to be seen. There never was anything to see behind those three stolid and blank expressions. They all look the same. I stop myself. I'm not going to think about them anymore.

With a stirring of love, I turn to my sister Martha, standing to the left of her mother. But Martha, look at you! Ranged up against me for the first time in your life. How could you have abandoned me and be standing alongside my parents? You were always my friend and confidante and the only person I could trust.

I speak to her, to this image of Martha that has appeared as clearly as though she were there.

'Do you remember, Martha' I say to her 'how we were always together as children and how we looked out for each other? Have you forgotten how in the prayers that seemed to last forever I would look across at you and catch your eye, or you would look to me with a secret smile? Do you remember our plain shared bedroom? how every evening after prayers we would whisper together in there, sharing what we had seen of the world on our short walks to and from the Meeting Hall?'

And now even *your* face is hardened and blank. Your arms are folded tightly as though to stop from reaching out.

Can it be that your heart is not conflicted? I look into her face, remembering the last time I saw my dear sister, hoping for a sign of softness and sympathy, but I can see none. I speak directly to her silent image.

'Martha,' I say quietly. 'I just heard you renounce your so-called sin and seek forgiveness from my father and the elders. Does that mean you are now at peace with yourself? How could you of all people have turned against me?'

The image doesn't change, and she doesn't seem to have heard. It is clear now, as it was then, that Martha has joined the chosen ones. Together they have declared me to be no longer a part of the anointed group.

17

Someone is talking to me. I wish they would bloody well shut up.

'Flora, wake up now. Hey Flora, can you hear me? It's okay, you are safe. I just want to know how to help.'

But I'm not going to talk, why should I? I'm going to stay curled up here in the warm until whoever it is goes away and leaves me alone.

After a while, the voice stops, and I sense the person moving away from where I am curled up on the floor. It was a nice voice mind, gentle and friendly. I'm sure I know that voice. I'm almost sorry he's gone.

The door to the sitting room has been left ajar and I can hear faint sounds of someone moving around. It sounds like papers are being shuffled, the turning of pages. Damn cheek. Whoever is here, in my flat, is looking through my things and not clearing off as they should. Or had I secretly hoped they might stick around? I listen carefully but the noises seem to get quieter. My brain fills with gluey clouds of vodka-fuelled oblivion, and I drift off back to sleep.

Much later I come round again. The sunlight is no longer chinking through the blinds and the room is cool and dim. I'm hungry. I am *really* hungry. I am also dry-mouthed, stiff and headachy and I desperately need a pee.

I listen again to see if I am alone. What a daft thing to do, to fall asleep with an unknown person in the flat.

I bet Elena let them in, whoever they were. She has a spare key so she can come in and water my houseplants and drop off the post when I'm away. I don't want to think about Elena right now. My head hurts. My eyes are loose in their sockets and pain shoots through them when I move. I must have drunk a lot of vodka. I took some pills too.

Footsteps come into the room. Childishly, I shut my eyes and scrunch back down into my nest of blankets and pretend I'm still asleep. I'm not ready to remember whatever is the bad thing lurking in the shadows of my mind. This time, the voice is quieter and less certain.

'Miriam,' it says, 'should I call you Miriam?'

This is too much. I'm not Miriam anymore; I'm not that frightened bible-spouting fool. How does he even know about Miriam?

I sit up suddenly. 'I'm not Miriam,' I say, my voice coming out louder than I expected. 'And I'm not bloody Flora. She was just someone I made up. But I need a pee and I'm going to go now.'

The voice laughs.

'Okay,' it says. 'Open your eyes then, whoever you are, and I'll give you a hand to the bathroom.'

It's Luke. Of course, it is. That is who the voice is. I have no idea why Luke is in my room, but I am surprised and pleased that it is him. I look him full in the face to see what he is thinking. He is watching me carefully, as though I might do something unexpected, as though he is cautious of me. Well, we can't just stare at each other. I must get to the bathroom quickly. I stand up slowly, realising how weak I am, and gratefully take his arm. I lean on him heavily and together we stagger to the bathroom, where he leaves me to it.

After the longest pee in the world, I feel a lot better. I

randomly splash water over my face and arms, brush my teeth and gargle away the dry-mouthed feeling and then catch a glimpse of myself in the mirror above the sink.

Shit, I look bad. My eyes are red-rimmed and puffy with smears of make-up in the creases, my skin is managing to be dry and spotty at the same time and my hair is limp, greasy and sticking out in odd lumps around my face. I badly need a shower; I can smell the dried sweat on my body, but the effort of just thinking about having one is too much. Finding a towel, getting undressed, getting wet. All these things seem impossible. I whimper pathetically with self-pity and like the answer to a prayer, Luke appears at the bathroom door.

'Eh, em, Flora,' he begins and then becomes still more uncertain.

'Or, Mir… Well, let's not worry about what to call you right now.' He clears his throat and becomes brisker. 'I think the first thing is to get you a nice hot cup of tea and some toast. When did you last eat anything?'

I cannot begin to think about this question. That means going backwards and interrogating my frozen brain. It involves trying to remember actions in the past and nothing from the past is safe. Better to stay completely in the present.

And in the present, I'm hungry. My stomach lets out a huge rumble at the mention of toast. Luke laughs again.

'Here we go,' he says and gently helps me to the sofa, tucking in freshly plumped up throws around me.

After a big mug of steaming tea, (Earl Grey, my favourite) and two thick slices of nutty brown bread and honey, I decide, firstly, Luke must have been out to the nice bakery down the street specially and secondly, that he looks as though the last few days have been hard for him too.

He's watching me with that careful expression again like I

am an unpredictable animal. I beam widely at him to prove that I am not going to bite, and this seems to galvanise him into speech.

'Okay,' he says carefully. 'I *am* a little bit confused. Can you help me out here? I've always called you Flora and I've got to know you as a charming woman who is go-getting and completely focussed on her work. But it turns out, from looking around here,' he gestures round my flat, rather disingenuously, because I hide any evidence pretty well, 'that you are in fact, *Miriam* Miller.'

He pauses to let this sink in, waiting to see how I react. He looks earnest and concerned, and that is quite cute. I give him a big beaming smile. I am feeling so much better. That tea hit the spot and now I want some more hot toast. I'm feeling warm and sleepy and ready to shut my eyes again. I am distracted though by wondering what day of the week it is and what time of day it is. Maybe it is not a good idea to ask this now?

Luke continues, feeling his way word by word.

'But, er, this is the tricky part. Sometimes when I'm with you, I think I'm with someone else altogether. Maybe someone a bit younger. Not the Flora I know, maybe not Miriam. Em, someone who is a total rule breaker...' His voice tails off and he looks uncertainly at me.

I can't help myself; he looks so comical and he's trying so hard.

'Well, durr,' I say loudly. So loudly that the sound of the noise I make starts me giggling. Once I start, there seems to be a lot of giggles to let out and I laugh for a while, in a snorting gasping kind of way. I look up at last to see Luke watching me with a slight smile on his face. Holding out my hand and still giggling and snuffling, I decide to introduce myself properly.

'Good day, kind sir,' I say in a fake posh accent. 'It is so very nice to meet you. You, my good man, may call me Chloé.'

18

Luke's eyebrows jerk up in surprise, but he recovers himself quickly. Putting down his mug of tea, he accepts my proffered hand.

'Nice to meet you properly, Chloé,' he says. His eyes then snap to the designer grey bag on my kitchen table.

'Ah, now I get it,' he smiles. 'That *is* your bag, it's Chloé's bag.'

I feel like saying, 'well, durr' again, but restrain myself. It is nice to be having a friendly chat. I vaguely remember I did something bad last time I was with Luke, but the details escape me now. Should I ask him? No, that would sound weird. I know that most people have more of a memory for what they have been up to than I do. It is better not to let on that I don't remember what I've been doing. People can be funny about this.

Anyway, Luke can't be too cross, can he? Because here he is now. I smile at him again with my biggest smile. He is very sweet. *And* he made me breakfast.

Luke looks like he is going to say something. I watch him closely, trying to get clues about what has been happening. My body seems full of the remnants of strong emotion. My belly is churning, there is a queasy anxiety in my throat and the top of my head is tight with tension.

I rub my forehead to ease it, which reminds me that my hair is madly out of shape and badly needs a wash.

Luke laughs as I exclaim with disgust. 'Um, yes,' he says, 'I was wondering if you might like to have a bath, now you are finally awake. You've been sleeping for days.' He sees my look of alarm at his last words.

'Okaay,' he says again slowly, as though anxious not to frighten me. 'I think you might have lost track of time recently. It is Wednesday today. I called you a couple of times to see if you were alright, after, you know,' he looks away slightly. I gaze at him, hoping for but also dreading more information.

'After, you know, Saturday.' He finishes baldly.

'And then, Elena let you in?' I prompt him since he seems to have ground to a halt.

'Yes, that's right,' he continues. 'Well, as I didn't get any answer from my calls or texts, I thought I'd pop round to check you were still alive and your very friendly downstairs neighbour, Elena, is it? Yes, she said she knew you were in but had been getting worried because she hadn't heard you coming or going for a few days. And she let me in. I hope that is ok?'

Typical Elena, I think. Always with half an ear on what is happening or not happening on the stairs. I don't have any privacy living here. But I can't spare the emotion to be cross. I'm still reeling from the fact that it is Wednesday, and I have no recollection of Sunday, Monday or Tuesday. This is not good. This is a lengthy lost patch. I'm going to have to do something about this.

After a bath though. Time for a bath first and to get my itchy filthy head clean.

Later, wrapped in my dressing gown and with my hair still damp and now fresh smelling, I curl up on the sofa and take stock of where I am. I've got skinny. I can't have eaten anything the past few days. In the bath, I found ribs that I

113

didn't know I had. Luke, who has been tidying my flat (the man is a total angel) stops putting bottles in a bag to recycle and sinks down gratefully beside me.

I've been doing some thinking whilst I was in the bath, as well as finding ribs. I can see I am in a real mess and that I have been for a while. I can't remember at all what has been happening over the last few weeks. This latest blank patch seems to have wiped out all memory of the time before.

This should be frightening and for a moment, it is. Losing your memory *is* frightening and I bite my nails in anxiety as I try to cast my mind back into the dreamlike state from which I have just emerged. But then indifference soaks over me. My mind wanders back to that lovely bath I just had and how nice that new soap smelt. Was it fruity or flowery? It was a great smell. And, I think, sniffing my arm in pleasure, how nice I smell now I am clean again. I wonder what there is in the flat to eat. I'm hungry again, even though I've just finished that toast.

It is time to focus though. Come on Flora, I tell myself. Get a grip and think about what you can remember.

I am pretty sure I have done something seriously wrong. Is it just me or can other people taste their own guilt? I can taste mine now. There is a distinctive flavour in my mouth that I know means I have messed up in a major way. I remember this taste from when I was a child. I don't want to be found out and punished now any more than I did then. How nice it would be to be able to forget about whatever it is and to lie here all day, snug and clean and warm on my safe, cosy sofa. With a slice of chocolate cake and some more tea.

Tiredness sweeps over me as my thoughts circle round and I reach a decision. I *will* find out what has been happening, but I'm also going to open up about how much I keep forgetting. I'm too tired of putting on this act of being in control of my life. I am too tired to keep pretending. Enough is enough.

So, when Luke and I are settled on the sofa sharing a packet of bourbon creams with a pot of tea, I decide now is the moment. My heart is thudding in my chest in fear and embarrassment, but I brace myself, put down my biscuit and take a deep breath.

'Um, Luke.' I say, so loudly and firmly that he looks across at me in sudden surprise.

And then I can't think what to say.

'Um, Luke,' I try again. He smiles at me, seeing I am having a struggle with something.

'Yes, Flora, what is it?' he says, over the rim of his mug.

'Well, that is part of the problem,' I say, not caring that I am not making sense. 'You called me Flora just now and I am Flora. And I know that I am 36 and a wedding planner, or maybe,' I add sadly, 'maybe I *was* a wedding planner. I messed up at the last wedding, didn't I?'

The memory of Saturday, the day that was the culmination of all my work creating Laura's perfect wedding and the disastrous and sordid final scuffle with Tom in the larder has all flooded back to me, leaving me hot with shame. Luke nods sympathetically but says nothing further, leaving space and silence for my next words.

'It is just that earlier today,' I say finally, 'was I Flora? Because it feels like I've woken up and that someone else has been here instead for a bit. Oh, I know that sounds crazy,' I add despairingly, hearing a high pitched and desperate note in my voice. 'It doesn't make sense. But I can't remember earlier this afternoon, or yesterday, at all. And earlier I couldn't remember what happened on Saturday. At the wedding I organised. Tom and Laura's wedding.'

My words come more slowly, as more memories of Laura and the weeks of planning and preparing for her wedding come back to me. I am scarlet with embarrassment and shame. Luke must think I am truly mad, and I do feel it. But I must carry on now I've started. There is more to be said.

'Flora, I mean, me,' I point to myself at this point, 'is a made-up person. I am really called Miriam.'

Did someone use the name Miriam earlier today? It feels now like they did. Well, only one person has been here today. So it must have been Luke. I can hear his voice now floating back to me...' you are, in fact, Miriam Miller.'

'Yes,' I say in answer to this remembered voice. 'How did you know that I am Miriam?' Owning up to the name given me by my parents and the name I renounced when I became Flora makes my legs start to shake. I put my hands on my thighs to steady them, take a deep breath and look up at Luke.

He is smiling gently at me.

'Well,' he says, 'you were asleep and so deeply asleep I was worried you were ill. And you were out for ages, longer than I've known anyone to sleep. I didn't want to leave you in case you were unwell, but you didn't seem to want to wake up. So, I got bored and started to look at your books.' He waves to the bookshelves beside my tall, shuttered windows.

'You have kept some books from your childhood,' he says slowly, to give me a chance to understand what is coming.

And I do understand. The only books from my childhood that are there are my Bible and some religious tracts from the Meeting. The old belief system was so ingrained that I couldn't throw out my Bible. It has moved house with me and has been sitting on my bookshelves for years now and not once have I opened it. Now and then, my hand has reached towards it but fear has stopped me from pulling it off the shelf. I have always been too afraid that once I open the cover, I will meet the thunderously proclaiming prophets and apostles again. I have been too afraid to re-read the stories that I loved as a child, of Noah and the flood and the Garden of Eden.

Luke will not have had the same fear. He will have opened the Bible and seen my mother's clear round handwriting.

'To our dear Miriam. On the occasion of her eighth birthday. May you always walk with the Lord.' There is a small, faded photograph of us, my family, tucked in there too. Jacob and Fidelma and my three older brothers, who would have been in secondary school in that photo. Matthew, John and Reuben. Before it all began.

And us two girls were there too. Martha and me. She was my big sister and was very conscious of being two years older than me, so in the photograph she is firmly holding my hand. I was tall for my age though and nearly the same height as Martha in the picture, though unlike her I stopped growing at just over five feet. We are both wearing scarves over our heads, from which our hair hangs in long plaits down our backs. Our bodies are hidden in long grey smocks. I am staring fiercely into the camera, refusing to smile. I was stubborn even then. My mother had tried to coax me to, saying,

'Come on girls, let us all make this a good picture so we can send it to my cousins in America.'

The Bible is in Luke's hand now and he opens it and gently removes the photograph. Looking at it closely, he says 'you haven't changed that much, you know. Not really. Same eyes and same determined expression.'

I swallow and try to speak. Luke is right, the girl in the picture, that alien-looking child from an exclusive cult, *is* clearly me. I can remember it being taken perfectly. And if I can remember that, then I can remember what happened next. All that happened next, up until how I lost my family.

There is a long pause. It is so quiet I can hear the faint ticking of Luke's watch. He has moved closer and is still holding the Bible open, as though he is about to read to me. Martha, I am thinking, where are you, Martha? And my mother, where are you? You who plaited my hair and sang me gently to sleep all those years ago?

My big brothers I remember always as a group, a six-legged, six-armed, always eating group, pushing and shoving at each other on the way through doors and banging dirty boots. They seemed fused together. They had moved diligently through the ranks in their private school, never excelling at anything, but turning into hard-working and outwardly faithful young men. Only Martha and I and those other two boys knew that all three were keeping secrets from their parents and hiding their guilty faces behind their Bibles in Meeting. I feel a sudden boil of rage and push the photograph away.

And all three had married. This happened while I was still at home, soon after they left school. The young men of our faith were encouraged to settle down quickly to discourage the risk of sinful sexual activity. Though of course for these three it was by then too late. Before I was sent away, I remember hearing that two of their wives, barely more than children themselves, had fallen pregnant. There were prayers for them around our supper table and meaningful smiles and glasses of water came from the older wives and mothers as the newly pregnant and sickened brides flagged during the long hours of prayer and scripture in the women's area.

I was, no I am still, an auntie. Now I wonder about my nieces and nephews. What, if anything, have they been told about their missing aunt? Are there photographs on mantelpieces that my parents or brothers struggle to explain? Family pictures with a stern-faced girl in their midst, who then disappears? Or maybe the photographs vanished at the same time as me and there is no record that I ever was a part of that family.

I look up again and Luke beside me has almost disappeared, in a mist of my tears.

'Fucking hell. What are you doing to me? I'm not crying, am I?' I jerk my hand up to my eyes.

'That is enough, mister, you are messing with my mind.' I wag my finger playfully at Luke. 'Come on, let's not sit looking at old Bibles,' I glance disparagingly down at the book in Luke's hand, saying, 'we both need a drink to cheer ourselves up. How about we open some tins? I've got a six-pack in the fridge. And you need to tell me more about your cat. What is he called?'

Luke looks startled, then almost scared for a minute. I'm not that frightening, am I? Small blonde woman causes fear and alarm, I think inconsequentially, and the idea makes me smile. Luke catches my mood finally and smiles back, to my relief. It was all getting a bit heavy there. He answers my question with one word.

'Flump.' Then we both get the giggles because it is such a funny sounding word.

I say it again, 'Flump.'

'He is a big softie.' Luke says, who enjoys talking about his cat. 'My mother and me, we called him that because he just likes to, er, flump down on the floor, or your knee, or on top of my laptop, or even all over my camera stuff. And he sheds fur everywhere. I'm constantly picking hairs off all my lenses. Nightmare animal, complete monster.'

He laughs. 'Anyway, I will have a quick beer, yes please and then I must get off, feed Flump and get some work done. But I'll come and see you again soon.'

19

I struggle out of the depths of sleep as though from drowning. My body is rigid with the fear that stalks my dreams and today the early morning light brings no relief. Not when the memories of the past few days come raging back. I start to repeat my usual mantra,

'I am Flora, I am 36…' then stop myself. There is no point finishing, is there? I am not going to be a wedding planner anymore. Sometimes I am not even sure I am Flora. Today there is something that I need to face. It is time to look online and find out what people have been saying about me.

My mouth is dry with fear at the thought, so I make a quick cup of supposedly calming chamomile tea and clenching my fists and toes with anxiety, log onto the comments section on my website. Reading the first few lines, my head spins. It is as bad as I feared.

'When we hired Miss Miller, who came highly recommended, we were open and friendly with her and hoped she would help to make our preparations and wedding the happiest time of our lives. She wormed her way into our lives and began to flirt with my husband to be. During the wedding party itself, instead of doing her job, she sneaked off with the man I had just married and was found performing a lewd act on him. The betrayal of trust was absolute. Do not use this woman, her business is a cover-up for her depraved behaviour.'

Well, that is clearly Laura. I try to swallow.

'This woman is pure evil. She comes across as sweet and

charming, but then she stabbed my best friend in the back at her wedding.'

That is probably Clare. She makes me sound like a murderer.

'We feel we should warn anybody looking for a wedding planning service that this one is entirely inappropriate. We have been left most disappointed.'

That sounds like Annabel or Gerald. Poor things. Their measured tone upsets me more than Clare's ranting.

'I'm sure this woman is a thief as well as a complete slag. Some stuff was nicked from the wedding and I'm sure it was her that took it. She ought to be in prison.'

Now that one I wasn't expecting. Another bridesmaid or loyal friend must have written that.

It is like watching an accident unfolding in front of me in slow motion, a ghastly pile-up of cars, with shattering glass, crumpled vehicles and mangled bodies. Terrible, but impossible to ignore. I go to my Facebook page and stare appalled at my previous 5-star rating, which is now on 1.5. The comments section bristles with new entries.

'Organised the worst wedding I have ever been to.'

'If you want a quick divorce, book this wedding planner.'

Ouch, that is harsh.

'Charming, sweet, very organised and an amoral slut.'

That is enough. I shut down Facebook but immediately remember Instagram. I am barely breathing and though my brain is telling my fingers to stop, they are ahead of my thoughts and before I can stop myself, I am logged on. Oh God, I didn't think it could get worse, but it just has. Someone has posted a picture. A picture of me and Tom.

Who would do that? Take a photograph at a wedding they were attending of the moment it all slipped into disaster and then put it online? It shows me from behind, on tiptoe and tilting my head up to kiss Tom. His face is hidden behind my blonde curls, but his arms are round me and oh shit, his hands are groping my bottom. The caption says,

'This wedding planner likes to make sure the grooms at her wedding are completely satisfied' and it has been commented on and shared over eight hundred times.

I'm going to go viral.

Feeling sick, I slam shut my laptop. I won't be getting any more bookings now. A tiny corner of my brain registers pity for Laura. Poor stuck up cow, she didn't deserve this public humiliation. Which can't be said for Tom and me.

My phone shrilly blaring startles me. I panic, drop it and then realise it is Luke. Though unable to speak, I answer the phone and he starts at once, sounding unusually stressed.

'Hi Flora,' he says. 'Just checking you are awake. I've had some bad news myself this morning. My landlord has been round, and he's decided to sell this house, the house I'm in now. I never wanted to be here that long, but it has been dead handy. And he wants me out as soon as possible so he can repaint it and stuff. God, I hate moving. I've got so much gear here. He didn't mind me filling up the garage and it's such a pain trying to find anywhere that will take a cat.'

I can hear a faint meowing sound in the background while he talks and am fleetingly distracted from my misery.

'Is that your cat now, talking?' I ask.

'Yes, greedy bugger is demanding his second breakfast. Aren't you, you great useless lump.' This is directed at the cat,

123

judging by Luke's tone of indulgent exasperation.

'Luke,' I say, summoning up all my courage and deciding that I must tell him what is worrying me. It is not like anything can get worse today, is it? I explain first about the social media storm that is just being unleashed and he goes quiet whilst he checks it out for himself.

After a pause, in which I hear him gasp, I plough on. 'But I've also been worried about something else,' I say, trying to steady my voice, which sounds high and shaky. 'I think there might be something wrong with me. I think, oh, it is hard to explain. I think sometimes I am a different person. And it is the other me who is doing things that I don't want to do. And me, I, can't remember them. Though I sort of can, sometimes' I finish miserably.

'Yes,' says Luke very slowly. 'You know, we did talk about this a bit yesterday. Maybe you don't remember?' He speaks very gently. 'I feel a bit out of my depth here, to be honest. But I think you could do with some help. Is it alright if I come round later? We could talk about it some more. And I have something to show you.'

20

Before Luke comes round, I decide it is time I went to see Elena. I feel guilty for blanking her when I came back from the terrible wedding. (And for stealing her father's favourite spread, my conscience reminds me). To stop myself thinking about the wedding and the stealing I focus on my relationship with Elena. I have been trying to avoid making friends for fear of questions I am unable to answer and yet, really, what can happen that is worse than what has happened this week? I find I want to go and see her.

I tiptoe out, frightened I'll meet someone on the stairs. Halfway down, I decide I should take a present and I bolt back upstairs again. Remembering that cupboard full of gift-wrapped food I select some packaged heart-shaped cakes. Returning, I knock on the Varelas' door.

Elena opens the lock cautiously, but her kind face lights up when she sees me.

'Oh darling, how lovely, how sweet of you to come down. I have been so worried about you' she clucks, almost pulling me into her warm and cluttered flat that smells deliciously of baking. Then she puts her hands on my forearms and stares into my face.

'But what has been happening? Are you ill? You look so pale and thin. Come in, come in at once and let me feed you up with some chocotorta I have been making this morning. I am trying to tempt papa with it. Yes, he is back from hospital, but a lot weaker. He and my mother have gone to the church for morning Mass and to thank God for sparing papa. They both want to say a rosary.'

125

I find I can't talk. My mouth cannot shape the words that are in my head and dizziness sweeps over me. I know there is something I need to say to Elena, but I can't remember what it is. And her kindness makes me want to cry. Awkwardly, I thrust the wrapped packet of cakes towards her. Luckily, Elena is unfazed, and she gives my arm a quick squeeze, sweeps up my little offering, puts the kettle on and pushes some sewing off the sofa so I can sit down, all in quick bustling movements. The tennis is on the telly and Elena busies herself in the kitchen, so I sit back and find myself being fed strong coffee and delicious chocolate cake, dark, dense and moist. After a thick slice, the tension and anxiety that has been clouding my brain recedes and I get absorbed in the match on the screen in front of me.

Two hours later, I am still sitting on Elena's squishy brown sofa, on my third coffee and second piece of chocotorta when I remember Luke said he would come round. And he had something to show me. I wish I could stay in this warm and chocolate scented room and forget all my troubles, but no, I'm going to have to find out what Luke has to tell me.

I send him a quick message and he replies that he is talking to his landlord and will be round in half an hour. Elena puts another wrapped slice of chocotorta into my hand and gives me a hug as I go back upstairs. As I leave, I meet her parents returning from church, carefully shepherded in by a dark-eyed Argentinian man who I don't recognise. We nod and smile shyly but I cannot face talking and bolt upstairs. Once in, I half-heartedly start to make the bed and pick up clothes from the floor. Inspired by Elena and her homely ways, I decide to make some coffee for Luke and as he comes in; he sniffs in appreciation.

'Hey Flora, that is more like you. I'm glad to see you up,

almost dressed,' he smiles at my mix of silk pyjamas and an oversized fleece 'and back to making fancy coffee.'

As usual, he is laden down with bags, satchels, photographic kit and also a large brown envelope, which he drops onto the kitchen table.

He seems ill at ease and though he accepts a coffee and sits down, sprawled in one of my dainty Queen Anne chairs, with boots akimbo, I can tell he has something that he needs to say.

'So, Flora,' he starts at last. 'You know, I've really enjoyed working with you this summer. You have such a knack for organising events and making people happy. And I like you too. But I've been feeling a bit worried. I'm a straight sort of a guy. I always thought I knew what was right and what was wrong. And if I caught someone I was working with doing something dishonest, I'd have reported them or else made sure I didn't work with them again.'

He pauses, sighs and looks over at me.

'But you've had me confused,' he says. 'Before I met you, I would have thought someone like you was up to no good; but I somehow don't think you are.'

This is too much. What is he going on about?

'Like me how?' I exclaim indignantly.

In answer, Luke opens the brown envelope and draws out some photographs. He has printed them out as A4 images.

Silently, he spreads them on the table.

Silently, we look at them together.

The first one was taken at that wedding back in the

spring, the first time I met Luke. I am in the photo, which looks like he took it by accident. It is a muddle of people setting up the dining room before the formal meal and there are no guests in the picture. I am turned away from the camera and I find myself admiring my back view. I should wear that green dress more often; it really flatters the shape of my bum. Has he been taking photos to admire me? Maybe this is what this is all about. Perhaps he is going to come on to me? Now that might be fun and a bit of light relief. I give Luke a cheeky look, but he shakes his head slightly and gestures me to look again at the photo. I look more closely. In my left hand is a small bottle of perfume. My bag is half open and I am clearly about to drop it into my bag.

Luke is following my eyes.

'Em, when I took that one, I wouldn't have kept it usually, but you looked really pretty,' he reddens slightly. 'And then I thought it was odd that you were putting something into your bag that looked like a guest's valuables. But I didn't think much of it at the time.'

The next photo shows a dim room, red and black. I look at it blankly for a moment, then remember it was the casino themed wedding party in Gloucester. Luke has had his camera pointing at me again and this time I am stuffing a pair of gloves into my handbag. I am struck by my expression, which is wide-eyed and furtive. There is another photo taken a minute or less later, in which I have whirled round and am rapturously embracing a tall man, my expression wiped clean of the furtive look and my eyes alight with mischief. I can't remember that guy at all. He must have been some guest at the wedding.

Well, these are confusing. There is a strange dislocation in my brain as I look at the pictures. A voice is starting up in my head.

'So fucking what,' it is saying. 'How does he know whose bloody gloves those were? Why was he taking photos anyway without asking? And that one with the guy? Why shouldn't I kiss a wedding guest? Is Luke jealous? Is that what is his problem?'

I am shocked that in none of these photos do I look as I imagine I do. I think I present a front that is calm, unflustered and professional, but this woman looks almost possessed.

The next pictures are worse. They were taken a couple of weeks later. In the first, I am outside on the terrace of a hotel. I am again wearing a nice dress, (scarlet prom style, with flounced petticoats and my treasured Louboutin heels). But I don't have time to enjoy how good I look because what is disturbing in this picture is that I am bending over someone else's bag and riffling through the contents.

I feel sick. I have seen enough. Rage, shame and confusion course through my veins and I am boiling hot and then icy cold. I cannot look at Luke.

'You abandoned woman, truly you have descended to the gutter. There you stand, dressed like a tart, whoring after men and stealing ungodly trinkets from the unsaved. Breaking the commandments again and exposing your covetousness soul. These are mortal sins, Miriam. Is there no way back from the fiery pit for you? Is there no depth of depravity too low for you to sink into?'

But actually, what the fuck is Luke doing taking all these pictures of me? It is like he has been spying on me. I mean, maybe he has got the hots or something, but he shouldn't be taking and then keeping pictures when I'm off guard, should he? I'm sure there is a law against it. A sense of righteous indignation rises up and triumphs briefly over shame.

I turn angrily to Luke to confront him, but his expression

silences me. He looks almost tearful; he is pale with anxiety and is biting his lip. This is upsetting for him too. I take a few gasping breaths, fighting down rage and trying to hide my shame and confusion. After a pause, Luke reaches out and takes my hand and holds it quietly for a while as I gasp and flounder in an incoherent storm of emotions.

'I am sorry,' he says quietly at last. 'I know it must look like I was stalking you and maybe, in a sense, I was. The first time I twigged what you were doing, I thought you were just some crazy dishonest person. But then I started to get to know you. There is something going on, isn't there, Flora? You are not just stealing to get stuff, are you? I mean,' he gestures around the room, 'I think you have enough bags and shoes and makeup.'

I smile despite myself and more of my anger dissipates. It is true, my little flat is as full as it can be.

Luke waits to see if I am going to speak, but I don't. There are a million thoughts rushing through my brain and different voices all trying to gain the upper hand. I could say three completely different things at the same time, and this has created a blockage like a traffic jam in my throat and I can't say anything at all.

Luke carries on slowly.

'I am not judging you, Flora. We all are a bit messed up I think. I mean, look at me. I'm about to be thirty-five in a couple of days and I'm trying to pretend I'm not having a birthday at all, as I have no one to celebrate with. I don't have *my* life sorted out, not even a little bit. I live alone with a cat that I didn't even choose to have. I don't have a relationship, I don't have many friends, I don't have much in the way of close family. Workwise, I barely make enough to pay the rent and I won't even have any rent to pay soon. I need to find a new place to live because like I said I've just been given notice.' he finishes ruefully.

I look up, surprised and distracted from my own misery. Luke has been so reserved about himself, so this is a lot to take in. I don't like to think of him with no one to share his birthday with.

'I can't bake, but I'll make you a birthday cake,' I say lamely. 'And you can come for a proper tea here.'

'Oh Flora, you are sweet.' Luke says. 'No-one makes me cakes! Not since my grandma died. But seriously, you need to get some help. I think you are having quite major personality shifts and maybe you don't always realise they are happening? Sometimes you seem so capable and organised, kind and in control of things. Sometimes you are completely mad and impulsive, though a lot of fun and sometimes you are serious and solemn and as though you are remembering something sad. Yeah, does that all make any sense?'

He looks at me and I nod. Words are still all jammed up inside my throat and I have no way of getting them in order to get them out. Luke continues gently.

'Here is what I think. I think it is the mad and impulsive part of you that does the stealing. I don't think the other parts of you would do that. Can you answer a question truthfully?' he looks at me seriously.

I nod. I'm not sure I can, but I can try.

'Whose bag is that?' Here he points to the grey designer bag still sitting on the kitchen worktop.

I feel the jamming up of my throat as at least three different answers try to come out at once.

'Well, Mr Nosy, it's mine, fair and square. You got a fucking problem with that?'

'No, I don't know why it is there. Whose is it? It is

131

making me very uncomfortable.'

'I am a wicked sinner and have committed a terrible crime. I must throw myself on the mercy of the Lord and His righteous servants and do penance.'

Choked by too many possibilities, I say none of these, but Luke can see something of the confusion that I am in as he pats my hand soothingly.

'Look, I don't think you are a bad person, though God knows, you do some pretty dodgy things sometimes. That guy, that Tom, what the hell was all that about?'

He reaches into his bag, scrabbles around a bit, pulling out a squashed supermarket sandwich, then a spare pullover, then some very dirty socks, which he looks at with surprise and finally digs out what he was looking for. He hands me a big sheaf of papers, giving them a quick wipe down before he does so to brush off any mud or sandwich remnants.

'You can certainly tell me to mind my own business,' he says, not smiling at all now 'and I will. But, here,' waving at the photographs, 'and here' at the papers, 'are problems you really should be thinking about. I do have a bit of an idea what is going on, but it is down to you to decide what to do about it. I have brought you something to read that might help to get you started.'

I am still silent. There is a lot of noise inside my head and it feels like I have been talking, but I realise I haven't said anything out loud for a while. I clear my throat.

'Um, thanks,' I start, my mind lurching away from thinking about the grey handbag; now taunting me with its continued existence in my kitchen, and those shameful photographs that he showed me that I cannot now will back into oblivion.

Searching for a way not to talk about any of this, I remember my earlier resolution to be interested in his life too. Yes, that's a good idea. Let's put the focus on him for once. See how he likes being on the spot.

And what had he just told me? Oh yes, that it is his birthday soon and that he has to move. Impulsively, I decide to help him out in return for all he is doing for me. God knows he's had enough to put up with.

'You know what you said just now about needing somewhere to live?' I blurt, my words almost ahead of my thoughts. 'Well, if you did need somewhere to be for a short while, you could always stay here. I've got a second room, just through there and there is space to store your stuff in the lockup out the back. And I suppose if that cat of yours can behave himself?' I look at him questioningly, 'he could come too?'

As soon as the words are out of my mouth, I can hardly believe I've said them. What am I doing? I totally hate having someone else in my space. And Luke probably has lots of unattractive possessions that he will lug in to clutter up my already full flat. And a cat. Will it pee in my orchids, shed fur and scratch the furniture?

On the other hand, I have felt better since he came round today, it is nice to have company. Left to myself I am not doing such a great job of my life.

Luke looks startled, nonplussed, then delighted and finally goes red. I watch the tides of emotions wash across his face, simultaneously pleased and terrified about what I have suggested. My head is in such chaos, how can I manage to live with and communicate with someone else? Would this ruin even the nice times with Luke? I am such a fuck-up.

But Luke has collected himself and is now smiling broadly.

133

'That is kind of you to suggest, Flora,' he says, 'and brave too. You don't know what sort of a weirdo I am yet, and you haven't even met Flump. Though it might be good for you as well. I feel like you could do with some company and someone to chat things over with?' he raises his eyebrows at me.

I realise one thing. He knows and he has known for quite a long time that I have been stealing. I don't like putting this idea into a clear thought, but there it is. I have been stealing and he does know. He has just shown me the photos that prove it and yet he is still talking to me and considering moving into my spare room. That is a big gesture of acceptance, and I momentarily feel brighter and more hopeful than I have for ages. Since you got off with the groom at a wedding you were organising and got thrown out and were shamed online and have been shown to be a thief, I tell myself vindictively.

My mood droops again. I'm exhausted and overwhelmed. I rub my hand over my eyes and sigh. Luke sees my expression and picks up on my tiredness.

'Try not to worry,' he says gently. 'You have certainly got some sorting out to do but give yourself some time. And read these,' here he bangs his hand onto the papers he has left me. 'These are important. Give me a call, when you've had a look at them and when you want a chat. Hey, thanks again for the offer of a place. I hope you mean it because I might well take you up on it.'

He gathers up his scattered belongs and leaves, banging the front door as he goes, which reminds me I need to call in again to see Elena's parents, who have probably been startled by Luke's heavy footedness. After silence settles back on me once more, I try to focus on what just happened. I'm finding it hard to hold onto the sense of the conversation. The words are slipping away from my memory, like drops of water

134

splashing into a pool of forgetfulness.

This should matter more but I am too tired. I *will* read what Luke has given me, but not now. Now I need to sleep, now I need warmth. The safety of my bed calls to me, the vodka bottle and the respite of oblivion

21

I am back in the clouds of sleep. Sweet, sticky, dream-soaked sleep. I force open my eyes to the pale grey light that filters through the blinds. If I stay completely still maybe I am not here at all. I am not ready to resume my life. Today I could be anyone at all or no one. I am part of the greyness and can disappear into it.

How do other people live? How do they get up day after day and shrug on their familiar personalities? Is it only me who becomes disconnected from myself in sleep? Now that getting out of a warm soft bed has ceased to be automatic, maybe I will never be able to do it again. Perhaps I will lie here forever in a soft nest of bedding and give in to warmth and oblivion. Why should I fight so hard to stay alive?

My stomach's demand for food grows more insistent after a while and force me to move. I am hollowed out with hunger. Careful to think of nothing at all, I concentrate on moving. I blindly lurch to the bread bin, where the remains of the loaf Luke brought is waiting for me. Frowning with the effort, I pull at the bread until a lump breaks off in my hand. Gnawing hard, I return to bed, back to downy warmth and safety in my blanket lair.

After the last crumb is gone, I realise I cannot stay here forever. The vodka bottle by the bed is almost empty and my emergency gin has gone as well. I will have to put on an identity along with my clothes to leave the house and shop. Who will I be? Maybe I can start again and create another new person, completely different to Flora. A person who hasn't already messed up her life.

'Stop it' I tell myself, 'there is no need to think about that now.' But my thoughts run on in a frenzied loop. I have no money and have no more drink. To get some, I will have to talk to people. I will have to look at my phone, at my post, my messages. I swallow the last dregs of vodka with a random handful of pills and sink back to sleep.

Another time when I wake there is a terrible sound in the flat. A shrill shrieking that startles me awake in fear. Sweat breaks out on my skin. The bad noise finally stops, and I try to return to sleep but my nerves are jangled and my muscles are tense. My mouth tastes metallic and foul and my eyelids are gritty and dry. Moaning with effort, I sit up slowly. The room pitches and reels as I straighten and then gradually starts to right itself. Once it has settled, I stagger to the bathroom. Halfway across the room, the noise starts again. Oh, this is too much. Not that noise, that frightening noise, not while I'm out in the open and unprotected. I make a dash for the cover of the bathroom door and slam it shut, hiding from a monster. I listen till the noise stops and the disturbed silence reforms around its echo.

Now I am in the bathroom I pee in a distracted fashion. I clean and clean my teeth until the taste in my mouth is fresh. I am very afraid that the noise will start again, with that sudden jerk from the safety of silence to unbearable volume, but as I tiptoe back to bed, I realise what it was. Of course, it has been so long since anyone used it. That is the sound of my landline phone ringing. And the evil red flashing eye beside it is telling me that someone has left me a message.

I edge up to the machine warily as though it is alive. I am afraid it will start blaring at me again. Up close the noise would be intolerable. I clutch my nightie around me and catch sight of someone in the mirror across the room, a hunched, wide-eyed and wild-haired ghoul. I touch my hand to my face and the reflection does the same. Yes, it is definitely me. But why am I creeping around my flat with the blinds drawn in the middle of the afternoon?

Summoning courage, I decide that whatever is on the phone message, I need to face it. It will only be a recorded voice. I won't have to talk to anyone. With clammy hands, I click through the options to hear the message.

It is a woman's voice, clipped, clear and busy.

'Good afternoon' she says 'This is a message for Miss Flora Miller. I am Pauline Stobbart DC of the Cheltenham and Gloucester police force. We are making some enquiries about an alleged theft at an event you attended on the 7th of this month and would be grateful if you could call back to speak to either myself or one of my colleagues.'

The message clicks off and I slump back on my heels.

'Fuck it all why does it have to be the police? And the bastards have left a message on my landline so they must know where I live. What did people call them in the old days? The coppers? Bobbys? The fuzz? No, that one can't be right, that sounds filthy.

Now how am I going to call that stern woman back with the word 'fuzz' in my brain? I'll get the giggles and that will make things worse. I feel like a naughty kid who has bunked off school about to get told off by a teacher. I don't want to deal with all this shit today. It is not fair at all, don't I have enough to cope with right now?

Maybe I should do nothing? It might be best to stay here and let it all quieten down. Meanwhile, I need a drink. There had better be some more vodka in the flat. I lie back down weakly and rummage through the pile of pills by my bedside, looking for something to make me feel better.

The noise, that bad noise, wakes me again. I jerk up once more, cricking my neck hard as I do so.

What time is it?

Where am I?

I am sweating again, and it smells like neat vodka. My skin crawls and itches and my mouth is dry and acrid. The noise stops at last and the flat creaks back to a resentful silence apart from my pounding heart, which is so going so hard I can hear the blood beating in my ears.

That was a different noise, not the terrible ringing sound of before. I know that sound.

Doorbell. That is what it was.

For a moment I feel clever to have identified it and then fear starts again. Who is out there and what do they want? Will they come and get me? After another peal of devastating sound, there is a long silence. I hear something being pushed through the letterbox far down in the hall and landing heavily on the tiled floor.

My heart rate gradually slows, and I realise I am tangled up in the bed sheets. I have been thrashing around in a nightmare and am now trapped in the bedding. I am chilled with cooling sweat. And I smell. These things are so distressing that, groaning and wincing from the light, I manoeuvre into a sitting position and begin to consider my options.

I catch the smell of myself again as I shift position. I must have a bath. And somehow change this bedding. But my legs feel too heavy to move from the bed and my head is full of buzzing, static interference, tinnitus and an incoherent babble of voices. I lie back down, slowly, defeated by the effort.

Later I will get up. Later I will move and wash and force myself to re-inhabit this awkward, alien and demanding body. But not yet.

22

Waking the next time is even harder. Why could I not have stayed unconscious for longer? Maybe if I have some more vodka immediately, I will go back to sleep. I reach out blindly for my supplies beside the bed. The pills have all gone. The vodka has all gone. There is no food.

The flat is dark. It smells very bad. A red light on the phone winks evilly at me.

My stomach rumbles, reminding me how empty it is. I have eaten nothing but bread since Luke left. How long ago was that? Where is Luke? Surely, he said he would come round. I slowly accept that I am going to have to leave the flat soon to buy more bread. Food as an entirety seems to have narrowed down to bread, dry plain bread. I cannot imagine making toast. Or coffee to go with it. Or frying an egg. How did I used to do these things?

Soon I shall have to buy more bread.

In the bakery where they sell bread, they also sell buns. And doughnuts and cupcakes. My hungry brain conjures up the image of the shop counter in its entirety and I can see all the baked goods and smell their aromas, warm and good. I spin off into a fantasy of doughnuts. Of pulling apart the yielding dough, sickly sweet and satisfying. Of biting into the jammy centre and licking the sticky sugar from my lips. And there will be cheese and onion pies there too, steaming under the hotplate. And fruit cake, flapjack and cinnamon buns.

Oh, I am so hungry. I will have to get dressed now and

brave the fear that is out there. I will have to go out into the street. Into the light that is too bright, among all the people, the banging and jostling. Moaning with the effort, with the sheer awfulness of being alive, I slowly get up and head to the bathroom.

Slowly I force myself to wash and run a brush over my tangled hair. By now the skies are lighter. The weather has changed, and rain is streaking the windows and puddling in the street. My window-box herbs, parched these last few weeks, are stretching towards the rain, which forms pearl drops inside their leaves.

I linger in limbo half the morning, before creeping out like a fugitive. When the door of Elena's flat creaks open, I jump in shock and then freeze into the shadows. I would do anything not to have to speak to anyone.

Elena of course has no such problems. She sees me cowering on the stairs and opens her arms with a cry of pleasure.

'Come down my little darling,' she exclaims, 'you look like a frightened cat up there. And where have you been hiding and what is going on with you, that you have not been back to see your neighbours, or even answer the door?'

It is all said good-humouredly, with no hint of reproach, but her comments trigger waves of remorse. I have been so self-obsessed I never came to see if she needed help. Nor have I contacted Luke who might be waiting for *me* to call. If he wants to hear from me at all. I can't imagine why he would. It is all too much. Pathetically, I start to cry, saltwater leaking helplessly from my eyes. My throat closes into a hard dry knot.

Elena comes up and gently pulls me down the remaining stairs. She cradles me in her warm arms that smell deliciously of cooking soup and then with tender cooing, steers me into

142

her flat. The scent is stronger in here, a rich savoury aroma and the windows are misted up with steam. My legs are shaking, and I make no protest as Elena settles me onto her squishy sofa, pushing Mrs Varela's pug dog onto the floor. She puts a hot mug of tea into my hand and then hurries away to give the bubbling saucepan a stir, giving me a chance to dry my eyes.

I sip the tea, sniffle, blow my nose and become aware of three pairs of eyes watching me. Mr and Mrs Varela, with the now deposed pug dog, are all focussing their attention upon me. I am glad to see Mr Varela home and attempt a weak smile. He nods kindly at me. He is so frail his body looks held together by pure spirit. As I struggle to speak, he puts a finger to his lips and turns his attention to the dog, fussing and murmuring in Spanish to her.

Elena returns with bowls of soup, bread and butter, salt and pepper. Mrs Varela pauses, crosses herself and murmurs a quick grace and we eat. It is so delicious. My body warms and relaxes with the sheer pleasure of warm and nourishing food.

We are all quiet. I am still choked with tears and the older Varelas are tired and ill. Elena looks after us all, drops titbits down for the pug and smiles across at me, but only when the bowls are cleared away and fresh coffee is brewing does she begin to chat. We slowly settle back into our usual ways.

'So, here is poor Papa back again. You haven't seen him since he taken to hospital,' she chuckles, smiling at him affectionately. 'He was so not happy about that, but those darling ambulance men were not going to let him stay here. Most insistent they were.'

Her mother, who has been fussing with the coffee cups and rearranging the tray, looks up and speaks for the first time.

'And a very good job too, isn't it? My Salvador.' She

looks up at me, her eyes widening, 'he was blue, just blue, and he could not breathe. They were all so kind, first the ambulance men and then the doctors at the hospital. Jesus, Mary and Joseph though, it was busy in there. They kept him in and got him breathing better, but,' she breaks off, her face clouding over.

Elena continues gently.

'They don't think they can do that much really, not long term that is. But the important thing is he is more comfortable now, aren't you, papa?'

Salvador Varela straightens up in his chair with an effort. He leans towards me.

'Don't they both fuss?' he smiles at me. 'I'm alright really. Hey, mija my love, fetch me another cushion, I keep slipping down here.'

Elena obliges and Mr Varela shifts and shuffles in his chair for a while until he is settled. He rubs his hands up and down his thighs as he speaks as though to ease a pain.

'I know I'm getting near the end, sweetheart. I know it is time to look death in the eye. It is the next thing.' He hesitates, catching his breath and searching for the words to explain what he means.

'You ever watch old American movies? My wife and I, we love the old black and white movies,' he smiles across at Mrs Varela, 'and sometimes in them, there is someone tied to a train track, and you know that the train is coming.'

He pauses to breathe, in deep rattling gasps that shake his frame. Seeing that he is preparing to speak again, I move to hush him, but Elena shakes her head at me gently and leans forward to catch his next words.

He takes a sip of coffee and continues.

144

'So, in the film, you see the train and you hear it and then the action shifts to the hero or the girl, but all the time the train is coming closer. Even if you stop thinking about it, it is still coming until finally it is round the next bend and you can see the smoke.'

He stops again, exhausted and breathless, but he has more to say.

Finally, he shifts in his seat again and looking at me he says quietly, 'we spend our lives avoiding it. The train that is coming. We act like we can't hear it whistling as it runs through the hills towards us. But now I can hear it close. I feel,' he hesitates, rubs his creaking legs and then chuckles faintly, 'well, relieved. I guess. I've dealt with my demons and there were plenty of those. I know soon I will be going to re-join my God. It has taken me a long time to get here, mind.'

He leans back, panting. His face is shiny with sweat. Wiping her own eyes, which glisten like dark marbles in the rain, his wife wipes his brow, resettles his glasses and takes his hand protectively.

I am so touched that I cannot speak for fear of my voice breaking. Elena and I both watch the old couple settle back down together in gentle, long–practised little movements. The room is very quiet.

And I understand something. I *am* able to be a friend to them. All I had to do today is be here and listen. But this awareness is followed by a sense of panic. This is what always happens. People open up but then they want you to talk as well. How can I do that? How can I get the noisy muddle of voices inside my head to stop for long enough?

The others are all looking at me now. It seems they too have decided it is my turn to speak. Elena has moved to her father and is holding his other hand and gently stroking the blue veins that stand out against his papery skin.

'Um,' I start. It's as though I've forgotten how to talk. 'I've messed up at work.'

I pause, remembering my many successful weddings, how many delighted brides have kissed me gratefully, how many relations have praised me.

'Well, work *was* good,' I qualify and then grind to a halt. I can't begin to explain the storm of fury and condemnation I have brought down on myself. Especially as it is my fault. How do I explain that at times, I become a stranger to myself? How do I explain about missing time and lost days? How do I explain about the objects in my flat that should not be there at all? How can I tell these straightforward people that I stole a husband on his wedding day and that I did it without thought or care for either him or his poor pregnant wife? How can I tell them this when there is a perfect example of love and fidelity and marriage in this room? And I can't stop thinking about the fact that last time I was here, I stole from them as well. Only a jar from the kitchen, but what a betrayal of their trust and kindness. My mouth is filled with the ashes of self-recrimination and disgust, and I can say nothing.

And watching Elena with her parents, I realise that this is another sin of mine. I have not seen my parents for years. I have no idea if they are in good health. Perhaps they too have grown old and frail and need my support.

'Miriam, Miriam, have you no care for your parents that you reject us in this way? Did not the Lord our God give this commandment to his prophet Moses "Thou shalt honour thy father and mother?" These are sacred family ties, and it has been ordained that you should respect and obey your father in all things. Who are you to know better than him and than all the wise and holy people who have gone before?'

146

It is my mother's voice this time, quieter in tone than the pulpit practised Jacob, but strained with emotion. When did she say that? How come these words are stored in my memory, intact and clear?

Perhaps it was the day I left when they all stood silently by. My father, secure in self-righteousness, my mother, grieved to be losing her daughter but resigned to the will of God, the Meeting and her husband. Martha, my beloved sister, tear-streaked but meekly resolute and my brothers… no, I won't think about them now. The hypocrites. Hiding their sins behind smug condemnation of mine.

But I clearly remember my mother's appeal to me. Maybe I *should* have listened to her. Maybe I should have stayed, along with Martha, in the kitchen, helping my mother look after the men, helping her to prepare and clean up after the wedding parties and praying every night in my cold clean bedroom. Would my life have worked out better or worse if I had? Despite myself, I shiver slightly at the memory of that room.

For how long have I been silent? Did someone ask me something? I sense the others are waiting for me to speak and grow flustered.

'Oh, it is nothing serious, just silly work problems,' I say dismissively. 'I let things get on top of me.'

Elena sighs slightly and glances across at her father, who shakes his head gently. With an effort, she brings the conversation back to safer ground.

'Can I show Flora what you have been making?' she asks Mrs Varela, who considers it and me, then nods decisively. They rummage together through a tangled mass of coloured wool, before shaking out a delicate lacy knitted object. I try to decide if it is a scarf, a shawl or even a small blanket. Mrs Varela is holding it up towards me speculatively, assessing its many colours against me.

'For you,' she says at last, decisively. 'You go out in all weathers like this...' Here she pulls down her high neckline, bares her sharp collar bones and shivers dramatically. We all laugh at her antics. Impulsively I kiss her thank you on her soft powdery cheek and promise to wear the thing, whatever it is. Now is the moment to leave. We have all brightened up but I know that my mood will plunge again and I want to be on my own before it does.

23

My flat seems chilly and unloved when I return. I should tidy, do some laundry, get some food in. Instead, I return to the table where Luke has left my Bible and look again at the photograph of my family. I study their faces carefully, touching them with my fingertips, whilst cautiously, as though I am testing for a possible broken bone, I start to remember them.

I start with my mother, Fidelma, whose voice I heard today. How has she aged in the last fourteen years? Has she changed and softened? Does her remaining daughter, Martha, smile and tease her gently, like Elena does, as they cook together? It is hard to imagine, but I delve deeper into my memories, trying to break through the walls that I have built around them.

Those last days were so terrible that I can hardly think behind them, to what went before. I push aside memories of the day when I was told that the Elders of the Meeting had sent me forth from the group and into eternal damnation. That is not for now. But perhaps I can think of my mother. What memories do I have of her? I have no photos apart from this one to help me, but slowly I begin to see her again.

She always had something in her hands; always. When I came back from lessons and wanted to talk, she would swivel towards me, a tea towel and bottle of bleach in her hand and frown slightly, before sitting down at the kitchen table and putting aside the bleach. On the stairs, as I rushed upstairs to whisper to Martha, I would meet her carrying loads of linen and hear her quiet sigh as I pushed past her. My dreaminess she found hard to bear. She would reproach me when she found me lost in a world of imagination, the world I shared with Martha. She would chide me to make my bed or to tidy my books. Empty time and idle thoughts were ungodly to her; and often, so was I.

Only in Meeting were her hands empty and I remember seeing them twitch as she sat beside me, keeping a watchful eye on us all. Her hands seemed to be moving against her will, as though there was some gesture they wished to make that she was suppressing. Her boys, my three big brothers, were across the room with their father and the other men, in a world of biblical and religious study that was closed to us. We would keep our eyes down, not wishing to be accused of pride; or of staring at the men; of not knowing our place. Soon I had no wish to look at that opposing line of males.

My brothers, Matthew, John and Reuben. And their friends who were always with them, James and Thomas. My mind spits those names out like shots of poison. Those doughy overgrown boys: sons of one of my father's friends, became inseparable from my brothers. Together they formed a gang of five. How could I look up and into their eyes? Not when I knew what they had seen. Not when the sight of them brought shame buzzing redly into my ears and flickering across my vision. It was safer to stare at the floor and my mother's twitching hands. To pretend to be deep in prayer.

I focus my memory on those hands. I can see them again. How her fingers would claw together and then the third long finger would shake up and down. I wonder now what it was that her hands were fighting to say.

I dig deeper, mining my memory for a nugget of gold, for a time of family togetherness and for some reason I remember Mr Paulus. He was a member of the Meeting, who lived nearby, so we would often be walking to a service at the same time as him. He wished to become an elder but lacked effectiveness and authority. Possibly to increase his chances by looking the part he had grown an impressively luxuriant dark beard that jutted from his chin at a raffish angle. He had a habit, whenever he spoke, of smoothing out his beard in a distinctive pulling away and out from his chin movement that Martha and I found fascinating, especially when viewed from below.

One dinnertime, after we had all said Grace and my mother was serving my father, he remarked that he had 'seen young Paulus in town, in the bank, this morning.' Without thinking I had raised my hand to my chin and mimed his distinctive beard-stroking movement. All eyes had turned to me. Martha's eyes went round with horror whilst her mouth worked with the laughter she was trying to suppress. There was a tiny silence in which I realised my mistake (disrespecting a man of the church, one of my elders and betters) and then to my huge relief, the whole family; even stern Jacob, even muted and obedient Fidelma, even my older brothers with their blank teenage faces; all of them together laughed out loud. Jacob even copied the movement himself to further merriment around the table. I laughed along the loudest of all, delighted to have caused this sensation and not to be told off until my mother gently reproved me.

'Mr Paulus is a good man and a devoted Christian; you must always be polite about him.' But she had laughed as well. I had seen it. And I knew then there was another side to her or at least the possibility of one.

I sit in the growing dimness of my silent room as the afternoon draws in around me, dragging back the veil of forgetting and letting light into the past.

Always the Meeting was there in our home, its rules in our heads and its strictures shaping how we were together as well as in public. I think of Elena's warm devotion to her parents and their obvious love for her. I feel a hunger for that love, a life-long yearning I thought I had subdued. Coming on top of the emotional shocks of the last days it is too much to bear. My spirit retreats into the dark, an unknown place of blankness and watches my body fall to its knees on the hard wooden floors without interest or compassion.

As darkness falls, I rise, chilled and stiff-legged, to draw the curtains and light the lamps. I have made a decision.

I will go back tomorrow. Back to my family home and to face my past. I wonder who will be there. Will any of my brothers? Will Martha? How will my parents be, and will they reject me again? With my life in tatters around me, it will be bitter indeed if I am turned away again, the prodigal daughter who has seen the world and for whom the seeing has not been good.

I push Luke's piles of papers to one side, unread. I am too tired tonight to find out what he was trying to tell me. Instead, I sit with my old Bible, feeling the weight of the Book in my hands and on my heart. Am I ready to carry that weight again? I am not going back because of any faith. I am going back because despite the coldness of my early life there is still a part of me that yearns for my family. And because of the voice, I heard in my head earlier, the plaintive voice of my mother, asking if I have forgotten my duty to my parents.

'No,' I silently reply to her, 'I never wanted to forget and never wanted to be separated from you, but you all pushed me away.'

Deep down I know my words will not have the weight of a sparrow's feather when weighed in the balance against my sins and that to be with them I will have to accept their life and their faith and to make it mine again.

In a flurry of renewed agitation, I fall to my knees once more and drop my head onto the Bible. Surely it will help me in my hour of need. But I have forgotten how to pray. I grasp for the words, for the form, for the mental readiness, until finally, I hear a quiet voice, is it the voice of my mother perhaps? telling me,

'Humble yourself before the Lord and he will lift you up.'

Prayer begins to flow. This, then, is the way through. The Lord in his goodness has brought me low, to this desperate pass, where I am despised and friendless, but only so He can show me the Way that I should take.

I listen to the voice in my head, and it tells me I should make ready in the morning; I should be sure to dress decently and modestly and then I should throw myself on the mercy of my family. They are good people; the voice tells me. If I repent sincerely and renounce all my sinful ways, they will have me back. I could return to the heart of my family, and they can help me to sort out my life. The thought of handing over the mess and the effort to God and my family and the other brothers and sisters in faith fills me with relief. I have been foolish and headstrong, thinking I could do this on my own. But now I have seen the way forward. I must be humble and penitent.

Silently, I begin to prepare for this great change. I start by cleansing my shame-filled house. I clean the kitchen. I tidy the bedroom and sitting room and hoover every surface, I scrub the sinks and the toilet. Finally, I run myself a bath, scouring my skin with soap and washing the dirt and sweat from my matted hair. I am weak and tired, but I force myself on. At last, I feel clean and with it comes calmness. I will become pure. I will repent and henceforward I will live a blameless life. My thoughts are focused on the Lord. I pray to Him for strength for what I must do tomorrow.

24

I wake early and lie neatly and calmly with my limbs arranged tidily beneath the bedding. I retired to rest after saying my prayers and slept soundly without waking. This morning I run through my morning checks before rising to pray again. I am Miriam; I am 36 and today I am going home to earnestly seek my parent's forgiveness. In a sober mood, I wash and dress. I choose my most modest dress, dark grey, long-sleeved and full-skirted. It is a cool damp day, so I add opaque tights and a short cardigan. I clean my lowest heeled black ankle boots and comb and tie back my hair.

Putting down the comb on my dressing table, my eye is caught by the make-up spread out before me. Such a tempting array of powders, tubes, creams and brushes. All of it to make me smoother of skin, rosier of cheek and brighter of eye.

Not today, I tell myself firmly; I do not need such things. Did not the Bible say "Your beauty should not come from outward adornment, such as elaborate hairstyles and the wearing of gold jewellery or fine clothes. Rather, it should be that of your inner self, the unfading beauty of a gentle and quiet spirit, which is of great worth in God's sight."

I am quietly pleased with myself for remembering every word of these verses and I repeat them as I prepare unsweetened porridge and herbal tea.

It is time. I look in the mirror before I leave, not to see how good I look, but to check that I do not see the degenerate woman that I was. I stare carefully at my neat and clean boots, demure hemline and well-covered arms. My eyes go to my unmade-up face. I am very pale and there are red rims to my eyes. My hair is a problem. They will know me at once for what I am when they see me at the door, bare-headed and blonde. They will understand what I have become and refuse to speak to me. I bite my lip in anxiety.

Well fuck it all, you are looking properly shit this morning. You might be trying out Shaker chic or some crap, but you are so not pulling it off. That is a look for the under twenties with peachy perfect skin.

How come I am dressed like this? Was I dressing in the dark? And no make–up at all? I drop my bag in dismay. I can't go out looking this rough. I rush to my dressing table. Yes, here are the tools to pull this whole look together. I start with the primer to get my dull skin glowing, then concealer for my dark circles. I layer on foundation, eye shadow, eyeliner, my best mascara and lip gloss. I finish by swirling on an expensive radiance creating powder that I picked up in the cloakroom of the grander hotels. Honestly, some people are careless, leaving their good stuff around.

Next, I turn to my hair and brush it out into flattering curls. I add serum, as it is dull as fuck and spray myself liberally with Black Orchid perfume.

I consider my reflection. Getting better, but why am I so bloody skinny? Clearly losing all your business overnight works as a crash diet, like divorce and shit like that.

With the memory of my lost business comes back shame. I stare at myself, appalled. I remember now what I am doing today. Hastily I wipe all the muck off my face, tie back my hair in a firm ponytail, grab my handbag, scrubbing frantically at my wrists to remove the slutty scent and rush out of the door, slamming it shut and running quickly down the stairs before I have another change of heart.

156

The fresh air makes me dizzy and I walk unsteadily to the car. For a moment I cannot remember how to drive, but somehow I start the engine and cautiously pull away. I drive slowly, clutching the steering wheel and anxiously scanning the street. I am afraid I will see Laura, one of her supporters, or the police. I remember now that I never replied to their message. Nor, I realise, did I read the pages that Luke had left for me, that he said were important. Where is Luke? I should call him later.

My hands grow clammy on the steering wheel as I realise that in all the fussing over clothes, I forgot to pick up my phone, which is still on my bedside table, plugged into the charger. I feel bereft without it. It is only really Luke or Elena I would call, but I should have told someone where I am going. For a minute I think of going back for it, but then decide I'm being silly. People managed without mobile phones for years. I'm only going to visit my family for a few hours. Surely the Lord will watch over me, guide my steps and keep me safe?

The roads I am driving down are familiar now, redolent with memory. I have arrived in Gloucester; I have been weaving through quiet suburban side streets and am now nearly at the turning to my parents' house. I am overwhelmed by the past. That is the path, narrow and grassy, that we walked on our way to the Meeting Hall. There is the corner shop to which Martha and I would be sent to buy milk when there were extra guests for a prayer group. There is the bus stop at which the ungodly children used to wait. I feel again the shame of facing them down and braving their stares and teasing. Suddenly I feel like I am going to wet myself. I do need to pee. That was something else I forgot in my rush out of my house.

This need triggers anxiety about arriving at my parent's

house and whether they will let me in. I should at least have brought a gift. And now I am worrying about how soon I can go to the toilet. Will it still be in the same place, just off the hallway beyond the kitchen? Of course it will, I tell myself, the house will be the same inside. My mother had no interest in interior décor, only in cleaning.

I spin off into memories of the inside of their home. What colour *was* the hallway? Magnolia? Pale grey? Lost in musing, I almost drive past the house altogether. My heart jumps as I see it, smaller somehow as if diminished, and I drive straight past, whimpering out loud with fear. I park badly, struggling to control my breathing. Maybe I should call at the corner shop first and buy a gift. Looking around furtively, I expect to see the same crowds of young people hanging around and I hear again their mocking words,

'Hey, it's the God squad. Watch out, they've got nits. Look at their hair. They never undo those plaits. Hey nit face, do you want a crisp?'

This all said mockingly, while the crisp packet was tauntingly waved in front of us. Shaking the memories away I force myself out of the car and onto the pavement. I am stiff legged with self-consciousness and can barely remember how to walk. This is the area in which all the brothers and sisters of the community live and I might have been seen already. What if someone warns my parents and spoils the unexpectedness of my visit?

In the shop, I panic and grab a bunch of cellophane-wrapped chrysanthemums, luridly yellow. I can't imagine my mother liking these, but it is too late to get anything better.

'Want anything else with that, love?' the blue–overalled woman behind the counter asks me indifferently.

'No thanks, that's all.' My voice is a croak and I hasten to normalise it.

'Nice flowers, aren't they? I'm just visiting my mum.'

The words sound much too loud. It is the first time I have spoken in days. The woman merely lifts one painted eyebrow and hands me my change, her fake nails scratching against my palm. Now I am in a rush to get to the house, before it is too late, before I lose my nerve. I gather up the flowers with fumbling fingers and hurry out.

In a minute I will not be able to go through with this. I will turn the car back to Cheltenham and scuttle back to my flat again. I think of the last lost days in which I have behaved like a wounded animal, afraid to leave my lair. There must be a better way.

This is my *family,* after all. We are bound by ties of blood. Everyone has a family and has something to say about them, even if only to complain. Everyone apart from me. After I was thrown out, I tried to pretend that I had no need of a family and or of a past. But look at the mess I'm in now. The only way, I tell myself, unconsciously echoing Luke, is through understanding how I got to be like I am.

I am so scared I have left my body. I watch the woman who is Miriam, scuffing her boot against the kerb. I watch her cross the road, keeping her head down and not looking at any of the windows of the seventies brick house she is approaching. I watch her walk up the short path. I watch her reach up her hand and hear the doorbell ring out clearly in the quiet street.

25

The doorbell chimes coldly inside the house. Peeping through the pane of frosted glass, I see a figure enter the hall and move slowly to the door. Which of my parents will it be? The door creaks cautiously open and I am at last face to face with my mother.

Except that it isn't my mother. It is my sister Martha. She looks exactly how I remember my mother. She has the same long faded plaits, the same unadorned face. She looks old, much older than the Martha of my imagining. Her hair has dulled from rich auburn and is mostly grey. She has filled out too. Whereas I am the same size I was at sixteen, she has become shapeless and solid. She has my mother's reserved expression with frown lines around her eyes. But there, now, is a familiar quick glint to her expression, an unguarded look of surprise and joy, immediately stifled. I glimpse a flash of the girl who gave me sidelong looks in prayers and giggled with me under the bedclothes.

Neither of us speaks or smile. We just stare; taking each other in. She is probably as shocked by my appearance as I am by hers. Despite my modest outfit and unmade up face, I must still look like a woman who cares about fashion and hair and nails, shoes and bags. All the temptations that Satan lays out to call us away from the path of our duty.

I hold out the hideous flowers to her and she takes them, frowning as though she doesn't understand the gesture.

'Martha,' I say at last. 'It is me, your sister. Can I come in?'

'Miriam, is it really you? Why are you here?' she answers, her voice huskier than I remember. An involuntary smile of pleasure hovers around her lips, despite her neutral words. She moves aside to let me in, then hesitates, remembering the rules and my expulsion, leaving me half in and half out of the doorway.

'Martha,' I say gently, 'is it alright if I come in, just for a minute? Please can I use the bathroom?'

I am embarrassed by my need for the toilet, but it helps us both because it gets me through the door. Martha motions wordlessly to the toilet under the stairs.

I am too strung up to pee at first, hyper-aware of my sister, both familiar and strange, just outside the door. The hall walls are the same shade of washed-out white and the house seems scuffed and unloved. Its evocative smell takes me back to the last time I stood in that hall, with my clothes and books packed in bags around my feet, waiting in a terrible silence for the taxi they had called to take me away.

I lean on the sink, dizzy and breathless, and stare at the pattern of tiles in front of me, recognising every chip and bump. Splashing water on my face I square my shoulders and exit with a deep breath. It is time to face my parents.

My hour of reckoning has arrived. From an upstairs room booms out a voice. *The* voice. The voice that has been in my head every night for the past fourteen years. I jolt in fear and Martha sees and shoots me a supportive but anxious glance. Underneath my fear are bubbles of joy at seeing her. I forget that the last time I saw her she had stood unmoving beside my parents while Jacob raged, shouting that he must pull out the evil weed from the wholesome garden and make clean the House of the Lord.

The voice that is calling imperiously to Martha, 'who is at the door?' is the same voice that uttered those words. I could never forget his loud and sonorous tones.

My body floods with adrenalin. Blood rushes from my head and I wobble where I stand, my palms and armpits pooling with sweat. I steady myself on the bannisters.

'Yes father, I answered the door,' Martha replies, playing for time. 'I will take our visitor into the front room.'

Automatically, I swing round to enter that room. She gently pushes ahead of me so that she is leading me in, as though I do not know my way, as though I do not recognise everything in here. There is the same landscape painting hanging over the fireplace. There are the same bookshelves beside the window. There is the small, cluttered table by the sofa. It is as familiar to me as the inside of my flat.

They have bought a new sofa though. I stop myself from commenting on it. An olive-green couch has replaced the beige one that I remember. Following Martha's lead in presenting my arrival as a harmless social visit, I perch awkwardly on the edge of an almost-matching green chair on the other side of the hearth.

My father's ponderous steps can be heard above. He is beginning the descent down to us, down to me, and my heart thumps ever louder in alarm. But before he arrives, another step is heard, quickly crossing the kitchen to our left and opening the side door into the sitting room. With a damp tea - towel in her hand and an apron tied around her waist, my mother enters the room as if to check if whoever has come to visit would like to be offered coffee.

I jump up to greet her and step towards her. Her eyes widen in shock and her mouth opens, but then she holds up a hand in a gentle remonstrance to check my progress. We both freeze as Martha and I had done, and stare at each other.

My mother is heavier too. Her body is doughy and round

and her back has bent. I think of her life consumed by cooking, kitchen work and prayer. She was always the woman in charge of organising food for the Meeting. She it was who would tirelessly produce after-service tea and biscuits, the harvest supper, a picnic for the yearly seaside outing. The food she produced was uniformly dull. Sliced white ham sandwiches, tasteless sausage rolls, industrial-sized quiches and pies in many shades of beige.

I had been telling the truth when I told Tom that I used to help her with weddings, but they were very different events to his and Laura's. Simple ceremonies in front of the congregation of the faithful were followed by a shared luncheon in the echoing social rooms attached to the Meeting Hall. In front of plates laden with my mother's food, the young new couple would sit together and shyly accept good wishes, with the watchful eyes of the Elders always upon them. The Meeting was at its best at these events, joined in loving if claustrophobic solidarity.

These thoughts rush through my head, triggered by my mother's passive solidity. She has become one of the old Meeting women I remember clicking their tongues at me as a child. I look straight into her pale blue washed-out eyes, whose colour highlights the uneven redness of her kitchen-scoured face. She is staring back at me with a mixture of longing and repulsion. Her hand is still partly raised against me and prevents me from moving closer.

We have no time to speak because my father enters the room briskly. He is clearing his throat as he comes through the doorway, but the curious tableau of Martha, his wife and I all frozen still stifles back his habitual smooth words of greeting.

He is the first to grasp the situation and react to it.

'Is this you, Miriam, my sinning daughter? he says coldly, looking me up and down in disbelief. 'What are you doing in my house?'

His words unfreeze us all. Martha slumps onto a seat behind me and my mother drops her hand but remains standing, lost in a storm of conflicting emotion.

'How is it that you feel you can walk into this house?' Jacob's voice is raised and angry. 'You have been with the ungodly all this time. Why do you dare to come back, bringing your contamination with you, as though you are still a part of the family? Do you not remember that the Elders forbad you from attending Meeting and us from seeing you?'

Behind him, Fidelma murmurs something inaudibly. He swings round to her. 'What was that you said?' he demands harshly.

'Maybe she has repented.' Fidelma murmurs again, her blue eyes lifting to mine.

'Have you?' she says slowly, looking at me appealingly. 'Would you like to come back to us?'

Words block my throat and freeze on my tongue. I hadn't expected this question so early. But what had I expected? I could hardly have thought they would just welcome me back. That is not in their nature. For a moment, I am confused about why I am even here. What good will this do?

Then I remember the mess I have made of my life, the shame of my disgrace at work, my debts and unpaid bills. I am so alone. I have nothing to show for my time away. I have failed in my attempt to break free. Why should I ever have felt better than these people? Maybe they are right after all and I am wrong. Surely I should try to meet my family halfway?

Ignoring my father's bluster, I hold my mother's gaze.

Her expression is unreadable, but she is waiting for my answer. Tears sting my eyes. What I would do for a soft look from her and for a warm motherly hug. The pain of my rejection feels as fresh today as it did fourteen years ago.

'I don't know,' I answer, looking just at her.

26

Jacob Miller is a man to whose clear and melodically cadenced speech people turn instinctively. He sounds like a natural leader and orator and people defer to him. As he starts to speak now, I sense the inexhaustible energy of the man, powered by his religious fervour. Fear stirs inside me. This was how I felt as a child when I was caught in some sin and made to seek forgiveness through prayer and penitence.

'When you lived with us before,' he begins, 'we always had grave concerns about your fitness to be among the Chosen ones. From an early age, you showed a rebellious and wayward temper. We hoped and prayed,' here his voice dips in volume momentarily, 'yes, we prayed mightily with the Elders and those who cared about us, that God would find his lost lamb and bring her home.'

Jacob sits down in his armchair, weightily, as though ready to pronounce judgement on me.

'But you persisted in your sinful ways,' he continues, 'and the company of the pure and the Chosen was not enough for you. You questioned the teachings that we hold most dear. You caused your mother and the whole family great grief and sleepless nights.'

He looks across at Martha here, who has pushed herself deep into her chair, as though trying to become invisible. Her face is pale, and her eyes are wide.

'Your brothers too, all fine and devout family men, have mourned the loss of their sister. And now you come back to us, to stir up trouble again, no doubt.'

Out of the corner of my eye, I see Martha make a sudden movement at the mention of our brothers. A look of fear, pain and anguish flashes across her face, as though she has bitten on an abscessed tooth. It is gone almost at once and her face resumes its former blankness.

I turn back to my father who is in full flow of righteous indignation. He is so sure of his own purity. But was he always so pure? Now I am seeing my mother again I remember some evenings hearing her choked back tears when Martha and I were in bed and seeing her reddened eyes in the morning. What was he doing to cause her such grief?

'So maybe the old man is not so clean after all. He's good at preaching at everyone else how we should all be behaving, but what was he doing, making his wife cry? And as for those fucking devout brothers. They make me sick. But I won't think about them, I won't go there.'

Lost in these thoughts, I straighten up impatiently in a restless movement. *'And it would be just common politeness to offer me a drink. It is bad enough that they are not pleased to see me, but surely they would at least offer anyone who came to visit something?'* As I think this, I realise my mouth is completely dry and I am desperate for a drink.

'Please,' I say quietly, 'could I have a glass of water or something?'

I'm hoping that the something might be a cup of tea but am not prepared for the consternation my words cause.

Both Martha and my mother flick their heads to Jacob and an expression passes between them. Fidelma murmurs very faintly, 'surely water is alright?' while Jacob frowns and considers.

'You should be aware,' he says at last, 'that since you left, we have had clear instructions from the Man of God. He has forbidden us, the Chosen ones, to eat or share a table with the ungodly and worldly. We must protect ourselves from contamination, you understand. We have taken enough of a risk opening the door to you, but that was Martha's doing.'

He glances at her with displeasure.

'We will have to take advice on how to proceed, should you decide to stay any longer, but for now, I think it is best we keep ourselves separate and are careful to uphold the correct way of dealing with outsiders.'

There follows an oddly formal moment. My mother leaves the room and returns with a glass of water, which she puts on the side table. Jacob then motions to her and Martha and the three of them retire into the kitchen, leaving me to drink the water unwatched, as befits a sinner in this holy house.

Left alone, I sip slowly and look around me. Apart from the green sofa and two armchairs, there is a desk in one corner. My father's leather-bound Bible is open upon it, on top of piles of religious tracts. On the mantelpiece over the gas fire are two china dogs that I remember from years ago and between them is a gilt-framed group photograph. I don't want to look at it, but I can't stop myself.

This photograph is the sequel to the one that Luke found inside my Bible. It shows the family, my family, grouped in solidarity. Those three early middle-aged men, one running to fat, another slightly balding and the third almost hidden by his glinting spectacles, must, I realise in shock, be my brothers. Martha stands unsmilingly to one side with Fidelma, and Jacob is at the centre. I wonder if they were thinking about my absence that day and if they sensed an empty space. Maybe all they felt was relief. They had cast out the wicked part of their family and they were the purer and safer for it.

I take a last mouthful of water and wonder what to do. I can hear voices in the kitchen, but for now, I am alone in my old sitting room.

So, is this an opportunity? Shall I take something as a keepsake? Have the miserable buggers left any collection money lying around? Because this lot owe me, don't they? They are so fucking rude. I get a glass of warm tap water and they all leave the room as though I've got the plague. Anger and need, deep primal need, rises inside me and I scan the room in agitation. As well as the china dogs, there is a small brass bell and a vase of plastic flowers. And the photograph, but why would I take that? There is nothing here I like but I want something, and I need it now. A hunger opens inside me, a gaping hole of need, demanding to be filled. Before I can reach for something, the voice is back in my head. It is louder than before.

'Miriam, Miriam, you have sinned and turned against your people and caused your family much pain. Repent now and turn to the ways of righteousness.'

The heat of my rage chills instantly. The voice is right. I *am* an evil sinner and I deserve nothing at all. Not even the glass of water these good people have given me. I shut my eyes in prayer and when I open them, my parents are back in the room. Martha is no longer with them. I had felt better with her there. The voice continues.

'Miriam, Miriam, *have* you come to repent at last? There must be a reason, as your mother suggests, for your sudden reappearance. *Have* you come to beg pardon for your sins and ask to be joined again in the community of the faithful? If you come in true humbleness of spirit, maybe the Lord God can find it in His heart to forgive you. But we must know if you come to us with a penitent heart. If there is any doubt, we must ask you to leave this house at once.'

My father pauses for breath and sits down heavily

169

opposite me. My mother sits beside him with hands tightly folded in her lap. Her eyes are downcast, so I cannot see what she is thinking.

But what is the miserable fucker referring to? These sins he keeps banging on about? I remind myself he knows nothing about my recent life, so he is basing his assessment on me as a child and teenager. Anybody in the real world would have thought I was an unnaturally perfect young person. It is only him with his fucked-up rules who saw sinfulness in my behaviour. Mine and Martha's. And wasn't it her that started it all?

I force myself to remember the weeks leading up to the final scene of my expulsion. It had all begun so innocently. My father's voice fades into the distance as I return to the past, remembering the girls we were.

27

At eighteen and twenty, it was "high time you were married" my mother said. Allowed a little freedom at last, Martha and I used to walk back alone from a prayer meeting on Wednesday evenings. We knew our time together could not last much longer and we clung to each other.

There was another, darker, subject that bound us together. We never spoke of it, but it was there in our thoughts every Wednesday as we set off on the short walk home. It caused us to hurry as we left the Meeting Hall before anyone could offer to "see us back safely." It was there as we anxiously scanned the street to see if that dreaded car was in the road. It was with us in our shared bedroom, and it wove creepers of shame into our evening prayers, into our choice of nightgown and into our restless and muttering sleep.

My parents chose their house for two reasons; that it was detached which removed the need to share a roof with unbelievers; and for its proximity to the Meeting Hall. So this was barely a five-minute walk. And every Wednesday night a girl would pass us in the other direction.

I perch on the edge of my chair and pretend to listen to my father's voice rumbling on but now I am thinking about that girl. Gina, who was the cause of all our trouble.

Gina was coming back from judo club at the same time as we were returning from prayers. When she first mentioned it, neither of us had any idea what judo was, but it sounded very heathenish. For the first few weeks, she merely gazed at us with bold and open curiosity. Then one day she smiled at us both, though mostly, I noticed jealously, at Martha. She looked about eighteen too and had shoulder-length dark hair, bright dark eyes and wore big hoop earrings. She was always dressed in sportswear and trainers.

Martha was in a fervour the night of the smile.

'What if that girl wants to know more about the Lord?' she asked me anxiously, over and over. 'Maybe it is our duty to speak to her? She does keep looking at us, every week, as though she wants to know something.'

The next week the girl smiled more readily, as soon as she saw us. She slowed down and as we approached, she said, 'Hi. Are you two sisters?'

She spoke to us both, but she was looking at Martha. All the time, she was looking at Martha. And Martha was looking back at her, and her face was flushing as she ignored the voice that must have been telling her 'do not mix with the ungodly ones, do not speak with them except when necessary.' She told Gina (who in exchange told us her name) that yes, we were sisters and with a little prompting, she told her where we lived and that, yes, her hair was right down below her bum when it was out of the plaits. Gina giggled.

'Ok Martha, maybe I'll see you next week?' and bounced off down the road, swinging her gym bag as she went.

For the first time in her life, Martha had a guilty secret. She had always seemed content to live within the constants of the Meeting. Unlike me, she was never caught fidgeting when the preacher spent over an hour haranguing us on an early Sunday morning. She showed no interest in forbidden fruits like youth clubs, television, or alcohol. But now she had a secret. She had spoken to a person from outside of the Meeting and had not stopped herself and nor had she told our parents. And I was keeping the secret with her.

Gina's youthful, flushed and smiling face slides from my mind and I reluctantly tune back into my father's voice.

'… I will contact the Elders to start the process of bringing you back into the fold, though it will be a long endeavour,' he is intoning, 'given that you seem to lack any sense of repentance or to show any proper humility.'

What the fuck is the old fart talking about? What have I missed? That wasn't why I came! Why is he going on about Elders already? I'd just wanted to see my parents, hadn't I? And see if I could understand when my memory gaps started. I glance at my mother in alarm. She is nodding calmly in agreement, but she is also looking out of the corner of her eyes at me. I try to smile at her, but she looks away at once.

I am suddenly exhausted by them; exhausted and depressed. Why had I thought this might work? Nothing has changed. But then I remember Martha, who had opened the door to me, and I think had been pleased to see me.

'Can I go and talk to my sister please?' I ask my father politely, slipping back into obedient ways.

'Martha is in the kitchen now,' he says, glancing at his watch. 'You cannot be there when she is preparing our food. However, we should ensure she is making a portion for you too. And I daresay the spare room could be made ready?' Here he glances enquiringly at my mother who nods mutely.

He looks at me again.

'We have to go out for prayers now, but on our return, you can eat upstairs and then perhaps join us for a short time in this room before we retire?'

I am both appalled and drawn in by his suggestion. Having to eat on my own in an unloved spare room is humiliating. But he does appear to be offering an olive branch of sorts. He has not hounded me off the premises at least.

So that is what happens. I sit quietly in the featureless front room while the family silently gather their Bibles, coats and shoes and set off to Meeting. I think of Martha, who has been walking that same short walk all her life and try to imagine how that must feel. Bereft of anything to do apart from read the Bible placed beside my chair, my mind wanders back to our earlier walks together and our meetings with Gina.

The following Wednesday both Martha and I were excited and edgy as we left the Meeting Hall. Would the girl, Gina, be walking down the street today? Would she stop again, or had she decided we were too weird? Should we talk to her? That last was easy in theory. We both knew perfectly well that we shouldn't. I was by far the more naturally rebellious of the pair of us, but Martha had surprised me last week.

And she surprised me again. Very soon we saw Gina, her dark hair dishevelled, and her cheeks flushed, sauntering towards us with an open bag of chips in her hand.

'Hey, Martha,' she called, not Miriam, I noted darkly, was it just me that was too weird? And Martha, my devout and obedient sister, called out as clear as anything 'Hello Gina!'

Gina offered us both her chips. That sealed her status for me as the ultimate temptress, surely sent by Satan himself. The taste of those chips. Salty, sour, crispy and fluffy. I had never eaten anything so good. In no time she and Martha were chatting away with animation. Gina's words were all accompanied by giggles. She was in constant motion, fidgeting with her earrings, tossing her hair, picking at the chips, swinging her bag and scuffing her feet. Martha by contrast stood very straight and still, but her cheeks had flushed and there was a light in her eyes I had never seen before.

After a few minutes, my sister seemed to collect herself. Her hand went to her head to check that she was not showing any hair other than the plaits. Gina saw she was about to move and lightly caught her arm.

'Why don't you girls come round next week to my house and hang out?' she asked. I was awestruck, both by the invitation, which was a first and by the audacity of the girl. No one had ever wanted to see more of Martha and me than they had had to, ever. But surely this was how Satan worked? He offered something so tempting and innocent and then before you knew it you would be sucked into the abyss. Both Martha and I knew a lot about the abyss and the fiery pits that Satan had prepared for sinners who he managed to lure from the path of righteousness. I was even more surprised when Martha hesitated and then smiled and said 'do you live really near? Maybe we could just for a few minutes?'

That following week, neither of us had spoken of it. We both hugged this secret to ourselves. Sitting in Meeting on Sunday and listening to one of the brothers preach, on and on in his sing-song tones, I thought about what we were going to do. We were about to be deliberately disobedient. The rules we lived by forbade us from mixing with the ungodly ones. Today I am on the other side of this terrible divide. I am the evil one, possibly the agent of Satan, who has come to my parent's Godly house and is tempting them.

How was it that Martha, who was much more involved with Gina right from the start, is still here and a devout member of the Meeting and it was me who has been cast out? Remembering the answer to this question, I get up and restlessly move around the house. I am sure to have at least another half an hour before they return. I am curious to look over my old home again and start in the kitchen, to see where my mother spends her time.

28

This kitchen is clean in the way only my mother could clean. She was devoted to the Lord and obedient to her husband Jacob, but Fidelma's true passion was hygiene. She would scrub and disinfect every surface, horizontal and vertical, every morning. She would vacuum the entire house daily and wash the windows every Monday. Spring-cleaning was an exhausting season we learnt to dread. Today my nostrils catch the scent of her preferred brand of floral bleach and at once I am back in this room with Martha. We would work fast to prepare piles of wedding food, sausage rolls, sandwiches, quiches and cakes, then carefully wrap them all in cling film. They are still using lots of cling film, and today there are four plates laid out neatly on the countertop. Each contains bread and butter, grated cheese, sliced tomato and cucumber and a spoonful of coleslaw, and each is wrapped in its own transparent and wrinkled skin.

So, is that going to be my fucking dinner? Talk about a chilly welcome. These people are insane. I am starving and desperate for a snack and I rummage through containers and cupboards but there is nothing, literally nothing, in this kitchen that I want to eat. Sliced white bread, instant coffee, the blandest of cheeses, bloody boiled beetroot. And fuck it all, I didn't think it could, but it just has got worse. There is absolutely nothing to drink. In a panic, I go back to the sitting room to check. No, there is nothing, not even a bottle of dry sherry in a side cupboard.

How the hell am I going to get through an evening here without any alcohol? Shall I escape to the nearest wine bar and call the whole thing off? I could go back to the corner shop and get a four-pack to put in this joyless fridge and see if I can get Mr Grand and Grumpy to lighten up later?

I walk slowly through the narrow utility room to the back door and after a momentary hesitation, I put my hand firmly on the handle to leave the house.

The door is locked, and I cannot open it from the inside. With rising apprehension, I walk through the house to the porch and try the front door. Same thing. Firmly locked, with a deadlock and with no way of opening it. I check the windows in rising claustrophobia, and they are all locked as well, with electronic alarms installed. Why do these people have so much security? What are they afraid of that they need to be so self-protective? Unless I smash a window, I am trapped here till they return.

Now I realise I am effectively a prisoner, my anxiety ramps up sharply and my breathing quickens. I struggle to stay calm. This is my family after all, not unknown kidnappers. Pacing from room to room, I finally decide to do what they wanted, which is to read the Bible. Idly, I turn the pages. One of them has been freshly folded down. The book opens at Deuteronomy chapter 21, and I read,

'If a man has a stubborn and rebellious son who will not obey the voice of his father or the voice of his mother and, though they discipline him, will not listen to them, then his father and his mother shall take hold of him and bring him out to the elders of his city at the gate of the place where he lives and they shall say to the elders of his city, "This our son is stubborn and rebellious; he will not obey our voice; he is a glutton and a drunkard." Then all the men of the city shall stone him to death with stones. So, you shall purge the evil from your midst and all Israel shall hear and fear.'

Well, I am a daughter not a son, but did my father turn

down that page before he left, so I might read these verses and see within them, surely, a veiled threat?

My palms are sweating, and I jump up to pace the house again. There is no way out and at last, I sit back, exhausted, and let my thoughts slide from my predicament and back to memories of Martha and Gina. I remember that week of excitement and guilty anticipation as we looked forward to the following Wednesday. The night we were going to Gina's house.

That evening the Brothers' droning exhortations to the Lord seemed to continue long after the usual time. Martha and I were in agony. What if we were too late? Would Gina wait for us? Martha's hands were fidgeting on her Bible in such an unaccustomed way that my mother, glancing down the row, frowned at her.

The prayers finished at last, and we set off rapidly up the road.

We saw Gina from right down the street. She was waiting for us. She was hanging by one hand from the railings at the corner, swinging her body in and out idly and prodding at her phone with her other hand. When she saw us, she jumped upright, threw her phone in her bag and linked her arms with Martha and me, in one easy and confident movement.

Now we had done enough to condemn us. We were walking arm in arm with one of the ungodly ones, a young woman so worldly that she possessed a mobile phone. We were doing it of our own free will, knowing that with every step we were sinning. The Bible I hold feels like it is burning my hand as I remember those first steps into a life of defiance.

We turned a corner and Gina gave us both a gentle tug

and led us through the metal gates of a small, terraced house. Pushing through the overgrown front garden she opened the door and ushered us inside. Once the door had closed, she turned to us both with a huge smile.

'I didn't think you'd come,' she said. 'Might you get into trouble?'

Perceptive enough to realise something of our situation but too impatient to wait for an answer, she had swept us into her kitchen and opened the door on a new world. In no time we were perched on bar stools and gazing around the messy, colourful room. A large black and white cat jumped up onto the counter and to my delight, headed for me. My secret longing was to own a cat and I had an imaginary grey one who I would summon onto my bed to warm my toes on wakeful nights. For me, this friendly feline was almost better than Gina herself.

Gina opened the magnet covered fridge and pulled out a bottle. Pouring red fizzy liquid into tall glasses, she handed them to us. I took a greedy mouthful that I almost spat out. The drink went up my nose and fizzed noisily in my ears.

'Eugh,' I gasped, 'why is it doing that?'

Gina let out a cascade of giggles.

'Have you never had cherryade before?' she asked. 'Don't you like it? We've got squash otherwise.'

She turned her attention back to Martha, leaving me to my fizzy drink and the purring cat. The two of them were soon caught up in whispering and giggling together. I was distracted by looking round the kitchen, so I didn't mind being left out. The room had been painted bright yellow and someone had stencilled tropical birds over the walls. Like the rest of the house, it was filled with plants. Trailing greenery tumbled from shelves, sweet-scented flowers bloomed on windowsills and herbs in pots stood on the wooden work surfaces. There was a bowl of fruit on the table and mismatched colourful cups in the sink waited to be washed.

On the counter in front of me was an open box of chocolates. Even today, all these years later, I can still see those chocolates. The shiny jewel-coloured wrappings, the rich sweet smell and the plump glossy chocolates themselves half bursting out of their wrappers, all sang to me with a siren call.

Turning to the others, I was surprised to see Gina leaning towards my sister and lightly brushing Martha's cheek.

'Your skin is so good' she murmured jealously, 'what do you use on it? I need something. I'm such a spotty cow!'

Martha had blushed as red as she could go. I studied her as though through fresh eyes. She did have clear skin, very pale, which brought out her green and currently shining eyes. The hair that peeked out from under her headscarf was dark auburn and curly, like a wet red setter. Gina switched her attention to me.

'Here, Miriam, you should try this. You are getting touched by the spot monster like me. Though you do have amazing eyes' she adds consolingly.

She handed me a tube of cream in shiny pink packaging. It was exactly the kind of frivolous and worldly item that made my mother purse up her lips when we went shopping. Martha had looked across at me and seen her little sister with cherryade pink lips, gazing in delight at the little tube of vanity in her hand. She jerked back to reality.

'We are going to have to go home,' she said breathlessly, 'we've been out far too long. We need to…' her voice trailed off. I understood that she didn't want to tell Gina that we had to go home to prepare my father's evening coffee and to gather for family prayers.

Gina had giggled sympathetically but then rounded firmly on Martha.

'I *have* to try giving you a makeover next week' she declared, 'no, don't say no, we can wipe it all off straight away, but you have *the* most amazing features and skin. I want to show you how you could look.'

There it was again, the voice of Satan, loud and clear. I had been taught how Satan could disguise himself to lure the unwary from the path of righteousness but had never known before he could be a skinny, giggly teenage girl with bangles round her wrists.

I had waited for Martha to refuse, but Martha had seemed to be in a daze.

'Ooh right,' she had murmured doubtfully, colouring up again 'We could just be here for five minutes I suppose?' She and I both knew that my parents and elder brothers always stayed behind after the evening prayer Meeting, Fidelma to wash up the coffee cups and sweep the Hall and my father and brothers to have a business talk with some of the other Elders. So, we did have a little time in which we would not be missed.

That night in our bedroom, Martha had been very quiet. The agonising of the previous weeks about how we should be trying to be saving Gina's soul had stopped. Maybe it was her soul that she was afraid for now.

Neither of us mentioned the evening's adventure. I had carefully placed the pink tube of skin cream in my top drawer, hidden underneath my plain white cotton socks, vests and pants. Beside it, I had placed a wrapped chocolate, shiny pink and as tempting as a baby's cheek, that I had found in my hand as I left the kitchen.

29

Remembering all this, I am suddenly curious to see our old bedroom. My parents had managed to buy the all-important detached house but always struggled for space. Martha and I had shared the same room until the day I left.

I don't know how long I have before the others return but decide that I can bolt back down quickly if I hear the key in the lock. At the top of the stairs is our old room. It is Martha's now. I wonder fleetingly if she prefers having it to herself at last. The length of the intervening years hangs heavily as I enter the room and I am sad for us both.

A single bed is pushed to the left wall and where mine stood is now a low chest of drawers and a small rag rug. The room fills at once with chattering memories. I sit limply on the edge of the bed, my mind replaying those times with my bright-haired and bright-eyed sister.

Over the next few weeks, we had called into Gina's house every Wednesday. Despite our fearfulness and guilt, the visits were the highlight of our week. I sensed that Gina would sooner have been alone with Martha, but she was always kind to me in her breathless way and would settle me in the kitchen with a drink. The cat Freddie would rub himself into my face, his tail banging the plants above us as the other two would disappear in a flurry of giggles to Gina's bedroom. It was not just Gina giggling now. Martha was joining in, sounding every bit as silly and worldly as her new friend.

Fifteen minutes or twenty later, no more, they would return. Gina would solemnly make me check Martha's shiny face to be sure no trace of any make-up remained. One week, in the bedroom after evening prayers, Martha hesitantly showed me her toenails, which had been painted a soft sweet pink. We had both gazed at them in awe. Her feet now belonged to that other world. The world of the outsiders.

My collection of treasures was growing too. Every Wednesday night I would add something to my top drawer, tucking the new acquisition under piles of underwear. As weak-willed as Eve, I had tasted the stolen chocolate, had nibbled and licked at it slowly over the week and had saved the wrapper which was too pretty to throw away. I often picked another from one of the boxes that seemed constantly open in Gina's generous kitchen. A tiny green glass pebble glinting in the afternoon sun on her windowsill caught my eye the following week. The next it was the turn of a sparkly heart-shaped hair clip, one of several that lay discarded beside her bag.

One week I asked to use the bathroom and tucked away a wrapped guest soap in my pocket. On another occasion I simply picked a few leaves from one of the houseplants and took them home to dry. I would gaze at my collection every morning and night, touching them gently. Knowing they were there gave me a jolt of pleasure and satisfaction each evening.

Martha too was nursing secret happiness. She moved more lightly and almost skipped along the garden path as she hung the washing out on the long clothesline. For both of us, this was an enchanted time. Loss, pain and disillusionment were just ahead but we dreamed our way through those autumn months, living from Wednesday to Wednesday, hugging our secrets tight to ourselves and delighting in the pleasures of a world outside our faith. We had almost

183

forgotten to worry about Satan. He had not forgotten us though and was busy working on our souls and tightening his grip.

30

The sound of the front door jerks me out of my reverie. I bolt downstairs with my feet clattering guiltily on the treads. I am only just quick enough and perch breathlessly on the edge of the armchair with the Bible beside me as my family walk in. To my alarm, they are followed by two men I do not recognise. One is thick-set, balding and wearing a suit that he has struggled to do up, the other man is younger but already stooped and has thick-lensed glasses and sandy hair.

My father waves them both to sit down and introduces them to me.

'Mr Paul Walters' (the heavy one) and 'Mr James Simmons' (the ginger one).

I try to catch Martha's eye over their heads as they settle themselves on the sofa. I'm half expecting her to look as I have been remembering her, a fresh-faced girl, alight with excitement. The glow about her was created by meeting Gina, with whom, I understand at last, she must have been in love. She gives me a stricken glance now and seems to be conveying a warning. The arrival of these men reminds us both of the last time men like this came to our house.

And, as before, my mother quickly leaves the room, and this time pulls Martha out with her. I can faintly hear them both making drinks in the kitchen. I know that we in this room will not be offered any. These holy men cannot risk their purity by eating or drinking with me. I think of the plastic skinned salads waiting coldly in the kitchen and realise how long it has been since I ate anything. I swallow to ease my dry throat. I remember this from before as well. The hours of talking, the exhortations, the prayers, the tireless way the men talked on and on until Martha and I were ground down with exhaustion and she became submissive.

My father Jacob begins the conversation, in a disarmingly gentle tone.

'Brothers' he begins, looking at Mr Walters and Mr Simmons, 'you may remember my youngest child, Miriam?'

Mr Walters clears his throat and smiles at me insincerely.

'Yes, indeed, I do' he says, 'I remember you with your sister, who is such a blessing to our little community,' this last comment is directed at Jacob, who smiles benevolently.

'I remember you both well as young girls, learning the ways of the Lord and growing in faith. Truly I am delighted to see how Martha has matured in her spiritual journey. She has proved a blessing to her parents. Of course, I am sorry that she never married and gave them the gift of grandchildren but at least your brothers have provided amply in that regard. Martha in the end took the right path.'

Again, he addresses Jacob.

'But there was something, wasn't there, brother? Involving them both? At the same time, we lost this young lamb to Satan?' He indicates me here. 'I was very junior then, but I believe you had counselling from some of our most respected Elders, Brother Matthew and Brother Joseph?'

So those were their names. The men who came before. After my mother had found the collection of treasures in my drawer and demanded an explanation. After my father had spent three hours alone with Martha. Sensing a story and a bigger sin than the theft of small items, he had taken her into the front room and not let up his questioning until the whole story of our visits to Gina and her house had come out. Then he had called on the elders, his brothers in faith, and they had come to find the truth of how Satan had been working his evil into our hearts.

They had questioned us separately, so I had no idea what Martha had said. On and on for hours, the questions had continued.

'Who had we been meeting? Why had we gone to their house? What had we done there? Who else had lived there?'

I remembered almost mentioning Freddie and then getting the giggles at the thought of confessing to meeting a dribbling and purring black and white cat. The two men had looked at me as though I had truly been infested with an evil spirit when they saw me struggling to suppress my nervous and mistimed giggles.

But fuck it all, there must be a *little* comedy potential here. The chinless ginger here, for example. He is clearly trying to behave like my father and Mr Walters but being a less impressive kind of man, he is overdoing it. He frowns at me in a way he must think is intimidating and he slaps his hand onto his Bible a little too often and too hard. Now I've noticed this, I can't stop focusing on it.

Mr Walters says, 'what have you been doing living among the ungodless for so many years?' *Smack* goes Mr Simmons' hand on his Bible cover.

Mr Walters again.

'Is there any part of your wretched soul that still remembers the ways of righteousness?'

Thump goes the other's hand. He has ginger hairs on the back of his hands and between his knuckles.

'What are we to make of your visit today? Do you earnestly seek forgiveness and to begin the reparation of your soul?'

At this last question, Mr Simmons' Bible receives such a pounding that I wonder if the spine will crack.

In the sudden silence after this last attack of Bible thumping all three men stare at me. How long have they been waiting for me? What was the question he just asked?

Mr Walters repeats his last question in an icy voice, and I consider.

Well, no, is the honest answer. I'm not thinking about the reparation of my soul. Souls are such an abstract and unlikely notion like that other thing they are always banging on about. The holy spirit. What is it even? My mind wanders at the word spirit, and I think how nice a glass of gin and tonic would be. Tinkling ice and a generous measure of the kind of spirit I do believe in.

Bloody hell, why am I even here? It must have seemed a good idea this morning, but what was I hoping would happen? I try to remember what I was thinking when I set off but instead with a shock of pain, I recall Tom and Laura's wedding, the vindictive messages on social media and Luke's disappointed and withdrawn face. But I've made up with Luke, haven't I? Where is he? I could really do with talking to him now.

Why did I leave my phone at home? I could have been calling him for advice. Should I leave now, go home and call Luke and try again another day?

I hear my mother say something inaudible to Martha in the kitchen and that reminds me of the reason for my visit. These people are my family and that was why I came today. It was nothing to do with all the forgiveness of sins and salvation stuff these men are talking about.

The silence has become uncomfortable. It hangs like a dark cloud in the room.

I clear my throat and look directly at my father.

'I am not here for the good of my soul' I say clearly. 'I came to see you and my mother and my sister because I miss my family.'

31

I should have remembered that family ties come very much second to loyalty to God amongst these people. And the One they worship is a demanding and narrow-minded God. My father's expression did not waver as I spoke, but he looked across at Mr Walters with a slightly raised eyebrow and Mr Walters rose to the cue and addressed me next.

'You must understand, Miriam,' he said, 'there is no question that you can be reunited with your family unless you *do* undertake to repent. Seek humbly,' he said these words with zest and I realised that he was enjoying this, 'humbly and in a penitent spirit, to be re-connected with the community of brothers and sisters to which your family belong. Your parents have much standing amongst us, your sister is a faithful handmaiden of the Lord and your brothers, once you have been cleansed of your sins, have indicated to me their willingness to meet with you again.'

Mr Simmons pipes up here. 'Your brothers are very devout men,' he says, 'and are all hoping to hear from us that you are beginning the work of reparation of your soul.'

"My brothers." The words punch a sickening wave of adrenaline and fear through me. How had I thought it would be all right to come here? I had been hoping to be reconciled with Martha and my mother and I had been trying to change my sense of myself as a hopeless sinner and failure. But I had forgotten to consider my brothers.

It sounds as though they are still as close as they were when we were young, and likely to react as one entity. Before of course, there were the other two as well, Thomas and James. Whatever they did, they did as a group, and membership of this group absolved each of them from individual responsibility.

Though I try to shut the mental door that has clanged fast on them so many times before, now I am back in my parents' house, it seems they can push that door open without effort. Though I want to, I cannot control my thoughts of those young men. As a gang of five, they would hang out after a meeting. James would, on occasion, be allowed to drive his father's car and all five of them would pile into it together on Thursday evenings after school. Sometimes they would see me and Martha.

Individually they might have had a conscience. Maybe Reuben on his own, or Matthew, or Thomas, would have seen us as family and to be protected. But the call of the pack was strong with them.

The door in my head begins to creak shut as I visualise that car driving down the street towards us. There are thoughts beyond, but they cannot and must not be reached. It is as though there is a box on the table in front of me containing my worst fear, from which I recoil in horror whilst also feeling a repulsed attraction and a crazy desire to lift the lid just a crack.

How close I came to opening the box! My palms are wet and the hairs on the back of my neck are raised. In my nostrils is the acrid smell of spilt oil mixed with damp lawn cuttings and overlaid is the scent of sweaty teenage boys. In my mouth is the taste of cider. The cider is sickly sweet and washes some of the terrible taste from my mouth. We are always given this afterwards, and it means that Martha and I have sinned as well. We have drunk alcohol and are complicit now. The door finally slams firmly shut, the lights go out, and I am in the darkness.

My head fills with an electrical storm like a computer rebooting. There is a stuttering of confused interference. Memories and thoughts jerk randomly, stuttering nonsensical and horrific images in front of my closed eyes. I am swimming in a soup of fear.

The room lurches sickeningly and then rights itself. I hear a child call to a friend in the street outside and one of the women in the kitchen clatters the dishes as she works. I open my eyes and look around. Here I am in my parents' house. I am a grown-up woman. I am not being touched.

And there are three men, in their smart and dull clothes and sensible shoes, watching me in silence. They are as immovable as the furniture. All is as it was. I swallow hard.

'Could I speak with my sister for a few minutes?' I ask again, beginning to adopt their style of speech. 'I feel her sisterly counsel would be of great benefit to me.'

'Martha *is* a good girl' my father responds in a voice laced with piety and condescension, 'but she is hardly qualified to deal with a matter of this sort. By having you here we are running a great risk. We are all being exposed to evil and to the influences of the godless world. There is no question that we can allow you to spend time with Martha. We must protect her first and foremost. She has such simple and pure faith and has led such a quiet life.'

I look at him hard then. I stare right at him. Because he must surely remember, as I do, that day, or night as it was by the time the elders had finished with us. In the end, Martha and I were standing together on the rug by the fire and both in tears. My father had been talking at us, in his too loud voice, for hours and hours. We were weakened and exhausted, having had no food or drink or respite all day. The other two men had taken it in turns as well. Very suddenly Martha had capitulated.

'I'm sorry,' she had sobbed, not looking at me. 'I am truly sorry. I was weak and sinful. I was tempted from the right path by Satan. He disguised himself so well I did not recognise him.'

Her voice was faint and shaky, and tears had splashed from her eyes to the floor.

There was a long pause and then Brother Joseph had slowly put his hand on her shoulder.

'That is what he does,' he had said. 'We understand that you consorted with the ungodly and were led into temptation by this young woman. Now you must realise the extent of the error of your ways. You indulged your feminine vanity and put the consideration of your physical and temporary appearance before the good of your immortal soul. As it says in Proverbs, "charm is deceptive and beauty is fleeting, but a woman who fears the Lord is to be praised." You could be that woman, Martha. You have gifts that you can bring to the Lord and into His service. But first you must tell us the full extent of your sins. And you must tell us as well what your feelings are now for this person?'

And Martha, my lovely truthful sister Martha, who had been hugging to herself the joyful secret of Gina for weeks; had dropped her head in shame and whispered that she had committed a further grievous sin and had been having

193

'unnatural and unholy thoughts.'

It was all over then for her and Gina. In that moment she chose the life she is living now. From then onwards she has stayed safely in the fold. She is the lost lamb who did return, and after being lost, is now frightened to ever lose sight of the rest of the flock.

Mr Walters returns to the attack. This is a pattern I remember. They will take it in turns with their different approaches.

'It is clear that you have missed your family and the communion of the righteous' he begins pompously. 'And you can have the joy of reunion with them. But first, you must accept you have been living in a sinful state for many years. There is hard and arduous work to be done on repentance. But we are all here to help you if you will let us.'

He glances briefly at my father at this point, who has made a sudden movement. Perhaps he remembers that I am stubborn enough to react against this kind of approach. He has seen me do it before, after all.

Martha had finally given in to the bullying of the Elders, but it had seemed I couldn't. Perhaps her emotions were more turbulent than mine and her judgement more confused. Heaven knows, she had more to lose. Gina had always been sweet to me but it had been plain that it was my sister she had wanted. I had been the awkward younger sibling tagging along. Despite that, when under pressure, I somehow couldn't abandon her memory and denounce her.

Gina had been my first real contact with the outside world. She had shown me it was not the terrifying sin-filled place that I had been taught. Those short Wednesday evenings and our tiny glimpses into another life had made me see everything differently. Now when I sat in our austere kitchen eating our evening meal, I was aware of the silence and of what was missing. We were all so quiet that after the grace was spoken, I could hear the sound of each family member chewing. The silence would only be broken by one of my father's pronouncements or my mother's gentle murmuring as she served him and her sons. At those times I pictured the colourful and cosy clutter of Gina's family kitchen. There was always noise in that house. The television was often chirping away unheeded in the corner, or Gina would be playing music. The cat would be purring, there would be giggling and chatting, and food being prepared and eaten in a relaxed way that I could not begin to understand but found intensely desirable.

Then there was the matter of my secret stash. Up to that point I had had no sense of it being wrong to take things from Gina's house. There had been such a hunger and desire in me for the tiny objects I smuggled home with me that their collection had seemed completely natural. But of course, it *was* a moral matter and a sin at that.

So, I had remained defiant even after Martha confessed and asked for repentance. She was given a tissue to dry her eyes and was then bundled back into the kitchen with our mother and some of the other Meeting women who had gathered to wait for this outcome, I knew that was not the end of it; that was only the start. She would now have to endure weeks of humiliation. She would be forced to sit separately from the other women, kept apart for their safety as well as to isolate her. She would have evening meetings with the Elders who would lecture her until the last vestige of any desire for Gina or to experience the wider world had faded away.

Back in the present, I shake my head. That had happened to Martha and explained why she looked so lumpen and joyless now. My arrival must have rekindled feelings and thoughts she had supressed for years. Unlike her, on that fateful evening, I had held my head high and had refused to apologise to the Elders. They had realised at last that they would not be able to make me break down. They had then gathered together, summoned both my parents and called me to stand in front of them. They had solemnly told me that I was no longer a part of the Meeting. I was formally cast out from the fellowship of everyone I had known my entire life. I was warned that I would never see or speak to my family again unless I repented.

From that day I shut another box tightly inside my head. And until all this trouble with Tom and the police and the involvement of Luke in my life, I had managed not to think about my family at all. I had closed my heart to Martha, who had been closest to me of anyone in the world. I never let myself wonder about what the next weeks must have been like for her.

I had moved to Cheltenham. It was only a few miles physically but seemed a world away from the claustrophobic life I knew in Gloucester. After staying in a cheap hotel for a couple of nights I had managed to rent a tiny room in a shared house, using the roll of banknotes my mother had quietly pressed into my hand as I left.

And I had changed my name to Flora. There is no one in the Bible called Flora. In that first week away, I was walking back to my rented room after buying food and essentials when I had passed a flowering lilac tree. The beauty of the flowers and their heavy scent on the evening air had lifted my heart in a way that I had been told only God would do. I decided I would not worship Him anymore, with His rules

196

and anger and cruelty, but instead, I would worship nature and beauty. I would call myself after the Roman pagan goddess of nature. Despite everything, I am pleased with the choice of name I made.

Now for the first time, I am wondering what exactly it was they had done to Martha in the weeks after I had left because that is surely about to happen to me now. I understand at last why she had given in that day. Guilt causes confusion and doubt, and doubts are creeping into my mind. Maybe what they are saying about me is true. I *am* sinful. I am a thief, after all. I have stolen so many things from so many people. I am lustful and immoral. I broke up the holy bonds of matrimony that had just been tied between Laura and Tom. Martha would have had this struggle too. She would have been aware of how unacceptable were her feelings for Gina in the eyes of the Meeting.

A dizzy clamminess creeps over me as the true realisation of my evil nature begins to settle in my soul. I am sickened by myself. Briefly, my head drops and my father senses weakness. He clears his throat and continues with renewed vigour.

32

What saves me from giving in at once is a sudden memory of Luke. Mr Simmons has a habit of taking off his thick glasses and rubbing his hands across his eyes that reminds me of my friend. Luke is no Bible thumper though. I feel a pang of nostalgia for our chats together; chats which had gradually been getting longer and more relaxed throughout the summer. Why oh why had I left my phone behind? And was it only this morning that I had tiptoed out past Elena's front door trying not to disturb her? How lovely it would be if she were to appear at the front door of this bleak house, bearing cakes and hot tea and bubbling her irrepressible warmth all over these dour men. Thinking of Elena and Luke pulls me up and reminds me that I have a life outside of this place.

But later, maybe three hours later, maybe five, these memories are growing faint. It is so late, I think dully, trying to catch a glimpse of the watch on Mr Walter's wrist. Are they never going to stop talking? My sinfulness, my unwillingness to admit to it and that the family can never see me unless I truly repent. These are the subjects that beat through my head like a deafening drum. I am questioned about every aspect of my life. Where do I live, who do I see, how do I earn my money? Was I living immorally? That means having sex, I decide.

At first, I fend off their questions easily. I tell them how I am working hard helping people to have the weddings they want and that I earn enough money to have bought my own flat. I imply I am using skills that I learnt from the Meeting, which surely should please them. As the evening wears on, my answers grow greyer and more confused. At times I remember things that do not fit with this picture of hard-working modest living. I remember the men who have wandered laughing into my bedroom on Saturday nights and then slipped down the stairs in the early hours of Sunday morning. I remember the full cupboards of wrapped gifts in my flat, the jar of cash, the bags of scarfs and shoes I never paid for. I remember Laura's white face as she faced the ruin of her wedding day and the scorching shame of my social media downfall. At least there is no internet here and without my phone, I cannot see what people are saying about me.

The seat I am on is hard and I shift uncomfortably as these memories wash over me. I should be glad of the physical discomfort; I tell myself firmly and see it as a penance for my evil ways. I force myself to tune back into the men's words, which rise and fall in undulating cadences. I recognise their sound from my long hours in the Meeting Hall. My body seems to be there again, in that high ceilinged and windowless room, perching on a hard wooden bench with this same aching tension in my limbs.

I try to fend off another question about possible sexual relationships. This is difficult because my brain is suddenly full of images of half-naked men who I have known for a few hours, and I am afraid this will show in my face or voice. I stiffen and speak in monosyllables, dropping my eyes to the floor to hide my embarrassed flush. Mr Walters senses the uncertainty in my answers.

Suspecting that I have had carnal knowledge of men, he declares with relish, 'in the words of St Paul, "to the unmarried I say that it is good for them to remain single as I am. But if they cannot exercise self-control, they should marry. For it is better to marry than to burn with passion." And you, my dear, have been burning with passion. And had much better have heeded the words of the apostle than defiled your flesh with sinfulness and fornication.'

Listening to Mr Walters, my shame increases. It washes over me in a sickly red wave, curling my toes and curdling my gut. Hotly following it is a wave of anger, burning and energising. Who the fuck is he to talk to me like this? And who the hell still says fornication? That's like something out of the eighteenth century. But the wave subsides leaving me shaky and chilled as Laura's words come back to haunt me 'her business is a cover-up for her depraved behaviour.' She would agree with Mr Walters. Mr Simmons now re-enters the conversation and for once he is on to something.

'I do not believe,' he says, 'that you have honestly earned every penny you have. Look at your bag and your shoes; these are luxurious items. You are running a flat in central Cheltenham, and you have a nice car. I have to question this,' here he turns to my father.

'I hate to suggest it, Jacob, but is there a possibility that some of this money might have been acquired by immoral means?'

I know Mr Simmons is thinking of prostitution. There is a lot about prostitution in the Bible and I can imagine these pompous men are enjoying the idea of me selling myself. Of course, that is not what I have done, but I *have* broken the law. Unbidden into my mind come the calls from the police. The official brown letter that arrived the day before I left. The expensive stolen handbag still sitting on my kitchen counter. My sense of unease last time I left Partington's department store, as though I was being watched.

I remember again Martha's capitulation. True guilt in the end is what will bring us all down. And I *am* guilty. Not of everything they are accusing me of, any more than she was.

But I know in my heart that I have done wrong, and my conscience rises up in support of the voices of the men who accuse me.

My head drops again and this time it stays down. Tears fill my eyes. They are right. I *am* a sinner. I have done many evil things. I thought I could manage my life on my own but that was a sin of pride. I have also committed the sins of covetousness, immorality and lust, theft and falsehood. I have not respected my father and mother. I have not worshipped the Lord my God. I am exhausted by the extent of my failings. I truly need these people to help me to manage my wickedness. I need to seek forgiveness for all the bad things that I have done. I need to try to atone.

My throat is so tight and dry I can hardly speak, but I force out in a croaking whisper 'I am sorry.' I swallow hard and try again 'So very sorry. I am ready to seek forgiveness.'

It is Mr Walters, not my father, who rests his hand on my bowed head.

'It is good that you are beginning to accept this, my child' he says. 'There is much work to be done before we can bring you back into the fold. But as the great psalm says, "They who dwell in the shelter of the Most High will abide in the shadow of the Almighty." You will say to the Lord, "my refuge and my fortress, my God, in whom I trust." For He will deliver you from the snare of the fowler and from the deadly pestilence. He will cover you with His pinions and under his wings, you will find refuge; his faithfulness is a shield and buckler. You will not fear the terror of the night, nor the arrow that flies by day.'

His voice has grown strident and triumphant, and his hand is pressing painfully onto my head. I am being crushed into my seat by his weight. Mr Simmons coughs slightly and Mr Walters comes out of his holy reverie. He looks across at my father.

'Well, I am glad we have been able to help you, dear brother. Do you want me to drive tonight, or will you? It is late already.'

What is he talking about? He can't just mean that he needs to go home, because otherwise why would he be asking my father if he would drive? I can still feel Mr Walters heavy hand on my head and his weight seems to have settled on my shoulders. My moment of calm resignation and acceptance is punctured by anxiety. What are these men planning to do now? And will it all stop soon so I can sleep? I am tired and drained beyond speech or thought.

Jacob is already in motion as he answers.

'We will go in your car' he says to Mr Walters. 'Is everything there that we need? I can ask my wife otherwise to pack another bag.'

A memory from before. The last time I saw Martha was when she had been shoved into the kitchen with the other women. I had been left to face the Elder's fury and she and I never got to say goodbye. Now I wonder for the first time if she had stayed there? I had been half-aware of busy activity in the house, of my mother's white face appearing at the sitting-room door and anxious whispering amongst her companions. Someone had rushed up the stairs and there had been clattering overhead of drawers and cupboards being opened. Then, while I was still defiantly facing down my inquisitors, I had heard the sound of a car parked outside starting up and driving away. Now, too late, I understand what it was I had been hearing.

33

"Shutting up" they call it. It is such an odd phrase that I find myself explaining it in my head, as though to Luke. "Shutting up" is removing a sinful member of the Meeting from their families and into a house owned by the Meeting. The supposedly guilty person would have no contact with anyone whilst shut up except for regular visits from Meeting elders. Money and food would be provided for them.' I can picture Luke's incredulity and realise that this is what must have happened to my sister the day I was cast out.

"Shutting up" had never seemed strange to me before, but now, sitting penitently with my head bent and my hands neatly folded in my lap, it seems like a historical relic, like the stocks or stoning, and not something from the 21st century.

The brief mood of tranquillity I enjoyed as I surrendered myself to God has gone and I try to calm my nerves by continuing to talk to Luke in my head. I can picture him, head cocked to one side and frowning slightly.

'How long it lasted was down to the Meeting, and how easy it was to break down the person.' I pause as I remember a time that shutting up had touched our family. There had been a friend of my oldest brother who had started seeing a girl from "outside." They said he had been missing Meetings too. His name was spoken at the dinner table in tones of condemnation and warning, until one Sunday lunch after Meeting I had heard my father say that he had been shut up. My mother gave a slight shudder and glanced quickly at my brother to see how he was taking this news of his former friend. We never heard what happened to him. From that day on it was as though he had never existed.

And now it was going to happen to me. Panic rises in my throat. How have I got to this place? How has my life lurched so far from its moorings that this morning I had left my pretty flat and driven here and now I was about to be swept away to God knows whereby these appalling men?

Could I, should I, even now, make a move and reject them again? This time it would be forever. There could be no more coming back. As this thought rises, I squash it at once. Who am I to question them? Am I so lost in sin that I would turn down this last chance of salvation? These good people are trying to help me. It behoves me to be calm, patient and grateful.

I am so tired. It must be long past midnight. My body is shaking with emotion, exhaustion and hunger. There is nowhere left to run and there is no way I could run even if I had the will.

The men return to the room and my father touches me on the arm to stir me. My body is leaden and numb. I look down at my legs stupidly and run my hands across my knees. Finally, I stumble to my feet and dazedly I let them gather up my coat and bag. My father collects a small suitcase from the kitchen. My mother and Martha must have been packing this earlier while I was with the elders. Do they also feel I am a sinner who must be cleansed before they can bear to be in the same room as me? This thought is so painful I shy away from it at once. The two women had long since gone to bed and the house is dark and quiet. I excuse myself briefly to use the bathroom and stare at my pale face in the mirror.

'Who are you, Miriam?' I ask the face. 'Who are you that you have so much sin inside?'

Maybe I *am* possessed by an evil spirit as they suspect and once it is removed, I will no longer feel the need to steal. I might no longer find myself coming round with gaps in my memory either. Can I blame an evil spirit for my problems and if so, could I be released from it? I splash water on my hands, take a deep breath and go back into the hall, ready to accept my fate.

Silently the four of us get into Mr Walter's car, a spotless Audi A6. I am in the back with Mr Simmons. It is clear that everyone but me knows where we are going. I have become a mere item to be moved about. Trying to reassert some identity I struggle to start a conversation with my companion and ask him about his family. He is uncomfortable with our proximity and shakes his head at me, sitting back forbiddingly with his Bible as a shield across his lap. I try to pay attention to where we are going, but I am unsure of the roads around this area and unable to focus. I am soon quite lost, but not long after that we do stop, in the driveway of a detached bungalow in a residential street. I peer through the dense shrubbery of the front garden as Mr Walters unlocks the double lock and I am quickly bundled inside.

The house is chilly and smells musty. Mr Walters turns on the lights and leads me through to a small bedroom where he puts down the suitcase.

'My child' he says, not unkindly. 'You should sleep now. You must be tired. You will stay in this house for a time. There is no one else here. We will visit you tomorrow. There are some basics in the kitchen for breakfast and suchlike and you will find what you need. Should you have to call me or your father in an emergency you may use the phone in the hall, which will connect to one of us.'

He gives me a business card. I am reminded wretchedly of my missing phone, with the numbers of Luke and Elena in it. Apart from work contacts, there are no other numbers. I realise how few people will notice or care that I have disappeared.

Perhaps this is the right place to be. I should be glad that I have a family. If I can accept the washing of my grimy soul and all that entails, I will afterwards be surrounded by people. I should feel comforted by that, but the thought of being back in the Meeting makes me sickened and shaky.

That momentary softening of my father's tone has reawakened a hunger in me, has made me want to grab his hands, to make him want to stay. I keep looking over to him hoping for a sign of affection and forgiveness, but he will not catch my eye and it is Mr Walters who gives me instructions on the heating system, after which they leave and I am alone. Dazedly I make up the single bed, drink a glass of water and despite the strangeness of my surroundings fall into an exhausted sleep.

34

Panic awakens me the next morning. Where am I? This is not my flat. It is dark, the smells are wrong, and the bedding is cheap and rough. My head spins as I jerk upright in bed and gaze around the magnolia painted room in disbelief. I struggle to the window and peer out. There are nets behind the floral curtains and the thick shrubbery blocks any view of the road. I could be anywhere.

But before I can think about *where* I am is another more urgent question.

Who am I?

Visceral fear grips me as I struggle to remember my name.

Am I crazy? Have I died and gone to hell?

I know who I am. I am Miriam.

Is my name really Miriam?

An echo floats into my head, on which I seize.

"I am Flora. I am 36, and I am a wedding planner."

Flora is a funny name, isn't it? And can I really be 36? I feel much younger. 36 is so old.

Do I have any identification with me? Maybe if I see my name written down it will all come back to me. What do I have with me? Shouldn't I have a bag? A phone?

I see a dark brown leather bag on the dressing table and grabbing it, I rummage feverishly, desperate for clues to re attach me to my life. Car keys. But where is the car?

With a lurch of dismay, I remember my cherished car is still parked on the street outside my parents' house. Fragments from last night return to me and I chew my nails in worry. I need to find out where I am. Should I dress and go outside to try to locate myself? Shall I keep trying to remember how I have ended up here? Shall I carry on looking through my bag for clues?

My stomach rumbles loudly while I am dithering, and I realise I am shaking with hunger and cold. Shivering in the dank air, I fling on yesterday's clothes. In the bag that my mother packed, I find a pair of very plain white pants and put them on, remembering my sister as I do so. Are they Martha's? They are too loose on me.

In the cold and spotless kitchen, I find tea bags and milk, a loaf of sliced bread, butter and jam. I toast the limp bread and hungrily tuck into thickly spread slices and two mugs of tea. The food fuels my brain and thoughts flow more easily.

The breakfast reminds me of the last time I ate toast. When Luke came round to my flat. How kind he was and how well he looked after me. After Laura's wedding. I force myself to say her name in my head, waves of nausea curdling my stomach as the past weeks flood back.

It is much nicer to think about Luke and I smile to myself as I remember him bringing me toast, and how he always looks at me carefully with a little twitch playing around his lips before he speaks. If anyone can help me now, it is Luke. But will he want to? Luke knows all about my stealing. It was he who showed me those photographs. He knows about that expensive handbag that I should not have. He knows too that I got off with Tom at the wedding. He knows so many shameful things about me. How can I ever face him again? And here I am in a complete mess once more. I would sooner he didn't know this as well.

I *would* like to speak to him though. Is there any way I can reach him? I don't have his personal number, but I do know the name of the agency he works for and there is a phone in the hallway. Pride might stop me from telling him about the trouble I am in, but is there another reason I could contact him?

Usually, I could call him on the pretext of discussing a wedding booking, but that is clearly not going to work now. I bite my nails, drawing blood as I try to remember everything I can about our last meetings. By the end of the talk, we had had in my flat Luke had been open and relaxed. He had been so helpful, looking after me and tidying up at the same time. He had told me that he was used to housework because his mother had been ill with MS during most of his teenage years and he had gradually taken over the domestic jobs. His father had disappeared when Luke was only six, he had said. I can imagine him as a skinny and spotty teenage boy learning to cook and clean and to keep his mother happy. He told me he was still not much good at making more than shepherd's pie and spaghetti but just the thought of a home-cooked meal makes my mouth water. These daydreams are all very nice, I decide, but not much use right now. I can hardly ring him up and ask him to come and cook me lunch, can I?

And then I remember that Luke had said he was having to move in a hurry. And that I had said he could use my flat to crash, even though the idea had freaked me out. Well, what if I rang him and said I was away for a few days but that he was welcome to stay there until he was sorted? I could make out he was doing me a favour, watering my plants and getting in the post. He could get the spare key off Elena.

Momentarily, the thought of the cat puts me off. It will need a litter tray and it will spread black fur all over my furniture. But this is the only way I can think of to contact Luke without seeming like a total failure.

I go into the hall, wrinkling my nose at the musty smell. This is such an old-fashioned house that it has a yellow pages book under the phone. I find the number of the agency that Luke works for and without letting myself think, I pick up the handset and make the call. There is a delay and some static on the line but just when I think the phone is not working, I hear it ringing.

'Regency Photographic Agency,' says a bored female voice.

'I, ahh, can I speak to Mr, er, Sanderson, please? Luke Sanderson.' I add, 'I'm, um, Flora Miller.'

Now I am on the phone, I am full of doubt. What if he doesn't want to talk to me? Maybe he thinks I'm too much trouble? I couldn't bear it if he ghosts me now.

'I'm sorry, but he's out on calls all morning. Can I take a message?' says the bored woman, slowly.

I freeze, unprepared. I can't tell her that Luke can use my flat as a temporary home as that is a personal matter. I should have thought this through better.

'Never mind,' I stutter. 'I'll try again later. Have a good morning.'

Well, that didn't go well. A hot flush of embarrassment is rising up my neck and chest and I dither with the phone still in my hand even though the office woman has rung off.

And then I hear it again, a buzz of static and indistinct sounds coming out of the handset. I drop it onto its cradle as fast as I can and stare at it in alarm. That sounded like there was an open line. But there isn't another handset in the house. Does that mean that my conversation was overheard by someone *outside* the house? Can the Elders somehow be listening in? Have they tapped the phone like the Government did with Communists in the eighties? Mr Walters did say it would go through to one of them, didn't he? Maybe it's not private at all.

Well, this is now a total clusterfuck. Firstly, I should have told that silly cow the number here so Luke could call me back. I have achieved nothing in terms of contacting him, but worse than that, I have probably given the Elders a whole load of information. They now know I want to speak to someone called Luke. I try to remember what else I gave away in that short conversation. How could I have been so stupid as to carry on the call once I heard those noises on the line? What the hell was I thinking? What have I been thinking the last few days altogether and how have I ended up in this hole?

I look round the room in despair. It is a depressing shithole that looks like the set of a suburban horror movie. All those religious books are creeping me out. There are hell and damnation tracts on the shelves, a Bible by the bed, a Bible and more tracts in the hall and then the main Bible in the sitting room. I mutter aloud in frustration,

'That's enough with all the Bibles, people. I get it that you are God botherers. But fuck it all, where is a girl to get a drink round here?'

There may be some alcohol here that I missed before. In a seventies horror-film house, there would be a couple of bottles of sweet sherry. I am still pissed that that call went so wrong, and I need something to calm me down. Wandering restlessly into the lounge I spot a dusty wooden sideboard to one side of the fire. Creaking the stiff door open I find old board games, ludo and draughts. Does that mean a family has been here? Perhaps someone hid a message for those who came after? I lean into the cupboard hopefully. No message; and no alcohol.

I sit back on my ankles in defeat, staring into the dusty shelves and a tide of fear begins to seep up my spine as it sinks in that I am a prisoner. This house is as secure as my parents is and all the doors and windows are locked and alarmed. The nearest house is too far away for anyone to hear me shouting even if there was anybody at home and the dense shrubbery around the house obscures it completely from the view. I am now much too scared to use the phone in the hall again. I don't know where I am.

In confusion, I grasp for my earlier certainties. I am a hopeless sinner who is here to be saved. My only chance of redemption then is staying here until the Elders return to educate me. Ashamed that I have been searching the house for alcohol I reach for the Bible, praying out loud as I take hold of the Word of God.

'Help me, Lord' I pray. 'I beseech You for help. Pity me in my hour of need. Forgive your humble servant Miriam. I call upon You to rescue me from the pit into which I have fallen.'

Penitently I kneel and pray and then I settle to the Bible, searching for words of comfort in the dusty pages. And as the day goes on, I wait. I wait in mounting anxiety, listening for sounds in the driveway outside, for the phone, for voices, or for anything to connect me to the rest of the world.

When the key at last sounds in the lock, I have lost track of time again and the room is filled with shadows. The three men are back. My father Jacob, Mr Walters, now wearing a grey tight suit with shiny black shoes and Mr Simmons, sweating slightly in a short-sleeved polyester shirt. To my surprise, my father hands me my car keys.

'We've moved your car into the driveway here, as you might be able to drive to the supermarket' he says, at the same time peeling three twenties from a roll of notes in his wallet and handing them to me.

I am confused and wrong-footed. Does this mean I am free to go? He must care for me after all because he is giving me money. Why did I think these men were my jailors? They are good people, and they are looking after me. The unexpected kindness makes me weak.

'Have you eaten today?' asks Mr Walters, again in a gentler tone. I think. Yes, there was toast this morning, but nothing since.

'There are sandwiches and fruit in the kitchen' he says, seeing my hesitation, 'sent you by your sister. She was most insistent.' He frowns a little at the memory and then smiles at my father as though indulging his daughter's unwonted assertiveness.

'Go and refresh yourself whilst the three of us have a preparatory prayer meeting. You will need all your strength for we have much work to be done tonight.'

Dully, I do as he suggests. I sit obediently in the Formica topped kitchen under the harsh overhead strip lights, forcing down the sandwich and grapes that Martha has prepared for me. The food is nicer than I expect, and I feel a pang of gratefulness to her, especially when I notice she has slipped in a wrapped chocolate along with the grapes. She remembers my love of chocolate then. I smile at her as I eat it. If only I could talk to Martha and my mother.

Finishing the food, I fidget on my high stool, swinging my legs as I try to decide what to do next. Should I join the men in their prayers, or should I wait for them here? I am scared to do the wrong thing. It is *so* quiet, too quiet.

No wonder Martha had found Gina's ordinary home life so alluring. I feel a wave of yearning for that lost glimpse of normality and for the times that I have been swept up in Elena's warm, sweet-scented and floury kitchen. She would be chatting constantly to her parents at the same time as preparing delicious food, sipping her ever-present matté tea and singing along to the radio. Today I slowly wash up my single plate and perch back on the stool, listening to the ticking of the oven clock until at last the lounge door opens and I am summoned back to the presence of the elders.

35

We take up our set positions. I am across the room from the three men. My father is furthest from me, Mr Walters is in the centre and gingery Mr Simmons is closest to me. The room is chilly and gloomy. Still caught up in nostalgia for Elena's warm home, I wrap my arms around myself and huddle into my lightweight cardigan. I should have appreciated her more. I was always too worried about keeping my distance or that I would say something stupid because of a memory lapse. But nothing could have been as bad as what is happening now. When I get out, I will tell her all about myself, I decide. If I ever do get out.

The men take it in turns to question me. They quote scripture and admonish me to repent. They tell me how distressed my mother has been not to have her daughter all these years. How Martha has suffered my loss in silence and channelled her grief into caring for others. It seems her only rebellion was against the Meeting's advice that she should marry. My father tells me that she begged to be allowed to stay at home and look after her parents in their later years and that they were glad of her support. My brothers have all married and they tell me that I have three nieces and a nephew. I try and fail to imagine these unknown children.

I am distracted by more memories of Martha and myself. Now I have opened that door a constant stream of images and recollections is filling my head. We were so careful to behave in the way we had been taught and would sit quietly in Meeting for hours without fidgeting. We knew our place and would leave the room after we had helped my mother wash up so the men could talk together and go upstairs to memorise the Bible verses we were set. But underneath our obedience, there was a hungry curiosity about the world that had us sitting up on the windowsill and peering out into the street at the other children, the ungodly children, who we could see playing outside.

My mother told us to pity these poor children because they were unsaved. At the final Judgement, they would go at once to Hell and burn for all eternity. Martha and I watched them with fascination, trying to spot the signs of wickedness, horrified that we knew their terrible fate. They had only a few short years maybe, till the End of Days.

At any point, we were taught, the Lord could decide it was Judgement Day and, on that day, the faithful and holy would be raised up to heaven. All the rest would be left behind, including these children who we watched kicking a ball through goal posts of jumpers and skidding their bikes in tight turns around the lamp post just outside our house. Then they would know that they had been abandoned. When it was too late to be saved, they would understand that they were going to Hell. I dreamed sometimes of them, the girl from three doors up with long red hair and freckles and her skinny younger brother and the Muslim family from further up the road, who we saw going to their heathen temple. I dreamt of them arriving at the gates of Hell, which I pictured as like my school gates but with a fiery pit just inside, stinking of sulphur and brimstone.

These laughing and squabbling children who could have been our friends would be sucked down into the depths where cackling demons would grab them, by the long red hair, by the colourful scarfs, by their tiny golden earrings and would drag them into the flames, to burn forever.

My waking mind shrank from these dreams and rebels

now from these terrible thoughts. An eternity of pain is too much to contemplate. Those poor children, are they going to go to Hell? And will I be suffering there too? I escape from these thoughts to the past again, remembering how I would freeze completely still in the Meeting and try not to listen, try not to hear, when the brothers were preaching about this with relish. After a while I could leave my body neatly sitting there apparently attending to the sermon whilst my spirit was somewhere else entirely. I would watch myself from across the room and then leave to roam freely in imaginary worlds. And I knew Martha did the same.

I must have done it again now, for I know I have been sitting for ages with a listening expression on my face as Mr Walters' voice rises and falls. But I have no sense of the meaning of his words.

A sudden noise makes the four of us jump out of our separate worlds and we stare at each other, united by a current of fear that pulses through the almost dark room. My father gets up abruptly and goes into the hall. He picks up the phone whose clamorous ringing has disturbed us. I listen to his half of the conversation through the wall.

'Hmm, yes, who is this?'

'Why do you think that?'

'I don't think that will be appropriate. I will pass on your message. Good evening.'

He comes back into the room, clearly rattled, and violently throws on the light switch, making us blink.

'Someone asking about you' he says sharply to me. 'I told him you were safe with your family and that we were looking after you. Honestly, people should mind their own business.' He stares at me again, more suspiciously this time.

'That phone is only for you to use to call us in an emergency, as was explained to you clearly last night. It is not there for you to make private calls.'

He hesitates, as though he would say more, and I am sure then that someone *did* hear my call to Luke's office earlier. It is odd they have not mentioned it. Maybe they are keeping it to use against me later. Thinking is too confusing, and my tired brain gives up trying to sort out what the Elders might be planning.

Who was that ringing though? How would anybody know I was here? Could it have been the police? Maybe they followed me here?

No, it can't be them, I tell myself firmly. The police only want to ask questions about the missing bag. I shut that line of thought down quickly. I'm in enough trouble here, there is no point worrying that as well. 'Him' though, he said 'him.' It *must* have been Luke who managed to trace my call.

'Was that Luke?' I blurt out eagerly, before realising that I have fallen straight into their trap. They didn't even need to tell me they knew I had called Luke. I have as good as confessed.

With a glint in his eye, Mr Walters rounds on me at once.

'Who is "Luke"?' 'Am I living in sin with this man?' 'Have I no moral code at all?' 'What happened to the values instilled in me by my upbringing?'

Concentrating hard on my answers, I try to tell them that he is a work colleague with whom I have become friendly but that nothing has happened between us.

And that is true in its way. We have not slept together. But now I am thinking of him, I find myself picturing his smile, which though slow to develop, is so warm that it is like a hug, his strongly muscled arms that he hides in baggy shirts

218

and his endearing energy. I think he fancies me too though he has not made a move.

But he knows too much, I tell myself, quelling my sexy daydreams. There is no way I can now flirt with him, screw him and discard him, which is how I usually relate to men. If I got it on with Luke, it would have to be the real thing and I would have to be honest and open with him. I am not sure I can do that.

I struggle to forget him and to focus on the men again. It seems like the questions will never end and I fear that my interrogators have divine energy as they never seem to tire. My eyes are gritty, and my mouth is so dry I can hear my tongue clicking as I speak before the elders finally stir in their seats and share a glance of understanding that it is time to depart. First though they bow their heads in prayer and without prompting I do the same.

'Lord, we pray that this sinning member of your flock, this lost lamb who has gone astray, will find her way home, with your Grace, Oh Lord. Look kindly upon her and forgive her many sins. In your infinite mercy lead her back to us, to her loving family and the society of the saints and prophets from whom she has turned her back.'

Declaimed in my father's rich and sing-song voice it is very poetic and I say 'Amen' as fervently as Mr Walters and Mr Simmons.

But it is me who is the lost and sinning sheep.

Why are they always talking about sheep? There are sheep in the psalms, sheep in the parables, flocks and flocks of woolly miscreants in every book of the Bible. I smile to myself, wishing there was someone I could share this thought with. Elena would get it. Although deeply religious she was always ready to have a little laugh at the pomposity of her priest and the rituals of her beloved Catholic church. How I wish she was here now. She would hold my hand and tell me that my parents do love me, they just want the best for me. The smile fades from my face when I notice Mr Simmons has been staring intently at me. For how long? I wonder uneasily.

The Elders leave at last. I am exhausted. I can barely remember what we have been talking about for the last few hours. My spine has locked in place, so I stretch and yawn and jump up to pace the house. They have shut me in again. Panic and claustrophobia rise in my throat, but I tell myself that I need to go to bed now and sleep. In the morning I can plan for escape.

36

In the morning I cannot understand why I wanted to leave. I should be happy and grateful because here I am at last near my family. I am being looked after and they will help to heal me and cure me of my sinful ways. Somehow today I don't feel anything at all; not a desire for freedom, not gratitude; I am numb.

Lifting the greying nets from the windows, I can see my car outside as though ready to take me home. But why should I go back to the flat I can now hardly picture to confront the lurking police, the piles of stolen items and the hostile messages? I am safer here.

In any case, I cannot get to my car as the doors are locked, which stops me from having to worry about it. It is kind of them to keep me so safe and secure. Again, I remind myself to be grateful. What was I doing driving such a showy car anyway? That was vanity pure and simple.

I wash and I pray in a trance-like calm. I make myself plain toast, rejecting even the tasteless jam as too indulgent and sweep and tidy the kitchen. After I have done, I am exhausted. Tiredness sweeps over me in a sticky wave that glues up my thoughts. I lie on the sofa and try to read the Bible, though the words make no sense. I am listening all the time for the sound of the Elders returning. It is so good of them to visit me every day. They must be busy men and their families will miss them. How many days have they been coming? After a while, I give up trying to work it out. It doesn't much matter.

They are kind to point out my failings. And they are right. I had turned my back on the Lord fourteen years ago and since then have thought only of myself. Not like Martha. She is my better half and she returned to the true path and gave up silly fantasies of her and Gina. She has lived a pure and perfect life ever since. I imagine her now, busy with satisfying tasks, cooking and cleaning and supporting the Meeting. She is looking after our parents too and I have never once helped her. She alone has kept the family together.

A wave of corrosive guilt breaks through my bone deep weariness and powers me off the sofa. My heart is pounding, and I pace the house, feverishly ripping at my nails, trying to escape the burden that is settling on my head and shoulders. I am longing now for the Elders to come so they can help me again and I can start to put things right.

At some point, the phone rings, shockingly loud in the silent house. I go to it uncertainly, my hand reaching slowly for the receiver. Should I answer it? Maybe it is Luke? But perhaps it is one of the Elders testing me and if I answer the phone, it will be more evidence of my rebellious ways. I hesitate too long and the phone stops. I am suddenly desperate to talk to someone, to anyone, and scrabble at it frantically. Checking the list of numbers brings up only 'caller id withheld.'

After the call, I cannot settle. My palms are prickling with sweat as I anticipate another night of questioning. There is a weight on my chest, and I cannot get a deep breath. I force myself to make a sandwich, but my mouth is so dry that I can barely swallow a bite. At last, I hear the sound of a car parking outside, hear keys in the lock and the heavy tread of the elders. I go into the hall to greet them with lowered gaze and quiet voice. My body is stiff and awkward.

'Would you like some tea or coffee?' I ask though I know what the answer will be. I am an outsider so they cannot drink with me. How will it feel when this ban is lifted? Will I be relieved and happy or sunk too deep in penitence to care?

Despite my efforts to listen my mind glazes over as soon as they start to speak. I shake myself firmly and manage to wake up a little.

'Come on Flora, you can remember who you are' I tell myself. 'Stay awake and look at these people properly. Look at the shoes Mr Walters is wearing. How can he wear sandals like that? And beige polyester trousers. Does his wife choose his clothes?'

Without knowing I am sure that both Mr Walters and the unprepossessing Mr Simmons have wives. They will be dutiful and quiet women who will not be asking where their husbands are going every night this week and why they come home in the early hours and stand in the kitchen eating from the fridge and drinking several glasses of whisky before lumbering heavily up to bed.

When they left last night, they had heard me apologise and had expected that today I was ready to renounce my evil ways and accept the salvation they are offering. But now I have lost all conviction and my mouth refuses to say the words it seems they need to hear. I am removed from them altogether and I watch indifferently from across a chasm as they argue passionately with the unresponsive woman who is reluctant to give them back her soul.

The hours slide by very slowly and I am gradually sucked back into their world. They are right. I *am* a hopeless sinner; I *have* made a mess of my life. As they point out, I have no real relationships, no marriage, children or connection with my parents or with my God. I have very few friends either, only Luke and Elena and I have only really started to get to know them this summer.

"How was your weekend? Are you going out tonight? Where are you from? Do you remember that TV show that was on when we were kids? What are you doing over Christmas?"

Whenever I became friendly with anyone these sorts of questions would come up. They were impossible to answer truthfully and so I had begun to tell lies. Lies to seem normal and to fit in and then lies to bury those lies, until in the end, I could hardly remember what I had said to whom. A new invented identity had split off from me and pursued her own life. Sometimes I would even believe that I had lived that life and had been that person. Right now, in this featureless house, cut off from all outside connections, I barely exist at all. Who am I without real memories?

I am brought back to the present abruptly by Mr Walters hitting his Bible with more than usual force.

'Pay attention Miriam!' he shouts suddenly. 'Your stubbornness and obstinacy will go against you, both now and more importantly, at the final Judgement Day. I say to you, "The Lord shall never be willing to forgive you, but rather the anger of the Lord and His jealousy will burn against you and every curse which is written in the holy book will rest on you and the Lord will blot out your name from under heaven.'

'Deuteronomy Chapter 29,' I say, surprising myself. It is all still there inside me, waiting to be remembered.

'Yes, Miriam' says Mr Walters, more quietly. 'I am glad you remember some of your lessons at least. So how can we countenance letting you back into our lives when those are the clear and unbending words of the Lord God himself? You must realise we cannot dare to disobey Him. We cannot let you back into your family and our assembly unless you truly repent and from henceforward hold fast to the right and true path. And you must allow us,' here he gestures at himself,

Jacob and Mr Simmons, 'to guide you in the ways of the Lord.'

My head is bowed, and I am close to giving in again, more out of sheer exhaustion and mental confusion than agreement. I think of my mother and my lost family life. I think of Martha and of my naïve hopes that I could spend time with her and get to know who she is now. Oh Martha, my long-lost sister, is this the only way to see you again?

Tears form in my eyes and silently roll down my cheeks, splashing heavily onto my hands which are neatly folded in my lap.

Jacob clears his throat.

'It is late' he says, quite gently. 'We are all tired. I think you should take time to reflect and to pray. Pray, Miriam, pray. Examine your heart honestly and humbly. I do hope that when we meet tomorrow evening you will be able to tell us that you are truly prepared to seek forgiveness and will not waiver from this right path again.'

The three of them depart quietly after my father's words. Mr Simmons passes me an open Bible as he leaves the room. I hear the car drive off, loud in the sleeping street outside and the house settles back into stifling silence. I am alone with my thoughts, with my tears and with the cold comfort of the long-dead words of a vengeful God.

37

For once, my sleep is not fractured by nightmares. I awake in peace. I lie in bed enjoying the quiet and safety of this house. It is time to stop my resistance. It is time to reconcile with the Lord, my Redeemer. I dress with quiet deliberation, grateful for the plainness of Martha's borrowed clothes and that I have no makeup to tempt me into vanity. I carefully make my bed and kneel beside it to pray. This is the right way after all, just as the Elders have told me. This is the true path to a good life and salvation. I *can* choose to reject the desires of my worldly and frivolous self. I *can* choose the better way and from today I will do that and live a pure and blameless life.

Cleansed by prayer, I move sedately into the kitchen to make a bowl of plain porridge and a mug of herbal tea. The only sound is the ticking of the oven clock. Sunlight filters in through the net curtains but I can neither see the world outside nor be seen.

After breakfast, I put on some laundry and clean the bathroom. I think of Martha and of the blessing of her simple life spent cleaning, cooking and serving the family, the Meeting and thus her God. Maybe I can learn to be more like her.

My trance deepens throughout the morning, and I become absorbed in Bible study and reflection until my peace is suddenly ruptured by the tinny ring of the doorbell. A shiver of alarm floods through me. Is it the Elders back so soon? I am not ready for them yet. But no, they would not ring the bell because they have the door key. This reminds me that I do not and so cannot let in whoever is at the door. The bell rings again and, curious now, I go to the hallway to peer through the smoked glass pane of the front door.

I can see a large, dark figure outside. When it sees me, it becomes animated, waving its arms widely. It moves right up to the opaque window and tries to look in and taps on the pane itself.

Both of us try to see more of each other and then the figure moves away. Next comes tapping on the lounge window and going through and lifting the nets I, at last, see who it is.

And it is Luke. Luke is beaming at me, jumping up and down and waving around a carrier bag that he is holding aloft. I take my first deep breath for ages, and Bible study quite forgotten, I laugh back in sheer delight at seeing him.

Oh, I've been so lonely! How lovely it is to see a friendly face. How welcome he is. We laugh and wave at each other. His mouth is opening and closing so he is saying something, but I can't hear him through the thick double-glazing. I frown and cup my hand to my ear to encourage him to shout but glancing round and up the street, he appears to think better of this.

He moves away again, and I hear a rattle at the front door, as though the post is being delivered. Clever Luke has opened the letter-box flap. Bending down I see his mouth and a portion of his face through the plastic fringing in the letter-box mouth. He looks so comical I laugh even more, and I must look the same because I hear him giggling too.

'You do have very good teeth, Flora, and it looks like your nose is probably fine' he says, 'but how is the rest of you?'

It is *so* nice to hear his voice. It seems ages since anyone spoke to me in a friendly and ordinary tone. The ponderous style of the Elders has invaded my brain and my thoughts are becoming couched in their speech patterns. And now, here is a familiar and welcome visitor who doesn't seem angry with me or like he is going to stand in judgement. I giggle again.

'Oh, Luke' I say, 'It *is* good to see you, well the little bit I can see. I'm stuck in here though; I don't know how to open the door.'

Once I say that, I realise how odd this sounds. Surely, I am a free woman, but yet here I am, a prisoner in this house. And *where* exactly am I? How did Luke manage to find me? The excitement of seeing Luke drains away as my confusion returns in force.

'How did you know I was here?' I ask more quietly, and Luke becomes graver too. His mouth settles into its usual turned down shape as he explains that he got the number from the work phone that I'd called and used that to trace the address.

'I *was* a bit worried, you know,' he says, 'because you seemed so low when I saw you last and then I didn't hear anything from you. I'm still worried. I don't want to interfere with your life' he tails off, gesturing at the locked door between us 'but shouldn't you be able to get in and out?'

I remember the reason I'd given for calling him at work and it seems easier than trying to explain why my visit to my family has ended up with me trapped in a place I do not recognise.

'I was wondering if you had found anywhere to live yet, what with having Flump and all' I say. 'That's why I called, and a very professional sounding woman answered the phone, and I didn't want to leave a message with her, but if you wanted, you could always stay at my flat for a little while, like I said. Elena has the key.'

'That's really sweet of you' says Luke, joining me in my pretence that we are having a normal conversation. 'I am in a bit of a difficult position right now. I've got a possible new house share but it doesn't start till next month so I'm living in my van and Flump is with a workmate. And none of us are too happy with this arrangement,' he smiles.

'But hang on, what about you? How long are you going to be here for? Won't you want to be in your flat? And are you sure you wouldn't mind my boots and bags and mess?'

What was that question he just asked?

"How long am I going to be here?"

Come on Flora, think. I should have some idea, shouldn't I? How long have I been here already?

I'm in a complete muddle. Shame washes redly over me as I realise I am once again in a situation that I don't understand at all. And a longing to be outside with Luke and able to walk away from this house and never look back.

'Luke, I, I'm not sure what has happened. I came to see my family. Do you remember we were talking about them?

The part of Luke's face I can see nods vigorously.

'And they, well, my father and some men from the church,' I try to explain in layman's language the intricacies of the Meeting hierarchy, 'are helping me, to, um, to be a better person, so I can see them again, to see my mother and sister I mean.'

I am floundering. This is harder than I expected.

Luke seems to have got the gist of what I am trying to say.

'Flora' he says seriously, 'is this what you want? Because if it is then fair enough and I hope you will get reconciled with your family. But it's just that when we were in your flat the

229

other day, what you said was quite different, so I want to be sure you know what you are getting into. And I don't like that you are stuck in there. That is how it is isn't it? You are locked in? That doesn't seem good to me at all.'

He's right. I know he's right. A window in my mind has opened into another room, a room in which I am relaxing on a sofa, with my feet on Luke's lap (how did that happen?) and we are chatting easily about my childhood, my family, the whole crazy-making business of growing up in the Meeting and all my worries about sin and damnation are fading away. I want to go through the window and into that world right this minute.

'I'm not sure, Luke,' I say. 'Part of me wants to go home, to my flat I mean.' I hesitate and then finish miserably 'but I can't, can I?' as with awful clarity, the events of the last few weeks rush through my mind's eye. My public shaming at Laura and Tom's wedding. The trashing of my business online. All the stolen property in my flat. The calls from the police who want to question me. The gaping hole that is my bank account. And worst of all I can no longer hide from myself that there is something terribly wrong with me. Something is wrong in my head. How come I can remember things one minute and then they disappear the next? How come I am stealing stuff and then forgetting what I have done?

Evading both these troubling thoughts and the problems of the present I let my eyes wander round the hallway and they fall on the Bible on the telephone table. I have an urge to open it at random as I have seen members of the Meeting do. I wish I could have their simple faith that the Lord will direct my hands and that the page will fall open at the exact passage of scripture that I need. It is such a comforting idea that my life is safely in the hands of the Almighty.

But what if I opened the Bible and He led me to read

another verse such as the ones they have been quoting at me full of fire and threats of damnation and eternal punishment for wrongdoing. What then?

I am split in two. Two worlds are colliding in my head and cancelling each other out. Who is right? Is it Luke, so kind and sweet and still patiently standing outside? Or is it the faith in which I was brought up? Should I return to the safe and enclosed world of my family and the Meeting? What does Luke offer, actually? He has no religious beliefs; he told me that in one of our late-night post-wedding chats. He said more than that. He said that he thinks that all religions are dangerous nonsense and the cause of violence, confusion and damage. My mind rebels from this nihilist view. It is too extreme a rejection of all I was brought up to believe. At the same time, I am repulsed by a faith that causes a family to turn against and reject their own child. I can't help but question the concept of a God who is so judgemental and hard on us inept humans, who He calls His children.

In the past, I would have distracted myself from this mental confusion with a drink or maybe a bout of stealing. An intense craving for a large glass of wine sweeps over me as I stand dithering in the characterless hallway. It smells of floor cleaner in here. and apart from the Bible and yellow pages, the only things to read are some old flyers for take-away pizza. There is nothing to take away the full pain of my situation. I am trapped. I am stuck in this miserable hallway, unable to move forwards or backwards. I am already in purgatory. Even if the door were unlocked now, I would not be able to leave. I am held here by my mind, by my indecision, my lack of conviction and by the ties that bind me to beliefs that I despise but from which I cannot break free.

A slight cough outside reminds me that Luke is still waiting. I peer through the letterbox, and he is standing awkwardly and looking uncertainly up the quiet street. He must have been there for ages. What a nice man he is to wait.

I murmur his name and give him a weak half-smile through the letterbox to reassure him I am back.

He grins back warmly, but before he has time to say anything, a movement and sound further up the street distracts us both.

38

It is a police car cruising slowly past. Perhaps it is just a patrol vehicle checking all is as it should be on this leafy street. But it slows down as it passes the driveway to the bungalow. I can't see into the police car, but I imagine whoever is in it is looking through the dense shrubs towards the house. They would be able to see my car parked in front of the locked garage, but not to the front door and so would not see Luke. Or me because I am inside. On the floor. At the sight of the car, I ducked down in alarm and am crouching in the dust and peeking out through the letterbox.

'Come back Flora' calls Luke. 'I lost you for a while there. You were miles away. Did you realise? And now you are hiding. Please come back and do try your best not to zone out on me again. We need to make a plan.'

He doesn't mention the police car which has now slid past and out of sight so maybe he didn't see it. I don't want to think about what it could mean but the sudden jerk of fear it generated has galvanised me out of hopelessness. He is right, I need to stop zoning out and I need to get out of this house. Suddenly I am ready. What is there to stay for here? The cold comfort of a Bible full of judgments that can be used as a weapon against me? The colder comfort of my family who have locked me up in this cheerless house, refusing to speak to me, to hug me, to welcome me back? It is enough, I tell myself. I have tried. And they have rejected me once again. It is time to let go.

'Luke' I whisper urgently. Why am I whispering? Who can hear me? 'I do want to get out. I don't want to be here anymore. I want to face up to all the things I've done. It's got to be better than this.'

Even as I say it, I know that this certainty and courage will slip away as fast as it came.

Luke nods and smiles broadly.

'Oh Flora, I know that you might change your mind again, but that is *so* good to hear. Ok, let's see if we can't get you out of this house for starters. And then we can do all the' he mimes speech marks with his fingers, still close to the letterbox "facing up to all you have done" from the comfort of your flat, which might have a light coating of black Flump fur by then!'

I laugh shakily, remembering my rash promise to house his cat. Well, it is a small price to pay for having someone to help me out. And the idea of Luke being with me in my home makes my heart lift despite my current predicament. He is already scouting around in the bushes looking for a way into the apparently impregnable house.

'Any windows you can open from inside? he asks, 'downstairs ones ideally.'

He lops off around the building, squinting into the morning sun and I can hear him systematically checking all the windows, doors and the small lean-to conservatory. I move off to search inside. Surely there must be one window that I can unlock. My eye is caught by more movement on the street. Through the thick shrubs, I can see another vehicle slowing at the end of the drive. Is that the police back again?

It is an expensive grey estate car and as it noses into the driveway, I see it contains my father, Mr Walters and Mr Simmons and that someone else is driving. Instinctively I dive down on the floor to hide once more. Why are they here in the morning? This is unexpected. Already I have felt there is a routine developing and that the Elders do not come till the evening. Surely, they have jobs and work to go to. Perhaps it is the weekend today? Think, Flora, you must know what day it is.

All this is racing through my mind whilst I am lying on the floor like a fool. Then I remember Luke. He might not have heard the Elders arriving and could walk right into them. The need to alert him propels me off the floor and I run around the windows looking out for him. From the kitchen, I can see his back view heading round the corner to check the back porch. There is no time to warn him now. I need to be ready for my visitors because I can hear the car doors shutting outside and the low murmurs of their conversation.

I bolt into the sitting room, grab the Bible and open it at random. Just like they do. Glancing at it I see it is upside down and I have just time to correct this as they unlock the door. Four sets of heavy feet are weighed down with unexercised and overfed bodies. I recognise the voice of my father, Mr Simmons' reedy tones and Mr Walters' plummy boom. The fourth voice sends an icy jolt lurching down my spine though I have no idea why it shakes me so.

I stare unseeingly down at the open Bible until the black lines and dots swimming before my eyes settle into words. I find I am reading the beautiful verses of Psalm 103.

"The Lord is merciful and gracious, slow to anger and abounding in steadfast love. He will not always chide, nor will He keep His anger forever. He does not deal with us according to our sins, nor repay us according to our iniquities. For as high as the heavens are above the earth, so great is His steadfast love."

I look up as the four men enter the room. The words of the psalm are whirring in my head, and I am struggling to reconcile them with what the Elders have been saying. The

God in the Psalm is a God I *could* love. And He is a God who might love me. A kind and forgiving God. Why do I hear nothing about Him from these people? These words are in the Bible as surely as all their hell and damnation verses.

My father and Mr Simmonds and Walters are acting differently. They politely defer to the new arrival, are silent when he speaks and usher him into the room before them. My body recognises him before my conscious mind has understood who I am seeing. My palms are damp with sweat, and the breath sucks out of my lungs. Dizzily I stare at him. He is tall, in his early forties and heavy now. His hair is still dark, but he is balding around a shiny crown. It is my brother, Matthew.

Matthew. He is married now and a family man. Unwanted images swim into my mind at the thought of him with a woman and bile rises hotly in the back of my throat. He looks unhealthy somehow, his face has an oily sheen of sweat despite the chill of the house. He does not acknowledge me at all. My father invites him to sit down on the best chair directly facing me. The other three seat themselves awkwardly squashed together on the new green sofa.

My father turns to me. 'We are pleased to be joined today by your brother Matthew' he begins, not giving me time to speak.

'I have been consulting with him about you, Miriam, and he has kindly taken time away from his business to come to help us here. My brothers in Christ,' he gestures to both sides of him on the sofa, 'feel that though you remain unclear and at times stubborn and wayward, the Lord is trying to reach you and you might be within salvation's blessed grasp. We are grateful for another wise voice today.'

He glances at me coldly. 'You will not know this of

236

course, but your brother Matthew is now a much-respected preacher. He lives in Birmingham and has come all the way down to pray for you today. It is a great favour from him and the Birmingham Meeting who have spared him so that he can be with us when we need him most. I expect you to listen with respect and in silence.'

Inside my chest, something is starting to boil. It catches me by surprise, and I focus on it, trying to identify what is happening. Yes, I am boiling, bubbling over with rage. My breath is coming in quick pants and my cheeks grow hot. I am full of energy and power. How dare he talk to me like that? What bloody right has he got to tell me to be silent and respectful? And my brother, how dare *he*? Oh yes, I know you well, my brother. Respected preacher indeed! My rage overwhelms even the intense shame that licks over my skin since seeing this man, this Matthew, this 'pillar of the community,' sitting there like a pompous fool and expecting me to be grateful for his poisonous interventions.

The whole damn lot of them can go to hell. I've had it with them all. I'm never going to get to talk to my mother properly or spend time with Martha. My fists are bunched up in rage.

But then a wash of sadness follows, putting out my angry fire. All I ever wanted was to be loved. To feel acceptable and for something to take away the sickening reek of shame and self-disgust that is constantly in my nose. A stink that no amount of stolen perfume can mask. And now I will never get that.

Barely ten seconds have passed since my father spoke, though I feel I have been struggling blindly through a storm of stinging sand for hours. Remembering Luke is just outside and that I have some support, I take a deep breath.

'No' I say loudly. 'No. I do not want my brother to help

me. You' I look at him directly for the first time, seeing the slight flinch as his eyes meet mine. 'Matthew, I do not want you to pray for me.'

I gain confidence as I speak, 'I do not want any of you here making me guilty and wretched. I do not want to be shut up in this house anymore. I came to talk to you' I turn to my father, 'but I can see it is impossible. Let me go at once. I want to go home.'

The men glance quickly one to each other and then my father and the two sidekicks all look at Matthew, waiting for him to respond.

He pauses, as though fighting an inner reluctance, but then slowly reaches out and puts his hand over my bunched fist. His hand is warm, smooth and fleshy and his aftershave fills my nostrils as he leans in.

'Miriam,' he says gently. 'My poor little sister. I can hear the voice of Satan himself loud and clear. You, poor girl, you have been taken over by the Evil one. You were brought up in a God-fearing household and your mother and sister are models of humble womanhood. Why did Satan want *you* so badly?

It is a mystery' he speaks to the three men now 'why for some souls we must fight so much harder. It will be worth it in the end when we see this lost and wayward one back where she belongs in the heart of her family, and we are all able to sit together on a Sunday and worship together as one.'

A furious sound, half snort, half sob, breaks from my constricted throat, but before anyone else can speak we all hear two different sounds outside which distract the Elders from the battle for my immortal soul.

One is a sharp crack, as of a breaking branch, followed by muffled swearing. It comes from directly outside the room we are in, from someone in the garden under the window. Luke, I think, with relief. He is so close. It sounds like he might have just hurt himself though. The other sound is slower and for some reason fills me with foreboding. There is another car pulling into the drive.

We freeze in a tableau. I am centre stage as the defiant sinner. Matthew still holds his oily hand over my rigid one and the three other men are in a line on the sofa, all looking alarmed.

The car outside stops and a door opens. We hear the crackle of a walkie-talkie breaking into life.

'Yes,' we hear faintly from the front drive, a male voice with a local accent. 'Lima, Alpha, sixty-six, November, Papa, Juliet. Yes, yes, parked outside. It looks like it has been here for a few days...a pause, more crackling and then the voice says, 'Okay, got that. I'll do it now. Thanks, mate.'

The doorbell's strident tone assaults our straining ears and makes us jump. United in uncertainty, we glance at each other, then Matthew removes his hand from mine and stands up. He has assumed control of the situation and the others seem content to sit and wait as he strides to the front door and unlocks it.

I am worrying about Luke. Did he fall off something? Is he hurt? Was he trying to get into an upstairs window? I want so much to rush outside and check he is unharmed that I start to stand. My father firmly gestures me back into my seat, frowning at me.

'Good morning, officer' we hear Matthew saying. 'How can I help you?'

I hear them talking outside and sit back as far into my seat as I can, wishing I could disappear completely. It was bad enough when the police were outside my flat but now they are coming into this house and will meet the Elders. This is going so wrong.

My brother lets the policeman into the hall, asking him,

'what is the name of the person you are looking for, officer?'

We all hear the reply.

'Is there a Miss Flora Miller here, sir? We are anxious to trace her,' replies the policeman.

My father shoots an incredulous look at me. Of course, I had forgotten. I never told him or anyone from my old life that I changed my name. 'Flora!' my father whispers, aghast, horror at my rejection of my given Christian name spilling out despite the situation.

'What heathen wickedness would cause you to choose such an ungodly name as that?'

His frenzied whisper causes both Mr Simmons and Mr Walters to twitch uncomfortably beside him but does not carry through into the hall, as we all hear my brother saying loudly and confidently.

'Flora? *Flora* Miller? No, there must be a mistake somewhere, officer. There is no one of that name here. Nor do I know anyone of that name.'

He is going a little too far in his denials. Maybe the policeman will have become suspicious. My car is parked outside, and it is going to be hard to explain that away. But I have a sudden revelation and my spirits rise up to greet it.

All this time, I have been worrying and panicking about the police catching up with me. I have a stolen designer handbag hidden in my flat, so I have committed at least one crime. I can remember that clearly now. I can picture the wretched bag in detail.

And I have been shoplifting. I am a thief.

Yes, Flora, I tell myself, it is time to give it a name. It wasn't just tidying up, or re-arranging shelves, or picking up items that I was entitled to. It was stealing. Despite the guilt, there is relief in finally owning up to this, if only to myself. So that does make me a sinner. And if I accept that, I should face up to what I have done and take the consequences. But it doesn't have to be like this. Not with these men, not this awareness of eternal shame, not this fear of endless punishment and the vengeance of an angry God.

I would be better to go with this policeman and accept the consequences of the law. Could I go to prison? Cold chills run through me at the thought of being trapped in a prison cell. Trapped like I was as a child, trapped like I was in that garage, unable to escape except through my mind.

But I am in a kind of prison here already, aren't I? Perhaps it is worse here. I can't go out or see anyone and I have nothing to do. Here I have no idea how long my sentence is. I know the "shutting up" can go on for months. I remember hearing of shut up people who had breakdowns and ended up in hospital, or who tried to kill themselves. Even if I was allowed back to my parent's home, in the end, I would still be a prisoner, held to ransom by my behaviour. Just a few days of being held here have been bad enough. What would I be like if it went on for weeks? It is an unendurable idea.

Talking to Luke this morning has cleared my brain of some of the cobwebby tendrils of sickly religion that have been adhering there. I must act while I can. I clear my throat and take a deep breath.

'I am here!' I try to shout. It comes out as a weak croak. I try again and this time I am loud enough for the policeman to hear. 'I am here. I am Flora Miller.'

39

My words hang in the silent room, shocking us all. My father draws back from me and emits a hiss of amazed disgust. The other Elders glare at me disapprovingly but their eyes slide fearfully towards the door as the policeman's firm tread approaches. Outside in the shrubs around the window, I can hear faint voices. That must be Luke. Who is he talking to?

'Flora?' my father is seemingly unable to let this go. 'What kind of pagan name is that? You were given a decent name. A *Christian* name. We called you Miriam as a symbol of our wish that you might become a wise woman, a teacher and supporter of other women in our community. And you throw all that away for *Flora?*'

Matthew enters the room while he is still speaking, followed by a tall young policeman.

'This is Sergeant Watson' he indicates the newcomer, who flushes slightly as he looks round at us all. 'Mr Simmons, Mr Miller, Mr Walters and Miriam Miller,' he finishes, pointing us all out one by one.

The policeman frowns slightly at the three men lined up on the sofa but nods his thanks and then turns to me.

'Good morning,' he says politely, 'is that your vehicle parked outside?'

I nod minutely. Should I even tell him who I am? That will mean he can charge me with theft if this is why he is here. But I don't want to stay here with the Elders and my brother either. Not one bit. I am frozen in indecision and stare at him dumbly.

'Okay miss,' says Sergeant Watson quite gently. 'It *is* your car? And can you tell me your name please?'

'Flora,' I whisper, almost inaudibly, at the same time as my father says loudly, 'this is my daughter Miriam. She has not been well. She is very confused, and we are looking after her. Is there any reason why you need to speak to her?'

Am I confused? Have I been ill? Is what he says true? I turn to Sergeant Watson, who is frowning again. Ignoring my father, he addresses me.

'Miss Miller?' he asks me gently. 'Miss Flora Miller?'

I nod mutely once again, in a tiny, controlled movement and he smiles at me, ignoring a clamour of comments from my father and the two Elders about how my name is Miriam and always has been.

They are a loud trio but not for nothing is Matthew their unelected leader. His booming voice cuts through the babble, silencing us all.

'Brothers, brothers, please, calm yourselves,' he orders. 'Let the officer speak. We need to know if this is a case of mistaken identity or if it is yet more evidence' he addresses my father directly 'of wrongdoing on the part of your daughter, my sister. An innocent woman would surely not try to deny their own name.'

'Thank you, sir,' says Sergeant Watson to him as the noise dies down.

'Please let me speak to Miss Miller for a moment. In private if possible.'

Mr Simmons has the first word in now.

'She needs our care and support' he blurts, adding triumphantly, 'she is a vulnerable person.'

I shake my head a tiny bit, as much to clear it as that I

243

disagree, and the Sergeant sees me.

'I think we will get along just fine' he says, 'but I will ring for a female officer as well. My colleague DC Johnson is in the area. If you will excuse me a moment, I'll radio through and then in a few minutes we can both have a chat to Miss Miller if that is okay with her?'

He looks at me questioningly and I nod again. Speech or movement is impossible. My body has set rigid in position and my brain has frozen over too. From a long way away, I watch as the policeman goes into the hall, from where we hear the crackle of his radio starting up.

'What are you doing, Miriam?' Mr Walters hisses angrily at me. 'Denying who you are will not protect you now. Only God in all His mercy can do that. This is the moment, surely, you wretched abandoned child, to repent sincerely. Then we and the Meeting and all your family will do everything in our power to protect you and keep you safe. They may let one of us, maybe your father, go with you.'

Go with me where? To the police station? Am I going to be arrested? Even as my stomach lurches with sick fear, I know that the last person I would want with me there would be my father.

'No thank you,' I say, my voice coldly polite. Mr Walters appears to be finally out of patience with me. Turning to my father, he shakes his head in sorrow and resignation.

'I am sorry, Jacob,' he says, 'there is no reasoning with her. I do think she may be,' his voice lowers, 'mentally unstable, if not possibly… ' lower still now and I struggle to hear. 'As we fear, infected by an evil spirit.'

I don't know whether my father can even hear Mr Walter's murmurings. My ears are sharper than his. But hearing that they think I have an evil spirit reconnects me with my earlier emotions.

I decide, in an energising rush of gladness, that this is an opportunity. An opportunity to escape. I cannot stay here a second longer, not while they think I am evil and impure and knowing that they will pray and fight over my soul till this imagined evil spirit departs. I have had it with being the wretched sinner. If I get arrested, then I will be able to get away from them straight away. It means exchanging one kind of captivity for another, but Sergeant Watson seems a better bet than the Elders if I want to find out who I really am. And how long did I hope to escape the police? They know where I live and what car I drive, and they have found me when I didn't know myself where I was. That is something I do want to know and just as Sergeant Watson, his call completed, re-enters the room, I blurt out 'where are we?' my words falling loudly into a sudden silence.

As five pairs of startled eyes turn to me, I continue. 'I mean, which part of Gloucestershire are we in? You see,' I explain to the Sergeant, whose frown has come back, deeper than before, 'I was driven here in the dark and then they drove my car here, so I don't know where I am.'

Sergeant Watson nods slightly.

'I see, Miss Miller,' he says. 'You are in Hardwicke, a few miles north-west of the city centre.'

He sits down on the edge of the sofa seat, blocking my view of Mr Walters and my father and leans towards me saying quietly, 'we have been looking for you as there are charges against you. And you have been reported missing. But it sounds like you may have some things you need to tell us as well.'

Turning to face the room but still addressing me he continues more formally. 'So let me go through the procedure with you. Firstly, the charges against you are that you are in possession of stolen property. Also there has been a positive identification of you stealing items from Partington's store in Cheltenham on three occasions over the last few months. Would you be happy to come with me to the station to answer some questions?'

I hear Mr Simmons take a gasp of horror at the mention of the police station and now it has come to it, I am frightened. It is with a dry throat that I reply.

'Yes, Sergeant. I will come.'

Before anyone else can speak, there is the sound of a car or cars outside, pulling onto the by now crowded front drive. The neighbours' net curtains must be twitching this morning with all this unusual activity.

The sergeant glances out.

'That must be DC Johnson' he says and heads back out to the door.

'May I bring her in?' He looks to me first and I nod, and then checks in automatically with Matthew, who speaks coldly.

'Yes, go ahead.'

My brother then turns to me.

'So, this is why you came to us, is it? Not to be reconciled at all but in a pathetic attempt to escape from the consequences of crime. Now you are dragging us, your honest God-fearing family, into your sordid life and forcing us to let Outsiders in to meddle in our ways. You should have been more repentant if you want us to help you now.'

The man is such a fucking hypocrite. My cheeks burn with rage but before I can retort I am distracted by hearing Luke's voice again. And it is louder this time.

'I'm here!' he is saying. 'Come round the side.'

Who can he be talking to? Ignoring the others, I jump up and run to the window and peering down, I can just see Luke's large and muddy boots sticking up at an odd angle from a flower bed. I crane my neck round further to try to see more. I am amazed and delighted to see Elena outside. Elena, red-faced and wearing a brown cardigan with the buttons done up wrong, is bustling around the side of the house.

In excitement, I tap loudly on the window. Mr Walters hisses his disapproval again. Stupid man, he sounds like an angry cat. Elena looks up but doesn't initially recognise me. She looks away but I tap again and mouth 'Elena!' to her until she sees it is me. She drops her bag and throws her arms up in the air and then blows handfuls of kisses to me. It is so lovely to have somebody properly pleased to see me that tears spring to my eyes. I wave back at her, and we both beam at each other.

She then remembers Luke and, waving once more and half pointing to where Luke is lying, she picks up her bag and disappears to his aid. What *has* Luke done to himself? The police have been a long time outside in the drive, but I finally hear the front door re-opening and to my surprise, I can hear them talking, in patient and encouraging tones, as though to the elderly.

They carefully usher in some new arrivals and I exclaim in surprise and consternation, for it is Mr and Mrs Varela. They must have been in the car with Elena.

I help Mr Varela, who is wheezing heavily and settle him in the chair I was in. The room is becoming crowded. Mrs Varela fusses over her husband and I glance at the newly arrived policewoman to find she is checking me out at the same time. I give her a weak half-smile.

DC Johnson is a tall, brown-skinned woman who returns my smile more warmly. Something inside my stomach starts to unclench ever so slightly. Maybe this isn't going to be too bad. Together we settle Mr and Mrs Varela down and I attempt to introduce everyone. The morning now reminds me of one of the Bible study meetings we used to have in this room when I was growing up. Should I offer everyone tea and coffee before they arrest me, or will one of the Elders decide now is the moment for a prayer? It would be just like my father to make the most of having an audience.

Sergeant Watson disappears into the garden and returns with a muddy-kneed Elena. Between them, they are supporting Luke, who is pale and sweating. His right foot is twisted up off the ground and seems not to work. The policeman curtly gestures my brother to stand up so they can help Luke into his seat and then disappears again to the hall, this time to call an ambulance.

I decide it *is* time to play hostess. This unlikely group of people are all here because of me, so the very least I can do is be hospitable. I am so delighted to see Luke and Elena. Finally, I have some allies here and I am not facing the forces of God and the law all on my own. I ask if anybody needs anything, 'tea, coffee, water? And would you like a painkiller? I ask Luke who is biting his lip and looking greyer by the minute.

He nods gratefully at me, and I go out into the kitchen for the pills that are in my handbag, and a glass of water. I seem to have taken control of the room now, which is odd, given that I am the one about to be arrested.

On my way back, I nearly collide with the hefty form of Sergeant Watson, who gestures me to go ahead of him politely. As I give Luke his tablets and water, I sense the atmosphere in the room has dropped several degrees. Matthew is standing stolidly in front of the window, legs akimbo, almost blocking the light and no one is saying anything. The Elders will be bothered about the contaminating effect of being in the same room as Luke while he is drinking. Luckily, he only takes a sip.

'Can you possibly explain?' Matthew swings from the window and rounds on Luke. 'Yes, is it possible to tell me quite what you thought you were doing in the back garden of this house, which is clearly private property? And what *you* were doing?'

He turns to Elena.

'Most people would have the courtesy to ring on the doorbell before charging through into someone else's back garden. And what are *you* doing here?'

He rounds suddenly on Mrs Varela, who has been staring at the two police officers with an expression of mixed fear and curiosity on her lined face.

I pat her hand reassuringly and nod to Luke to answer.

He returns Matthew's cold stare without flinching.

'I was worried about my friend,' he says quietly. 'I don't think she wants to be here. I came to see if she wanted to leave.'

His eyes flick slightly towards DC Johnson as he says the last words, who raises her eyebrows slightly.

'And then because she appeared to be barricaded into this house,' he continues in a stronger voice, 'I was looking to see if there was a back door we could open. And I slipped and have twisted or sprained my ankle,' he finishes, looking down with a rueful expression. I think he missed a bit out there. He didn't do that damage just walking round the garden looking for a back door. He must have been climbing to get on the porch roof or something. He was being quite heroic. That is the most gallant thing anyone has ever done for me. My insides go warm and glowy as I think what this might mean.

Luke looks up from his sore ankle, feeling my eyes on him. A big smile breaks out on his face as we stare at each other. For a moment, it feels just like it did when we were hanging out together late at night after a successful wedding. Luke is here and I can be me with him and that is all that matters. I feel other eyes on me and see DC Johnson watching closely.

That woman has got some well-groomed eyebrows going on. I check her out more carefully. Yes, she definitely has style, masked by the hideous uniform. Seeing as she has to wear sensible black shoes, she has probably got the best you could find. I can see a small tattoo just visible on her ankle bone. I wonder if I should get a tattoo. Just a little one. Maybe on my shoulder blade, or, like her, on the ankle. Some flowers, for Flora, tendrils of something exotic like passionflower, or hibiscus. I look again at DC Johnson's ankle but can't see any more. This time I take in the whole look; she is a professional in police uniform. She has not come to chat about body art, but to ask me questions and take me to the police station. When do they do the actual arrest? Will I be put in handcuffs?

Flora, focus. I tell myself. I had drifted off again. What is everyone talking about now? I try to tune back into the conversation. DC Watson is checking the ETA of the ambulance they have called for, and Elena is midway through explaining how she and her parents came to be here.

'I've been ever so worried about dear Flora' she is saying, in her bubbly confiding tones. Her voice is so familiar and welcome after days of religious language or silence. I want to just curl up next to her and have a cuddle, safe and warm and sweet-smelling.

'She's been having terrible trouble at work' she continues

diplomatically. 'Recently she has been very depressed. And then she disappeared completely. And the pol….well,' she gestures to the two in uniform, 'your people have been round and there have been *lots* of official letters and calls for her. And then this young man' she waves to Luke, 'he calls me and says Flora is with her family, which is what I know she wanted' here she gives my father a cross look 'she wanted so much to be part of a family and to belong. But Luke here, he says she is not having a good time. And then he rings this morning, and it is him who is not having a good time. I couldn't really understand him because we kept getting cut off, but he says something about being stuck in someone's garden and it being about you and how he knew I was a good friend of yours. So naturally, we came right away. We were just on our way to put some flowers on my aunt's grave, weren't we?' here she fondly addresses her parents, who nod mutely back at her.

'It was the first day my father had felt well enough to go out for ages and so we all rushed here, getting a bit lost on the way in all those little streets. And very glad we are to have found them both. But Flora my love,' here she turns to me, 'are you okay? How are you feeling now?'

She has noticed me tuning out again. I shake my head to try to clear it and smile at her, wishing I could just go back to her flat and be safe and warm in her kitchen again.

We lock eyes and I edge closer to her, but my father chooses this moment to take the floor.

'My daughter,' he says to the two police officers as though he is explaining the ways of the world to them, 'my daughter is undergoing some intensive spiritual nurture and teaching at this time. She is under our care. As you have probably understood by now, she has some problems.'

'Vulnerable person,' interjects Mr Simmons again, trying

to get a man to man look going between himself and DC Watson, who is watching them all with a calm but sceptical expression.

'This very untimely interruption has come at a crucial time' says Matthew, in his confident and ringing tones. 'This poor young woman; my long-lost sister, has been resisting the power of the Lord most strenuously. She is now at last beginning to show signs of repentance and we hope to bring her back to the heart of her loving family. And back to the centre of our community, which has its own traditions and is set apart from your world. We cannot sanction your request to take her with you. We do not recognise your laws over the laws of the Almighty God. In His name we are keeping her here and it is His work we are doing.'

He stops for breath and the room falls silent. The two police officers look carefully at my brother and then at me. While Matthew was speaking, I found myself agreeing with him. I do belong here. I certainly don't belong anywhere else. I should be more grateful that my family want to look after me. Now he has stopped though I feel again the physical, visceral repulsion I experienced when I saw him first this morning and cannot help contrasting that with how Luke is making me feel.

The silence is broken by tooting outside on the street. Luke's ambulance has arrived, but the drive is so full of cars that it cannot get close. Mr Simmons visibly winces at the sound. For an intensely secretive group, the morning's events must be torturous. All this unwanted activity and so much interaction with outsiders. And now the quiet careful anonymity of the house is being destroyed by the arrival of police and ambulance crew.

'This is all most unfortunate,' Mr Simmons mutters to my father. 'I know we have to do our duty to our families, but this is all going to set us back you know. We should conclude this matter as swiftly as possible.'

Two cheery paramedics enter and after checking Luke over, help him into the ambulance. I watch him go sadly, wishing I had a twisted ankle as well and the friendly crew would carry me out at the same time. He gives me a final smile as he is wheeled out and mouths, 'I'll see you soon.' Elena is murmuring gently to her parents. The two police officers go outside briefly to talk to the ambulance crew. Mr Simmons and Mr Walters are both glaring at me angrily whilst my brother and father have adopted expressions of pained and self-righteous resignation.

I am stunned by the events of the last hour. Luke being there had made me feel safe and the room seems cold and empty now he has left. I look sadly at my father. He is right, of *course* he is right. I *am* a burden to my family. I *have* disgraced them before and have just brought unwanted attention and grief to these good people who just want to be able to live according to their own moral code. So not only have I made a mess of my life, not only am I a thief and a marriage wrecker but I have now dragged my sordid self here to harm and contaminate. There can be no way back for me now, I can see. I have transgressed too much. I am too full of evil.

My head drops, my hands fold together, and I begin to quietly pray. I pray for my family in their trouble and that they may find peace without me. I pray for forgiveness for my stealing and for my selfishness. I pray to a harsh God who hears me not. His silence increases my despair.

40

My eyes are closed in prayer. As I come round slowly, I realise the room is very still. How long have I been like this? I can feel eyes watching me and hear quiet breathing and a gentle snoring wheeze from Mr Varela. A warm hand is covering mine. Who is it? It feels like a man's hand. It is not Luke, which is who I wish it was because he has left. It is not Matthew either. I would smell that one, and I still feel branded by his oily unwelcome touch. I force my tear swollen eyes open a crack and look at the hand. It is wrinkled and lined, the soft hand of a man who does no manual work. It is my father's hand. I can see faint marks on the skin that I used to stare at across the dinner table as a child.

My father! How gentle he is. A deeply familiar scent fills my nose; old wool, woody cologne and the unique smell of the man himself. Does this mean I have been forgiven? Will my father love me now? I long so much to fling my arms around him and sob, but I am frightened this will make him drawback. This nearness is too precious. I hardly breathe in case he moves away.

How did this happen? I was so angry and hurt just now and ready to leave and now I would do anything at all my father wants, if only he will stay beside me and keep his warm, large hand on mine.

Mr Simmons breaks the charged silence, clearing his throat and saying 'Praise be to the Lord. I think you are reaching her now, Jacob, at last.'

He turns to the police officers and speaks.

'I need to ask you to leave this house. This is a private matter between us and this man's daughter.'

He speaks to me, eagerly now, seizing a chance for a moment of religious grandeur and significance.

'So, Miriam, *do* you repent? Do you humbly seek forgiveness for your sins? Will you come back to us, accept your penance and be made clean again?'

Mr Simmons's voice buzzes irritatingly in my ear, but I am focused only on the man sitting beside me, whose warm firm hand still covers my praying ones. My father. At last. A lifetime of longing rises inside me. Will he finally accept me and love me if I just do this one thing? If I agree that I will be guided by them all and re-join the Meeting? I look up at him shyly, hoping for a loving smile.

'Miriam' he says. Not in the affectionate and forgiving tone I am longing for, but coldly.

'Miriam, my daughter. You have a chance now to save your immortal soul. We will fight with you for your salvation and try to cast out the demons from your heart. Please tell these people,' he nods towards Elena and her dozing parents, 'to leave us in peace now. If you return to the faith in which you were brought up, we will support you in your dealings with the law. At some point, we could consider re-instating you into the Meeting, under close and ongoing supervision.'

Such a carefully metered out measure of Christian charity. It opens a hollow void inside me through which the cold winds of abandonment blow. It is not love this time, no more than it ever was. This is the chilly response of a man doing his painful duty.

As this sinks in, I finally and permanently forsake their God. All of me rejects Him. Not just the Flora part of me, but the dark side of me too and the young and trusting Miriam.

We all turn away from the God that they tell me to call 'Father.' A God who is, like my own father, unforgiving and indifferent.

I have spent far too much time trying to be loved and trying to belong. I choose to turn away from it all and this time I hope I never turn back.

My head goes down again, and I withdraw my hands from underneath Jacob's and rest them shakily on my knees. The unheated room and the ice of rejection flowing through my veins has chilled me to the bone.

But I am not left cold for long. Warmer small hands are wrapping themselves round mine and though my eyes are closed again, I recognise the homely scent of dear Elena. Spiced baking, her father's forbidden tobacco and a perfume of carnations blend into a comforting mix. Elena begins to murmur to me consolingly,

'Oh Flora, my love, don't listen to him. He is just a silly man, and he is so hard on you. Darling, don't cry now, ignore them all.' She moves nearer and almost whispers into my ear.

'What a lot of miseries this lot are. No wonder you are down. This is *not* how your own family should treat you.' Moving away slightly, she says, more loudly,

'Now dry your eyes, sweetheart, because the police are still here and need to get on. You do need to sort this stealing business out once and for all. Mum, do you have any tissues?' Seeing her mother is fast asleep, she turns to me. 'Maybe you have some in your bag? There you are,' she continues, gently wiping my cheeks and I submit meekly as a child.

'You'll be fine. Go with the police. They will try to help you. Tell them the truth now, remember. That is the most important thing.'

'Thank you,' says DC Johnson, who has also moved

256

closer in the last few minutes. She smiles at Elena.

'Thank you,' she says again, in gentle dismissal. 'Now we need to ask your friend some questions. If you could just let me?' this last is directed at my father and with a firm gesture she encourages him to relinquish the seat beside me and she moves into it.

Matthew clears his throat now and slowly begins to speak, as though Elena was not there at all.

'This is a private matter between this young woman, God and our society' he addresses Sergeant Watson. 'Our laws are not your laws. We do not abide by the laws of the world.' He takes a deep breath and I feel myself sinking again. He is about to unleash another avalanche of words.

Luckily however, Elena and her parents *are* here, and their presence gives me strength. And the police, who are about to arrest me. Absurdly at this thought my spirits rise. I will get out of this house for certain today. Even my brother and father cannot in the end stop the police from doing their job. And as my brother is filling his lungs for his next declamation Sergeant Watson cuts across him.

'It has been really helpful to get your views' he says quite genially to the group of men, 'and we are happy, in a general sense, to let you follow your religion undisturbed.' He pauses.

'However, when an individual's actions may have broken the laws of the land, which we are bound to uphold, then we have a right and a duty to step in. On this basis can I now ask Ms Miller to accompany me and my colleague to Gloucester police station to answer some questions?'

He looks directly at me as he says the last words and I nod silently. He seems less friendly now and I dread what is to happen to me.

'Get your coat or anything you might need' says DC

Johnson. 'And we will drive you there straight away.'

I numbly grab my handbag and stumble out into the hall to find my jacket and shoes. Elena follows me. To my surprise, she takes my bag from me.

'Really darling, I know your family are awful but do have some taste' she says, removing some silver spoons, a packet of coffee and one of the china dogs from my bag.

'You don't want the police officers finding this stuff later, do you?' She hesitates and then says, 'oh pechina, I am so sorry, but there is something I need to tell you. I'm worried you will be upset with me.'

She sounds so anxious that I try to smile at her.

'It is okay' I say slowly. 'What is it?'

'Well, darling' she begins reluctantly. 'You know I always pop into your flat when you are away to do the plants and such? I didn't know then that Luke was going to be staying at your place, so I didn't need to, but I realised you had been away for a few days and I know how much you love all those orchids and succulents. Also, there was a pile of post building up and some of it looked, well' she hesitates, 'I thought it was better it wasn't left lying around.

So, I just stepped up to your flat. Oh darling,' she is distracted suddenly. 'I love that cat. Is it Luke's? He is just the friendliest thing; he was all over me the minute I walked in the door.

Anyway, what was I saying?' She collects herself, still smiling slightly. 'Well, I was just doing the window boxes and there was a ring on the bell. And then another. And when I looked down there were two police officers, not these two nice ones,' she nods back into the sitting room 'and I thought I had better let them in because they were making quite a lot of noise and you don't want people talking do you dear?'

I shake my head gently, encouraging her to carry on, though the cold sick feeling is back in my stomach.

Police, in my flat. Angry official letters. Oh God. I remember now why I left in the first place.

'Well, these two, again a man and a woman,' Elena continues, 'they came in acting all very official. I don't generally like the police you know, what with my father being here and all. But they didn't ask me much. I told them you were away and I was looking after your flat and they said alright, but that they needed to look around a bit.'

She pauses; to give me time to think. I know what she is going to say.

'The handbag' I say flatly, not trying to explain or excuse myself.

'Yes, darling, yes' says Elena, sadly. 'They took it away and they took some photographs and fingerprints from all over the flat as well. And they kept asking me where you'd gone, but of course I had no idea.'

She breaks off as the door to the sitting room opens again, then waves me off quickly.

'Go and get your things together, I'll keep them talking.'

41

When I return to the sitting room, I am ready to leave. I have my jacket over my arm and my bag now has a change of underwear and toothbrush inside. I wish I had my phone.

The mood in the room is tense. Mr Walters is again asserting that they, as a religious group, have the right to deal with their own affairs between themselves and should answer to the laws of God ahead of the laws of the land.

'What you don't understand' he is saying to Sergeant Watson loudly, 'what you *can't* understand, maybe, is that it is this young woman's soul we are concerned with here. Her immortal soul is what is hanging in the balance today. She is turning back to us, I can see it' he says this triumphantly, looking at my father, 'she *is* going to return at last to us. But you' he glares at the Sergeant, 'you must not take her away now. In due course, she will have to face the consequences of those of her sins which concern you. But today is about a chance for redemption and we must not be thwarted from doing the work of God.'

He pauses to draw breath and I see a glance pass between DC Jameson and DC Watson. Nodding to her and drawing himself up slightly, DC Watson turns to me and says formally.

'I believe you are consenting to come with us willingly, but nevertheless, Ms Flora Miller, also known as Miriam Miller, I should tell you that I am arresting you on suspicion of theft. You do not have to say anything. But it may harm your defence if you do not mention when questioned something which you later rely on in court. Anything you do say may be given in evidence.'

I'd wondered how it would be to have these words said to me. I am suddenly weak, as though I have not eaten for a day. Fuzziness is in my brain and my vision dulls. DC Jameson puts her hand on my arm, though whether as a sign that I am now captive or to steady me, I am not sure.

I am watching my father as he watches me being arrested. I see his face harden and his expression go blank. I turn to Elena, who is holding her mother and father's hands.

'Can you tell Luke where I am?' I say, 'and maybe, please, keep in touch?'

DC Jameson gives my arm a little pat, to get me moving.

I turn to my father.

'Goodbye.' I say. I mean to say more, but once the words are out of my mouth, I realise there is nothing else *to* say. I cannot look at Matthew. He does not deserve even one civil word. I nod at the two Elders, wondering what they are going to do once I've left. I blow a kiss to Mr and Mrs Varela and trying to control my sudden trembling, leave the house under arrest.

On the short drive to the police station, I can hear three different voices inside my head. I focus on them to quell the rising panic and shame at being in custody and bundled into the back of a police car. The two officers at the front answer the radio and murmur to each other, but make no contact with me, so I am left to my thoughts.

'I am a sinner. The Elders and my father were right. Who else but a sinner would be arrested and taken away from their loving parent's house? Now I will be cast out again and I will never join the communion of the good and devout. I am doomed and I will go to Hell.'

'Bloody hell. Those churchmen are fucking annoying. Patronising twats. How do they all end up talking the same way? With those fucking sing-songy voices, like they are miles above you giving a sermon? I hate them.'

'I have lost Martha. I will never get to know her or my mother now. And will Luke still want me? I've caused him so much trouble. He has hurt himself as well. And poor Elena, she shouldn't be caught up in my chaos.'

Martha barely even spoke to me, I realise. She was almost mute throughout my time there. I could tell she was pleased to see me, but we never had a conversation. And that chance that I have been longing for, the chance to talk to my sister, has slipped away from me. What Martha thinks or feels will remain a mystery to me, as much as I must be to her.

I look a complete mess, I realise, catching an unwelcome glimpse in the driver's mirror. How unfair that I must face whatever is coming with no make-up, lank hair and wearing someone else's clothes. What happens in a police station? Will I be searched? How long is this all going to go on?

I should pray. I should be praying right now. I must pray for forgiveness for my sins and for my poor family who have been cursed with such a stubborn wayward harlot of a daughter. Truly I am a bitter curse to them all.

42

When PC Rowlands opens the door of the car the police station looms over me. Rows of blank and gleaming windows glare down in the midday sunshine. He is cool and business-like as he ushers me in and as the main door creaks shut, he sends me into an office to be processed. Indoors the building is dingy, as though its insides are older than its outside. Before she leaves DC Jameson turns to me and asks, 'do you want to be known as Flora or Miriam? Okay, I'll make that clear. And is it alright if I tell them there are some family issues? Also, you might want to speak to a mental health professional while you are in here. How do you feel about that? It might help your case. Do you want anybody to be with you?'

She is being kind and I do wish I could have someone with me, but there is no one. Elena has got enough to do looking after her parents, who both seemed even frailer today. Luke is in hospital. There really is no one else in the world who would care what happened to me, apart from Martha, I think with a pang of sadness. And now this woman is asking if I need to speak to a 'mental health professional?' That means she already thinks there is something wrong with me. My palms are sweating again in fear and my heart is thumping painfully as I struggle to keep my composure. If only I was back in my safe little flat, with all my treasures around me and the door firmly shut on this frightening new world.

And now even the two officers who brought me in are about to leave me alone with strangers, probably hostile ones at that. DC Jameson has been kind and gentle and I am more comfortable with her around.

Giving me a slight smile, she says, 'good luck Flora. Just tell the truth, like your friend said; it is always easier in the end,' and with that she heads off, her radio crackling into life, her thoughts moving away from me and onto the next problem of her day.

I have been sucked into a machine. I am repeatedly asked my name, date of birth and address. I am hustled into a small drab room where my photograph and fingerprints are taken. A briskly unemotional woman asks me for my bag and itemizes the contents, placing it in a locker afterwards. I am grateful to Elena for removing the stolen spoons. She then approaches me and asks me to lift my arms, searching through my pockets, checking my shoes and reaching into my underwear. As I feel her hands scrabbling across my body, I zone out completely.

I come round to find myself in another dingy room sitting across a desk from a tired-looking police officer. He has thinning grey hair and grey grizzled skin. Another new person. There have been so many today.

This man is sitting back in his chair and looking at me carefully. When I catch his eye at last, he nods and opens some papers on the desk.

'Right, Miss Miller, er, Flora Miller' he says, in a slow, grey voice. 'I'm here to read the charge sheet against you. Do you understand why you are here?'

Is this a trick question? If I say I am in for stealing a handbag, haven't I as good as admitted it? Don't I get a lawyer or something?

The new police officer, whose name I haven't been told, seems to read my mind. Greyly he recites.

'You do, of course, have the right to see a solicitor. Do

264

you have one of your own you would like us to call, or would you like to see the duty solicitor? They can give you advice, which will be independent of us, the police.'

Should I have a solicitor? I did have one who helped me to buy the flat. But that is conveyancing so altogether a different thing. How am I going to explain to someone new and official that sometimes I know there is a stolen bag in my flat and sometimes I don't? I can't even explain it to myself. How much is that bag worth anyway? They must think it is valuable to be going to all this trouble.

'The duty solicitor would be perfect, thank you,' I murmur, realising I now sound like an upper-middle-class lady graciously accepting a coffee. Oh well, it can't be helped and why am I worrying that I sound too posh to be a prisoner? Get a grip, Flora.

And listen. He's talking again.

'….the charges against you are for the theft of a grey leather handbag, valued at £1,500, found at your address on July 10th and the property of a Miss Lucinda Spenser and eleven counts of shoplifting from Partington's store in Cheltenham, between May and July this year. Do you accept these charges?'

Fucking hell. £1,500. How can that bag, any bag in fact, be worth that much? And what idiot would take such a stupidly valuable thing to a wedding and why did that have to be the one thing that caught my eye? It's her own fault, Lucinda whatever the fuck her name was, that she got it nicked, stupid cow. And what else did he just say? Something about Partingtons?

'I'm sorry, can you repeat that please?' I say, still in my overly polite voice. I don't know where this has come from, why since I've come here I'm suddenly channelling the Duchess of Cambridge.

The grey man in front of me raises his eyebrows slightly and repeats the whole list of charges in exactly the same tone as before. This time I'm ready for the shock of the handbag's value, so hear the end of the sentence. Shoplifting, at Partingtons? Eleven times?

I think quickly. Partingtons, mmmmn. What a cosy old-fashioned shop that is. I picture the sections of soft furnishings, the piles of cushions, the glassware. In my mind, I wander round the departments, until my pulse rate slows back to normal.

But shoplifting. That is what he just said. Can that be right? I know I've done a lot of *shopping* there. I try to remember the last time I was in there and come up uncomfortably with the unwelcome memory of shopping for Laura and Tom's wedding. Could I have been stealing as well?

I hear a cough from across the table and look up at the officer opposite.

'Yes, I do have the handbag' I answer slowly. 'I know I shouldn't have picked it up, but I had no idea it was so valuable. But I have only ever *bought* stuff from Partingtons. I am in there a lot for work. Maybe there has been a mistake?'

The grey man sighs, loudly and slowly.

'You are saying you do not accept these charges?' he asks flatly, as though even an inflection at the end of the sentence is too much effort for him.

'I do accept that I have the handbag' I reply slowly and clearly, hoping it is true as I say it, 'but I have not stolen anything from there.'

Mr Grey lets out a long slow breath. 'You are sure about that answer?' he asks. 'I am recording your response. This means that you will need to wait here now as you deny some of the charges against you. You will kept in overnight, whilst a detective looks into this.'

Oh that's not good, is it? Overnight? This has all got serious suddenly. And why *am* I being accused of shoplifting? Is there someone else doing it who looks like me? I can tell from the grey man's face that it is going to be pointless saying anything else, pointless to protest my innocence. And I wish I felt surer that I am innocent. Something about that last memory of being in the store is niggling at me, like a dream that I am trying to remember that keeps sliding out of my grasp. Things are bad enough already. I am going to be tried and punished for stealing a fifteen-hundred-pound handbag at a wedding that I was working at, and from a guest at that. What are they going to do to me?

For a minute I wish I was back in the Meeting's secret house again. Perhaps I should have hidden when the police came round this morning. I can still see my father's expression as I was being escorted out though. Disgust. As though I was something dirty and unwanted. I am a defective and faulty daughter that he will be glad to be able to wash his hands of. Like Pontius Pilate. But wasn't Pontius Pilate on the wrong side?

Oh, it is confusing, and this place is freaking me out. I tell myself firmly that it is better to be out of that house and away from those men. All the time I was there, I was dragged down by sinfulness and shame. Now I am actually a criminal. I am under arrest, and I have been charged with a crime. Curiously, I feel lighter now, clearer-headed and cleaner.

43

I don't have much time to enjoy feeling lighter and cleaner though, as the police service is determined to keep me in my place. As soon as the grey nameless man has written down my partial admission of guilt but my denial of shoplifting, he calls for a policewoman.

As she enters, he says brusquely, 'we need to contact CID. Get them to pull up some CCTV footage or whatever they have in relation to offences 1 to 10 and 12.'

He nods to her and then turns back to his computer.

The new policewoman checks my details. She then asks if I would like a sandwich. I realise that I am starving, and my throat is dry.

I nod eagerly and she asks in a bored tone, 'do you have any dietary requirements? Tea or coffee?'

'Vegetarian would be lovely' I say, not because I am vegetarian, but because I want to be able to make a choice.

'And coffee please.' I hear myself sounding middle-class again. Is it a reaction to police procedure or am I like this all the time?

The female officer gestures me to follow her down a long grey corridor that smells of floor cleaner. I try to pay attention to where I am going but the building is huge, and I am lost almost at once. There seems to be no daylight anywhere and we might as well be underground. We change corridors to one which is full of offices or interview rooms and then past swinging doors that lead into industrial kitchens.

'Here we are' says my companion as we enter yet another corridor harshly lit by overhead fluorescent strips. Down either side are lines of doors; painted dark blue and each with their own small window that looks into the cell beyond. The policewoman unclips the bunch of keys from her belt, selects one and unlocks a cell, telling me curtly to 'come on in' as I hesitate on the threshold.

'Okay,' she continues briskly once we are inside. 'You'll be kept here until we have got all the information we need about your case to charge you.' She looks at her watch. 'That means overnight. Someone will be down soon with some food. And the duty solicitor will see you as soon as they have time, probably in the morning.'

She doesn't acknowledge the other person in the room. But I am very aware that there is a girl, who looks to be about nineteen, perched at the other end of the cell and glaring at me in an unfriendly way.

The cell door closes with a rattling of keys and clangs heavily behind the policewoman. I hear her steps and the rattling moving away up the corridor. Back to where the free people are. The cell is very small and seems too full already. I sit down on a battered metal chair beside the door, breathing hard and trying to ride the waves of claustrophobia. It smells very bad in here. The girl and I look at each other.

'Hi' I begin uncertainly, 'I'm Flora. What's your name?'

'Tiff' the girl replies shortly, spitting out the syllable. She looks like the kind of girl I used to be terrified of at school. Skinny and dressed in a tracksuit, she has cats-eye flicks of eyeliner emphasising her darting eyes and her hair is shoulder length and black with washed out pink at the ends. I try to smile at her, but she looks away and mutters something. To my surprise, she then turns back to me, and looking at me appraisingly asks, 'you got a fag on you?'

I am sure we are not allowed to smoke in here, but there doesn't seem any point mentioning this, so I merely shake my head.

'Fuck it,' Tiff mutters and lapses back into gloomy silence. I watch her covertly as she fidgets with her hands, ripping at a hangnail, pushing back her cuticles and turning her rings round and round on her bony fingers. She feels me watching her and gives me a hostile stare. I look away at once, flushing. This is worse than being in a cell on my own. Although I am now staring fixedly at the floor, I can feel Tiff giving me a long once over. I wish I was wearing anything other than my sister's over-large and shapeless grey skirt and navy jumper, the only clean clothes that almost fit from the bag Martha packed for me. I stop myself trying to explain why I am dressed like this, as though I am middle-aged and have no style.

Imagining what she sees when she looks at me makes me aware of how much I don't look like myself. Apart from the terrible clothes, I have no makeup, my skin is dull and spotty, my nails are chewed and bare and a couple of centimetres of dull brown roots are showing through my blonde highlights.

'Nice boots', Tiff comments finally and all credit to her, she has spotted the one thing I am wearing that belongs to me. They are black and simple, but they do have a nice short heel and are well made and classic.

I look up, still afraid she will scowl or bite my head off but deciding I had better respond.

'Thanks.'

'What you in for then?' she asks, her darting eyes sliding away as I glance at her.

'Nicking a baby or something? You look like that sort.'

I give her credit again for a good guess. I probably do

look like the kind of woman who would steal a baby from a pram in a fit of desperate hunger. I've never had the slightest interest in babies, but she is not to know that.

'Stealing, yes' I answer honestly. 'But not a baby. I took a handbag from a wedding. And, they say I have been shoplifting' I add, remembering the list of charges, though I can't imagine myself doing that.

Tiff looks at me again fleetingly.

'Where from?' she demands. 'Partingtons?! You fucking crazy? There are cameras everywhere in there! You are better off in supermarkets. And you can always flog on stuff that is branded....'

She loses interest in me and sinks back into herself, sniffing, twitching and pulling at her nails again, before jumping up and pacing the four steps she can manage across the cell, rounding on her heel and pacing back. She continues doing this like a caged panther while I try to take in what has happened to me.

My memory problem is back again. It always happens when I'm upset or stressed. The result is that I can barely remember the events of today at all. There are hazy images of my father, with men, a whole group of men, all staring at me. Then Luke. Now that is a nice thought, and cosy comforting Elena was there too, I think. Why isn't Luke here now?

Police asking questions, that damn handbag. The mystery of whatever it is I seem to have been doing in Partington's department store. There is a sickly feeling in my belly; too much emotion, half-swallowed tears and choked back shame.

I shake my head to clear it and look round the cell for clues about the time of day. The room is dim, with one small, iron-barred window through which only a high brick wall can be glimpsed. There is an overhead strip light though that is

271

not turned on yet. My stomach is telling me it is a long time since I last ate. It must be mid-afternoon, perhaps early evening. I am in a police station, locked up. This is real and serious, and I can't get out of my head like I usually do and think about something nice.

Because there really isn't anything nice to think about.

This room is the ugliest I have ever been in. The walls are a dark yellowish-brown. I try and fail for a name for their colour. There are two fold-back bunks, presently flat against the wall and covered in some kind of plastic material. I think of spending the night on one of them and shudder.

Tiff has been alternately pacing, then stopping to check by listening if anyone is coming and then going back to pacing. Suddenly she turns to me, hunched up on the single metal chair. She hesitates, coughs and then says, 'you know, people like you think it is *such* a big deal getting arrested. It is like the end of the world. But it is not so bad. They are not going to beat you up in here, you know. It is just boring. And it is so fucking annoying they won't let us have a fag,' she returns to her own discomfort abruptly, before considering me again.

'See, this bit, the being processed, or whatever the fuck they call it and being in here and then meeting the solicitor and whatever, is just like really slow. And *fucking* boring,' she says again for emphasis.

'But it is like, oh I don't know, going to Argos or something with your nan who wants something totally lame, like a pedal bin or whatever. And you have to queue in this horrible hole for like ages and then look through a book that is chained up and then wait and wait and then your number gets called and you go to a big cage thing at the back, and someone checks stuff… yeah, just imagine this is like being in Argos, but maybe like, for a week…

They are always picking me up, though, they're like "oh hi Tiff, back again?" those boys out there. They are not so bad really. Though this room does stink, like of what? piss, or something.'

She tails off and begins pacing again, banging her trainers moodily on the wall each time she turns on her heel.

I consider her words as I watch her. I can't quite believe that one of the scary girls is talking to me. But she is. And she has just given me some good advice.

44

Before I can respond to Tiff, we hear rumbling in the corridor, which stops outside, and our door is unlocked. A very young orderly bustles in.

'Flora Miller? Vegetarian option?'

I stand up and take a plastic tray from her, containing a pre-packed cheese sandwich on white bread and a polystyrene cup of instant white coffee.

'Thank you so much,' I say. The Duchess again. It isn't very much though, is it? Is this all I'll have till tomorrow?

'Hey, can I have a sandwich too?' asks Tiff quickly, with a new wheedling tone in her voice. 'And a coffee?'

'I couldn't eat the shepherd's pie earlier,' she says loudly.

'It was like shit. At least they can't fuck up a cheese sandwich.'

The orderly looks displeased, and I worry that if Tiff doesn't get a sandwich, I will feel I have to share mine but to my relief, she nods and fetches another tray from the trolley, identical to mine, which she bangs down on the bench beside Tiff. I stop myself thanking her again, as Tiff doesn't, but simply grabs her sandwich and rips off the wrapping.

We eat in silence, united by hunger. Tiff finishes first, loudly crunches up her coffee cup and moans, 'fuck it, now I need a fag even worse,' before dropping down one of the metal bunks and moodily flinging herself on it, trainered feet dangling over the edge. The food has made her more relaxed, and she carries on talking.

'Fuck I'm depressed,' she mutters. 'I'm sure I'm going to get time again. I've been banged up before and it bloody stinks. All that having to be a good girl to get points and having to share a fucking cell, the last cow I was in with was such a bitch, and no Wi-Fi… and I'm bound to get longer this time.'

She grinds to a halt, close to tears. She looks so young and scared when she isn't scowling that it hurts me to look at her. I almost wish she would revert to her earlier surly manner.

I stop myself asking her what she has done, as it is not going to help either of us at this point. Instead, I ask, 'what *does* makes you feel good? What do you like doing?'

As soon as the words are out of my mouth, I feel foolish. What a pointless and condescending thing to ask. I half expect a sneer in response, or her to tell me that shooting up heroin makes her happy. She looks away and kicks her legs, but I can feel her thinking about her answer.

'Music', she says at last. 'I like listening to songs, but also, I like, you know, make up tunes with me mates sometimes. They say I've got a good voice. It's probably shit though.'

'Sing me something' I say softly, even though I expect she will react with scorn. This girl was a stranger to me this morning. She was rolling her eyes when I walked in, but now, in this cut-off-from-the-world bubble, she is opening up to me. Yes, I'm afraid I will say the wrong thing and Tiff will turn from me in disdain, but I am lonely and scared enough that the chance of making a friend, even if only for one night, seems worth the risk.

And I would like her to sing. If anything could improve our grim situation, it might be music. Shut up in this airless and fetid cell, we have nothing but the contents of our own heads to keep us from going mad. And I don't want to listen to the voices in my head at all, nor do I want to listen to the sounds around me. Harsh metallic clattering from the distant kitchens echoes from down the corridor. There is the occasional sound of shouting, maybe from another inmate and the scream of a siren from the town.

Tiff stares hard at me, to check if I am serious. I hold my breath and smile at her. Suddenly it seems terribly important that she will sing. Maybe she can't sing at all, and it will be awful. Or maybe she will become emotional. I know nothing at all about her.

There is a very long pause in which we both hear a door banging shut further down the corridor and muffled thumps and yells.

'Do you know this one?' she says at last. To begin with, she hums almost inaudibly but gaining confidence a little, she begins half speaking and half-singing a song that has been on the radio all summer. When she gets to the chorus, I join in very softly. My timing is out with hers though and she breaks off awkwardly, as though one of us has got it wrong.

'Great voice' I say, trying to be encouraging, as so far I have hardly heard it.

'Can you sing me one of yours, something you've written?'

'Fuck, I don't write them down. I'm thick as shit. It is all just bollocks in my head' she says with a sudden return to hostility, flopping back and banging her trainers on the wall again. I am worried I have ruined the moment, but after a long silence, she starts again. This time it is something of hers and she shuts her eyes as she sings.

She has a husky, sweet voice and though she is imitating the vocal quirks of her favourite singer, something of her own personality comes through.

> 'And I am waiting
> Waiting to be free
> And I'm sat here wishing
> I was out of here
>
> And I'm lying here waiting
> For the open door
> And my heart is outside
> Flying free
>
> And I sit here waiting
> Waiting to be free
> Let me go home
> And leave me be'

There is little melody to her song, but the words are so right for how we are both feeling that when she stops, I cannot speak because I am choked up. I hope she can see how much she has touched me.

In the silence, the prison sounds return, but they bother me less now because we have made a place of music in this room. Tiff comes to life suddenly.

'Your turn now, yeah. What is your name? Did you tell me, and I forgot? I'm always doing that.'

'Flora' I answer, and she smiles at my name.

'That's better than bloody Tiffany at least…my mother watches fucking Eastenders all day long,' she sniffs.

'I don't know any songs' I say, weakly. Then I realise this is not true. Of course I listen to music on the radio and enjoy the bands and DJs I book for weddings, but that is not the kind of thing I want to sing right now. What I do know very well, word perfectly, are lots of hymns, and this seems the moment for one of those.

The Meeting would sing together every Sunday. When it was just our local congregation, it could sound quite weak. There were some good voices, my father and brothers among them and their strong baritones would boost the sound from across the hall, but there were many uncertain, weak and mispitched voices and the general effect was ragged and patchy. Martha and I would join in enthusiastically though. Singing was one of the few enjoyable activities allowed on a Sunday, or any day really, and my mother would permit us to sing at home as we washed up after the evening meal, as long as we were practising the hymns for the next Sunday.

But it was when we met in larger groups of several congregations together that the singing became extraordinary. On occasions we were all packed into huge halls, seating upwards of five hundred and when the first hymn began, there would be a powerful intake of breath from us all, in unison and then glorious melody, amplified by spontaneous harmonies from the more musical, would rise up like a lion roaring and shake the timbers of the roof. It used to bring tears of joy and pleasure to my eyes, and I remember the pride I felt at being part of that huge and sonorous monster of sound.

Quietly, and quite on my own now, I begin to sing my favourite hymn. I am as uncertain as Tiff was, both of my voice and my choice of song. The familiar words and tune strengthen and comfort me and my voice grows stronger.

> 'Amazing Grace, how sweet the sound
> That saved a wretch like me
> I once was lost, but now am found
> Was blind, but now I see.'

Tiff is huddled on the bunk, cuddling her knees. Her hair is half over her face, hiding her expression, but I catch her giving me a surprised look and try to explain my choice.

'I'm not a Christian or anything, but we sang this all the time when I was growing up, so I know all the words.'

Taking a deep breath I launch into the second verse, filling the miserable room with my voice.

> 'Through many dangers, toils and snares
> I have already come
> 'Tis grace that brought me safe thus far
> And grace will lead me home.'

I stop then because I don't want to sing the next verse, which is all about the Lord being my shield and portion. Grace can be anything. It doesn't have to be about God, but once you get onto verse three, it is a clearly Christian song. A wave of longing sweeps over me for my childhood self and the sister with whom I used to sing, as I remember Martha and me belting this out as we scrubbed the dishes and wiped the pans in my mother's chilly kitchen.

I had thought this morning I could walk away from my childhood, my faith and my family without missing a thing, but it is not that easy. There had been something incredible about that feeling of singing together in the larger Meeting, of the strength of numbers, the way we breathed and voiced together. I had been uplifted and held by the people around me in a way I never was by the Almighty. Mostly He seemed elusive and resolutely invisible and inaudible.

'Oh, I think I know that one' says Tiff. 'It's been on X Factor, or one of them shit-fest shows. But you sing it real nice.'

279

We smile at each other. I am happy and relieved that we have started to bond over the singing, and Tiff seems a lot less frightening now. I am starting to feel uncomfortable, though in a different way. It has been a *really* long time since I went to the toilet. In fact, when did I last go? Have I been since I got arrested? I can't remember and that makes my need to pee even more urgent.

There is a problem. It shouldn't be a problem, because a very obvious item in this tiny cell has been the toilet. Its lid is up, there is loo roll next to it and its smell is all too plain. But how can I possibly pee in front of someone else?

What about Tiff? Does she need to go? I'd feel better if she showed me how I was supposed to manage this. Perhaps there is some special prison etiquette. I wish I hadn't just drunk that cup of coffee. Oh, this is all so uncivilised. We are being treated like animals. We have not been found guilty yet, so why can't we be allowed to use a bathroom?

Tiff has spotted my constant glances towards the toilet.

'Do you need a piss?' she asks bluntly. 'Go ahead, I won't look.'

She is probably one of those people who can go anywhere, in front of anyone. She will have had to, by the sounds of it. But I don't think I can. What if I sit there, on the loo, and then nothing happens? It is going to get super awkward. After the clatter of daytime activity, it is quiet in the station now. Perhaps this is a downtime before they bring in the late-night drunk arrestees to be dried off overnight. I picture myself trying to pee and failing and having to get up again, abandoning the attempt, feeling even more desperate. Oh, this is so unfair.

'Well, I can't exactly leave the room,' says Tiff reasonably.

'So you are either going to have to use the bog in front of me or else sooner or later, you are going to piss yourself.'

She laughs out loud at this thought, but I don't feel like laughing at all. Suddenly, everything that has happened today is too much if I can't just have a moment's privacy. It is unbearable that I am shut up in a tiny stinking cell with a stranger who is laughing at me.

'Um, you could sing, to cover up the noise...'I mutter at last, flushing hotly.

'Bloody hell,' snorts Tiff. 'Madam wants serenading on the bog.'

Now she is going to get nasty and after we've just been getting on so well, but then she glances at my scarlet face and relents.

'Oh okay,' she says, drawing the words out slowly. 'I'll sing if it makes you happy. But you better fucking well sing for me too, and I might be having a dump later.'

There is nothing but to go through with it now. I fumblingly pull down my sister's shapeless and sensible white knickers and perch on the toilet, while Tiff, bless her, turns around, puts her hands over her eyes and sings, this time quite loudly.

'Onward Christian So -ldiers, marching as to war.
With the whatever-the fuck- the –wo -rds- are
Going on before.'
'Carry on,' I squeak, and she sings it again and halfway through my bladder decides to cooperate and I pee for what feels like three minutes. Once I've started, it is easier. I realise that eventually, like everything else, I would get used to doing this. If I end up facing a jail sentence and locked in a cell with some other woman. Oh God, what a horrible thought.

Stop it, Flora, don't worry about that now.

'Hey thanks, Tiff,' I murmur, sorting out the loose grey skirt as best I can. 'How come you sang a hymn that time?'

'Oh well, I thought it might be nice for you, seeing as how you did that holy song first,' she says, adding, 'I'm gonna take my trainers off now, excuse the pong, and try and get some sleep. I could die of boredom right now and fuck all is gonna happen now till after whatever pile of crap they give us for breakfast.'

She is correct about having smelly feet. She also loosens her jeans, wipes her face and armpits with wet tissues, moans again about needing a fag and about not having any toothpaste and then rolls herself into a ball, with her back to the room. I should be tired as well. It must be late, though it is hard to tell. The lights are left on all night and there are now regular thumps, thuds and shouts coming from other parts of the building.

I listlessly pull down my plastic covered bunk, give it a sniff and then wish I hadn't. The solicitor is not going to find me looking or smelling my best tomorrow morning.

45

In the end, I do sleep a little, even through the glaring overhead light and the unsettling sounds of banging doors, shouting and heavy feet in the corridor outside. I huddle on my narrow, plastic-coated shelf with my eyes shut whenever the hatch is lifted and some unknown person peers in from outside. Tiff is an extremely restless sleeper. She mutters and scuffles and scratches and on one occasion sits up suddenly, shouting out 'no, no, stop!' before dropping back into a deeper sleep and beginning to snore.

In the morning we are quiet; our connection from last night lost as we both struggle with anxiety about what the day will bring. Waking in custody is awful. Coming back to the reality of this tiny stinking cell is so depressing that I lie motionless in my bed even after Tiff is up and stretching and grumbling. Everything that will happen to me today is out of my control. I already know that most of my day will be spent waiting.

I force myself to sit up and tell myself that I chose to be here. This form of incarceration is still preferable to the one I have just left. I am not alone, even if my only company is a moody teenager. Facing up to the law, in all the chaos of its application, is a less mentally sickening prospect than the thought of another night of those religious thought-police coming in, full of their sanctimonious sincerity.

Tiff cocks her ears to the rumble of the breakfast trolley and brightens up with the arrival of the same young orderly this time with paper cups of tepid tea and bowls of cornflakes for us both. I give Tiff my sugars and she pours all four sachets over her cornflakes and starts eating noisily. Sipping my tea and watching her, I feel myself relaxing again. We are both in the same cell today, but I probably won't see her again and I have an unusual urge to try to talk about what has been happening to me. Maybe to start to make sense of it. So I begin to tell her about the 'safe' house I have just left and then, in order to explain that, I have to tell her more about my family and upbringing.

She listens wide-eyed as I tell her about the hours of prayer and the restrictions on us all, but especially on the girls. Her face darkens as I talk about the Elders, both as I remember them from my childhood, beings of extreme importance and unpredictable wrath and the trio of men who visited me in the last days while I was 'shut up.' I wonder as I talk how long I would have stayed if it had not been for Luke and then the police, finding me. Do people just disappear sometimes? I wonder. Do they go mad? Or do they in the end submit out of sheer exhaustion and re-join the fold, with their spirits broken?

'God, I hate all them fucking Godsquad Nazis' Tiff mutters. 'Evil tossers. What about your sister though? Are you going to go back and rescue her, once you get out of this place, I mean?'

I think of silent, solid Martha. Of the flicker of pleasure that was in her eyes when she saw me, of the care with which she had packed for me. I remember us as children giggling furtively in our bedroom when we thought we were not being heard. I remember her face flushing with delight at the sight of Gina walking down the road towards us.

'She has to choose,' I say slowly. 'I can't rescue her unless she wants to be rescued.'

Yeah, I guess, fuck it' Tiff agrees. 'Hey, listen, that is someone coming. Who's going first I wonder?'

In the end, it is her who is summoned by a new policewoman, full of start-of-shift briskness. To my surprise, I am grabbed for a quick hug by a visibly shaking Tiff as she is escorted out.

'Take care, singing girl' she says. And then, more loudly, clearly for the benefit of the smart new police officer.

'Tell all the poncey-faced cunts to suck it up!'

And then she disappears out of my life. Before I can say anything back or wish her luck. Before I have found anything out about her or why she is here.

The cell seems smaller now she has left and is more oppressive. I am glad, an hour or so later, to hear footsteps stopping outside my door again and to hear the clatter of keys in the lock. The same police officer is back, already slightly less brisk, as though wilted by the mid-morning heat down here in this airless corridor.

'Miss Miller' she says formally. 'You are to come with me to see one of our detectives.'

I had thought I would be seeing my solicitor next, so question this.

'Yes, you are on this morning's list for the duty solicitor' says my companion as she escorts me at a rapid pace back up the long corridor of locked doors, 'but it might take a bit of time to get to you and CID have some questions now.'

She brings me to the door of a small interview room, opens it and half pushes me in, saying to the large man sitting behind the desk,

'Good morning, sir. This is Miss Miller.'

She backs out, shutting the door smartly behind her.

The detective, who is black and late middle-aged, with short, grizzled hair and glasses perched on top of his head, looks up at me.

'Hello Miss Miller,' he says quite pleasantly. 'I am DS Okafor. I have a few questions to ask you.'

He motions me to sit down opposite him, pushes his glasses down onto his nose and looks at his computer screen, frowning slightly as he reads.

'So, you have understood the list of charges against you?' he looks back up.

On my nod, he continues, 'and you admit the theft of a handbag from Prescott Manor Hotel on June 27th. The same handbag that was found at your address and has been taken into safekeeping by the force. Currently valued at £1,500.'

He looks up at me.

'This is a quite distinctive item' he says. 'Were you planning to sell it on?'

I shake my head vehemently in denial. He waits for me to say more, but my thoughts spin and tangle themselves up inside my head. I don't know how to explain why I took the bag. I can hardly remember doing so now, or what I thought I was going to do with it. As I consider this, I remember the photographs Luke took of me picking up other items at other weddings. A cold sweaty lurch of fear alerts me that my gut has understood before my conscious mind has worked it through, that this means that I *may*, in fact, have been shoplifting. Because if I didn't remember those occasions until I saw the photographs, how do I know that I haven't been stealing from the department store as they say I have?

I almost blurt out this fear but check myself. There is no use making the situation worse than it is. I should find out what evidence they have.

The detective is still looking at me carefully across the

table. His dark eyes are intent. His is a look of calm and unhurried appraisal; with something else behind it. Something softer.

I resist the urge to spill my confusion and anxiety in an uncontrolled flurry of words. This is how they work; I tell myself. This guy is the good cop and will be gentle and calm and suddenly someone else will come in and start shouting at me and accusing me and the two will work together in tandem until I have confessed to everything they can think of.

There is a long pause and then the detective sighs slightly and clears his throat.

'Alright, Ms Miller' he says.

'Looking at this charge sheet, there are eleven counts of shoplifting, all from the same store, Partington's in Cheltenham, and all between April and July this year. Are you saying that you didn't commit any of these offences? I would like you to think about your answer very carefully. Take your time.'

Again, I have that cold lurch in my stomach. I think of my many visits to Partingtons. I think of how much I enjoyed wandering round the shop and moving between departments. Maybe I just spent too long in there and they got suspicious. That would be typical, wouldn't it? Some over officious security guard starting to suspect and then persecute a perfectly innocent shopper. A good customer whose only crime was that she also enjoyed a bit of window shopping and browsing along with her legitimate business. But then I remember the boxes and boxes of things in my flat; the bags of wedding favours, the candles, the glasses, ornaments, jewellery and scarves...

I shake my head to clear it. Normally, when my mind begins to move along these lines, I distract myself and start to think about something more upbeat. My usual distractions all fail me now, stuck in here. Unwillingly my attention is forced to stay in this small room, with its hard chairs and cheap Formica table. And behind that table is sitting a man who I am beginning to feel is my nemesis.

What shall I say?

He is still waiting, and still watching me, and looks like he could wait all day. He doesn't need a shouting sidekick. This quiet approach is effective enough. I sense that the muddle and confusion in my brain has now encountered a slow implacable force that is determined to shine a light in there and to find out what is inside.

46

After a pause, Mr Okafor asks again.

'Do you deny that you have committed any of the shop-lifting offences with which you are being charged?'

His voice is low, gentle and oddly reassuring, despite the actual words.

Don't get taken in, Flora, I tell myself. This is how they get you to confess to crimes. He is only pretending to be understanding and on my side. Yet, despite knowing I should stay on my guard and suspecting that this man's demeanour could change at any moment, despite all that, I do want to open up to him. To share my confusion. Because right now I do *not* know what I might or might not have done. Horrible though it is in here, I am almost afraid to be released because who knows what I might do next?

'I don't know.' I say at last. Elena told me to tell the truth. I look up into Mr Okafor's face.

'I'm sorry, but I can't answer your question.'

He makes no comment, merely nods and then pushes his laptop across the table so we can both see the screen.

'This might help' he says, neutrally.

As I brace myself for what I might see, images appear. He is showing me a low-resolution video of a small blonde woman (wearing high heels and a nice jacket) moving around a rack of sunglasses. I must be the most stupid person alive because I don't immediately recognise myself, until the camera angle shifts, and I see my face. My onscreen expression is intent and focused as I appear to choose between two pairs of glasses. Mr Okafor and I watch in silence as the woman who is me tries them both on, smiles at herself experimentally in the small mirror on the stand, puts one pair back and the other disappears, not onto the rack, but into her open handbag.

I say nothing because I literally cannot. My throat feels as though it has been burnt dry by the caustic acid of fear and shame rising from my gut. As I watch, I see myself exposed. Caught completely red-handed. One of the dark corners of my life that I have hidden from myself is here, then, captured by camera. I was not invisible. I was being watched all along. I cannot pretend it didn't happen, because here is cold, hard evidence. This is even worse than when Luke came over to my flat and showed the photographs of me at weddings, stealing from my employers. My body is drenched in the shame I felt then and it is so unpleasant I would do anything to escape it.

And Luke knew. He has been so patient and seems to understand me even though I don't understand myself. Why haven't I been in touch with Luke? I have been so caught up in my own drama and the strangeness of everything and with sharing the cell with Tiff, but I could have tried to contact him. I could have phoned him last night; we are allowed a phone call. Why didn't I think of that? Am I losing my mind? I hope he wasn't hurt too badly in that fall. My mind wanders off into a fantasy of visiting him in hospital and bringing him gifts of books and fruit and music. What *would* Luke like brought to hospital?

'All the footage you are about to see has been collated by the security staff at Partingtons over the past few months.' Mr Okafor, still in the same neutral tone, interrupts my daydreams and brings me back to the unwelcome present, as he clicks on the next video clip.

'They consulted CID who made a positive identification of you,' he adds relentlessly, banging another nail into my coffin as he presses play.

In this next clip, taken the same day, I see myself leaving the store. For a second, I feel relief. Surely if I could stroll out of the building looking so calm and relaxed, I cannot have committed any offence? Don't they have people on the doors?

I see first myself from behind, a slim and stylish woman and then as I exit into the sunny street, the viewpoint shifts and a camera at the front catches me full in the face. Now my hair is pushed back off my face and is being held back by a pair of shades. The same shades that had dropped into my handbag twenty minutes before, according to the running clock displayed at the bottom of the screen.

I look so good in that picture. My blonde waves bounce and catch the light and the jewelled arms of the shades add glamour. They were the right pair to pick. They look perfect. That is a woman who knows how to put a look together. Now I can remember that day and that shopping trip, quite clearly.

It was genius to pop into the ladies, cut the security tab off the glasses with the little nail scissors I always have in my handbag, chuck that in the bin along with my used paper towel and simply slide them onto my hair. I couldn't wait to try them on anyway, they were so cool.

I toss my hair back in a half memory. If only I had some decent products and my diffuser in here so I could get that look back. I watch my past self, envy mixed with self-satisfaction, as in the grainy film she looks up at the camera and gives a distinct but cheeky wink.

I can't help myself now but let a snort of laughter. I look so funny, winking straight into the camera before sauntering out. I can remember the rest of that day; it had carried on being bloody brilliant. From Partingtons, I had gone to an upmarket perfume store. I had been given free samples and then when I left a small bottle of Gucci Bloom eau de toilette left with me. I wouldn't have taken the perfume oil, that would be too expensive, but the eau de toilette is, as its name suggests, mostly water. Those shops make all their money on packaging images and dreams. I must go back and get some more of that soon; it is a lovely scent and that day it made me happy.

I realise that Mr Okafor is looking at me, with quite a different expression on his face now.

'Ms Miller' he is saying. 'Can you hear me?'

And then after a moment, 'I'm surprised you think this is funny.'

Now he is not so gentle and calm, but puzzled, a new uncertain note in his voice and he leans forward to try to catch my eye.

'Well,' I say, quite sarcastically and deliberately, looking away. I am not going to join in with his competitive staring game. 'It's not like they make it difficult, do they? Surely if people don't want things picked up in their shops, they should take reasonable precautions. I'm only doing what millions of other people do. It was just bad luck that silly camera happened to be there.'

I look back at the image on the screen, which has frozen onto my face, up tilted and slightly flushed and I can't help but snigger again.

'Ms Miller, I must ask you to take this more seriously. You are under investigation for a string of offences, and you don't seem to realise the seriousness of your situation. I can assure you that we will prosecute each and every theft with great vigour.'

"A string of offences." Into my head comes a picture of a line of crimes hanging on a string, maybe attached to a kite. There is murder, arson, petty theft, larceny, whatever that is, and what else? Perjury, fraud… you could call your dogs those. 'Come here Fraud, drop it Perjury.'

Mr Okafor's voice continues in the background, getting further away as I focus on my kite. I am out of this grim little room altogether. I don't like it in here. It smells. Why can't they at least get rid of the horrid stink in these places? There is a gap at the end of my string, so I add some more crimes, '…. adultery, sexual assault, rape….'

I sober up as I move along this list. A marsh of sadness and tiredness slowly begins to pull me down. I rub my eyes blindly to try to clear them. He is still talking, what is he saying? I can't understand all the words.

'Ms Miller, do you admit that this is you in the video and that you committed the offence of theft from Partington's store on May 8th this year?'

I nod dumbly, as that seems to be the answer he is looking for. I am suddenly too tired and too far away to make a sound.

'For the benefit of the tape, please, can you answer out loud?' asks Mr Okafor.

'Yes,' I say slowly. 'Yes, I can see that was me.'

'Thank you, Ms Miller,' says Mr Okafor. 'Let us look at

the next piece of evidence.'

He pauses and then looks carefully at me.

'Are you alright though? You don't look well. Do you want to take a minute? I will get you some water.'

He stops the recording machine and walks out of the room, leaving the door ajar. The small part of my awareness that is still here registers this with surprise. What has just been happening? Why is the detective being nice to me now? I've just confessed, haven't I?

I have confessed to stealing and I am guilty. I am a wretched sinner. I have brought disgrace on myself and on my poor family. I have shamed my whole community. I will never be allowed back now. If it were not a mortal sin to kill myself, it would be better by far that I ended my useless disgusting life and went straight to Hell, where I undoubtedly belong.

'For the cowardly and unbelieving and abominable and murderers and immoral persons and sorcerers and idolaters and all liars, their part will be in the lake that burns with fire and brimstone, which is the second death.' I murmur to myself, first quietly and then louder. I am back in the windowless hall now, with not just one man, but rows and rows of men facing me. And they are all accusing me of my crimes. Worst of all is that I know that I am guilty. But surely they are guilty as well? 'Sexual assault, rape, incest...'

My hands are clutching convulsively at the table and then clasping together in a rigid semblance of prayer. Overcome by the realisation of the depths of my iniquity and finally understanding that phrase and what it means, I fall off my chair. I am on my knees on the floor, where I belong, prostrating myself in prayer. I can hear someone weeping loudly. Not just weeping but howling out loud, in animalistic wails. Desperate, throat twisting and gut-wrenching sobs echo round the building and bring with them a ringing bell, running feet and slamming doors and finally hands that lift me up. A needle that slides into my arm, followed by the sweet welcome of black thick clouds of oblivion, rushing into my brain and smothering the voices, till they run out of breath and fall silent at last.

47

This morning, looking back on that moment in the police station, I realise I don't know what happened next. Somehow, when I woke today, I found myself lying on my own soft sofa in my own pretty flat. I shut my eyes quickly and then open them again. Yes, I am definitely home. Now, still lying here, afraid to move, my head is throbbing painfully. I am drowsy and confused but there is no doubt where I am. Relief sweeps sweetly through me. Once more I seem to have escaped, though hardly by my own agency. I force myself to try to remember the recent past, but there is just a blur. Gradually fragments come back, though each one makes the pain in my head still worse as though I am having to mine out the memories with an axe. Crying, praying. A lot of praying. Kind people helping me. Doctors. Luke. A tired official giving me a lot of forms to be signed. My jacket and bag handed back to me. A silent drive back through the late evening streets.

I have buried my head deep into the pillows and throws, but even so, I can tell it is daylight outside. So, a night, at least one night, must have passed. I am in no rush to re-join the world. It is much safer to stay here with my head under the covers slowly letting sensation return. There is a sick sense in my body of spent but powerful emotion. The painful ache of a storm that has passed. A dragging sense of shame.

I force my memory back further. I can remember the cell now. I can remember Tiff. The summons to meet Mr Okafor. His face, quiet and watchful, floats back into my mind. Yes, it is there somewhere in the face of Mr Okafor that the memories will be held. But clear memory eludes me. I have lost the sense of who I was in that moment and the awareness that should go with it has been lost too.

Giving up on this futile introspection, I allow myself to indulge in the simple joy of having made it out of the police station. Not just the police station, but also away from those awful Elders and that depressing house. And by some miracle, though surely not a miracle of God's agency, I am back on my own familiar sofa.

I stick my head out from under the covers and peek at just a few centimetres of the room that are in my eye line. I have been gone a little while; I can see. Long enough for the orchid that was fully in bloom on my mantelpiece to begin to wilt and drop a few heads of petals. There are quite a lot of small changes in my flat, I register hazily, but I am distracted by an unfamiliar sensation somewhere around my knees.

Warmth, softness and a rumbling vibration. I reach out my hand and touch the softest silkiest fur. It is a cat. Lying on my legs on top of all my coverings. I stroke its hot small head and the cat doubles the volume of its purring. It rubs against my hand and offers up its ears to be scratched. As I oblige, a memory stirs. Another cat, another time, but the same delight in this simple exchange. Rubbed ears equals purring, warmth and friendliness. If only people were so easy.

I remember the other cat now. That was in Gina's cluttered and cosy kitchen, all those years ago. The cat was, what was he called, yes, Freddie. Martha was there too. I find I don't want to think about Martha and concentrate on this cat instead. This cat who is here now and definitely real. I count his toes for him as he spreads out his paws in pleasure.

'Oh, I see Flump is making friends' says Luke, coming into the room with a clatter.

Luke. Luke is here. Of course, he *would* be. And this must

be his cat. Things are beginning to make sense. Didn't I offer him the use of my flat while he was between rentals some time ago? I can't think of anyone I would sooner see right now.

Wincing with the pain in my head, I sit up a little more, being careful not to dislodge Flump.

'Oh Luke, what's happened to your foot?' I cry. He has one foot in a heavy plaster cast and the other one in socks.

'Yeah,' he grimaces. 'I did a bit more damage than I thought. I cracked a couple of bones and sprained my ankle quite badly, um, falling off that roof.' He tails off and then looks me in the face.

'There has been some very weird stuff going on,' he says at last.

'That house, those men. What the fuck was going on there? When you feel up to it, I think it would be good if you told me everything that you can. There was some strange shit about your brothers you've been shouting about the last couple of days as well.'

My mind slides away from this. I don't want to go there; I don't want to think about those men, nor about my father, certainly not about my brothers. It is too painful. I can't remember anyway. But then I look at Luke, wincing as he moves and realise that I owe him at least an explanation. He has carried on being friends with me even after finding out I am a thief. He cared for me after the disaster of Laura and Tom's wedding. He came looking for me after I disappeared and then injured himself falling off a roof trying to rescue me. He must have then come to me at the police station and somehow managed to bring me home.

That is a lot of kindness and support from one person. And I realise how pleased I am that *this* time I am not alone in my flat when I come round after losing time. How much better to have someone here. A person I am happy to see. I look up at him and smile. He is hovering over me uncertainly, trying to balance on his painful foot, but smiles back with real affection.

Maybe it is time I took care of him for a change.

'Ok,' I say very slowly. 'I will try and tell you about them. But first, I'm going to have a shower, put on some clean clothes and make a pot of tea and some food. For us both.' I add firmly.

'You are going to sit down, cuddle this daft animal, put your foot up and let me wait on you for once.'

Luke's smile broadens and he obediently sinks down into the nearest chair and calls to Flump, who stretches, arches his back and jumps off the sofa onto his lap, where he starts to knead his paws into Luke's belly vigorously and purr with renewed enthusiasm.

Eyes still half shut in pain, I head to the bathroom. It is subtly changed as well. There is man smell in here. It is not unpleasant. Sniffing deeply, I decide it is quite nice. Some kind of herbal potion has been splashed around, but the room looks quite tidy. I have a blissful shower, washing away the sweat and fear and grime of the police cell, rinsing out the nasty cheap shampoo that poor Martha had packed for me from my hair and finally putting on clean underwear and clothes that actually fit. Oh, that is so much better. How can those people live like that? How can Martha stand it?

I don't want to think about Martha, so why does she keep coming back into my mind? There is an unswallowable hard lump of sadness in my throat as I picture her standing silently with that slow dawning smile on her face when she opened the door to me at my parent's house. She looks so different to how I remember her, so placid, bovine and lumpen. But I had seen the occasional spark of the quick-witted and lively girl that she had been. And she had packed me chocolate along with all the dull food, as though she were sending me a message.

I know though, with sadness, that unless she decides for herself to leave the Meeting and to reject the rest of her family, I will never see her again. I can accept this is the truth, but it hurts like hell.

Coming out of the bathroom, with damp hair and in jeans and a floppy shirt, I catch a glimpse of myself in the mirror. I am pale and thinner than usual but look surprisingly bright-eyed and clear-skinned. Not bad, I think, considering everything. Not bad at all.

With a new spring in my step, I head to the kitchen. Someone has been shopping and the fridge is full of unfamiliar food. There are breads and pies and lots of packets, bacon, cheese, eggs. Luke clearly believes in getting enough protein.

Deciding to cook something that he would enjoy, I pull out the eggs, some mushrooms, bacon, bread and beans and decide to make a proper fry up. Looking for the first time at the clock on the cooker I see it is after three in the afternoon, but that just makes it a perfect time for an all-day breakfast.

48.

We eat the fry-up, which is delicious. I am absurdly proud of myself for cooking something that Luke so clearly enjoys. He washes up while I make a second pot of coffee and we head back to the sofa. It is a grey and rainy late summer evening and for a while we sit in companionable silence, drinking our coffee, watching the rain splash onto the overfilled window boxes and both stroking Flump, who has settled down between us.

'So, Flora' says Luke finally, 'I think that it might be good for you to start talking about your past a bit. That nice woman in the police station who talked to you at the end. Do you remember her?' he asks me and when I shake my head, carries on, 'never mind, I'm sure you will. Anyway, she said that you should try to talk about when you were a kid and, umm, the Meeting and all' he adds, looking at me quickly to check I am still on board.

'You are out on bail at the moment,' he explains.

Oh good, I'm glad I didn't have to ask. In the last hour or so I had been getting worried that the police might be going to return and take me back into custody. Bail sounds good, though I'm not quite sure what it all means.

Luke continues gently. 'The detective, CID and the psychologist all need to prepare some reports. And then you will get a date to go to court.'

Oh right. That sounds scary. I must try to deal with this calmly. Of course, something was going to happen. They weren't just going to forget all about it, were they?

I take some deep breaths.

'Court' I murmur faintly.

'Yes, Flora', says Luke rather dryly. 'You do have a few charges against you. But the psycho thingy woman, she said, that if you,' he changes his voice to a caring professional one, '"undertake to engage in sustained therapy" and also check in with them for a while, it is likely they will give you a suspended sentence only. But you are not off the hook,' he continues firmly.

'It will all be on your records. You will have to at least pay costs.'

He reaches out and puts his hand over mine. I am shaking and icy cold all of a sudden. This is very real and serious. Was I just in a fantasy bubble before in which I pretended that it wasn't really me doing the shoplifting? No, it was more than that. It *wasn't* me. At times, I *was* someone else.

I make an inarticulate sound and then find my words are jammed up in my throat. Luke pats my hand reassuringly. His is warm and dry and it is so lovely feeling him there that I start to breathe again and look up at him with a crooked smile.

Encouraged, he continues.

'There is a legal process that you will have to go through. But the most important thing is for you to start understanding how it happened. And *what* happened. She, the psychologist woman, she said that was the key.'

He reaches out his hand to touch my cheek.

'Hey, don't look so worried' he says softly. 'We'll get through it.'

I absentmindedly nuzzle my face into his hand. He smells so good. Fancy someone saying "we" about me and them.

And after me ruining that wedding, acting so unpredictably, getting taken in by the Elders and then getting arrested (and rightly so, I remind myself, for theft), he still thinks there might be a "we." What a nice man he is. I wish he would keep stroking my face.

His hand moves away as he looks at me, but his voice is still warm as he says, 'Flora, can you concentrate for a moment? You need to start talking to people. No one can help you unless they understand what you are dealing with. So, as you are going to have to why not start with me? I know you can. Why don't you tell me a bit more about those men that were in the house with you to start?'

And so I do.

I tell him about the Meeting and its rules. I try to explain its hierarchy and the importance given to the Elders. I tell him how much time we used to spend praying. About the Hell we were told about that haunted my early years. About my silent and regimented home life. About how Martha and I shared secrets as well as a room and how we looked after each other.

I tell him about my obedient and exhausted mother and about my pompous oratorical father. I explain the system for men and women to pray apart in Meeting. I even tell him about the rules of shunning to which I was subject.

'If someone has broken the rules or mixed with worldly people, then they cannot be accepted back into the meeting until they have repented. They are "shut up" in a special house until they learn the ways of God. And no one can eat or drink with them until they are declared clean again. It is all in the Bible, all these laws' I tell him.

'Not the Bible I remember' Luke disagrees with me; gently but shaking his head in horror and denial of what I am telling him. 'Whatever happened to loving your neighbour and turning the other cheek and all that stuff?'

I can't answer him. But suddenly I want to stop talking. We are getting too close to something, too close to a place of danger. I try to distract him from questioning by turning my other cheek to him. I turn away, smiling with the side of my face he can see, until he understands. I want him to stop asking questions and I want him to touch my face again. And he picks up on this but gently and sweetly he takes my chin and moves my face back towards him, then taps me very lightly on both cheeks and mock sternly says, 'stop playing Flora. We will have time for that. But I think it would really help you to try to talk a bit first.'

Before what? It felt like something nice might have been about to happen. Why did I not realise before how much I fancied Luke? Something seems to have happened to him. Or maybe to me. Or even to us both. But now he seems disappointingly determined to keep talking.

He reaches into the bookshelf behind us and pulls out the Bible that was there. I think he is going to ask me to find the passage about shunning and I am trying to remember the verses to find, but instead he pulls out the photograph of my family that we looked at before.

Silently he points to my brothers, ranged in order of age. A heavy set and expressionless trio standing to one side of my parents. I look away instinctively and then look back, drawn to them against my will.

'What about them?' he says. 'You haven't mentioned them. In fact, you never told me you had brothers. Though you did mention your sister before and today you have talked about her a lot. What about them?'

I am silent. Luke looks at me. Watches me struggling to speak and struggling not to speak.

'What is he called?' he asks finally, pointing to the brother on the left.

'Matthew' I manage, seeing the older man who visited me recently in the face of this unformed youth. I continue along the line, reciting facts baldly and blankly.

'He is the oldest, he is eight years older than me. Then next is Reuben, a year younger, then John, a year or so younger than that. Then there was a gap till Martha. And then there was me.'

Something has happened to my voice. I can hear it from far away, faint and high. I am struggling to breathe. A weight is pushing on my chest, yet at the same time I feel like I am drifting out of my body and looking down on myself.

'Hmmm, um,' says Luke, sounding distracted. He gets up and crosses the room to my speakers and scrolls through his phone, searching for something.

'Some music may help' he says, turning up the volume, 'I know you like this tune.'

The sonorous and melancholic first notes of Miles Davis 'Blue in Green' quietly fill the room. Luke comes back and sits beside me again. How does he know I love this piece? Did I ever tell him that? We listen in silence. I have no idea for how long. The music washes over us, sad, sweet and yearning. The whole album plays, and my minds spins back.

Back to the past, to Matthew, Reuben, John and their friends James and Thomas. To that group of boys with their smart haircuts and their names from the Bible and their bodies full of a force they could neither understand nor control. To the terrible consequences for Martha and me. At some point, I realise Luke is holding my hand.

I begin to talk, in muttering incoherent sentences. About a garage. A garage full of men, still boys in age, as unformed as raw teenage cadets, but they seemed like men to us. Fear, pain, Martha crying, the taste of cherryade, the feel of my wet and soiled underwear.

It is all there, after all. Every single second of it. Carefully stored away in a safe box deep inside my brain. Underneath the boxes of stolen cash, the handbags, underneath the drawers of wedding favours. Underneath the touch of all the men who have tumbled in and out of my bed. I could never get rid of the feel of *their* touch. My brothers. Burning their hands onto my flesh.

Later still I realise my face is soaked with tears. Tears that I had not noticed were falling. And Luke has his head against mine and his face is wet too. Our tears mingle as we sit, huddled together and completely still, like two children hiding from the monsters who are just outside.

49

After all the lies and the evasions, once I started talking, it was easier than I expected. I tack back and forth, telling the story in sections and stopping for breaks whenever pain threatens to overwhelm me. I tell Luke that it was not just what they did, those afternoons after prayer meeting when my brothers and James and Thomas would pick us up in Thomas's father's old car as we were walking home. It was that there was no one to tell. Martha and I were caught between two realities and when we were in one, there was no way to access or even to understand the other.

The family and the Meeting would not have listened to two silly young girls like us. Not set against the word of five of its most promising young men, clever and able scholars, soon to be married, soon to be family men. The Meeting's best and brightest Elders of the future.

We never even considered telling our mother. She was totally obedient to Jacob and her greatest pride and joy was in the rearing of the three young men by whom she had been blessed by the Lord.

So, we both kept quiet. Our secret was shared only with each other. We were far too ashamed to want to tell anyone. Who would *want* to try to explain that your brothers, your own brothers, (though much older than you and part of a different and more important world) had laughingly sat you up on the worktop of their friends' fathers' garage and pulled down your white cotton panties? That they would hand you a bottle of cherry pop whilst you sat there, exposed and helpless and tell you they had brought you a little treat? That those brothers, (who you had seen at the breakfast table that morning, helping themselves to cereal and milk) and your brother's friends, (strange smelling and prone to sudden bursts of awkward laughter) had put their hands there and put their hands on themselves as well, not meeting your eye, but somehow seeming dazed and agitated, working themselves into some kind of jerking frenzy? That they would chase you round the garage and of course catch you easily, in some twisted version of friendly horseplay and when you were caught, you would be tickled, by hands that crept inside the bodice of your long full dress and explored your developing young breasts with damp and rough nailed hands? That they would tell you that you were good girls and to be sure to tidy yourselves up properly and not to say anything to bother your mother, because she had enough to be thinking of without our silly stories.

And then you would see James, or Thomas, or Matthew, sitting with the men across the hall later on that evening, or at the Sunday services, serious, scrubbed, minds intent on the Lord and at one with their peers. And you would be burning with shame and with the sense of dirty hands on your skin and in your knickers, and you would keep your eyes downcast for fear they should see you.

'It is them who should be ashamed, not you' Luke says hotly. 'The whole system is so fucked up. Nothing excuses what they did, but they were young men driven half-crazy by hormones. They should have been out, I don't know, drinking and playing footie and trying to chat people up. Not stuck in some God box for hours, pretending they don't have bodies. And then you would have been safer. Sorry,' he says. 'Go on, I'm stopping you.'

Shame is the killer. It leaves you dead inside and separate from yourself. Left to myself I would never have faced up to this degree of shame. I am still in shock I have told someone.

As I talk, I understand that I have been inflicting more of this shame on myself ever since. Why else would I have got caught in that stupid clinch with creepy Tom and been thrown out of his wedding with all eyes upon me? Then I was outed on social media as an unreliable slut. And when I returned to my family home the shaming continued. I was considered too unclean to be even in the same room with them as they ate and drank and then I was arrested in front of them and my friends for theft, searched, charged and locked up in that horrible cell. One way and another there doesn't seem like there is much more degradation I can inflict upon myself. It is time to turn around and face up to the jackal of shame that has been skulking behind me, stalking me down the years.

Luke moves closer and puts his arm round my shoulders and waits till my tears and panic subside. Handing me another tissue he searches my face till I reluctantly meet his eyes.

So, you *were* christened Miriam?' he says musingly. 'And all those things happened to Miriam? I can see now why you changed your name. Flora is a much better name for you anyway. So, you switched back to being Miriam when you went back to your family home.'

I nod uncertainly. Is that right?

I'm not sure though,' he frowns. 'Was it Miriam that was doing the stealing? Only once you told me you were called Chloé, and I always thought it was when you were her that you were the thief.'

Did I tell him I was called Chloé? I don't remember that. Chloé. I think hard. Oh, this is uncomfortable. Something is hurting my head. Sharp stabs of pain sear across my temples and blur my vision. I shut my eyes against the pain.

'Yeah' continues Luke, looking across the room as he thinks so he misses my changing state. 'She is a right Miss

309

Sassy. If you were her now, we would be halfway down that bottle of gin and you would probably have gone out to the off licence for some Sambuca and come back with a load of stolen cash in your bra or something.

I quite like that side of you' he continues, ' it is not bad to have fun, though that is when you do the thieving and illegal stuff.'

'Flora, are you feeling alright? He turns to me at last, a note of alarm in his voice.

Now, did someone just mention gin? That seems like a very good idea. All this fucking tea and sympathy stuff will get you so far but sometimes a girl needs to kick back a bit. And we can do better than gin. It is the perfect time to break out those highball glasses I picked up recently. And suddenly I am remembering a drink I tried the other day after a wedding. Blueberry something it was. Like a Moscow mule but with fruit.

'Hey Luke,' I say impulsively, 'can we lighten up here? That is enough talking. It's time for a drink. I want to try making blueberry Moscow mule cocktails, can we do it, do you think?'

'Oh babe,' Luke half laughs, half moans. 'What have I just started? Um, sure, a blueberry doodah sounds pretty nice. Do we have the ingredients?'

'Oh, I bet I can get close,' I respond confidently. This is a good idea. I head out to the kitchen and hunt around for ingredients. The most important thing is to get some alcohol in my system straight away. No wonder I'm feeling so pissing low, I haven't had a drink in days.

'I've got blueberries!' I shout triumphantly, reaching into the very back of my little freezer.

'Ice cubes and we need vodka which I've certainly got. There must be something else…Look it up.' I order Luke who is still sitting on the sofa looking shell shocked.

He scrolls through his phone for a recipe. It turns out we also need ginger beer, basil leaves and lime, none of which are here. I tease Luke for buying bacon and eggs but forgetting the basil and limes. But we make a pretty good drink with the vodka, blueberries, crushed ice and some lemonade and he leads me back to the sofa to drink it.

'So, Chloé,' Luke begins, chinking glasses with me. He stops with his glass in mid-air and looks at me closely.

'Chloé?'

The pain is back in my head again.

'Er, I think I'm Chloé.' I hear myself say rather lamely.

'Alright, I'll be quick' says Luke with a laugh. 'Why do you come out sometimes?'

Oh honestly, he is cute, but he can be quite slow, can't he?

Why would I want to be going round feeling ashamed and dirty and like there is something terribly wrong with me, when I can be upbeat, having some fun and also, fuck it all, getting some stuff I damn well deserve. I already said we'd done enough talking now, so why is he going on? I am sleepy and want to chill. I lean against Luke with a small sigh.

'Ok Flora,' he says gently, 'you're doing great. Did you ever read those papers I left you? Do you remember when I came round after Laura and Tom's wedding?'

Remembering them, I shake my head guiltily and move as though to try to find them in the clutter of papers and unopened envelopes still on the table. Luke stops me.

'Don't worry now,' he says. 'It's probably not the right

311

time. I'd been trying to do some research,' he continues, unable to stop himself it seems, 'on people who have more than one personality. It *is* a thing; it is not just you. It is called dissociation. And it is usually caused by stuff like you are talking about from childhood.'

Dissociation. I've heard that word before recently. Was it the woman at the police station who used it? I don't know. I can't really remember her at all. I shake my head drowsily, wishing he would stop talking.

Luke puts his arm round me. It feels like the nicest, most familiar thing. As though he has been doing it for years.

'You are right' he says. 'I'll shut up now. I think things are moving quite fast anyway. But I expect that whatever therapy they want you to have will be looking at that quite a lot.'

His arm is heavy and warm over my shoulders. And his hand is dropping down and lightly touching my collarbone, stroking my neck and caressing the very top of my breast. It feels gorgeously sexy.

'I think breaking your foot or whatever you did down there' I say, pointing down to his injured limb, 'has done you good in other ways. I never realised, um, how.' My words fade out. I had been going to say 'hot you are' but then I had looked into his face and seen his eyes, dark and intent and my mouth has gone dry with lust.

He leans down and kisses me, for the first time, properly, full on the lips. He tastes of blueberries, of vodka and best of all, of Luke. It is the nicest thing that has happened to me, for, oh I don't know, maybe just the nicest thing that has ever happened.

50

I'm not sure what to make of this. Luke and I are now lying entwined on my sofa. To my delight we have kissed some more, languidly exploring each other's mouths and sharing breath. The lipstick I slicked on this morning after my shower has all come off. His hand is gently stroking my collarbone and neck in a way that is sending sympathetic tingles of pleasure up and down my spine. But this is unusual. Normally, things move more quickly when I am hooking up with a guy. I would have expected us to be down to underwear, at least by now. With a fast mover, we might have been back in our clothes and brewing up coffee or leaning over the balcony for an illicit cigarette. And I would have virtually no memory of what we had been doing for the last hour or so.

But Luke doesn't seem to be in any kind of rush. For a moment, I am worried. Maybe I have messed up again. Perhaps he doesn't fancy me that much now that we are physically close?

Somehow, I don't think that can be right. Even though he is moving slowly, there is a sureness and confidence to his movements. And he does *seem* turned on. I decide that for once I should let him set the pace and even try to enjoy it.

So, we lie cuddled together in a comfortable languor. Luke's hand has moved down to cup my breast under my silky shirt. Resisting a sudden urge to pull away, I focus entirely on the sensation of dry, slightly calloused fingertips stroking, circling, admiring. I didn't know hands *could* admire, but there is no other way to describe what Luke's are doing. I relax again and am moving closer, shutting my eyes in pleasure when we both are startled by sounds just outside the flat.

Footsteps are running rapidly up the last flight. There is a volley of volatile banging on my front door and then a voice, clearly Elena, calling,

'Flora, Flora, are you there? Please come and help. I don't know what to do!'

We both sit up quickly. I re-arrange my bra and top, aware that Luke is watching me closely. My hair is messed up and I'm sure I have stubble rash, but there is no time to worry about that. I've never heard Elena sound like this before. I squeeze Luke's hand, shout 'come in' and jump up to unlock the door.

Outside is a tear-streaked and incoherent Elena. For the first time in our relationship, it is I who is comforting her. I put my arms around her jerking shoulders. She is crying and out of breath from running up the stairs and trying to speak all at the same time. I lead her back into my flat and push her gently onto a stool in the kitchen. She reaches out to me almost blindly and I hold her tight against me and stroke her hair.

Luke comes in quietly and after a moment he asks, 'is it your parents? Your father?'

Elena nods wordlessly and then bursts out, through renewed tears, 'he has been really struggling to breathe all day. I don't know what to do. He is determined not to go back to that hospital again. He was so frightened in there last time. I know they were trying to be nice to him and everyone was so kind.' She looks up at us anxiously, worried she is being critical. I nod to encourage her to continue.

'It is how he is; he finds it hard to trust people he doesn't

314

know. He thinks they will call the authorities and deport him. He is getting quite confused, bless him, and so all these nice kind nurses and doctors were coming in and out and with every new face he was getting more agitated. And he hated being on the monitors. It all got so distressing. He was getting worse, and I was terrified we were going to lose him in there while he was so frightened.'

I nod again, more sadly this time. I don't want to think of dignified Mr Varela in this state of terror and confusion and I am sorry that I have not been here to help Elena at this time. I can make up for it now, though.

She is still talking, words spilling out in a rush. She has been holding everything inside for too long.

'He made me promise that I wouldn't let him get taken back into hospital. And in the last week, he has been getting sicker and more depressed and really...' honesty fights with love and loyalty, ' a bit impossible. And mama is not helping at all. She keeps saying 'call the doctors, call the doctors. Why are there not doctors like the ones at home? Why can't we all go home?'

She grinds to a halt, exhausted. Luke puts a comforting hand on her other shoulder. I remember him telling me that he looked after his mother in her final illness. At least one of us might have some useful experience.

'So how is he doing right now?' he asks calmly. 'Why are you more worried tonight?'

Elena looks up and registers Luke properly for the first time.

'Oh Luke, bless you,' she says through a fresh shower of tears.

'I am so glad you are here.' Aside to me she murmurs. 'He is so nice, isn't he?' And then surprises me by giving me a

315

little wink, unnoticed by Luke.

I smile back broadly, warmed by her approval. She is calming down. She takes a deep breath and continues.

'Yes, poor dear papa, today he is having so much difficulty breathing,' she says to Luke. 'He looks quite blue. He can't eat, he doesn't want to drink. I'm having to coax anything down him, just water now. He feels so cold. I wish, you know' she says slowly, 'and it sounds awful, but we all know he is not going to get better, so I wish that he could let go and go to sleep peacefully here, with me and mama, because I hate to think of him being back in hospital.'

In my mind's eye, I picture Mr and Mrs Varela as I saw them last in their flat, sitting cosily together on the sofa. Mr Varela with his tobacco box and Mrs Varela always with her rosary beads entwined in her fingers or on the table beside her.

Rosary beads. They are both devout Catholics.

I don't want to say this, but I know I should.

'Um, Elena,' I say quietly, 'do you think you should call a priest?'

Luke looks at me sharply at the mention of a priest. Perhaps he is thinking this is what Miriam would say. I check myself. No, I am still Flora, and that I thought about Miriam then is a good sign, surely? I don't think a priest is needed for Mr Varela's salvation; I am certainly not worried about the Lord having another soul to collect for His celestial scoreboard. But for a devout couple like the Varelas, the presence of a priest is a needed ritualistic element for the rite of passage of death. And a death sounds close, from what Elena has been saying.

'Darling, you are so right' she cries in gratitude. 'I should have done that already. I haven't been thinking straight. It is such a blessing you both are here. I was so caught up in deciding whether to call an ambulance and I couldn't bring myself to do it and I forgot that what papa would really like would be to see a priest. Oh, I do hope dear Father Morrigan is available. Papa does like him so much.'

'Is that the one you like the look of?' I ask her, cheekily, remembering a previous conversation.

'You are naughty!' exclaims Elena, flushing as she laughs it off. 'I would never think of a man of God like that, not really. But no, he's a different man altogether. Father Morrigan is old, very old.'

You are going to have to watch this one' she adds to Luke, who smiles his agreement.

'I shouldn't have left papa at all,' continues Elena, frowning again. 'I know mama is there, but she is so anxious and fragile. She has been too worried to sleep for days.'

'Let's all go down' says Luke with authority. 'You can call the priest from your place, while we look after your parents for a few minutes.'

51

I am glad to be able to help Elena for once and it is lovely to have Luke by my side, but as we leave the flat together, I feel bereft at the abrupt curtailment of that very sweet time of connection. My skin is tingling as though I have come back to life after being frozen for years and I am longing for more of his touch. Who knew that the shy and gauche Luke would turn out to have such hidden depths? Also, I am nervous to be seeing Mr Varela near to death and in pain.

Luke is maybe feeling the same way because as we round the stairs to Elena's front door, he catches my hand in his and pulls me in close.

'Flora,,' he said, touching me gently on the cheek, 'that was special. You are fantastic. Please can we get back to where we were later?'

I nod so hard I almost crick my neck, beaming a smile of happy relief and anticipation. He drops a tiny kiss on my lips and murmurs 'later' into my hair. It tickles and I giggle and then catch myself sharply. What am I doing? We are about to visit a man on his deathbed.

For once Elena's flat lacks cosiness. It is by now late evening and the light is fading from the sky, but her curtains are undrawn, the lamps are unlit, piles of dirty cups and dishes fill the sink, and the stale smell of sickness is in the air.

Mrs Varela shuffles out of the bedroom in which her husband is lying, worried that we are an ambulance crew come to take him away. Trying to hide my nerves, I touch Elena on the arm and say, 'I'll pop in to see your father. Why don't you call the priest now? Do you have a direct number?'

Luke heads into the kitchen and runs the taps to start on the washing up and I tiptoe into the sickroom. Mrs Varela hovers by my side like an agitated ghost, clutching my arm for support.

The last time I saw Mr Varela, he had talked of his impending death but had been lucid and present. Now it seems as though the train he foretold is almost upon him. The wind of its coming is sucking the breath from his old and tired body and the sound of its roar is filling his ears. His eyes are shut, and each breath is pain filled. Too loud, too slow and filled with the crackles and whistles of failing lungs.

I take his ice-cold hand and sit watching him quietly. His wife moves opposite and takes his other hand. I understand why Elena doesn't want to move him. It would be an act of violence to disturb this almost translucent form any further. But I share her anxiety. What if he gets worse? What if his breathing becomes yet more laboured? Are we going to be causing him the very pain we are trying to avoid?

Elena comes quietly into the room and makes a small sound when she sees the tableau around the bed.

'Oh, he is more peaceful now,' she whispers. 'He was uncomfortable and restless earlier, but…' Her voice trails away as she stands and watches her parents and we are silent together.

Faintly in the background, we can hear Luke clattering in the kitchen. He has turned on the lights and the kettle on the range begins to hum.

We hear the doorbell, but none of us move. We are all caught up in a spell of stillness. Quietly the priest, the Father Morrigan that Elena had hoped for, comes into the room. With a minimum of words, he assesses the situation.

He begins to move slowly around the bed preparing for a ritual. While he gets out bottles of anointing oil and lights a candle, he talks softly to Elena. Luke comes into the room to watch. By some unspoken signal, we all gather around the bed as Father Morrigan begins to pray.

The words are unfamiliar to me, though well known to Elena and her mother, who murmur along. Calmness and peace return to their tired faces. He does not pray as the Elders do, as though in direct if halting communication with the Almighty. His prayer is the recitation of an age-old script, the words worn soft by use. Its strength is in its familiarity. He has no need to infuse it with passion or to convince us of his burning faith. Touching old Mr Varela's forehead gently with the warmed oil, he speaks softly.

'Through this holy anointing, may the Lord in his love and mercy help you with the grace of the Holy Spirit. May the Lord who frees you from sin save you and raise you up.'

Mrs Varela begins to pray, her quavering voice for once clear and steady as she repeats words that she has used since she could speak. Words so familiar they have almost lost their meaning. After a breath Elena and the priest join her, whilst Luke and I, unfamiliar with the prayer and without the simplicity of their faith, listen silently, with bowed heads.

'Hail Mary, full of Grace

The Lord is with thee.

Blessed art thou amongst women

And blessed is the fruit of thy womb, Jesus.

Holy Mary, Mother of God, pray for us sinners, now and at the hour of our death.'

'Amen' breathes Elena and her mother devoutly and Luke and I, taking our cue from them, also murmur 'Amen.'

We are all silent after the prayer, except for Mr Varela, whose laboured breathing is louder and slower than before. We listen to the air moving in, through and out of him, each time with such effort that each breath is a triumph of life over impending and imminent death. I can hear the ticking of the priest's large and old-fashioned wristwatch and the occasional muffled sound of traffic in the street outside.

Father Morrigan straightens up and smiles at Elena. He has a sweet smile. Also, he has the look of a man whose job is done. Elena understands and giving her father's hand a little squeeze, she leads us all into the kitchen.

Luke has worked fast. The table lamp casts a warm pool of light across the red and white checked cloth. Mugs, cream and sugar are all set out and a pot of fresh coffee is filling the room with its warming aroma. Elena pulls down small ornate glasses and a bottle from a high cupboard and wordlessly pours us all a glass of brandy. She hands the first one to Father Morrigan who receives it with the solemnity of a sacrament.

We are each caught up in the mood of the death room and no one speaks. Even Mrs Varela's distressed fidgeting has calmed. Luke smiles across the table at me. I think it is a look of assessment as well as affection, to see if I am in danger of a personality switch.

I check in with myself. Though the rituals we have witnessed are religious, they have not triggered the fear and rage that those of my birth religion would have done. I am respectful of this tired eyed priest who has come out so late on a Friday evening. Father Morrigan himself is sitting back in his seat and now contentedly clinking his brandy glass against Elena's.

'Bless you my child' he says, in a soft, educated Sligo brogue. 'I don't think it will be too long now. You are keeping him here?'

Elena nods mutely, her earlier anxiety about needing to call an ambulance soothed by the priest's quiet authority.

'Quite the best thing,' he murmurs. 'There is nothing more that doctors can do for him now and the right place is here with his family.'

He smiles kindly across at Mrs Varela.

'Your husband is safe,' he tells her. 'And soon he will be in the presence of his God.'

52

I am hiding in my car, slumped down in the seat. Even though I have driven round the block slowly three times, I am *still* too early for my appointment. There must be a succession of hovering nervous people doing what I am doing every day. All the nearby office workers will know I am going for mental health treatment. Telling myself firmly that what other people think doesn't matter at all, I finally get out of the car and walk into the anonymous buildings of the psychology department I have to attend. Checking my appointment slip, I see that Constance Fraser is the name of my given therapist. I can't imagine ever being able to call anyone Constance.

I wait, flipping blindly through an out-of-date interiors magazine, in an overheated and crowded room. We all avoid each other's eyes and try to look busy and normal. My palms begin to leak in panic. When I am finally buzzed through into an office and a woman opens the door, my heart sinks. She looks so much a therapist, in her pale oatmeal A-line skirt, neat light brown jumper and sensible beige court shoes. She isn't my kind of person at all. And she is short too, an inch shorter than me in my three-inch heels. How will someone so muted and insignificant-looking handle the strength of my emotions? I am too full of evil and messiness. I have been with the devil these past fourteen years and before that, I was living with devils disguised as men of God. Will she be able to deal with what I have to tell her?

Do I have to do this? I don't want to let this woman inside my head. How will she understand? Struck dumb, I hesitate in the doorway, almost ready to turn and run back to the safety of my car. But then I brave a glance and catch a better look at her face. There is kindness and warmth in her eyes. And sadness as well, perhaps from a lifetime of looking at pain.

She greets me warmly.

'Flora, how nice to meet you. Do come in, I'm Connie,' and ushers me into her quiet room. Even though it is a health service office, she has brought in some of her own things to personalise it. There is a white orchid flowering on the sunny windowsill. I sit down clumsily, feeling too large and too messy for the room. My head is so full of voices my body can hardly contain them, us, all. I glance across at the strange woman who I will get to know. Can she hear them too?

The idea of having to open up and tell someone else what all the voices are saying is terrifying. I talk to myself firmly.

'It is only for an hour. There is no need to talk about anything difficult to start. And then I can go get a coffee and chill out with Luke.'

The Chloé voice in my head has already kicked off.

'This is going to be a fucking waste of time. How can this silly cow say anything useful? And what does she know anyway? She can't even dress herself properly. Who the hell wears those colours? And her shoes are ugly as shit.' I try telling Chloé that she needs to give this Mrs Fraser a chance. I have to be here; it is not like we have a choice. I can think about shoes later, but I need to do this first.

The Miriam part of me is anxious. I am going to have to talk about my father and brothers and the Elders and say bad things. Also, there is a small statue of a Buddha on the windowsill next to the orchid. Is this woman not even a Christian? Should I be in a room with someone who keeps graven idols as ornaments?

I tell this part of me, the voice of my Christian upbringing, to keep an open mind. I am not here to talk about Mrs Fraser's beliefs or lack of them. I let the voices quieten and settle and look up again. The therapist is watching me patiently, with a slight expectant smile.

Taking a deep breath and trying to relax my shaking hands, I say very faintly.

'I am here because I've been told my memory loss is due to trauma.' I see compassion in the gentle face opposite me, which emboldens me to go on. 'And I was involved with the police because I was stealing from everyone. I am a thief.'

53

It is a warm late afternoon in early September and the hall is full of sunshine. I look around in satisfaction, admiring my work. Bunches of late summer flowers, yellow rudbeckia, purple Michaelmas daisies, late-flowering blowsy headed dahlias, are standing in white jugs on all the tables. The walls are draped with brightly coloured cottons and hung with photographs. Tables laden with food line the back wall and a three-piece Tango band are setting up at the front, strumming chords and adjusting mics.

It had been Elena's idea to have a party to celebrate the life of her father. Luke and I had attended the sparsely attended service in the local Catholic church, officiated over by Father Morrigan. Our nostrils were filled with the bitter tang of incense and the musty smell of damp old buildings. The mournful notes of a disembodied organ had exhorted the scattered congregation to sing and attempt to raise the tired spirit of Mr Varela heavenwards.

Elena, always polite, had warmly thanked Father Morrigan as he shook hands with the mourners in the draughty porch but turning to me as we left the graveyard she had said, 'well that was all very nice. But I'm not quite sure it was what Salvador would have wanted.'

A few days after the funeral, Luke and I were sitting in my front room in friendly silence, reading the papers together. Flump was perched on my knee, every now and then steadying himself against my bare skin by flexing his claws. Hearing a knock on the door and having checked that there were no suspicious vehicles parked outside, I tipped the cat off my lap, rubbed Luke's hair in passing and opened the door to Elena. We hugged warmly and I made coffee while asking how she and her mother are faring. Taking the coffee through to Luke and opening the box of shortbread that Elena has brought, I noticed a tiny secret smile on her face. Despite her sadness, there seemed a new lightness to her movements.

Sensing news, we looked at her expectantly. She begins by telling us that her father had used to go to an informal club for expat Argentinian men.

'It was all very macho, of course,' she says, 'they all sat and smoked and drank and talked about the old country, but it made papa happy.' The men had sent a wreath for Salvador's funeral and, wanting to thank them, she had braved the all-male enclave and called round 'just last night, once mama was settled, to thank them for their kindness.'

'I couldn't stop thinking,' she had said 'that correct though the church service was, it wasn't quite enough. My father was a great man in Argentina. He made many new friends over here too. It was only in the last couple of years when he was so ill that his world shrank to just his close family. I have been thinking that we should have a proper celebration of him, as well as the church funeral. And then when I called by his club, I met that younger friend of his, Tomas. Well, he and I had coffee yesterday and we were talking about how we could do this and now I have a plan.'

I look at her sharply and notice a faint blush staining her cheeks as she mentions her father's friend.

Keeping my expression serious I ask, 'so, who is Tomas? How could he help?'

Elena explains that Tomas is a tango musician in a professional trio. 'I think you saw him here once when he brought my parents back from church? He and his band are quite busy, my dear, you would be surprised how many people

327

want to dance Tango. Not just the homesick oldies, it is popular. Anyway, he suggested that we could hire a hall and have a little party and he and his band would play for nothing as they were so fond of my father.'

Privately I wonder if it is just her father's memory that is motivating his kindness, but the idea is a good one.

'What does your mother think?' asked Luke.

Elena had smiled at him indulgently.

'She is already full of ideas for food that I should make. She wants a proper Argentinian feast. She wants me to make his favourite Carbonara Criolla and lots of special breads and all the salads. She is already telling me to order enough wines and to be sure to have Fernet for all his friends. It is lovely to see her getting interested in something. But I don't know how to throw a party really. I've never had to plan anything like this before.'

'Flora does though' said Luke, glancing at me.

They both turn to me and then Elena flings her arms round me.

'Oh, would you do it darling?' she cried. 'You are the perfect person to help me arrange it. You know how to make a room look lovely and how to get a party going. I don't understand all these things. But I can make food. And I could bake all his favourite cakes.' her voice had trailed off as memories of her father overtook her and I had hugged her back warmly.

I am not sure if I can do it. Apart from attending therapy, I have mostly been hiding out in my flat since I got back from the police station. Even strolling down the street to the little park nearby is frightening. I am content for now to stay home in a little bubble with Luke and Flump while I try to make sense of what has been happening. I don't want to do anything that might draw attention to myself.

Every Tuesday morning, I must go back to the police station to sign in as a condition of my bail. I am waiting for a date to attend court for my trial and sentencing. Last week I met with a brisk young police liaison officer. She was quite kind and said that, following a report and assessment from the mental health team and so long as I keep to certain restrictions, it is most likely that I will only get a suspended sentence, as Luke had hoped.

'It will all go on your record,' she had said, 'but there is a recognition that you have suffered a lot already. In their opinion, the work you will have to do in therapy will be sufficiently arduous. Everyone expects you to engage fully with that. Let us hope that the Courts look at it the same way.'

But there is something about Elena that is hard to say no to and so reluctantly I agreed to help her to plan her remembrance party. I insisted that she come shopping with me to buy what we need. I certainly don't trust myself in a shop yet. Together we bought crimson wall hangings, gold table decorations and votive candles. Looking around the room this sunny morning, I am pleased with the effect. The room is colourful and distinctively right for Salvador.

The Tango trio have now arranged themselves to their satisfaction and, nodding to me, they begin a gentle acoustic version of 'Indio Manso' starting to warm the space ahead of the first party guests. I take a moment to study Tomas, who is playing bass. He is middle-aged, grizzled haired and looks quite ordinary but as I watch he glances across at the lead violinist, throws him a riff and they begin to play off each other. Suddenly Tomas's dark eyes are sparkling, and a smile is lighting his unremarkable face. I watch him grooving for a few minutes, my feet beginning to move in sympathy and decide that he might do very nicely for my friend. My reverie is interrupted by the side door to the hall swinging open and Luke staggering in. He is struggling to carry an enormous metal cooking pot, by its aroma filled with some of Elena's prize-winning beef stew. He gives me a big smile and after dropping off his burden in the kitchens, he comes over to me. Taking my hand, he impulsively pulls me to him and starts to dance in a very rough impression of tango style. The violinist gives us an encouraging whoop and together we spin around the almost empty church hall.

I look at the room as we swing around it. I am pleased with what I have done. Funerals and memorial parties are very different to weddings, but they still need to be stylish and individual. The very beginnings of an idea start to form in my head. I am distracted by the nearness and warmth of Luke though, who is now pulling me into a bad imitation of a salsa dip. He follows this by an over-ambitious attempt to pull off a one-handed coin swooping drop, which results in us both landing on the floor in a heap of arms, legs and giggles.

The musicians are still playing, so I wave my arms in the air in time. Luke joins in with his feet. Just for a moment, we are playing like children, until I remember the occasion and pull myself and Luke to our feet. I glance around guiltily for Elena, worried she might think we are being disrespectful, only to find her smiling broadly from the kitchen door, a tray of freshly baked plaited loaves in her hand. We bow and clap the musicians, who nod good-humouredly and make our way over to a nearby table to recover.

"How are you really doing today, Flora?' asks Luke. 'It must feel odd to be back organising events.'

I look up in surprise at his serious tone and then drop my eyes down, considering the question. I spot a few stray long black hairs on his sleeve and absentmindedly pick them off. Flump is as much of a fixture in my flat at present as his owner.

'Well, a funeral is a bit different to a wedding,' I tell him, still with my mind half working on my new idea. 'Much less likely to be bad behaviour. And though some people get married more than once, we all only get one shot at this.'

Is there a market for a funeral planner? I wonder. Would I be able to rebrand myself? No one flirts at funerals and there would be a lot less temptation. I can't imagine wanting a flat full of black edged place mats and funeral meats.

'Talking of bad behaviour,' Luke breaks into my train of thought, smiling at me reassuringly. 'I had a weird email this morning, from that mad wedding woman, you remember, the pregnant one. Laura, that was her name, who was marrying Tom…oh yes, of course you do remember' he says as he sees my face fall.

After a beat, he continues, 'well anyway, she messaged me, to my surprise, to thank me for taking the photographs at the wedding. I hadn't sent her all the lovey-dovey ones' he continues hastily, responding to my look of amazement. 'But there were some nice ones of her and her parents and their place all done up. Her mother had worked so hard in that garden and so it was easy to get good shots, especially early morning before things kicked off. And I thought as they wouldn't be any use to anyone else, I might as well send them over. I knew she wasn't going to pay me, but it was either that or delete them.'

'Anyway,' he continues, pulling me up and towards the bar area of the room, grabbing a Peroni and trying to pull the top off with his teeth while he talks, 'she emailed back at once. And, oh yes, she said she liked the photographs,' here he gives a little smirk of self-satisfaction, 'and also that she and Tom were having an annulment on grounds of non-consummation. So, I don't think she will need to cite you in a

331

divorce. Sounds like they never shagged again.'

At this his smile becomes broader and although I am slightly shocked and disturbed to be reminded of that terrible day and my, (was it my?) insane behaviour, I still can't help smiling back.

'Oh well, after all she got to have a baby and mummy got to do up the garden and they now have your lovely photographs to remember it by. I did her a favour really,' I continue, warming to my theme, 'at least, I saved her from marrying that total creep.'

Acknowledgements and thanks

In writing The Wedding Thief I have been very generously helped by many people. I'd like to especially thank Rachael Whitfield, Bryn Bazzard, Karen Whiteside, Caroline Yeates and Nadelle Langley for help with research.

I'd like to thank my mentor Eleanor Lees for her patient encouragement and editing suggestions, my friend and musical partner George Whitfield for sharing observations at the hundreds of weddings we have worked at over the years, Emily Hinshelwood for reading an early draft as well as designing the front cover so beautifully, and my son and daughter Sam and Bea for their constant encouragement.

It was important to me to present an accurate picture of the much-misunderstood condition of Dissociative Identity Disorder and the effects of early trauma on personality. The following books and resources have been helpful, as well as other first-person accounts.

PODS (Positive Outcomes for Dissociative Survivors.) An organisation that supports those affected and increases awareness and understanding of the condition.

Recovery is my Best Revenge: My Experience of Trauma, Abuse and Dissociative Identity Disorder. Carolyn Spring.

The Family Inside: Working with the Multiple. Doris Bryant

The Body Keeps the Score, Mind, Brain and Body in the Transformation of Trauma. Bessel van der Kolk

In Therapy: The Unfolding Story. Susie Orbach

Instrumental. James Rhodes

In the Days of Rain. Rebecca Stott